CLAUDETTE WALKER

C STREET

A Novel

Abacus Books, Inc.

P.O. Box 55302
St. Petersburg, Florida 33732-5302, U.S.A.
www.abacusbooks.com

First Edition
Second Printing

Library of Congress Cataloging in Publication Data
Walker, Claudette
C STREET
I. Title

ISBN# 0-9716292-5-0
EAN# 978-0-9716292-5-7

Printed in the United States of America
Set in Times New Roman

This is a work of fiction. Names, characters, places, and incidents either are the product of the author's invention and imagination or are used fictitiously, and any resemblance to actual persons either living or dead, events, or locales is entirely coincidental.

For NeCole

Chapter One
Splendid Isolation

JACQUELINE ROSE committed the premeditated murder of a federal agent. Crimson flames ravaged her mind amidst a haze of smoke – without denial, she was acutely aware that she bore responsibility for the son of a bitch's apocalypse. His survival would be her Armageddon, his demise her albatross.

Jacqueline Bovia was born in a small, lovely, water-surrounded suburb of dreary, factory-filled and smoke-infested Detroit, Michigan. Her teenage years intertwined with burning cities, forever scorched by the hate-induced race riots and turmoil of the late sixties. The smoldering racial discontent had barely ceased when the Anti-War movement took hold of the country with a fury. Jacqueline wove flowers into her hair, marched on Washington in protest of the American involvement in the Vietnam War, and followed the hippie movement to the legendary Haight Ashbury District of San Francisco.

Marriage, divorce, and single motherhood made the foundation, shaky at times, of her life. The Anti-War movement, the Equal Rights movement, and the mind-altering times of sex, drugs, and politics all had led Jacqueline into the arms of the one she would love and marry. He was Solomon Rosenberg, a Jewish man from

New York, an Ivy League lawyer. His death and the secrets left in her hands would be the catalyst for Jacqueline's sabotage of technological developments born of political subterfuge and nurtured by the CIA.

Even several years later, she could recall Solomon Rosenberg in almost perfect detail. He was the man she loved. His tall, slender, beautiful body, bronzed from the sun, resided clearly in her vision. His wavy coal-black hair laid parted to the left once again. A free-spirited intellectual with an Ivy League education, a member of Mensa, he dazzled her with prose, music, and the theory of everything. Everyone called him "Rose." That was appropriate, because he possessed charm and wit no woman could resist. Her love for him still swept her away.

However, as usual in her vision, his eyes still had that last hollow, empty, vacant look. Those were not the eyes that held such promise, the face she desired to remember. Jacqueline shook off her thoughts of Rose with contempt. Better to banish the memory of him than see that diminished, devoid look again. Splendid isolation, peaceful anonymity was her heart's desire. However, one last thing stood in her path before she could slip into obscurity. Understanding the need to stop the continuous, burning flow of her unwanted memories, Jacqueline knew she could have no rest until she tended to that last piece of business. She knew unparalleled tranquility would come from easing her burdened mind.

Jacqueline Bovia Rosenberg had become Jacqueline Rose with the simple stroke of a pen. She needed to leave behind her life with Solomon Rosenberg, as well as his name. She fled the ramifications of loving Rose – a man, a lawyer, and an assassin for the CIA – by quietly slipping into London's boroughs. Naïvely, she believed that after Rose's death the government would cease to pursue her and the information she had obtained. Jacqueline's unworldly assessment could not have been more wrong. Just when she thought that the pain and fear were over, something or someone would draw her back into that dark world of deceit.

Leaving the misty, fog-covered streets of London would not be easy, for Jacqueline had found calm living outside of the United States. The allure of London remained astounding, from the Tower of London on the mystical River Thames to the magnificent mosaics of St. Paul's Cathedral and on to the iron gates of Kensington Palace. Her eye remained eternally captivated. The city was overflowing with history, royalty, architecture, art, and culture. At first London seemed a little overwhelming, but over time, Jacqueline realized that she could travel easily as just another transplant from the States.

London has thirty-three boroughs split into five distinct areas – Central, South, North, East and West. Each borough, being so unique, is like a city in itself. Jacqueline had lived in hostels in three of the boroughs after she arrived in London. Each hostel was slightly different, depending on the character of the innkeeper. Every hostel had several beds to a room, shared by strangers, all of whom seemed to be traveling on a budget.

It was the same at every hostel – people were short of cash.

Jacqueline found during her time in the hostels that she could blend into any of the boroughs quite easily. The London hostels were a perfect way of devising where she would settle. While acclimating herself to London, she discovered that thirty percent of the city is green space, and her visits to the city's parks and gardens allowed her to feel free. Jacqueline had lived in cities as diverse as New York and San Francisco; she understood her need for open spaces.

The writer Samuel Johnson once said, "When a man is tired of London, he is tired of life; for there is in London all that life can afford." Jacqueline was surely not tired of life, and she had discovered the most important thing that London had to offer – a peaceful existence. A bonus of living in London was the security of fast travel to the rest of the world from the international hub. She knew that if she needed to flee, she could go anywhere fast from Heathrow Airport or by using the extensive tube and rail systems of Europe.

In Europe, people travel from country to country like Americans travel from state to state. She felt at peace in London, or at least she would, as soon as she could clear her mind with a final trip to the United States. Once she made this trip, Jacqueline believed that she would return to London and then slip into a life of quiet obscurity in a country far away from the United States. Jacqueline had already decided to make another move while she was living in London. She would move to a tropical paradise

– maybe an island. For all of London's wonders, the weather was surely not one.

To board an airplane at Heathrow Airport seemed the only solution to her feeling of things unfinished. Just one short trip and then maybe she could begin to feel life again. It was so simple – eleven hours to Tampa International Airport and another thirty minutes to her old friend Sid Shelly's front door in Saint Petersburg, Florida. Their paths had crossed in New York while Jacqueline was alone in the city and Rose was still alive. A simple conversation in the Shakespeare and Company bookstore had rekindled a connection from an earlier life. Thirty years ago, they first met in a hospital in San Francisco. They ran into each other in the New York bookstore nearly twenty years later, spent some time together, and promised to meet again.

Jacqueline knew that Sid was living in the Old Northeast section of Saint Petersburg, and writing freelance articles. The area where Sid lived was near the part of town where Jacqueline's house had been before her move to London, and she knew it well. While dining at street cafés in England, with the London Times as her only companion, she stumbled across a few of Sid's newspaper articles. Those stories would be the catalyst to bring Jacqueline back to Sid's door one more time. It was time to honor her vow to see her old friend.

Sid would never expect Jacqueline's arrival – of this there was no doubt. Jacqueline was filled with trepidation as she returned to the United States. She believed it would be her final journey home – one last trip to close that chapter of her past. When she was finished in the States, she would go to that far-away place she had discovered in maps while relaxing in the taverns of London. She was determined to slip away to sixty-eight square miles of scenic coast, palm trees, and tropical breezes. The maps had shown Jacqueline the island where she had decided to live out her life.

Before she married Rose, Jacqueline would not have considered living outside America. She was a small-town American girl who loved her country, and she had never dreamed of leaving it for more than a vacation until recently. However, London had opened new avenues to places in the world where she could simply disappear on foreign soil. Circumstances beyond Jacqueline's wildest imagination had been the inspiration that determined where she would live out her life in isolation and tranquility.

It was just before daybreak on a somber, foggy London morning. The engines roared. Rain bounced off the jet's windows and fog coated the glass as the plane took off from Heathrow. Jacqueline was disappointed that she had not been able to book a direct flight, knowing that she would face a delay of several hours at JFK. That meant she would arrive at Sid's door at an uncivilized hour. Nevertheless, maybe this would be better, after all.

Long after dark, on a clear, warm summer's night, the taxicab pulled down an old red brick street. It was delivering Jacqueline to a yellow Victorian house with tall white pillars reaching toward the sky. The front of the house overlooked obviously well-kept homes, and two palm trees soared high above the house's roof. The palms swayed in the breeze from Tampa Bay, which lapped at the beach only a few blocks away.

Jacqueline paid the driver. She slowly stepped out of the taxi, her backpack in hand, and walked up the red brick sidewalk leading to the steps of the terra-cotta tiled porch. She glanced at her watch, which was still set to London time. It was 5:27 PM – that made it nearly 1:30 in the morning, Florida time.

For all practical purposes, Jacqueline's hesitant knock at Sid's door made no sound. Yet the door slowly opened, and in absolute astonishment, Sid stumbled back. "Long time," were the first words Jacqueline could think of to lessen the trauma of her unexpected arrival. Obviously fresh out of bed, her long cranberry robe barely tied, Sid wiped her eyes, expecting to clear her vision of the ghost that appeared at her door.

It only took a moment for Sid to realize that this was not a dream that would go away. Sid's eyes focused on the beauty in Jacqueline's unchanged face and the emerald green sweater that softly intensified the shape of Jacqueline's braless breasts. Jacqueline's trademark blue jeans framed her still small size. Her backpack and the loafers she wore told of her journey. Sid opened the door wide then pulled Jacqueline through the door and into a lingering hug.

"My God, Jacqueline, it's you! It has been so long. Jesus Christ, I heard that you were dead. Woman, you are a vision for sore eyes at my front door. The news of your death was devastating, and I found it impossible to write that ending to your story. Obviously, the rumors were not true. Sit down. May I offer you a drink? I know it's either too early or too late for a cocktail, but I think I could use one."

"The usual, Sid – some things don't change." Sid smiled as she pulled a hand-carved crystal snifter from the shelf and reached for the bottle of Grand Marnier that sat unopened on the old oak buffet. The bottle was on top of the buffet, not in the back of a liquor cabinet – almost as though Sid was still hoping for Jacqueline's return to life. Sid could see Jacqueline's reflection in the beveled mirror that hung high on the wall behind the liquor bottles. The view in the mirror showed Jacqueline's image surrounded by a blue haze. Was she really sitting there, or did Sid's need for something to open her writer's block just conjure up Jacqueline?

Sid turned slowly, snifter in hand, almost expecting Jacqueline's chair to be empty. Their hands gently touched in the passing of the snifter. At that moment, Sid knew it was not her imagination. Jacqueline was real and not some mirage created by her writer's need. Suddenly, Sid realized why she had never written the tragedy of Jacqueline's death, a death that did not seem a befitting ending to Jacqueline's story.

Jacqueline spoke in her low, deep voice. "Sid, we're alone aren't we? Can we talk?" "Yes, we are alone." "Sid, my demise was intentionally over-reported." Sid knew that Jacqueline's unexpected arrival must signify an important part of her story. No writer could imagine a life more colorful than Jacqueline's. Sid felt an immediate connection with Jacqueline on the first day they met in San Francisco, when Jacqueline was just a young girl. That same connection was there when they ran across each other in the New York bookstore, many years later. Years after the brief renewal of their friendship in New York City, Sid was intrigued when Jacqueline contacted her, asking that Sid come to New Orleans about a story.

That day, Sid began writing the journey of Jacqueline and her love for Rose. Jacqueline had asked Sid to bury the truth of the story between the lines of fiction, for someone to find a hundred years hence. This was a concept that Sid, as a writer, had never considered but found intriguing. Jacqueline again had arrived at Sid's door. Why was she there? After all, Rose was dead, and that story was told. Sid suspected that Jacqueline would not have come back in the still of the night unless there was more to the story than anyone could imagine.

Suddenly, all of the years that had passed since Sid had last seen Jacqueline evaporated, and it seemed like only yesterday. Yet, it was long ago that they sat together for weeks in a New Orleans flat and the local taverns in the French Quarter, as Jacqueline told Sid of loving Rose. Sid recalled the story of their love's journey, the passion of two souls loving one another with an unequaled intensity. She remembered how Jacqueline had fled from the keepers of deceit, lies, and mistrust when she left Rose and hopefully, his CIA connections. Sid thought of Rose's bipolar insanity – insanity intensified by chemotherapy, and of Jacqueline having nearly died at the hands of a government assassin – her damaged husband.

In the beginning, after hearing Jacqueline's story, Sid realized how tragic it is that the American government will train agents and tell those agents to carry out orders that no one belonging to the human race should have to follow. Sid knew all too well, how the trainers of deceit were then unresponsive when the years of explosives, murder, and more destroyed the agents' minds. God, it seemed like only yesterday they talked of this story, and yet it was so many years ago.

Slowly, Jacqueline lifted the snifter to her wine colored lips, took a sip, then lowered it as she sat back in the chair and began to talk. She had found Sid's Florida address on the Internet while living in London; Jacqueline knew then that she would one day make this trip, to tell the rest of the story. She had just arrived back in the States and would only be there for a few days to speak with Sid.

Sid smiled as she asked about Marie, Jacqueline's only child. "Marie is grown up and doing well, a humanitarian, activist, and artist. However, like Rose and me, Marie has an interest in technology. She attended the Vienna Institute, MIT, and other science universities, always under the assumed name Rose had prepared for her before his death."

"You know Sid, America will never feel safe to me again, not after knowing the men of C Street. It's hard to believe that one group of men can exert so much power. Even though the faces are different over time, nothing really changes. They cover up sex scandals, prostitution, drug abuse, and payoffs. It's all to maintain power. They gain control over people with the promise of money and power for them; if that doesn't work, they threaten people with disclosure of their sins. If their victims have no sins, the men of C Street create some. If that doesn't work, people die.

"It's only a matter of time until some connection to the world of Solomon 'The Rose' Rosenberg will come looking for me if I'm in the States. I think they know that I cannot be bought. I'm not a public figure, so that leaves manufacturing some criminal activity for which I can be prosecuted, the threat of violence to me or Marie, or killing one of us. The knowledge I have is so dangerous to them that I shouldn't stay in the States – not even for a short visit. In fact, something just happened that nearly made me cancel this trip to see you.

"I thought of returning to Israel, where I have spent some time, but I'm sure the violence in the Holy Land will never end. I'm sure you've heard the old prophecy, 'When the holy lands walk hand and hand, the destruction of the earth will follow.' I assure you Sid, after my time in Israel I'm convinced that we have no fear of the prophecy of world destruction coming true, because the violence in the Middle East will never stop. Sid, let me start by telling you about my last night in Israel. A laugh is always a good way to break the ice."

On the night before she left the country, Jacqueline was saying her final farewells to her friends at the training center. She had spent the last months with them, and had grown close to most. One man, Ishmael, a thirty-two year old Israel military trainer, had given her a special goodbye. Jacqueline had been unable to locate him, despite looking everywhere. Finally, she gave up and retired for her last night in Israel, knowing that she had a long journey ahead the next day. Just as she was falling asleep, a soft knock came at her bedroom door. It was Ishmael coming to say goodbye. Within minutes, he had her body against the wall of her room. His raven black hair framed his strong, fine features and lovely brown eyes.

It started as a simple goodbye kiss, but his luscious lips were hot. Before Jacqueline knew it, the t-shirt she had been sleeping in was gone. Ishmael's strong six foot five body, honed by his military training, had lifted her into his arms and against the wall. She could feel her body seeping. His lips were all over her with warm, wet intensity. The power of the soldier lifted her up and down on his hard, erect body. They spoke not a word, but it was a farewell to remember.

Sid giggled and said, "Jacqueline, some things never change! This guy sounds gorgeous! Jacqueline laughed and agreed, "Yes, he was strikingly handsome." Sid just shook her head, saying, "Men just throw themselves at you. I just can't understand how they all find you. No one else I know has that kind of luck – only you! I'm surprised you didn't stay just for his talents."

Jacqueline told Sid that she knew remaining in Israel assured a life of fear, so she decided to make her home in London. However, she was unable to shake the feeling that things were still unfinished. "Sid, I kept coming across your articles in London, and knew I would not be at peace until someone knew the whole story. That someone is you. I know you will once again find a way to write the truth of the story woven into the lines of fiction. At least we will have left the truth for someone to find."

Jacqueline admitted that America felt strange to her after all she had gone through with Rose. It seemed her love for Solomon Rosenberg had sealed her fate. Jacqueline often wondered what she would have done, had she known in the beginning where that love would take her. Would she have run away from him on the very first day they met? She believed, even if she had known everything that was to be, it would not have stopped her from loving him. Nothing could have stopped that love – Rose was her destiny and she had accepted that fate.

"How ironic," Sid thought, as she watched Jacqueline lift the snifter again, "We make such strange bedfellows. Writing Jacqueline's tale has forever inextricably intertwined our lives." Jacqueline told Sid that during her time in London, Jacqueline had tried to write the second part of her story herself, as she had always dreamed of doing. However, she kept running across Sid's articles, and Jacqueline knew that it was a sign that she needed to seek out Sid again.

Jacqueline knew her unfinished feeling was that Sid needed to write the end of her story. After life had calmed down for Jacqueline, she knew that she needed to come back to the United States and tell the rest of the saga to the one person who could truly encompass the scope of her experiences and put them to paper. Sid told her, "To say the least, I'm honored to be that writer again."

Sid watched as her friend lifted the snifter to her lips one more time, taking another sip to calm her nerves. The late-night moon was shining through the windows and lit the few lines that had formed around Jacqueline's eyes over the years. Still, Jacqueline was like the fine aged liqueur she was sipping, with a beautiful golden hue to her olive skin. Sid remembered the New York college roommate of Rose who she had interviewed for the first book. His description of Jacqueline was, "Helen of Troy, the face that launched a thousand ships." Looking at her in the moonlight, Sid realized that Jacqueline's beauty was still bewitching, even after all these years.

Sid smiled. "Jacqueline, do you mind if I take notes? The fact that you are here talking with me means we are not finished together, especially after what you've said. I'm assuming that you only have a short time, so I would like to turn on my tape recorder and make notes." "Unfortunately, Sid, I can't allow a recording of my voice, but please get your note pad. I'm sorry, but I think you will understand why later. You are right though, our time together is limited – I'm not comfortable in the States." "I understand, Jacqueline. Just give me a minute to turn off the telephone and make some coffee." "Thanks, Sid. No one else must know that I'm in the country." Sid nodded, as she said, "You have my assurance, no one will know."

"Jacqueline, you must be exhausted. Lay your head back for a few minutes while I put on the coffee." "You are right, Sid. I'm exhausted – from life." Jacqueline sat quietly gazing out the window at the palm trees blowing in the wind, as Sid made coffee. Jacqueline's thoughts drifted in peace, and told Sid she found comfort in being with her "old friend." Jacqueline was surer now than when she began her journey that the need for this conversation with Sid was her unfinished feeling. After she told her story to Sid, maybe she could close this chapter of her life.

Sid returned, carrying an antique silver tray that held a pot of coffee and two cups. She sat it down on the old cherry wood table next to Jacqueline's chair. Then Sid eased back into a matching Victorian high-backed chair covered with gold tapestry, and only the table separated the two. With great anticipation, Sid was ready to listen to whatever Jacqueline was about to tell. Sid knew only that Jacqueline's unexpected arrival was the open doorway to free her writer's mind.

At that moment, Sid realized that Jacqueline was her destiny. She watched as Jacqueline laid her head on the back of the chair, her emerald green eyes and long auburn brown hair shimmering brightly in the moonlight shining through the window. Jacqueline began speaking even more softly, "When I lost Solomon, the pain was relentless. However, I realized that my life had to continue." In her low, sensuous voice, she began to tell the rest of her story....

Chapter Two
The Catalyst

JACQUELINE BEGAN rebuilding her destroyed world after Rose's death. Marie had grown up, and they had survived Rose's bipolar, drug addicted hands and the claws of the CIA. The government had kept Jacqueline in complete fear until Rose died. Once Rose was gone, she believed the CIA would lose interest, but she also knew that she could never let her guard completely down.

Because Jacqueline was unsure if the CIA knew that Rose had kept a diary of his life on C Street and had made tapes of his CIA missions, she lived in fear. If the CIA did know that the tapes existed, she had no idea what the government might do to get them. Jacqueline also knew that she could never truly rely on anyone for protection, for she would surely endanger that person's life if the government were to come looking. Besides, she now realized that the government was capable of anything, so she could never know whom to trust.

Within a few weeks of learning of Solomon's death, Jacqueline made the decision to return to Florida from the mountaintop where she had been hiding. She had lived quietly, hidden high in the mountains, to protect herself from Rose and the CIA. Jacqueline had relied long enough on GI Joe, a very handsome and strong Marine, to protect her. He had become her guardian, her friend and her lover, but Jacqueline's heart was so alone she could never love another. Their lives had become intertwined by her need for safety and not by her love. She did not want anything in her life to remind her of the days with Rose, even if that meant leaving her protector and setting out on her own.

Jacqueline had also begun making strange observations during her last days on the mountain. GI Joe had come back into her life from nowhere. He was the Marine she met on the trip with Rose to the State Department, and then he had shown up some years later at the ski resort while Jacqueline was vacationing alone. He arrived there at a time when she was most vulnerable, and worked his way into her life. Although he appeared to be an honorable man and Jacqueline was attracted to him, he always seemed preoccupied. He seemed almost unconcerned about the strange car periodically driving past her mountain home. That car terrified her.

It seemed strange to Jacqueline that just after the mysterious car with its white license plate made its last trip down the mountain road in front of her home, the call came that Rose had died. Immediately, the Marine had become very inquisitive about Rose's work. He suddenly began asking if Rose had told her about his government work. Jacqueline began to wonder if he had only been there to watch over her, and if the CIA were that resourceful. She was beginning to think more clearly, refusing to discuss anything about Rose with GI Joe over the next few weeks. As he became more insistent in his attempts to get information about her knowledge of Rose's work, the tension between them increased.

She no longer trusted GI Joe, nor did she want to be near some of the "hill folk" she had discovered so high up in the mountains. Her mother had clearly described some of the hill people. "Jacqueline, they are not like the kind old southerners you meet. Some are just uneducated and mean. High in the mountains, they are so isolated – they can get away with things that good folks would never consider doing." While Jacqueline was living in her hideout on the mountaintop, she had discovered that their illegal trade had changed from moonshine to methamphetamines, and she wanted nothing to do with the drugs or those who trafficked in them.

Jacqueline was afraid to live in the mountains alone, and thought that she needed GI Joe to protect her from the CIA and the drug traffickers. She knew that the CIA was watching her. She couldn't use a cell phone there – there was no cell service. She had to have a telephone, so she had a landline phone in the house. She knew that the hang-up telephone calls, the delay before a dial tone, and the occasional click meant that the CIA was monitoring her communications.

She felt that GI Joe would fight any of the drug traffickers and other criminals to keep her safe. However, she was not as sure that he would protect her from the CIA. She wanted to banish all memories of Rose, and GI Joe would not let the topic of Rose rest. Jacqueline began to believe that she had been sleeping in the arms of the enemy. Had she been in bed with the CIA?

Leaving a short goodbye note, she left the mountain while he was on a "hunting trip." Alone with her personal belongings in her car, she decided that she would sell the mountain house later. The only way out was sixteen miles of steep, winding dirt road. She wound down that treacherous, narrow, snow-covered road, never to return.

It was early morning when she finally arrived at her Florida home. The air was so still that the palm trees looked like statues as she walked up the sidewalk. Tired from the long drive, she was relieved to turn the key in the lock of her home. The long journey from the mountain had been exhausting, and Jacqueline was ready for a peaceful night's sleep and the glorious view of Tampa Bay from her bedroom window the next morning.

As she turned on the light, disarray greeted her eyes. Someone had ransacked her home! She quickly stepped back out the front door, ran to her car, jumped inside, hit the lock and started the car. With the doors locked and the engine running, the ransacking of her home overcame her emotions like a bodily attack. She pulled the car down the street and parked where she could see the front door of her house.

Jacqueline sat in complete disbelief, watching the front door of her house from inside her car until daylight and even longer, until her neighbors began coming out of their houses for work. She did not want to call the police and draw any attention to her return from the mountain. However, she did not want to go back into her home until it was daylight and the neighbors began to circulate, even though she thought whoever had done this was long gone.

Jacqueline sat for hours watching her house for movement, but all was quiet.

She drove her car a few blocks away and parked. Well after daybreak, she removed the blue steel Colt .38-caliber revolver from her car's glove box. She had the gun's coil cut back for rapid firing. She had only shot this gun on the mountain at cans, but if anyone was inside, she knew her aim was true.

Slowly, she walked the few blocks to her home, her hand nestled in her pocket, tightly holding the .38. Everything still appeared quiet around the house. She opened the front door quickly and left it open as she searched, gun in hand, every inch of the house. Jacqueline searched the showers, closets, and under the beds. When she was sure that no one was in her house, she walked carefully from the back of the house to the front one more time, then closed and locked the front door. Sitting down in a chair, her back against the wall, she placed the gun within easy reach on the table. Stunned, she began to look around at her belongings. She had left her home immaculately clean in preparation for her return. Now it was in shambles. Jacqueline began cleaning up the mess, while looking to see what was missing.

Her eyes scanned everything. It did not take her long to realize that every computer was smashed; VCR tapes, CDs, DVDs, and all recording devices were gone. The computers they destroyed were clearly a sign of frustration, as all of the hard drives were carefully removed by Jacqueline before she went to the mountain.

Gone were pictures of Rose, select papers, and books. Her antiques and art were still there, although some were smashed to pieces. As well, all of her paintings and pictures were sliced from their frames.

More interesting were the items that had not been taken by the burglars. Jacqueline's jewelry and coins still sat in the box on her dresser. Her large collection of silver flatware and trays was untouched. That told her this was not just a random burglary. She knew that it had to be the CIA, looking for information Rose left behind. She also knew that if they wanted to burglarize her house without her immediately realizing it, they would have done it differently. The ransacking told her that they wanted her to know they were still looking. Jacqueline was petrified at the thought of the CIA leaving such a clear message.

She checked every window and door, looking to see how the CIA had entered her house. The only sign of forcible entry was a few tiny scratches on the back door lock. Obviously, it was a professional job. That only confirmed what she already knew – it was most likely the CIA, or maybe NSA – what difference did it make? They were all involved in the C Street Complex. Jacqueline decided not to report the break-in to the police; instead, she decided to clean up the damage from the burglary quietly over the next few days.

She already knew that the burglars had found nothing. They discovered nothing because the diary, CDs, tapes, and other information about Rose's work were not there. The only documentation of where the items were located was stored in her head. The burglars had damaged many keepsakes, including a piece of art Rose had given Jacqueline on the day they married. They had not just cut the canvas from the frame but slashed through the center of a waterfall painting. It was as if they knew the painting had sentimental meaning.

Jacqueline had barely begun cleaning up the mess that the CIA left, when a man arrived unexpectedly at her door. A tall, strong man, with Mediterranean dark skin, yet only slightly tanned, stood on her porch. He wore a Bond Street suit, and was clearly articulate. He was extremely polite in his request to speak with her. "Allow me to introduce myself. My name is Adel Youssef. May I have a moment of your time? I believe we have someone in common. It will only take a few minutes." Jacqueline listened closely to his voice, but he spoke without an accent. This did not reconcile with his obviously Middle Eastern appearance. Nothing about the man's appearance would have told her whom he represented. Jacqueline, cautious, escorted the man to sit in the chairs on the front porch, avoiding bringing him inside her home. "I represent an organization that is interested in Solomon Rosenberg's work."

His topic shocked Jacqueline, but she showed no surprise. Until that moment, she had no clue what his business with her might be, but she did not expect that he would want to talk about Rose. "Well, I don't know how I can help you. Rose is dead." Those words still ripped through her heart. "Yes, we are aware of his demise. Please accept our condolences. However, we believe you have information that could assist our organization in the fight for a free Palestine. We would be willing to pay well for your assistance." "I have no information for you, nor any interest in the Middle East." Jacqueline regretted admitting that she knew Palestine was in the Middle East.

Jacqueline listened to him speak about the struggle for a free Palestine for a few minutes more, before explaining to him that she knew nothing about any connection Rose may have had to the Middle East. Youssef still believed that Jacqueline could be "an asset" to their organization. He explained that obtaining information about the work that Solomon did for the CIA and the Israeli Government would be of great help to them. Although he never actually said the name of the organization that he represented, she had little doubt from her years with Rose that the organization he was speaking about was the Middle East fundamentalist group Hamas.

Jacqueline played dumb to Youssef, but she was far from ignorant about the problems of the Middle East. Rose had followed the turmoil in the Middle East closely when he was alive, and she spent many hours discussing with him the issues involved. In fact, Rose followed the news from all over the world by television, newspapers, and magazines. He even listened to worldviews of current events on BBC, Voice of America and Radio Russia. Rose also had a "hobby" – talking on radio and telephone in different languages. He would tell Jacqueline, "Languages skills have to be used or they will be lost – it's use it or lose it."

Jacqueline had never really thought about how much equipment Rose had in the safe room behind the library of their home or how much he followed world events until just that moment. She had been aware of the mainframe computer he had built in the safe room of their home. They spent many hours in that room together. Rose had simply closed off the door to a windowless fourth bedroom and reconnected it with a secret door behind a section of a wall-to-wall bookshelf in the library.

It was there that he kept all of his electronics – how he loved being in that room, like a child in a candy store. Toward the last days they spent together in that home, Rose had dismantled and destroyed a great deal of the equipment in a manic rage that lasted for weeks. Eventually, he sealed the entrance to that room. At the time, she could not comprehend why he had closed off the things that gave him so much pleasure. Jacqueline did not understand many things about Rose until it was too late.

Gaining her interest in world affairs from Rose, she was well aware of the current situation in the Middle East. Youssef repeated that they would pay generously for any information about Solomon Rosenberg's government work. Jacqueline again firmly explained that she knew nothing about Rose's work. "Rose never spoke of his work or of any Palestinian organizations, and I'm afraid I can be of no assistance to you." She followed that statement with an invitation for the man to leave, and he did so without further conversation. Jacqueline watched from the porch as he climbed into his shiny black Mercedes and drove away without looking back.

His attempt to obtain information for his radical organization had failed, but it caused her to wonder if it was the CIA or Hamas that had burglarized her home. She turned and walked back inside, quickly locking and bolting the door. Jacqueline noticed her hand was shaking as she poured herself a cup of coffee. Sitting down at the table, looking out her living room window, she felt pleased at how well she had handled Youssef. Although she regretted saying Middle East, she thought that anyone would know that Palestine is located in the Middle East. After all, she could not turn on the news or open a newspaper without reading about the Middle East these days.

Considering his unexpected arrival in the early morning, she was pleased with her reaction. Jacqueline knew that the sole purpose of Youssef's visit was to try to obtain the tapes that Rose had recorded about his life's work with the CIA and possibly the Israelis, as well. At the least, Youssef's intention was to find out if the tapes existed. It had nothing to do with her being an asset to their organization – it was those damned tapes! The visit made her nervous; she could feel her body shiver. She was no longer sure who had turned her home upside down. Jacqueline had no interest in the movement to free Palestine, but she did make a decision after Youssef left that morning. If she was going to stay safe, she had to know the contents of Rose's tapes.

A long time ago, she made the decision not to retrieve the tapes until things calmed down. Now she realized that interest in Rose's tapes would never wane. Rose had left them with someone he trusted, and Jacqueline was worried about trying to retrieve them, because she did not want to reveal the keeper's location. She really thought that if she let time pass, interest in the tapes would evaporate. Then she could retrieve the tapes and avoid further involvement with the CIA. Jacqueline now knew time had not diminished the CIA's and others' interest in Rose's information, and it was time for her to find out just what Rose had to say.

Later that same day, Jacqueline booked a ticket for New York. She would leave the following day and stay two nights at the Hyatt. She booked the trip online in her maiden name. Finally, after all these years, she had made the decision to get Rose's tapes. He had told her years earlier that she would know when the time was right. As far as she was aware, only two people on the face of the earth knew for sure that the tapes existed.

Those two people were Jacqueline and the keeper of the tapes, Mark Steinberg, Esquire. Rose had told her that Mr. Steinberg was an old law school friend, and that he had chosen Steinberg because his ethics were above reproach. Rose knew Mr. Steinberg would follow his instructions to the letter. She hoped that Rose had instructed Steinberg to give her the tapes, and soon she would find out.

Jacqueline had only the vaguest idea about what the tapes contained, and she needed to know more. She had so many unanswered questions. Günter, Rose's old buddy from the CIA, knew she was living on the mountain. While she was there, he monitored where she was by driving down the road in front of her home many times, yet he never stopped. Now, a representative of Hamas or someone from the Middle East came to her Florida home looking for information he thought she possessed. Jacqueline realized there was still a great deal of interest in Rose's work.

She was ready to find out the truth, and she believed the answers were contained in the tapes held by attorney Mark Steinberg in New York City. Jacqueline had committed his name and address to memory many years ago, when Rose was still alive. She never told anyone that the tapes existed, let alone where they were. Now the time had come to relieve Mr. Steinberg of his responsibility, and Jacqueline knew that she would have to use extreme caution in retrieving the tapes.

She lowered all of the blinds in her home, and then Jacqueline began packing a small rolling suitcase. She moved her car back into the driveway at the front of her house, and she began loading the trunk of the car during the afternoon. She was filling it with empty suitcases. Jacqueline hoped that they were watching her load, and that they would not take their eyes off her car. Before dark, she made sure that the front porch, living room, and bedroom lights were on and that the back porch was dark.

The telephone rang a few times during the day, but she did not answer. That evening, she finished packing her rolling suitcase with the last few items that she would need and turned the television on for noise. Shortly after nine, leaving the lights on in her home, Jacqueline picked up her small case and went quietly out the back door of her home through the palm trees, hibiscus, and other shrubbery of the neighborhood.

She stayed away from the few streetlights that illuminated the neighborhood by walking through alleys and yards. Jacqueline moved quickly and crossed streets only where they were the most dimly lit, watching over her shoulder throughout. When she was sure that no one was following her, she came out on a sidewalk six blocks away from her home, on the edge of the downtown entertainment area.

Jacqueline knew she could no longer hide in the dark. There were too many people around and no way to walk to Three Beach Drive without being in public view. So, she decided that she should hide in plain sight. Walking swiftly, watching behind her, she headed to the basement restaurant. Descending the street level stairs, Jacqueline could hear the jazz playing inside the dark, brick, smoke-filled room.

She walked directly to the pay telephone and called to reserve a room at the Airport Marriott Hotel. Stepping to the bar, she ordered a Grand Marnier and took a booth seat against a wall in the darkest area of the restaurant. It was near the front door, where she could easily see anyone who entered. Jacqueline listened to the piano man playing music, as she watched through a window set high in the wall to see if anyone appeared to have followed. Everything appeared normal outside the window and no one had entered the restaurant.

Just as the piano man finished his third song, she asked the bartender to call her a taxi. He smiled at her and reached for the phone. A few minutes later, a taxicab pulled up in front of the restaurant window. Jacqueline finished the last of her drink, grabbed her rolling case and purse, and walked up the stairs to the street. Climbing into the cab she said only, "Tampa Airport," as the taxi pulled away in the night. Jacqueline could not see anyone following, as the cab drove the twenty miles to the airport.

Jacqueline paused and leaned back in Sid's chair. Sid looked at her guest and asked, "Would you like another drink?" It looked to her like Jacqueline was terribly stressed and could use another. Sid rose from her chair. "No, I think it will be a long night, and I want to stay alert. But I will take some more coffee." Sid picked up the elegant coffee service, headed for the coffeemaker, and returned with filled mugs for each of them. "I figured that we needed serious coffee cups." Jacqueline smiled and nodded. She told Sid, "Caffeine will be our friend for the time that we're together. It won't calm my nerves, but it will keep us awake."

Sid asked, "How – how bad is this?" Jacqueline told her, "Sid, at this point I'm not sure if I even have any emotion left in me – but I know that I do. I've been afraid for so long, I can no longer remember what it's like to live without fear. I'm to the point where I'm just numb." As soon as Sid sat down, Jacqueline began again....

Chapter Three
New York

JACQUELINE WAS sure that no one had seen her leave from the back of her home. At least she was trying to convince herself. The trees and brush were thick, and there were no lights in the back yard or the alley. She had been extremely quiet, and had moved quickly out of the area of her home before coming into the light, to avoid detection.

Even if someone had seen her leave, she knew that no one could possibly know where she was going. Jacqueline had never breathed a word about Solomon's tapes to anyone. Not even her family knew, because she decided long ago that anyone who knew the tapes existed would be in grave danger.

As the taxi pulled up to the curb at the departure level of Tampa Airport, Jacqueline stepped from the cab and joined a rapidly moving crowd headed through the terminal to the shopping area on the third floor. Then she began walking slowly around the airport looking for reflections in the shopkeeper's windows, reflections of people who might be following. Every fiber of her being was on high alert for danger. Her thoughts were louder than the noise of the terminal passengers; she had begun the journey of no return. Suddenly, she noticed armed men with automatic weapons headed in her direction.

Immediately, she realized they were there to protect the passengers from hijackers, but any government affiliation made Jacqueline's blood run cold. Finally, she rolled her suitcase into an airport lounge and took a seat near the back of the bar. Jacqueline watched the comings and goings of people for a while, as she ate her dinner and sipped a cocktail. She could not spot anyone who appeared to be following her. After an hour or so, she rolled her case toward the Airport Marriott hotel and checked in for the night.

Exhausted, she quickly hung out the clothes for her journey in the hotel bathroom, and within minutes fell asleep. Waking early the next morning from an unsettled night's sleep at the hotel, she still felt somewhat rested for her journey. Jacqueline found herself ready for the inevitable, but hesitant about the sojourn, as she brewed a pot of coffee in her room. She stood with coffee in hand, peering out the 12th floor window, dreading reentry into Rose's world.

It took her two cups of coffee in front of the window to accept her return to the dark side. Then, clearing her head of those thoughts, Jacqueline showered and put on the camel hair suit and monochromic accessories that she had chosen for her return to New York. It was slightly cool, but still a beautiful Florida morning, when she prepared to board the plane at Tampa International Airport for LaGuardia Airport in New York City.

At the airside terminal, Jacqueline waited until the last minute to go to her gate. She wanted to make sure that no one found out where the tapes were located. She continually but surreptitiously looked everywhere to see that no one was watching. With only her small rolling suitcase packed with a change of clothes, laptop computer, micro recorder, and some extra batteries, she began her journey for answers.

Jacqueline was not looking forward to this trip to the Big Apple. She was scared to death. However, at least her attire would shadow Vogue's current style for her return to New York. She hoped that her clothing would let her blend into the crowd on the streets of Manhattan. With only a couple of hours flying time to New York, she spent the plane trip planning her approach for seeing Mr. Steinberg without an appointment. Jacqueline did not want to reveal to his staff the purpose of her meeting. She decided to start with a simple request and increase information to the staff only as necessary for them to decide to advise the attorney of her presence. If she could get past the staff, Mr. Steinberg would recognize the name Rosenberg.

She arrived in New York shortly before noon, and took a taxi straight from LaGuardia Airport to Manhattan. She knew that it would be best not to arrive at Steinberg's office at lunchtime, since New York attorneys usually leave their offices for power lunches in Manhattan. Jacqueline already knew that she might have a problem seeing Mark Steinberg without an appointment. She did not want to complicate the situation further by arriving at his office while he was out. The cab pulled to the curb at 150 West Fifty-Seventh Street.

As the taxi pulled to a stop, Jacqueline once again saw the large red canopy with gold writing reading, "Russian Tea Room." She had decided on the flight to have lunch before going to Steinberg's office. The Russian Tea Room was a place Jacqueline loved to visit every time she was in New York. She had recently heard that the rumors about it being sold for its real estate value were false, so she expected this would not be her last chance to enjoy the Manhattan landmark's wonderful cuisine.

Frames of brass twelve inches wide surrounded the mammoth glass doors. The Art Deco crest high on the building was like an old friend, and she felt welcome as the maître d' took her case and escorted her to a table near the bar. Mahogany floors and high mahogany ceilings studded with multicolored crystal skylights surrounded Jacqueline in this mostly French inspired palace of glass. The deep green walls with their gold carved moldings were filled with pieces of antique art as big as ten feet tall, and yet more art – sculptures, crystal, and samovars – littered the room. At noon every Monday through Friday, the most determined minds in the business world sat at the white linen covered tables nestled inside red leather booths. Both the environs and the occupants were an inspiration to the viewer. This was especially true for Jacqueline, who had a fetish for men in power suits.

The ceiling soared some forty feet above, lit by its multi-colored skylights and sculpted glass chandeliers; the light flickered like rays of sun off the golden Russian samovars that adorned the room. With dishes such as borscht, duck, and caviar, the food was to the palate what the dining room décor was to the eye. Jacqueline relaxed and dined in peace, as she watched the power lunch set coming and going. She found herself wondering if one of the men lunching at a table near her was Mark Steinberg.

Jacqueline smiled as she pondered the thought that Steinberg might be in the restaurant. She found the idea amusing, to say the least. He would not know her and she would not know him, since they had never met. However, within minutes their lives would cross. Was he one of the men giving her a second look as she dined alone, possibly?

Maybe he was the tall thin handsome man with the blue eyes and slightly receding hairline. Alternately, was he the one with the quiet smile sitting just ten feet away? She had noticed that man's glance from time to time. On the other hand, maybe he was the loud-mouthed, short man who kept interrupting others while they were speaking at his table. She doubted that man would be him, knowing Rose. Jacqueline found the possibility that Mark Steinberg might be sitting only a table or two away from her intriguing.

Jacqueline finished her lunch of pâté de foie gras, salad, and champagne. She thanked her server, paid her check, picked up her rolling case, and walked back onto the Manhattan sidewalk. The door attendant signaled a taxi and Jacqueline slipped inside, looking back to say goodbye to her old friend, The Russian Tea Room. She told the cabbie, "Third and Fifty-Eighth Street," and sat back as the taxi took her to Mark Steinberg's law firm on Third Avenue. It was about two in the afternoon.

To Jacqueline, New York never changed. People, people, people packed the streets, all in a hurry to go everywhere and nowhere. The city, like the world, is filled with the good and the bad, the rich and the poor, the intellectual and the intellectually lacking. There is no other city in the world like New York City. Every lifestyle, every nationality, and every socioeconomic group – they have all melded into some kind of semi-peaceful coexistence. This city amazed Jacqueline, especially when she considered the sheer volume of people per square block.

No city could be more proud of the way its people reacted to the tragedies of 9/11. Residents of Manhattan and the surrounding cities came together, helping strangers without a second thought, without gain and without violence. It was as though the clock had stopped on evil. After terrorists hit the World Trade Center, only goodness prevailed in the survivors.

Jacqueline had always enjoyed New York, with its museums, restaurants, bookstores, and, of course, the nightlife. Day or night, even in the wee hours, there was always something to do to stay amused and feel alive in Manhattan. To her, the city still had its mystical excitement. However, the sounds of the city at the end of its lunch rush were almost overwhelming to Jacqueline after her years of reclusive living. The quiet of the mountain and the muted sounds of sleepy Florida could not prepare her ears for the din.

After her days in New York with Rose, she had never wanted to return. That was her last trip to the city until now. To Jacqueline, New York was her Paris, for she had loved her husband even more deeply during the New York days they had spent together. She could barely live with the pain of losing him, and she wanted those memories left buried deep inside. Seeing the city from the taxi window opened the floodgate of painful memories, memories of love lost.

Just as Jacqueline was becoming absorbed with those anguished thoughts, the cab came to an abrupt stop in front of the large smoked glass doors of a high-rise office building. She paid the cabbie and stepped onto the sidewalk, her breath taken away at the very sight of the building. Those doors led to Mark Steinberg's office, and hopefully Rose's tapes.

Jacqueline took a deep breath as she slowly entered a twenty-foot-high rotating door that opened into a magnificent lobby of brass and marble. Overcome by the soaring ceilings covered in mosaic art, she paused as a tourist would on first impression. Catching her breath, she walked over to the directory of office names and suite numbers. She scanned the list until she saw "Steinberg, Rosenthal & Ginsberg, et al, P.A., – Suite 1801."

She waited, looking at the art on the walls, until she could enter an empty elevator car. Once inside the elevator, Jacqueline pushed the button for the seventh floor. The elevator doors opened and closed on seven. She hesitated and chose not to exit. Instead, she pushed the button to the twelfth floor. On the twelfth floor, she exited the elevator, found the fire stairway and walked down to the tenth floor. Arriving at the tenth floor, she again entered the elevator, and pushed the button for the eighteenth floor. She felt that she had now taken every possible precaution to protect the location of the tapes.

The law firm was stately and polished, with marble floors, thick emerald green carpeting, and deep cherry furnishings in a reception area that was at least six hundred square feet. Although there was seating space for a dozen, no people were waiting. To Jacqueline, this appeared to be a very large piece of expensive Manhattan real estate for a receptionist. A nine-foot tall portrait of Jacqueline's favorite Supreme Court Justice, Benjamin Cardozo, hung on the wall to her left. She walked slowly across the marble floor of the immaculately kept foyer. Behind a fifteen-foot long finely carved reception desk atop an oval oriental carpet of gold and green, was seated a beautiful, smiling young woman.

"Welcome to Steinberg, Rosenthal & Ginsberg. I am Brie. May I help you?" "Yes, good afternoon, Brie. My name is Jacqueline Rosenberg, and I'm here to see Mark Steinberg." "Do you have an appointment with Mr. Steinberg?" "No, I do not." Jacqueline noticed a subtle change in the receptionist's demeanor and in her voice. "Can you tell me what this is in reference to?" "Mr. Steinberg is expecting me. Please just check with him."

The receptionist was still polite, but it was obvious from the expression on her face that she was irritated that Jacqueline would not explain her business with Mr. Steinberg. "Mr. Steinberg seldom will see anyone without an appointment, but I will see if he is available." Jacqueline had thought of a dozen ways to approach this meeting with Steinberg. She hoped that she would not need to say anything more to see him without an appointment, but she suspected that this haughty receptionist would do whatever she could to impede Jacqueline's progress.

The young woman picked up the telephone, "Anne, a Jacqueline Rosenberg is here asking to see Mr. Steinberg. She does not have an appointment." Brie hung up the telephone with a pleased look on her face, "I'm sorry, but Mr. Steinberg is not available. If you like, his assistant will schedule an appointment for you. She will be with you shortly. Have a seat." Jacqueline walked across the huge reception room and sat in a Louis XVI tapestry chair to wait, wondering if it was real or a reproduction. Her conclusion was that it was real. All of the furnishings looked to be antique – Jacqueline was sure that in status-conscious New York, all of the pieces were authentic.

In a few minutes, a well-dressed, lovely, middle-aged woman appeared in the reception area. She approached Jacqueline, "Good afternoon. My name is Anne Slosberg. I'm Mr. Steinberg's assistant. How may I help you?" Jacqueline stood, and again explained that she was here to see Mr. Steinberg. Again she was rebuffed, but more politely. Jacqueline was unsurprised by this. After all, she knew from working in Rose's law practice that part of the job of the staff was to protect lawyers from intrusions.

Jacqueline looked directly into Anne's eyes, "I will only be in town this afternoon, so please check with him before I leave. I think you will find that he has been expecting my arrival." There was a moment when

Jacqueline thought that she was not convincing enough, but then she saw a subtle change in Anne's face, and she knew that she had succeeded. Anne walked to the receptionist, "Brie, call Mr. Steinberg and see if he has a few moments for Jacqueline Rosenberg, and be sure to mention her name."

Irritated at Anne's request, the receptionist picked up the telephone, "Mr. Steinberg, I know that you are too busy to see anyone without an appointment, but Anne told me to let you know that there is a Jacqueline Rosenberg here to see you." The receptionist hung up the telephone with a shocked look on her face and in a very pleasant tone stated, "Mr. Steinberg will be right with her, Anne." Jacqueline laughed to herself thinking, "You never know who may be important, dearie." Anne walked back to Jacqueline and with a warm smile said, "I had a feeling that he would see you. Call it intuition." Jacqueline smiled back. "Thank you very much, Anne." Anne walked away as a man came out of large, cherry-paneled arched doors in front of Jacqueline, walking directly to her as though he had met her before.

He was shorter than Jacqueline had imagined, about five feet six inches tall. He appeared to be in middle age, and had a hairline that was receding. His weight was a little excessive, but carefully hidden inside his crisp Brooks Brothers suit. He was not any of the men she had wondered about in the restaurant. His hand met hers in a firm handshake. "Mrs. Rosenberg, please step into my office." Jacqueline noticed a single bead of sweat on his brow.

He turned and walked a few steps as he escorted her through the grand doors, not engaging in any further conversation as they proceeded down the hallway. Jacqueline immediately knew that she had met this man before, a long time ago. He stopped at the hall door to his office, "After you." Then looking to his assistant seated at the desk near the door, "Anne, I'm not to be disturbed." "Yes, Mr. Steinberg." Jacqueline smiled and thanked Anne again, as she entered his door.

Once inside his office, he offered Jacqueline a seat and closed the door. "Mrs. Rosenberg, you look very familiar. Have we met before?" Jacqueline was certain at that very moment where she had met Mark Steinberg, but she replied, "No we have not." She was unsure why she said that, because after all, she knew exactly who he was. "It must be my mistake. I'm Mark Steinberg. How can I help you?" Without hesitation, in a firm but polite voice, not knowing what resistance she was going to meet, Jacqueline looked straight into his eyes and said, "You have a package that belongs to me."

Mr. Steinberg's face did not move a muscle, his eyes staring straight at her. "I'm not sure what you are talking about." She noticed a second bead of sweat forming on his forehead. "May I please see some identification?" Jacqueline did not want to show the panic she felt when he said he did not know about the package. Calmly, she pulled out her driver's license, the one that still carried the Rosenberg name. She handed the driver's license to the attorney; everything appeared to be happening in silent, slow motion. She said nothing, however her mind was preparing for a fight with this old friend. Jacqueline knew Rose had sent the tapes to him; she had even mailed one of the packages.

Jacqueline remained quiet and waited for his response. Her mind was clicking into Sun Tzu warfare mode – "When strong appear weak, when weak appear strong." She would retrieve Rose's tapes. Mark Steinberg looked carefully at the driver's license then passed it back. Slowly, without a word, he reached into his inside coat pocket, pulling out a chain with a single key. Steinberg unlocked his lower desk drawer. "I had to verify you were Jacqueline Rosenberg. I am glad that you have come for the box; I have held these items for far too long. I do not want to be responsible for them any longer." Jacqueline noticed the sweat disappearing from his face. At the same moment, she relaxed. He had the tapes.

"I agreed a long time ago to hold this package, as a favor to my old friend Solomon, who is now deceased. Solomon and I started law school together at Columbia University in the early sixties. We became fast friends in the three years we were classmates. As you may know, our school divides each entering class into sections, and the students in each section take all of their classes together for the first year. Solomon and I hit it off immediately. He had a king's wit and we enjoyed studying and socializing together. Even after the first year, we took many of the same classes. We saw each other daily for those three years.

"Of course, after I went to San Francisco and Solomon left New York for Jamaica, we saw each other less but spoke often. Then he received the margin call on his stocks and returned to the United States to practice. I returned to New York a few years later, and began building my practice. We saw each other infrequently; by then, the time constraints of our busy practices estranged us some. With Solomon spending most of his time in Washington, our paths seldom crossed. My fondness for him never dimmed, although over the years our contacts became less and less frequent. While Solomon was ill, we spoke and I casually mentioned that I like Shakespeare. Two days later I received Shakespeare's entire works from Solomon by mail."

Jacqueline could tell that Mark had true affection for Rose – he became almost misty-eyed while talking about his old friend. She saw his demeanor change again, "But getting back to business, my instructions were to maintain the packages and letter as they were delivered to me, never to open them, and to release them only to you as long as I am alive. I must say I'm happy to be turning them over to you. I do not know what is contained in the packages, and I do not really want to know. However, I must admit I'm curious. Do you know what is inside?" She replied, "I have an idea. They contain personal effects." Mr. Steinberg looked doubtfully at Jacqueline after her statement, but said nothing more on the subject. "Mrs. Rosenberg, as you can see, the boxes and envelopes came to me sealed, and remain unopened. I was beginning to become concerned. I'm no longer a young man, and I worried about what would happen when I died."

He passed Jacqueline a box. She was surprised that the box was not sealed. When she opened the lid, she saw that the box contained a number of sealed packages. Each one bore a red wax seal, including the very package she had mailed for Rose. Shivers went through her as she looked at the packages and their seals, realizing immediately that Rose's fingerprints were impressed in those seals. She had seen Rose make that very same red wax seal fingerprint when he finished reading documents on a wooden clipboard. That was the day a soldier arrived at their home with Rose's CIA call-up orders.

It seemed that the incident had happened a lifetime ago. However, her memory of the Washington trip that followed was as fresh as yesterday. The evening began with a limousine driver by the name of Harry picking up Jacqueline and Rose, heading to Tampa International Airport the same evening Rose received the CIA's orders. It was a whirlwind weekend. Günter, Rose's college friend, greeted them at the airport. A beautiful needle-nosed white plane, with only numbers on its tail for identification, stood ready to whisk them to Washington.

Another limousine was waiting for them at Washington National Airport, to take them to a beautiful furnished house on C Street in Washington. It took Jacqueline only minutes to realize she was in Rose's house. She did not know her husband owned this house in Washington until that night. When she asked Rose about the home, a house obviously filled with his belongings, his response was simple, "Need to know baby, and you do not need to know about this place. When we leave

Washington, I want you to forget this house, just as I have been trying to do for years."

There she waited, while Rose and Günter went to a meeting at the Pentagon. While she was waiting, she walked around the house looking at duplicates of books, glasses, clothes, chess games, and more, that Rose had in their Florida home. The third floor and basement required pass codes for keyless entry; Jacqueline was not privy to them. Finally, she fell asleep waiting for Rose. He returned from the Pentagon in the morning hours, with clothes for her to wear for a State Department Dinner that night.

Someone had purchased a strapless dress of solid black, with a floor-length full skirt in size four. The material was made of fine silk with tapestry trim. A diamond necklace and earrings were in a separate box. Black heels, a clutch bag, and a fur coat were there to adorn the dress. Everything had been prepared for the evening ahead. A limousine would be waiting.

The lights of Washington were shining brightly through the raindrops. As the water beaded off the windows, the limousine headed to the State Department. When the car arrived at its destination, a Marine opened the door for Jacqueline and Rose to exit. Rose took her arm and said, "They are going to announce our arrival, so just enjoy it." As they entered the reception area, someone called out, "Mr. and Mrs. Solomon Rosenberg, Esquire."

Everyone seemed to know Rose, and they all seemed delighted to see him again. Jacqueline sipped on a glass of champagne as they mingled with what appeared to be old friends of Rose's. Musicians playing violins roamed the rooms, filling the air with music. There were cocktails, dinner, and dancing. After dinner, at Rose's request, the band began to play *La Vie En Rose*.

This was all because a briefcase had been stolen from Günter in Hungary. It had been sold to the Hungarian Embassy, and it was to be returned by the Hungarian Ambassador at the dinner in Washington. Rose was called up because the case was armed with Astrolite. Since an attempt had been made to open it without a code, it needed to be disarmed and Rose's expertise was needed. This is the kind of thing Jacqueline could never forget.

She gently rubbed her finger across one of the seals, trying to feel something – something left of Rose. "May I call you Jacqueline?" "Please do, Mr. Steinberg." "Mark – please call me Mark. Jacqueline, when I received the first packages, Rose told me if anything unusual were to happen to him, that I was to turn it over to *The New York Times*. He told me that it was the only paper he trusted.

"Many years went by before I received any further instruction from Solomon. He called me at my home from a pay phone in Florida, advising me that he was dying of cancer. Solomon advised me that other packages and a letter would be coming, and that I should handle them in the same way, with one exception. He spoke of you, and said that one day you would come for the packages.

"My instructions were to turn over all of the packages and the letter to only you. I promised Solomon that I would tell you that he loves you very much. He made me promise not to use the past tense – he was adamant about that. I will be honest with you, Jacqueline; I have wondered for all these years what you looked like. His description of you was perfect. I want you to know that never before or since have I heard a man speak with such love for a woman. That is the way I heard Solomon speak of you, with such fondness and excitement in his voice, on the final day we talked.

"I have waited many years to meet you. After a while, I began to believe that you would never come. Solomon asked that I not initiate contact. My instructions were to wait for you to come to me. He said that you would know when the time was right to come for the packages. If you did not come, my instructions were to have the packages and letter turned over to the Times upon my death. I provided for that eventuality in my instructions to my office staff and in my Last Will and Testament.

"However, I only advised my staff that any documents or packages marked 'Times' should be delivered to *The New York Times* at my death. I never told them what was sealed or from whom they came." Jacqueline noticed that the outer box was marked "TIMES" in black marker, and it was not Rose's handwriting. Steinberg continued to speak. "Frankly, I was concerned about fulfilling that contingency, not only because it meant that I was dead and would never have the opportunity to know what was in the packages, but because it meant that I would never have the pleasure of meeting the woman that Solomon loved – correction – loves so much!" Mark chuckled, "Rose made me promise, no past tense."

Once again serious, he handed Jacqueline a letter with the same red seal. "I have thought a lot about this, and decided that I never want to know what is in the packages. I am sure that you will know what to do with the contents. This letter and the final package arrived to be placed with the others shortly before Solomon's death." A red wax seal was on this envelope, as well. The envelope read only, "Mrs. Jacqueline Rosenberg." "After it arrived, I wondered if Rose wanted me to turn this letter over to the Times as well. I was not sure, as my instructions were for everything to go to the Times. I'm so glad that you arrived to collect the packages, and especially the letter.

"I was sure that I understood the instructions regarding the packages, but I was never comfortable with turning over that letter to anyone but you. When I spoke to Solomon that last time, he made it clear that I should only release the letter to you. He told me that I would never be able to reach him again. He was going to a hospital in Europe and did not believe he would come out alive. I did not ask any more questions of my old friend, and we said our final goodbyes that day."

Jacqueline removed the items from the box and placed them in her rolling luggage, as she thanked Mark for all of his assistance. As she rose to leave his office, Mark offered Jacqueline his hand again. "I know that this sounds strange, but I once knew a Jacqueline while I was in San Francisco. Have you ever been to San Francisco? "No." Her voice was calm, polite but firm. "I am amazed at how much you remind me of that girl." "Well, I have never been to San Francisco and I assure you we have never met before." Mark looked a bit disappointed. "I have often wondered if I would recognize her, if I did see her again. I was so young, and she was even younger. I doubt that she could possibly recognize me. I look nothing like I did back then. Besides, I don't think that I'm very memorable.

"It has been a pleasure meeting you Jacqueline. Are you staying in town? If so, perhaps I could take you to dinner while you are here." Jacqueline hated to lie, but she did not want to cause any problems for Mark, nor did she want to reinforce his memory of her as someone from his past.

She knew if they saw each other again, he would confirm that she was the girl with flowers in her hair from San Francisco. That was a lifetime ago, and his curiosity about her would require her to tell him even more lies. Besides, at this point he was ignorant of the contents of the packages. Jacqueline knew that the packages' contents were dangerous, and she had no desire to endanger Rose's old friend (and her old opium den friend) more than he had been already by holding the tapes for so long.

"I appreciate the invitation, but I'm going directly back to the airport." "Well, Jacqueline, I think it is safe to say that this is the only business we will ever do." She nodded curtly as she said, "Yes, I assure you Mr. Steinberg, this will finish any business we will ever have.

I just want you to know that I loved Solomon with everything in my being."

"Jacqueline, it is obvious to me that you and Solomon had the greatest love that I have ever had the privilege of knowing. I've never married, maybe because I am still looking for love like that. I wish you well." "Thank you, Mr. Steinberg. Also, please do Rose and me one last favor. Please delete any reference to these items from your Last Will and Testament, and from your mind."

"Oh, wait – I have one more envelope for you, and my instructions were to allow you to open it in private, immediately before you left the office. I will step outside." He handed her a manila envelope with another red seal, and closed the office door behind him. Jacqueline opened the last envelope. Inside was a new passport in a different name, additional ID, credit cards, cash, and a letter. The letter included the instructions, "Use this ID, once you leave this office with the tapes and documents."

Jacqueline placed that envelope in the front pocket of her case and walked slowly out of the office, pausing only briefly to give her thanks to Anne, and to say farewell to Mark. Then she rolled her case down the marble-edged, green-carpeted hallway and out through the French doors she had entered. Saying a polite goodbye to the receptionist, she pressed the elevator button. It felt as though it took forever for the elevator doors to open. Her mind was racing – she had the tapes. And Mark, of all people on the earth, was the one Rose chose to hold the tapes!

No one was in the elevator when she entered. She took it to the third floor and then walked down the fire escape stairs to the first floor. When she reached the lobby, she left the building through a different set of doors than the ones through which she had entered. She was on Forty-Ninth Street, and immediately hailed a cab outside the law firm. She slid into the back of the cab and told the driver, "Lexington and Forty-Eighth Street." Jacqueline could not believe it! Mark Steinberg was not only Rose's old college friend and the man who had been holding the tapes for all these years. He was also the same man she had dated a few times in San Francisco, when she was still a young flower child!

She was now a woman, and although he thought that he recognized her, she was sure she had dispelled his belief when she said she had never been to San Francisco. Everyone, including Mark, was stoned during the Haight Ashbury days. His recollection had to be foggy. She just wanted to disappear with the tapes and to leave him no hint of their ancient past together. Nevertheless, a smile did come over her face with the memories of Mark and the opium den. It was a time of freedom and innocence.

As the cab sped off, Jacqueline looked back for a few blocks through the distorted taxicab mirrors. Then she began looking around as though she were a tourist enjoying the sights of the city for the first time. It was all to see that no one was following. Jacqueline had made her decision to go to New York for the tapes quickly. Then she went without a scheduled appointment to see Mark Steinberg, so she doubted that anyone had followed her either to New York or to Steinberg's office. The thing that made her nervous was the visit from Adel Youssef. That was the catalyst for her decision to come for the tapes. She was still of interest to the CIA and now to Palestine, as well. She had a strong feeling they were watching her home and likely her movements. That is why she had left so carefully under the cover of darkness.

Jacqueline rested her head on the back of the seat and thought of the opium den where she and Mark had gone together so many years ago. She was shocked when she immediately knew, even with the age on his face, that he was her Mark from San Francisco. She wondered if he believed her when she said that she had never been there.

It appeared by his question that he thought he recognized Jacqueline, but the hesitation in his voice made her believe that he was not sure. After all, she was sixteen, with flowers in her hair, when they met. Now she was a grown woman in a Chanel suit. Would it dawn on him later that she was really the same girl he had known in San Francisco? She simply could not believe the man Rose spoke about so fondly and with whom he had entrusted his tapes was the very same Mark she walked with on the wharf in San Francisco. That was years before she even met Rose. She did feel badly about not acknowledging her history with Mark. However, she had too much on her mind to deal with Mark Steinberg, and she did not want him to know any more about her than was absolutely necessary. She told herself that she was withholding the information about their previous connection for his safety.

Within fifteen minutes, the driver had maneuvered his way through the horn-honking, bumper-to-bumper Manhattan traffic and pulled over at the corner of Lexington and Forty-Eighth Street. Jacqueline paid the driver without a word. Then she exited the cab with her rolling case and watched as the driver pulled back into the heavy Manhattan traffic. She began the three-block walk to the Waldorf Astoria on Park Avenue, stopping along the way to call for a reservation in her new name and cancelling her reservation at the Hyatt. Now if anyone did find out she had traveled to New York, she would be almost impossible to find. She just smiled. Rose had thought of everything.

The street was bustling with pedestrians, and Jacqueline slipped into the stampede within seconds. She could hear the conversations around her and had the feeling that all of their lives were normal. Two women walking in front of her were discussing how they wanted to find doctors or lawyers to marry. Jacqueline thought that if only they knew what trouble marrying a lawyer could be, they would decide to shoot for pharmacists instead. "If they had an inkling of the intrigue surrounding the woman directly behind them, they would turn and stare in open-mouthed wonder." She could not lose herself in thoughts like that – there was too much to do that would demand her full attention.

As she neared the grand street entrance of the historic Art Deco building, she saw the massive sign reading "Waldorf Astoria" soaring high above the street. Jacqueline walked slowly toward the American flag flying high over the sidewalk entrance. Finally, she began to feel some relief from the stress of the trip. The bell captain was awaiting her in full uniform, complete with shiny gold buttons. He greeted her with a smile as he took her small rolling suitcase and escorted her into the hotel's elegant lobby of dark wood and fine marble flooring.

Massive columns of white and black marble rose to the high ceiling. Imbedded in the ornate plaster of the ceiling was a large medallion of mosaic tile. That medallion was easily recognizable as Renoir's "Circle of Life." Jacqueline's eyes soared up the columns, to where a crystal chandelier cast golden light upon the mosaic and painted ceiling. Between the columns stood a two-ton clock embossed with the faces of Benjamin Franklin and Queen Elizabeth, and topped by a miniature Statue of Liberty. To her right she could see Cole Porter's Steinway grand piano surrounded by enormous oak walls and carved chairs upholstered in rich blue velvet. She handed her new passport and credit card to the clerk, who stood proudly behind an antique caved desk as long as a train. "I have a reservation for two nights."

Within minutes, a bellman in his mid-sixties escorted Jacqueline to the doors of the elevator, hand carved with goddesses, while making casual conversation. He continued to chat as they exited the elevator and he led Jacqueline to her room. After he opened the door, he followed her into the room, and placed her luggage on a holder near the closet. Then he opened the heavy blue drapes to show the view of Park Avenue through the floor-to-ceiling window. He graciously pointed out the bar, bath and amenities on the premises. Finally, he asked Jacqueline if she would like him to unpack her suitcase. Politely refusing, her eyes never far from her luggage, she tipped the bellman generously as he left. She then immediately locked and placed the security chain on the door.

The décor of the large room was an understated grand old elegant style, with a massive wooden canopy bed. A matching desk and a thick tapestry sofa formed a separate seating area that included a small, overstuffed, ox-blood leather chair and ottoman, carefully placed on an old oriental rug near the window that overlooked the city. The bathroom was white marble with veins of gold. It contained a large granite Jacuzzi tub. Towels monogrammed WA rested, perfectly placed, inside a marble towel warmer. This Shangri-la was just what Jacqueline needed before she began the long journey down memory lane, narrated by Rose's own voice.

She quickly slipped into the hot Jacuzzi tub; with the room service menu in hand, she made her choices for a long night's stay. She was beginning to relax. That was something she had been unable to do since the stranger arrived at her door the previous day. Reading the room service menu while resting in the warm jets of the Jacuzzi, the tension began leaving Jacqueline's body and mind. Thoughts of Mark as a young man played in her head. She was simply unable to believe that it was Mark at the office today.

Jacqueline placed her relaxed, warm, wet body into the terry bathrobe. Picking up the telephone, she ordered a bottle of Grand Marnier, a dinner of seafood, a few desserts and two large pots of coffee for later. She expected that she might need the coffee to stay awake while listening to tapes. She was planning to be awake late into the night. Even though the Waldorf had twenty-four hour room service, Jacqueline did not want to be disturbed once she settled in with the tapes. Looking out the window while waiting for the room service waiter, her memory slipped back to the days in New York with Rose.

She recalled the time spent at outside cafés along Manhattan's West Side, laughing as they checked for spelling errors on the chalkboards listing the cafés' daily specials. The days spent buying books at Shakespeare and Company came rolling back into Jacqueline's thoughts. She could still see Rose in her mind's eye. He was sitting on the floor of Shakespeare and Company when his body was too weak to stand, as she passed books down to him from the shelves.

Memories of his weakened body, his collapsed lung and the hours in the emergency room waiting for the doctors came flooding back. How they had waited to begin the experimental treatment to save his life from lung cancer – it all flooded into her brain. He had so much pain; his agony caused her so much anguish. She re-experienced the pain she felt as she watched the bipolar disease that affected his mind intensifying just before he became violent. He then had committed himself to a hospital and refused to tell anyone his location. His mental condition came roaring to life from the drugs and the chemotherapy, and it ended their life together. It was all inside her again. She had tried so hard to secrete those memories away in the deepest recesses of her mind, so that she could remember only the good about Rose.

Jacqueline's mind was lost in the old memories of love and pain when a knock came at the door, followed promptly by the announcement, "Room Service." She glanced through the peephole and then opened the door for the waiter to set up her dinner. He was a little more talkative than her mind was capable of handling at that moment. Realizing that she did not care to talk, he quickly placed the rolling table next to the leather chair in front of the window and left.

She locked and chained the door behind him. Then she sat down to her dinner while looking out at the movement of the people on Park Avenue. It was a way of taking her mind off loving Rose. From her window high above the city, the people look like ants rushing a hill. Jacqueline quickly let her mind drift to escape the memories of Rose, imagining that the women were proudly scampering from store to store, carrying their shopping bags from Gucci and Saks Fifth Avenue. The men, more serious, carried their briefcases, hurrying to the next meeting. Although she was far too high to see such details of the people far below, she was able to conjure up a marvelous dream of escapism – sexist, but amusing nevertheless.

When Jacqueline finished her dinner, she poured a drink and relaxed with a snifter of Grand Marnier, trying to let time pass and bad memories of the old New York days fade back into the depths of her subconscious. This was why she had not wanted to return to New York. She knew that her days of loving Rose in New York would all come flooding back into her mind.

Rose's need for cancer treatment had brought them to New York that summer. After months in the hospital, they returned to Florida. However, the chemotherapy, the drugs for his bipolar disease, and the painkillers had induced a manic period in Rose. At the same time, Rose had decided to be honest with Jacqueline about his work with explosives for the government. This happened after his psychiatrist was killed by a hit and run driver in his office parking lot. Rose was sure the CIA had found out he was seeing the doctor and had murdered him. Jacqueline had become more convinced as the weeks went on that Rose was correct about the death of Dr. Pillar.

Jacqueline stood and stretched, telling her old friend, "Sid, Rose persuaded me that they killed Dr. Piller, and later I found out that he was right. But I have to tell you the story in order, or I'll forget something." Sid nodded, as she shifted in her chair. "I understand." It seemed to Jacqueline that the only part of Sid that had been moving was her writing hand, but Jacqueline went on....

Chapter Four
Man Unknown

NEVERTHELESS, SHE shook off thoughts of her life with Rose. She walked over to her suitcase, opened it, and removed the package and envelope she had received from Mark Steinberg. At the same time, she took out her computer, recorder and batteries. Jacqueline removed the inner boxes, ran her fingers one more time over the red seals of the envelopes, desperately trying to feel his love again. Perhaps she could conjure up Rose, if only she wished hard enough.

There was nothing, no feeling, just the ridges of a fingerprint molded into the red wax. Jacqueline needed to cry, but she gathered herself together. She knew she was accomplishing nothing – crying was merely a waste of time, and there was no time to waste. Jacqueline broke the seal of the smallest envelope, almost angry that she could not feel his presence again, and opened the letter. A single tape and key chain with an electronic fob fell on to the bed. She placed the tape in her recorder, looked at the key chain, and then at the letter. She knew Rose's handwriting immediately; as she began to read, Jacqueline felt his presence in the room as though he had never left her side.

Jacqueline my love,

If you are reading this, you already understand the danger you will always face. I am so sorry that I brought you into this cold, dark world of my work, but I will never be sorry for loving you. After you have listened to all of the tapes, keep this one out and secure the rest in a bank safe with my journal and other evidence. Keep the key fob with you at all times. Slide the panel back and push the button, then speak into the microphone with a question or location. I hope that I will have anticipated what information you will need and programmed the response information. This computer chip is set up with answers to questions you may have; I'm trying to guide you from the grave. The envelope that contains this letter also contains one tape. Contact Meier Finch, and play for him parts of the tapes that describe his information and participation. Place a New York Times newspaper where he can see it when you are playing the tape. Tell him that you want an income for life in Israeli Zion Bonds and training in Israel to protect yourself. Do not hand over the tapes or documents to anyone. Never release the tapes! Never trust anyone completely, not even Meier Finch. However, as long as you control the tapes, Meier will feel the need to protect you.

I am also deeply concerned about Günter's obsession with you. So be very careful if he shows up in your life again. I am including a list of names and descriptions of people involved in C Street. I do not trust any of them. You may not recognize them now, but if they appear in your life, you will know to be wary and carefully follow all the instructions I am leaving. Jacqueline, wipe your eyes my love and be strong. Listen to the remaining thirty-five tapes now. When you have finished the recordings and documents, push the button. I'm sorry for everything. This is why I waited so long to marry you. It

was selfish of me to love you, but I believed that I would always be near to protect you. I will be waiting for our next dance under the statute in heaven, if Christ allows me to redeem myself.
I love you,
Solomon.

The tears flowed down Jacqueline's face like water gushing from the waterfall under which they had once made passionate love. She fell to her knees and began praying to God that this was all a nightmare and that she would soon wake in Rose's arms. As the tears slowed and reality sank back into her mind, she broke the red seals on the packages and dumped microfilm containers, a journal, and thirty-five recordings out on the bed. Most were computer CDs or micro-cassettes, but some were full size cassettes. Wiping her eyes with the bed sheet, she fumbled with the recorder as she listened to the first tape from the envelope that contained the letter. The tears came to an immediate stop as she became captivated with the sound of Rose's voice once again.

"Expect the unexpected, Jacqueline. The CIA is aware that these tapes exist and the Agency will want them. However, they can never be sure that they have the only copies, so you cannot turn them over in exchange for your freedom. Besides, the fact that you know about the tapes makes you a liability to the Agency, even if you no longer have the tapes in your possession. As long as you retain the evidence, the governments, unsure what it contains, will not harm you for fear that everything would be exposed automatically on your death."

Rose went on to say he had left a letter for Günter to find after his death, advising Günter of some of the material and telling him that an automatic release of all of the documentation would occur if anything unusual happened to her. The letter to Günter explained that even Jacqueline did not know who held the trigger on the auto-release of information.

Jacqueline was stunned at the words she was hearing. Rose said he knew that they would search everything after he died to look for any loose ends that connected him to his work as an agent. This was SOP (standard operating procedure). He told her that he believed telling Günter about the tapes and setting up an auto-release, if her death appeared suspicious, was the only way to protect her after he was gone.

Jacqueline was shocked that the CIA knew the tapes existed. Did Rose know what he was doing when he left a letter telling Günter about the tapes, or was he just in a manic, drug-induced state when he made that decision? Had he unwittingly placed her in more danger by his letter to Günter? Shaking off her questions, she again concentrated on Rose's voice on the tape.

Next, Rose's voice on the tape began to recite the names of agents he felt might be employed to retrieve the evidence that she had. As the tape continued, Jacqueline did not seem to recognize any of the names until he said, "Joe Kelly, the Marine from the State Department dinner." Jacqueline quickly ran the tape back and played it again. She could not believe what she was hearing. The tape repeated Rose's last sentence. "If I were running the CIA operation and I wanted to get the tapes and the other evidence from you, I would have him seduce you. They know that you met him at the State Department dinner, and he was an extremely handsome man." She stopped the tape again.

Jacqueline was furious. She should have gone for the tapes earlier! Then she thought that if she had gone earlier, she would have surely have led the CIA right to the tapes. After all this time, maybe they no longer believed that the tapes existed or that she did not know where the tapes were located.

Jacqueline had a feeling, during her last days on the mountain with GI Joe, that he was not the man she thought. She was right. GI Joe had seduced her at the ski resort and stayed on her private mountain until Rose died. He lived with her, claiming his love, sleeping in her bed and watching her for the CIA. Günter came to the mountain to let GI Joe know it was over – that Rose was dead. That is when GI Joe started asking questions about Rose's work. Once Rose died, Joe was determined to get the tapes as soon as possible. After all, she was his job assignment. It all made sense now – she had been sleeping with the enemy.

The only comfort Jacqueline found was that she had never admitted to him where the tapes were, or that she even knew of their existence. GI Joe was really CIA Joe, and he had failed his mission. She took a little pleasure in that thought. Besides, he was not bad in bed on a cold winter's night. However, she had suspected in the last days on the mountain that he was not all that he had claimed. She had trusted her instincts and left the mountain just in time. Now, she wondered just how long she could stay ahead of the group of professional killers and spies.

The tape also explained the documents on the microfilm, as well as what she was about to hear on the other thirty-five tapes. He had recorded some of them during his career and some after his retirement. This information was about past actions for the government agents participating in the events. Everyone involved felt safe, until Rose made it clear in his final letter to Günter that he had made the recordings.

Rose's tapes contained proof of all that had occurred, and her possession of the evidence meant safety for Jacqueline. Without the tapes, she was fair game for the CIA, because the Agency could not be sure what secrets Rose revealed to her during their marriage and his long illness. Rose had given his best to protect Jacqueline to the end. At least he thought revealing the existence of the tapes would protect her from the CIA.

She had been shocked when she opened the box. Inside were CDs of digital documents and computer code, as well as microfilm with optical copies of documents. Some of the items were from the U.S. Government and others were from the Israeli Government. Some of the tapes in the box were full size cassettes that he had obviously recorded earlier in his career, and some were on audio CDs. She thought about how to listen to the tapes, as she stared out the window overlooking the bustling Manhattan streets.

Of course, she could listen to the micro-cassettes and CDs now, but she suspected that the oldest tapes had information that she would need to understand the tapes that Rose had recorded later. She could go out of the hotel and purchase a regular cassette player. After all, the New York streets are full of electronics shops. However, if anyone had followed her, it might give away that she had the tapes. She decided to listen to the CDs and tapes that were his most recent recordings on her computer and micro-cassette recorder, and hope that she could make sense of them without the background that the older tapes might provide.

She listened, painful and shocking as it was, to the CDs and micro-cassette tapes that Rose had recorded. After the first tape, she realized that she had made the right decision. She would not need a regular cassette player right away. Each of the tapes or CDs described a separate incident, so the order that she listened to them was not so important, after all. However, some of the micro-cassettes were recorded at very low volume, and she knew that she would have to download them on her computer to enhance the sound. Nevertheless, she listened to what she could play and hear. That would have to do for now.

In her possession were the details of Rose's covert operations, headquarter locations, names of participants, identities that the government had changed by surgery, as well as contacts, dates, and locations of the events. He even described conspiracies for future operations on which the governments were working.

On one tape, Rose told her the story of a massacre of German university students. The violent, vicious kidnapping and murder of nine Israeli students by Palestinian terrorists in Germany caused shock around the world. Immediately, the global community responded in sadness, condemnation and outrage. While the world mourned the lost children of Israel, a group of senior Israeli and CIA officials met secretly in Bern, Switzerland to discuss retribution for the murders. What followed was one of the most aggressive and deadly covert assassination campaigns ever conducted by joint government intelligence agencies.

Shortly before nightfall, eight masked men dressed in civilian clothing silently entered the campus grounds. They quietly made their way to a dormitory housing Israeli students, and took the students hostage. Within minutes, the eight members of the Black September Organization had taken nine hostages, and killed one bystander. The students who managed to escape alerted the authorities to the attack.

After dumping the body of a murdered hostage onto a crowded street, the terrorists released a list of demands to the German government. The demands included the release of 300 people – Palestinian terrorists and non-Arab radicals – held prisoner in Israel and Germany. The list included the leaders of the German-based Baader-Meinhof Gang. The terrorists also demanded that three planes were to be fueled and ready for takeoff at a nearby airport. When the terrorists arrived at the airport with the hostages, they would select one of the fueled planes to fly them to Iran, where they expected to meet up with the released prisoners.

Negotiations with the Palestinian terrorists, said to include offers of unlimited money and German officers in exchange for the Jewish students, failed. In an attempt to save the hostages, there was an order issued to open fire on the terrorists at the airport. In response to the rescue attempt, one of the terrorists tossed a grenade into the open airplane door, where it exploded and ignited a catastrophic fire of jet fuel. Within an hour, after the smoke finally cleared, the massive scope of the failed rescue was clear to the world. Eight hostages, a German police officer, and five of the eight terrorists died at the airport.

Israel's retaliation for the massacre was massive, creative, and swift. Twenty-four hours after the airport fire, an air strike launched from Israel. There were approximately 78 Israeli aircraft involved, and it was the largest attack since the 1967 Arab-Israeli Six Day War. Israeli fighter-bombers struck guerrilla targets in Lebanon, Syria and the surrounding Middle East, killing 66 and leaving hundreds more injured. The casualties were damage collateral to the planned executions of those involved in carrying out the attack on the Israeli students.

Despite the large, aggressive military response to the terrorist actions, and in spite of the collateral damage and political fallout, the retaliation was not complete. A group of high-ranking Israeli officials decided to send a clear and firm message, not only to those who participated in the massacre, but also to those who might consider future attacks against Israel. An operations team was necessary, and that team needed to be independent of the military. The group, designated "Committee IX," was to consist of Israeli assassins and the American B6 unit.

The American government had assigned B6 to assist in the operation. The B6 unit was an elite group of six American assassins and Meier Finch, who coordinated their assignments. Committee IX was at the command of Israeli Premier Golda Meir. The group's mission was to execute the assassination of every individual involved in the Germany attack, whether the person's involvement was direct or indirect, minor or major. Because of the message that Israel wanted to send to other groups that considered attacks against Israeli targets, all of the executions had to be in public places. Israel would neither confirm nor deny involvement in any of the assassinations. Still, Israel wanted the message to be clear. There could be no doubt that the killings were not random acts of violence, but absolute retribution for the attack on Israelis in Germany. There would be no questions, no captures, and no arrests.

In order to carry out this task, the Israeli Mossad activated its assassination unit, known as the Kidon. The CIA supplied the explosive experts of B6, including Rose. Both teams underwent special identification training in Israel. Deposits made into Swiss bank accounts supplied the payment for personnel, travel expenses, and equipment. The money was available to the operatives – part of it during the mission, and the balance to be paid upon completion of their assigned mission.

Instead of informing all of the personnel involved in the operation of the goals, team structure, targets and other information, the teams were compartmentalized and had only two handlers, Golda Meier and Meier Finch. No team was aware of the existence of the others or their targets. The Swiss bank accounts provided financial support for the assassination teams, both operationally and individually. In this way, they would be able to operate with complete autonomy, and completely outside the Israeli and American governmental structures. The only mutual point of contact between all the personnel of B6 was Meier Finch. He would provide the list of target names and all other information necessary to hunt down the terrorists and kill them.

Meier always allowed B6 operatives great latitude in their operations, encouraging them to be clean but creative with their assassinations. Meier did have one ironclad rule on this mission. Targets would only be terminated after the surveillance team had attained one hundred percent identification. If absolute identification was not possible, the operatives' standing orders were to abort the hit and cause no collateral damage.

Israeli death warrants were issued for thirty-five targets. The first assassination attempt of the joint Kidon and B6 operation would result in collateral damage, a mistakenly identified local man. Rose was not on the team that misidentified and killed the local man in an explosion. This event set the stage for a firmer procedure to ensure no more mistakes. Meier Finch would thereafter verify every target's identity himself. But the damage was clear from the media; television news repeatedly ran the explosion footage of the mistakenly identified local man. This did not deter the mission of Kidon and B6.

The terrorist targets then were divided amongst the assassin teams of Kidon and B6. Rose's assignment was a terrorist known to have played an active role in the massacre, Ali Hassan Mustafa. After the killing of the Israeli students, Rose described himself as, "primed for this assignment. My only regret was that for my security, I would have to take him out from a distance. Explosives are the safest method for the assassin and the most reliable means of exterminating with extreme prejudice."

Operating from a covert location in Bern, Rose's team began tracking down their assassination target. Ironically, Mustafa was also the final target, and the subject of the very first failed Kidon-B6 assassination attempt. Rose finally caught up with him on the streets of Beirut. Following a short period of surveillance, the team positively identified the long-sought terrorist. Meier Finch himself confirmed the target.

Rose's voice continued, "Alone, I drove a 1977 Mercedes 230 sedan and parked it on the street shortly before 7 AM. I had already purchased a copy of a daily newspaper at another location, and brought it with me. I walked just over a block to a nearby café. Café Livonia Reef was my activation point. I took a seat at a low-rise outside table, at three minutes before seven in the morning. To my left, two men sat looking at a map. They appeared to be just visiting the Middle East. To the right, a group of three sat, including an American woman with a high-pitched voice, who was using the words, 'Yada, Yada, Yada,' repeatedly. Her shrill voice was piercing my ears.

"The table I chose was near the gated entrance of a low fence that surrounded the outside tables. I picked this seat in order to assure a clear exit, and because the chair was already out so I would not need to touch it to sit down. Placing my Arabic-language newspaper on the table, I walked inside the café and ordered an espresso. I walked back outside at seven minutes after seven and returned to the table where I had left my newspaper. This was to prevent a server from getting a good look at me or getting friendly. My Russian ancestry and suntanned skin made me blend in with the dark haired, bronze-skinned people of the Middle East. My dress was a simple muslin suit. Suits like it were common garb for any man in that area. I wore no tie and my shoes were sandals that I had purchased in the same town three years earlier.

"I sat with the local newspaper, that day's copy of *An-Nahar*, waiting and watching. Calmly, I took an alcohol wipe from my pocket and wiped my hands. Then, I slowly wiped the handle of my coffee cup in the one place I had touched. I never picked up the cup again. At fifteen minutes after seven, the target, Ali Hassan Mustafa, began his daily walk to the Grand Hotel. Each day he had made this walk. Some days he would walk on the right side of the narrow road and on others he would take the left side, completely at random. From his apartment, he had to pass by the café, and then pass the car I had parked. As usual, he was alone. He passed my table at seventeen minutes after seven. At eighteen minutes after seven, I turned slightly to the left in my chair. At nineteen minutes after seven, the target chose the wrong side of the road as he approached the parked car. No one else was near the car.

"At that moment, I pushed the button on a remote control in my right pocket. The car was armored on only one side. It was designed to explode out into the street, and it contained a high explosive charge of Astrolite, which I remotely detonated with the push of that button. People began running everywhere, running away from the blast. I stood looking at the explosion scene for only seconds to confirm the target had to be dead. Then I picked up the newspaper, to make sure that no clues remained of my identity. I joined the crowd fleeing the area, newspaper in hand.

"Meier picked me up within the first block. It was not Ali Mustafa's lucky day. Meier drove straight to the airport and we boarded an airplane marked with the logo of a humanitarian organization that was on the runway ready for takeoff. I was in the United States and at my office the following day. The blast killed Mustafa and ended the six-year campaign to kill and terrorize those responsible for the university massacre and those who would follow in their footsteps."

Jacqueline knew that Rose was an assassin, but she had never heard this story before. She hated to think about the hands that held her – the man she loved – pushing the button that ended the life of another. Somehow, hearing the details was much worse than just knowing that he had killed before. She was beginning to think that she did not really know him, at all.

Sid shook her head. "Jacqueline, I knew Rose worked for the CIA as a bomb expert. It's really not a leap to think that he was an assassin. However, when I look back on my interview with Rose's roommate Günter for the last book, I knew he was hiding something. I also knew that he wasn't about to tell me the unvarnished truth. Do you have any idea how much Günter knew about Rose?" Jacqueline told her, "Sid, you need to wait – just let me talk. There's a lot to tell you. We can't get off track. If you still have questions about Günter when we're done, I'll answer them."

"Jacqueline, what was Rose's demeanor while he was talking on the tape? Did he seem emotional at all?" Jacqueline turned her head, looked out the window and said, "His voice was flat – he showed no more emotion about the deaths of those men than we would show about squashing a bug." When she looked back at Sid, there was a tear in Jacqueline's eye. "Do you want to take a break?" Jacqueline took a deep breath, shook her head, and continued....

Chapter Five
Tape 35

THERE WAS a part of Jacqueline that was glad she could not listen to all of the tapes. By the time she had finished the last audible recording, she was simply stunned. That tape contained the story of a very strange mission that had been planned some twenty-plus years in advance. She could hear it in Rose's voice – even speaking of this mission upset him greatly.

Jacqueline reached for the key fob, and after hesitating, she pushed the button. A recording filled the room. "Sit down; I have programmed a hologram so you will never be alone. Suddenly, a six-foot hologram of Rose appeared before her eyes. "Hello, Jackal, I love you so. By now, you must have listened to the recordings and reviewed what I left behind. Go ahead and replay Tape 35, I will be right here with you, always." The hologram stood only feet away from Jacqueline, calling her Rose's pet name for her, and she no longer felt alone as she heard Rose's own words:

"Solomon M. Rosenberg, CIA, December 27, 1998, Sarasota, Florida: I hereby state this as my deathbed declaration. My diagnosis is terminal, inoperable lung cancer. My treatment in New York seems to have extended my time, but I do not know how much longer I will live. Although I have many more stories to document, this one is the most significant of all, because it details a plan that has the greatest risk of changing the future of the world. This plan is so far-reaching that I cannot risk failing to document it. As with each of the tapes, I will begin with a preamble, since each tape must stand alone, in the event of destruction of the others. The listener needs to understand some background information.

"It all began on February 9, 1963, at Jerome L. Greene Hall of Columbia University – It was my senior year at Columbia Law. I was deep in thought about the International Treaties lecture I had just attended. While I was walking alone near the large bronze Lion that stood in front of Havemeyer Hall, a man in a gray tweed suit and gray Fedora hat approached me. 'Excuse me, could you tell me how to get to the Sacred Cow restaurant?' Being a native New Yorker, I knew the restaurant well and was happy to oblige him with directions. As I began to speak, he interrupted me, 'Mr. Rosenberg, my name is Meier Finch and I am with the CIA. I would be pleased if you would join me for lunch.'

"I was stunned by the serious look on his face, and I asked him what he wanted from me. Mr. Finch replied, 'The United States Government would like to offer you a position when you graduate.' I told him that I had already accepted an associate position with a law firm, so I really did not need a job. He told me that the government position was in addition to the job that I had already accepted, and that it would not interfere with my practice of law. Pleased, proud, and innocent, I accepted Meier Finch's invitation for lunch.

"We walked together in silence until we were just off the campus grounds. A limousine pulled up beside us. Meier quickly opened the door and invited me to step inside the car. As we got into the car, Meier told me that the position would not begin until after I passed the bar examination. That ride forever changed the course of my life. The limousine did not take us to the restaurant, but it did take me to lunch at a Manhattan apartment on Fifth Avenue. Meier told me it would be my apartment at no cost while I studied for the bar exam, and for as long as I chose to practice law in New York. I knew it was only a block or so away from the firm where I would be practicing, and it was a great apartment in a great area. That seemed a deal too good to pass up. That day I took an oath of secrecy and signed my life away.

"The day after I graduated from law school, I moved into my new, fancy apartment and began studying for the bar examination. I heard nothing from Meier Finch until the day after the bar examination. That morning, he called me. That evening, Meier flew me to Washington. To my surprise, my taking-the-bar present was a house on C Street, for when I was in D.C. No mortgage, utilities, taxes, or insurance – it was all paid by the U.S. government. Of course, it, like the apartment, was all accomplished through a shill corporation. Once I had accepted Meier's offer, the preparations must have begun. When it was time for the government to bring me to Washington, my life was already prepared for me.

"The house on C Street held a complete office on the third floor. There was an entrance to a tunnel in the basement. That tunnel connected the C Street house to other homes and government buildings in Washington. I could go from my house on C Street to Meier's residence next door, to many federal buildings, to the Capital, or even to the White House without being seen on the street. All I needed was the pass code to exit my basement and the ten-digit codes to exit the tunnel at my destinations. During my years there, these tunnels were expanded all over Washington. All of the technological advancements we created for the government were incorporated into to the C Street house. My next-door neighbor was Meier Finch, who referred to our houses as the future base for the C Street complex. During my years in the CIA, we developed a massive, powerful complex on C Street.

"My office on the third floor housed a staircase behind a bookcase that led to the tunnel entrance in the basement. Meier had arranged everything, and nothing was left to chance. Of course, at that time I had no idea of the plans they had for me. I was still wet behind the ears. I spent a week in Washington furnishing my new home on the corporate account, and another week of long days and nights with Meier. His teachings made me realize the broad implications of the oath of secrecy I had signed. I realized that whatever happened, I was stuck in the job forever. That house on C Street in Washington would be the location where I worked for my entire career, except when I was on assignment.

"One day, Meier told me that my life of leisure was over, that the bar results would be out in the next week, and that I had passed. I returned to New York the following week to begin my new job at the New York law firm. My first assignment for Meier was as an associate in that firm. The firm was very selective, so I had worked hard in school to obtain a position. I had accepted an associate position just before Finch first approached me. The firm's offer was contingent on my having passed the bar exam. Meier's fringe benefits seemed too good to pass up.

"For the first three months after I started my new job, I thought that I was on top of the world. I had a nice home in Washington, a high-end Manhattan apartment, an unlimited expense account, and a good salary for my work at the most prestigious law firm in New York. In addition, the CIA was paying me three times my lawyer's salary, asking only that I do my job at the firm.

"Then reality reared its ugly head. Meier contacted me at home shortly after 10 PM, a few months after I began work at the firm. He instructed me to duplicate the file of one of the firm's high profile clients and turn it over to him in 48 hours. I completed the assignment. That would be the first of many moral and ethical questions that I would face in my life at the CIA. A client's file is sacred to lawyers, and to release the client's confidential information and the firm's work product is unforgivable. Once Meier had the file, he instructed me to give two weeks' notice at the firm and report to

Jamaica for training. After six months in Jamaica, I traveled to Israel for another year.

"I have often wondered if the catalyst for my being offered the CIA job was my having obtained that prime position at the New York law firm. If some other law student had beaten me out for the position in the firm, would he have been the one who signed his life away with the CIA? I do not know. My ego would like to believe they spent a lot of time choosing me as a CIA agent and the firm file was just a test. After all, the most important part of picking an assassin is a strong sense of moral flexibility, which I seem to have. Until my cancer, I had no problem compartmentalizing my CIA work and the rest of my life. However, cancer changes the soul of a man.

"Israel is where I would become the CIA's foremost expert on the explosive Astrolite and a trained assassin. When I came back from Israel, I returned to my house on C Street. That house and the neighboring homes on C Street would become the base for many of the CIA covert operations. As the years went on, the houses of C Street were outfitted with the most advanced technology available in the world. In my last years, I hated the C Street Complex; it had become a stronghold for the 'Christian' World Power Organization, the CWP, and barely tolerated Jews, Muslims, and other faiths. In addition, CWP was manipulating many Christians, using them like puppets for the profit of CWP and its powerful members. We always believed that CWP really stood for Corporate World Power, an organization created by the founding families. We never could find the evidence to prove that.

"Had it not been for Meier's and my skills, knowledge, and information, they would have had us eliminated. Each time the political climate allowed, the group's stranglehold on B6's developments got stronger, yet it did not weaken when the political winds were unfavorable to CWP. Eventually CWP had complete control, with full access to the code and other developments of B6. Never again did they intend to give up power in Washington.

"Although I had tunnels built and I developed security devices and technology that no one else understood, I knew my time on C Street was limited. My choice to retire rested a great deal on the CWP getting too great a hold on the technology we had created. It was not until my final year in the government that I realized who was using the B6 work and why. By that time, it was too late to prevent the damage from my work, so I retired. Today's C Street Complex residents only know part of what they have; however, the damage they are doing with what they know will destroy America. It is only a matter of time.

"I no longer remember my life before I was an agent. Moreover, I barely remember the days before I became part of the B6 operation. We were an elite group of men in a covert branch of the CIA. Some of us were members of other intelligence agencies, as well. I received all the benefits the CIA had to offer: money, drugs, sex. This is where it began and I'm leaving this information so you may somehow begin to understand how I became the man I am. However, I ask no forgiveness for my work on C Street. Men like me believe God is our judge, or more honestly stated, we believe we are gods. These questions are of more interest when you are dying – anyway, I guess it doesn't matter for me now. I expect that I will find out soon enough.

"The six men of B6 were strangers who knew each other only by code names and who submitted all communication through Meier Finch. Instead of informing all of the operatives involved in the B6 operation about overall goals and other information, the individuals and their respective assignments were tightly compartmentalized. No member was aware of the existence of the others' true purposes or identities.

"I had never met or talked with any members of the group until our first meeting in Geneva. We were a United States think tank made up of NSA operatives and CIA covert operations experts. The meeting in Geneva was the first time we even knew the group's actual name: Black 6.

"To the best of my knowledge, in addition to the think tank, each of us had cover jobs that paid a good government salary and required no work. My title in the US government was "Appellate Lawyer, Energy Administration" in the Department of Energy. Our real paydays were in cash, for operations such as Geneva. We were six men, forbidden to acknowledge our existence as an organization. Ever.

"Meier gave each member part of an assignment. We would work on our part of the problem, submit questions to the other members through Meier and present our individual results for him to combine and analyze. I knew that the other members existed, but they were completely unknown to me until the Geneva meeting.

"Personally, I found this method of filtering all of our discussions through Meier to be a very unsatisfying way of problem solving, and I often felt as though I was the only member of the 'Group.' Until the first Geneva meeting, I really thought that the group might only be Meier and me, with Meier playing multiple roles. This train of thought is all part of the paranoia that a CIA assassin feels.

"Very early in B6's mission, I began secreting documents, evidence, and computer code. When highly effective drugs were created, like those used for killing or those used for mind control, I would borrow a few vials using my clearances. I always maintained a supply of Astrolite and other powerful small weapons.

"On my last trip to Washington, I entered the secure underground bunker I had built in Arlington, Virginia, and removed the case of items. The cool temperature of the underground storage and the need to combine two ingredients to activate the explosive Astrolite made everything perfectly preserved. Through my connections, I left Washington on a diplomatic flight and I secured those items out of the country. I never expected that I would live long enough to tell this story.

"During my years working with Astrolite, each explosion was somehow a release of frustration from the work I did in that group. Not until later years did I realize that we were six of the best CIA assassins. We were thinkers, all with exceedingly high IQs and post-graduate educations. We were trained to kill one-on-one, but preferably by explosives, to take out large numbers of targets at once, or if necessary, a single person with extreme prejudice. We strategically planned covert operations from our solitary think tank jobs in our high dollar suits until we were called upon to kill on command. We were the perfect CIA assassins.

"I had assumed that our purpose would continue to be assassinations, and although the elimination work continued, B6's primary focus changed to a less violent and more technological mission. Now, I will detail the operation that has been the most damaging to our American way of life. It is the subject of this tape, the Computer Language Intelligence Presidency Program, or CLIPP.

"In late December, 1969, I received only three hours' notice to report to the Pentagon. That call came shortly after 2 AM, Eastern Standard Time, December 27, 1969, to my highly secure C Street office line. I was sound asleep, but when that telephone rings, you learn to answer fast and wake up even faster.

"At the Pentagon, each of the six participants was given time to change into ski clothes. No introductions were made or conversation allowed. Charles Dahl assembled us and advised that this operation would replace our current assignments but that this project was a 'lifetime commitment,' so if we chose not to participate, we should say so then. No one chose to leave.

"He stated that we were to have no communication among ourselves until we arrived at our destination and he called the meeting to order, at a predetermined location. This plane ride was a Code One Silence, Q Clearance – above Top Secret. We were told nothing about the destination, and we could bring no identification or personal items. An unmarked Boeing 727 waited on the runway. Once we were inside, it was clear that this was more than an oversized executive jet. It housed more electronics than I had ever seen aboard any CIA plane. The plane took off at 5 AM.

"As I record this, I think back on the history of B6, and my reason for agreeing to become involved in this operation, no matter what it entailed. Advanced Research Projects Agency – ARPA – was instituted in 1958 to jump-start U.S. technology and discover safeguards necessary to protect against a space-based missile attack. The U.S. military was particularly concerned about the effects of a nuclear attack on its communications infrastructure, the Pentagon and Cheyenne Mountain, because if our troops could not communicate, they would not be able to regroup or respond to attack. The solution was ARPA's mandate: to build a survivable computer network to interconnect the Department of Defense's main computers at the Pentagon and Cheyenne Mountain.

"ARPA had unique authorization and direction to make quantum leaps in technology using any means believed appropriate. One man from this original group was the creator of B6 after ARPA developed and deployed the first U.S. satellite. In the early 1970s, the word 'Defense' became a prefix to the name, and ARPA became known as DARPA. By the late 1990s, DARPA reported to the Director for Defense Research and Engineering, it had about 250 staff members, and it had an annual budget of five billion dollars. Typical projects had guaranteed funding between ten and forty million dollars. Black Six was an early spin-off of the original ARPA group by Dahl in 1969. We were each handpicked by Finch for B6.

"DARPA's mission is to assure that the U.S. maintains a strong lead in applying state-of-the-art technology for military capabilities and to prevent technological surprise from its adversaries. B6's mission was to use this same technology to control America and thereby control the world. DARPA was as unique as its mission; its program chief reported directly to the Secretary of Defense and it operated in coordination with, but completely independent of, military research and development – the R&D establishment. No person had more power than the DARPA Program Chief did unless the Secretary of Defense issued a specific mandate, which he did for B6.

"B6 was operating under Dahl, the Program Chief of DARPA and the creator of CDI, the Cyber Defense Initiative. But the Secretary of Defense gave total operational control of B6 and CDI to Meier. B6 flew so far below the radar with the CDI program that it reported to no one except Finch.

"In 1969, tension between communist China and Russia was reaching its height. The President of the United States decided to use that conflict to the U.S.'s advantage and shift the balance of power towards the West in the Cold War with Russia. Later, this episode would become known as playing the 'China Card,' The President deliberately improved relations with the Chinese in order to blackmail the Russians. I worked directly with the President on the 'China Card.'

"It had become clear to me toward my final days on the China Card project that the President had moved into a manic phase, sleeping only in short intervals, not eating, playing the 1812 overture loudly while goose stepping in the oval office. He was talking in paragraphs, demanding everyone sleep on premises, moving his 'hidden' microphones five or six times a day. It was pure hell. We all recognized that we were only seconds from being fired in one of his paranoid rampages. In the preceding week, two of his staff had been escorted out by White House guards and he announced the immediate transfer of another to Siberia. It took me a half hour to convince the President that he had no authority to send anyone to Russia. At least we had pre-signed blank Presidential Orders, just in case we needed to overturn anything the President had signed in a manic phase.

"To say the least, I was relieved when I was called to this meeting. I knew no matter what the project was it should permanently take me away from the mania in the White House. It had to be better than working directly with 'Mr. President' on the 'China Card' project.

"We all signed our National Security Agency task force placement orders as soon as the plane was airborne. I also knew whatever assignment I had accepted, the price for backing out now was the loss of my life. I never considered that a viable choice, since I have always placed a great value on my life.

"On the plane were wooden boxes with 'Top Secret Q' marked on the covers. Charles Dahl announced, 'This is your reading material. Study it well. You should try to commit as much of this material to memory as possible.' He handed each of us a sealed box. The only other thing that he said was to remind us that conversation could not occur, because the plane might not be secure. As he handed me a box, I recognized what it was; I had seen boxes like this before. I opened the box, and found another box inside. Inside the inner box were about five hundred pages for me to read, digest and commit to memory.

"Even with my photographic memory, it was clear that there would be no time for chatting during the flight, even without our orders. The plane flew from Washington to Geneva, Switzerland. We arrived at 2:03 AM, GMT + one. It was a bone-chilling –25°C. A limousine took the participants directly to Hôtel Les Nations, where a suite was waiting. Charles Dahl scanned the rooms for listening devices, and then the meeting commenced.

I have included specific details regarding each of the persons participating in the meeting and the location where we met. I have also included the affiliations of each of the participants, as best I was made aware. I am the only person about whose affiliations I can absolutely swear accuracy. This group consisted of people whose connections were secrets from everyone. Every single member of this select group had a security clearance well above top secret. Considering my past work it seems strange to me, but I felt that this was the scariest and most dangerous group of men, of licensed killers, that had ever been brought together around one oval conference table. Here are the details:

"Meeting: December 28, 1969 – Hôtel Les Nations, Geneva Switzerland
DARPA: Defense Advance Research Project Agency
Code Name: Black 6
Subject: Computer Language Intelligence Presidency Program (CLIPP)
Purpose: Organization of Task Force for Technology Development and Voting
Status: Black – Total Organizational Deniability
In Attendance: B6 Members (Black 6) and Meier Finch
Meier Finch: Agency Not Specified; Q TS Clearance
Charles M. Dahl: CIA; Q Clearance
Carl S. Hallwick: OMB, CIA; Q Clearance
Randolph P. Heiss: CIA; Q Clearance
Melvin D. Lord: CIA; Q Clearance
Albert J. Carlson: CIA; Q Clearance
Solomon M. Rosenberg: CIA, NSA; Q TS Clearance

"The Geneva meeting opened at 3:20 AM, local time. Dahl controlled the meeting. 'There are three reasons that we could not discuss the protocol on the plane. The first is that because of the electronics on the plane, security for conversation was not at the QT-21 level. The second is that our discussions cannot occur on American soil. The third is financial.' At that point, Dahl handed Charles Hallwick a draft for sixty million dollars from the Office of Management and Budget.

"Dahl went on to say, 'This task force will be a groundbreaker of developments in current technology. This year, Control Data Corporation has built the next generation of supercomputer, and AT&T has developed the UNIX operating system. You should be familiar with that and more from the materials you received on the plane. Due to these recent developments in the science of computers, it is now a real possibility that in the not-too-distant future, the American vote will be controlled via a computer network.'

"Dahl continued, 'Other countries will surely follow the American lead. This presents the real possibility for us to manipulate election results. If phase one of our operation is successful, this group will be in a position to control Presidential elections, and thereby, the United States of America.' Most of us shifted in our seats. The tension was suddenly palpable. Dahl's soliloquy sounded uncomfortably like treasonous talk.

"Dahl assuaged our fears. 'You may think that this sounds like treason, but our task is twofold. Our first task is to develop the method for controlling the outcome of elections. This technology could be implemented to strengthen America's position vis-a-vis other world powers by influencing elections of those countries. Our second task, our ultimate goal, is to develop and implement protections to avoid such an attack on our political system. I'm sure other countries are thinking along the same lines as us, and we cannot allow foreign control of our presidency. Our mandate is as patriotic as apple pie.' The tension that had developed in the room just as suddenly dissolved. Dahl's assertion of the necessity of this project for national security was the justification we needed to hear.

"Although the meeting continued for several hours, the details of the rest are not critical to your understanding of its purpose. Hallwick, from OMB, was the only person who had the authority to sign and deposit that check. He deposited the money in a numbered account held by Meier Finch for B6 at the Deutsche Dresdner Investment Bank. Before we left Geneva, each of the members received a stipend of cash in U.S. dollars and a private numbered account to be used for annual operational money.

"Each member of the group would follow the research and development of technology. When the group decided that implementation of the plan was technologically feasible, we would begin the task of developing the products necessary to complete the objective. Meier Finch supplemented the members' numbered accounts annually from the account he held, and in turn, OMB deposited funds into the primary account.

"Participation in this CLIPP group was a lifetime appointment. The group met at least once a year. Group meetings were initiated by a telephone call from Charles Dahl. He would tell us where and when to report to be transported to the meeting. No other member-to-member contact could occur. It was clear to me that Dahl was Meier's right hand and the fall guy, if necessary. Each member would be prepared to bring with him his individual status report about recent technological developments worldwide, as well as his budget for the following year's research. At this point, I believe it was the project rather than the results that interested me. The mental challenge of creating such a supercomputer, network and the programming necessary to complete the assignment was exciting. I knew the ramifications of creating the monster, but I ignored the obvious since the challenge was an intellectual's utopia.

"Discussion of these meetings or the CLIPP project outside the group was strictly forbidden. There would be no discussion among group members until the next Geneva meeting. Each time we met at a different location in Geneva. Each year, we received cash and deposits from the B6 account to finance our work for the following year. As the years passed, we took even more security measures for each meeting. Some members would take one plane and other members would take another. In the event that one plane crashed or was intercepted, the project could continue with the remaining members. Later, each member flew alone, partly for security, and partly because our work took us to worldwide locations. The members spoke to each other only about the project, and only as a group.

"If any one of us felt a development required the attention of the CLIPP group, we were to notify Meier

Finch, who would decide whether to call a meeting. Our trips to and from meetings were spent in complete silence. If we happened to cross paths elsewhere, we were told never to acknowledge knowing one another.

"All members returned to their posts around the world and went about their development duties with a virtually unlimited budget. Shortly after the first meeting began, I realized that the CIA, NSA, B6 and C Street all were convinced that they were indestructible. I did not buy Dahl's blather about developing protection for our political system. I suspected that the true purpose was to be able to assert control over America, and I have always believed that America can only survive if its people control its future. However, my ethical concerns no longer mattered. I was into this thing, and I had no way out with my life.

"I stayed actively involved and remained valuable to the operation, but I decided to do what I could to document the operations and to thwart CLIPP, by making it public if necessary, hence the contemporaneous journal notes. However, I remain silent even to my deathbed, for each day of life is too valuable for me to lose, even for the greater good. Once I bought time with the cancer treatment in New York, I changed as a man, and as an American. However, if I were to release this information, I would be dead in twenty-four hours. So, I made these recordings and I began preparing an arsenal for a counterstrike.

"The members of B6 held twenty-nine additional CLIPP meetings over the next years. After each meeting, each member left with a new assignment. We never talked except at a secured meeting site off American soil. I never knew any of the men before the first CLIPP meeting, although we all worked for the government. I often wondered if the B6 members were assigned to different parts of the world for security purposes. When you are in a program with this much secrecy, you spend a great deal of time thinking about what is really going on in the mission. You know that you are only a small piece of a bigger picture.

"B6 decided to employ multiple code writers within the government to begin writing pieces of the code for CLIPP after the infrastructure had been created. Various technical people from numerous agencies were carefully chosen because of their expertise by B6, and supplemental assignments were given within their existing employment. None of them realized that the assignments were for use by anyone other than the agency for which they worked. None had any idea what the completed product was to be, or how their work was to be used.

"A much smaller group of code writers, heavily vetted, finished the development of the project by assembling the patchwork of code portions written by the first group. Those unfortunate souls would be 'terminated with extreme prejudice,' upon completion of the programming. There could be no chance of loose ends. The member assigned to take care of the final programmers was Albert Carlson. Late at night on the evening the code was completed and the final simulation successfully run, the final programmers left C Street together in one vehicle. They had been told to take Pennsylvania Avenue to a facility in Suitland, Maryland for one last test of the program on another computer system. A front tire on their vehicle blew out and the brakes failed, so they say. As a result, the vehicle crashed on the John Phillip Sousa Bridge and then plunged into the Anacostia River. All of the occupants perished, yet no one else was injured. Carlson did his job well. There were no survivors to tell tales of their work, and the deaths were ruled accidental.

"I was one of the last to have access to our material over the years and I kept copies of everything possible. Within a few months after the programmers' deaths, Carlson died in a Beirut bombing. I retired, as much as any assassin ever retires, and opened a private law practice in Florida to keep me busy. Six months after Carlson died, Randall Heiss died of natural causes, as far as I know – from a heart attack. Only five of us are still alive at the time of this recording, inclusive of Meier Finch.

"The remaining members of B6 met one more time. This time, the meeting was in Tel Aviv, Israel, after the deaths of Carlson and Heiss, by order of Dahl. The programming was complete, the simulations successful. It had become obvious over the years that CLIPP was never intended to be used against foreign powers; it was intended solely for use domestically. Those who controlled CLIPP could launch the program any time they decided that they did not like the possible results on election night.

"The religious right organization CWP had assumed total control over the C Street complex, and I had to assume, the CLIPP project as well. This meant that a select few men located within the C Street Complex in Washington, and therefore the CWP, have the ability to maintain control of the Presidency of the United States forever. What B6 did was the computerized hijacking of America. Of all the horrible things I did for the U.S. and Israeli governments, this will have the most lingering, damaging effect.

"Whatever you do with this knowledge will be better than what I have done – nothing. I have the skill and power to do so, but fear of my own death paralyzes me, even in the face of certain death from cancer. I ask no forgiveness from the listener, as only God can forgive my work on CLIPP and my failure to do everything in my power to rectify the consequences."

Jacqueline was trembling by the tape's end. She knew that if the CIA had carried this plan out, it was the complete corruption of America's government. She just kept replaying the facts over in her mind. Rose participated in the Geneva, Switzerland meetings, where this long-term mission was conceived and executed. Only B6, those few CIA and NSA trained analysts assigned to the defense department, knew about the plan. At the time Rose made the tape, two of the men in the meeting had already died. Now with Rose dead, there were four men from that meeting who may be still alive, including the leader, Meier Finch. This also made her wonder if Rose had confided any information to Günter, or if Günter was pursuing her for general information about Rose's work. She had far more questions than answers.

Jacqueline flipped open her laptop computer and did a search for the remaining men of B6. She found that two of the men that Rose had named on the tape, Charles Hallwick and Melvin Lord, appeared to be still alive and involved in some activity overseas. Jacqueline knew what part of the government the two were in – it was the CIA. However, it appeared Charles Dahl and Meier Finch simply did not exist. She could find no reference to either man in government, social, or college records.

Jacqueline picked up her snifter and walked to the window overlooking Manhattan. She left the hologram on, so Rose was still standing in the room. She had no idea what she could do with this information. Rose had done nothing, and he had this information for years. Before she knew it, tears were pouring down her face and she was beginning to choke from crying. Jacqueline now understood the dark world of Rose, and how deeply involved he was in the CIA. She just wanted to be that little girl with flowers in her hair again. Now Rose's connection with Mark Steinberg had altered even that memory of innocent times. It seemed that he had touched everything in her life, and he would not let go, even from the grave.

She had listened to the earlier micro-cassette tapes, as Rose spoke of lives destroyed around the world in the name of America. One tape detailed a mission he had told her about while he was ill with cancer. That mission resulted in the death of a college girl at a café in Ireland.

She was killed in an explosion during the early days of America's involvement with the IRA, Shin Fein and the explosive Astrolite. Rose had miscalculated the amount of explosive needed to accomplish the objective, and the girl was an innocent bystander. Jacqueline remembered Rose's remorse for the death of that young, innocent girl.

Nevertheless, there was mission after mission described on the tapes. In each mission, people had died in the name of America. The first tape, the one in Rose's letter, was a recording just for Jacqueline and it was full of information, cautions and instructions for her to consider, including the part that talked about Meier Finch's involvement. The other recordings seemed to be all information about CIA missions.

Some of the tapes she would not be able to hear until she could quietly purchase an old cassette recorder, and for others, she needed to enhance the volume by downloading some of the microcassettes to her computer. She knew that Rose had begun stealing the documents and recording some of the tapes long before Jacqueline knew him. It must have taken a lot of thought before Rose decided to reveal the plot to hijack the American political system, because he did not record the tape with that information until after his cancer diagnosis.

The recordings also explained that at any time the CIA could create a new identity for a person, complete with passport, social security number, birth certificate, credit cards, and driver's license. She was aware that those documents could be altered, but the most interesting to Jacqueline was altering identity with surgery, too. Rose told her on the recording he made just for her that if she looked carefully enough, she would be able to tell if the identity of someone she had known was changed by surgery. She should judge not by how they looked, but by their actions, the things they said, the things they owned, and by watching their pattern of behavior. Jacqueline could not believe what she was hearing, but she heard the ring of truth in Rose's voice.

She had no idea of Rose's connection to the Israeli government, nor did she know that the CIA and NSA were tied to Israel, until she had heard the tapes. She wondered if that was the reason Hamas or Hezbollah had approached her at home, looking for information. They probably believed that she already had the information about Rose's work with Israel. They must have thought after all she had gone through with Rose, his drug addiction, his madness and his violence, Jacqueline would be so bitter that she would turn over information to them. Maybe they had just expected to buy what she knew. However, even if Jacqueline had known what was in the package when they arrived at her home, she would have never turned it over to a foreign country.

Of all the recordings she had listened to and the documents she had reviewed so far, it was the information about the Geneva meetings that shocked her most. She took a deep breath in front of the window, as she looked into the lifelike eyes of the hologram. Jacqueline thought about happier days with Rose. She thought of the times when they made love on the conference table in his office and beneath the stars in a waterfall. Her mind wandered back to the kitchen of their home and their spontaneous lovemaking after a victory in court. It was like a movie playing in her head. All of the memories came rushing back. Memories like the day Rose asked her to marry him, and then within minutes of her acceptance, telling her that he was retired from the CIA.

It seemed like yesterday that the soldier delivered the call-up orders from the CIA that brought Rose out of retirement. Maybe it was last week that they attended the grand ball at the State Department to retrieve Günter's stolen briefcase from the Hungarian Ambassador. On the other hand, maybe it was last month she took her walk with Rose down the ballroom stairs and was introduced to the partygoers as Mrs. Solomon Rosenberg, Esquire. Every memory was flashing before her eyes like the flickering of a star-filled sky.

Jacqueline still found it hard to believe that the kind, gentle man with whom she had fallen so deeply in love was the creature who had carried out the horrible acts of murder and destruction on the tapes. However, she had also seen him in a full-blown manic psychotic episode the day in April that he tried to kill her with a ten-inch knife. How is it possible to still love someone after that violent rampage? Love is chemical and highly explosive, and often uncontrollable. It was strange how Rose's voice on the tape became different, more matter of fact, when he described his covert operations. It was almost as though someone else took over to tell the horrible details – a person he created to cope with his work requirement of moral flexibility.

However, she knew it was Rose on the recordings and the hologram. There was more than one man inside him. She found this out so very clearly after his bipolar condition came to light. The cancer, the ensuing drug addiction, and the years of government work had driven him insane. Jacqueline had survived the ten-inch knife he wielded madly at her head. That was the day his beautiful dark brown eyes became black, hollow, and empty. It was the day he completely lost his mind. Jacqueline knew returning to New York for the tapes would bring back the terrible memories of Rose that she had so carefully buried. She wanted to remember only the good in the man she loved. She clicked the button shutting off the hologram. She was alone again. Her mind was racing, and she did not sleep much at all while she was at the Waldorf. After two long nights of tossing and turning, and rousing to thoughts of the tapes and Geneva, she was ready to leave New York. There was so much evil on these recordings! It shocked her conscience.

Sid asked, "Jacqueline, how do you feel about Rose after all the things you now know about him?" Jacqueline smiled. "That's a complicated question. You have no control over the chemical response you have to another person. It's that thing we call love. Rose was a sad and lonely person until he fell in love with me. I'd like to think that I was the best part of his life. He was a complicated man who showed great intensity in everything he did in life, including loving me. Yet, with him gone, his chemical not present any longer, the idol worship is over. I see him as an interesting genius with an uncertain moral compass. I now understand him better than I ever did while he was living." Sid got up, refilled their coffee mugs, and sat back down, pen in hand....

Chapter Six
Vieux Carré

THE THIRD day after her arrival at La Guardia, Jacqueline was more than ready to leave Manhattan behind. A day and a half of listening to recordings and reviewing documents and two restless nights had left her more exhausted than she thought possible. She put on her blue jeans and packed her belongings. Her roll case now contained the recordings, the documents, and the letter that she had collected from Mark Steinberg. Checking out of the Waldorf Astoria, she headed for the airport. She purchased a ticket, this time with the passport and pre-paid credit card Rose had included for her in the package. Then Jacqueline boarded a plane for New Orleans.

She arrived at Louis Armstrong airport just after lunchtime, and within minutes she was in a cab headed to the French Quarter. Getting out on Bourbon Street, Jacqueline walked, her suitcase in tow, through the streets enjoying the music until she found the Hibernia National Bank and Trust. The bank was completely unknown to her. Walking in from the street, she opened a large safety deposit box in her new name; she paid three years in advance, obtained two keys, and named her daughter the sole beneficiary with full access. She placed the tapes, CDs, journal, and microfilm inside the box and thanked the bank manager. As she left the bank, she looked up at the address on the front of the building. It read, "137 Royal Street."

Then she walked into a local bookstore to buy a book. She decided to buy a copy of *Aristotle on Ethics*. Jacqueline's life was becoming nothing but a montage of ethical questions, so the book made it a good choice for a reread. She continued walking and listening to the sounds of blues music spilling out of the taverns onto the streets of the French Quarter, until she reached the small Acme Restaurant she adored.

With its checked tablecloths, wood floors, oyster bar, and windows overlooking the Quarter, the restaurant reminded her of how much she had always loved New Orleans. Finding a quiet corner table near the window, she ordered a bowl of seafood gumbo and a shrimp poorboy sandwich. Jacqueline was glad to be away from New York and all the memories. Now she just wanted some time to think, and New Orleans was a perfect place to disappear for a few days.

Looking out the window, Jacqueline saw the old French architecture that had always pleased her eye. That architecture was one reason she had taken a flat in the French Quarter as an extra residence after Rose died. She kept her life in New Orleans a secret, just in case she ever needed a place to disappear. No landlord in New Orleans asked for identification to rent, not if one rented for cash in advance. When she first rented the loft apartment, she had paid a year's rent in advance. The landlord had never required a written lease. That was handy, now that she had a new identity. There was no paper trail of leases that anyone could link to Jacqueline Rosenberg. She could be whoever she wanted.

While she was waiting for her food, Jacqueline took the book that she had purchased from her rolling case, a pencil from her purse, and she began to read. After a few minutes of reading, she wrote in the middle of the book, along the inside margin, 137 Royal Street. On the second-to-last page of the book, she wrote the box number, 3007. She continued to enjoy her dinner while she read.

Jacqueline watched out the Acme's window for hours, looking directly at the apartment she had rented long ago. Nothing seemed unusual and no one seemed to be watching her flat. That was what she wanted to know. Had anyone figured out that she had the French Quarter loft or that she was coming to her apartment? Everything appeared to be safe, so she placed the book inside her case and walked across the brick street to her loft.

She had decided a long time ago that it was best to keep additional residences in several cities under different names, for her safety. Only Jacqueline's daughter knew of this apartment. As she entered the loft, she was happy to be home again, glad to see the few personal belongings that she kept there. Most of the items in the apartment were antiques Jacqueline had purchased in the Quarter. Local artists' paintings adorned the walls, a music box that played *La Vie En Rose* sat on a shelf, although she had not been emotionally capable of opening that box in years. New Orleans seemed to be the one place she could come and escape from the world. Exhausted, she fell asleep on the old fainting couch in front of her window and rested peacefully until late the next morning.

Waking the following morning, she had the recordings on her mind; the first thing she did was grab a large and a small padded envelope. She sealed the Aristotle on Ethics book in the larger envelope, and one of the safety-deposit box keys in the smaller, for mailing to her daughter, Marie.

In a third, regular envelope, Jacqueline placed a note she wrote that read, "Marie, please place the book on your shelf at home. It has information inside it about a safety deposit box in New Orleans. Place the key in another bank box. If I need you to access it, I will let you know. If I don't close the box, when I'm gone the contents will be yours. You should immediately release all of the contents of the box to *The New York Times*. I will call you next week to say hello, but I never want to discuss this matter over a telephone. I'm going to be traveling for a few months; we will talk about this when I get to California. Destroy this letter once the packages arrive. Burn it and then run the ashes down your garbage disposal." Jacqueline knew that Marie would understand. She had lived with and through the CIA, ever since she was a teenager.

Jacqueline took a long, hot shower, dressed in some of the clothes that she kept in the loft, and placed a few more pieces of clothing into her bag. Then she turned on the hologram. Rose's image appeared and said, "Hello, Jackal." She spoke into the microphone. "Is it safe to contact Meier Finch?" The hologram began to speak.

"Meier Finch can only be trusted because of the fail-safes I have installed to protect you. I'm sure that you are questioning whether to contact him. Do it, and then go with him to be trained. Get the money he has from the B6 operation. C Street and B6 owe us, and you are going to collect." The sound stopped and Jacqueline turned the hologram off, knowing what she must do.

She locked the loft up tightly, and then she stopped by to see the property owner, Jean-Baptiste Bouchard, at his apartment. He was an old Creole man in his seventies, who still played the saxophone in front of Absinthe's, an old bar in the French Quarter that was named for a now-illegal hallucinogenic liqueur made from wormwood.

They visited for a few minutes, and Jacqueline told him that she would be away on business for a while. Then she paid the rent on her small flat for the next year. Although Jacqueline did not get to New Orleans often, she always made sure to pay her rent well in advance, always in person, and always in cash. Jean-Baptiste had never even asked her last name when she rented the flat. Maybe because she offered cash rent, always six months or more in advance. That is just how things are in the French Quarter. Everyone minds his own business; the prevailing attitude is to live and let live.

She began her final stroll down Bourbon Street, stopping for a traveling cocktail, wondering what journey lay ahead. Within a block, she ran into an old Cajun woman, Dorr, who spent her days on the streets of New Orleans chanting and speaking of the future. Dorr was a fixture in the quarter, with her bright colored clothes, big hats and the strange but kindly aura that surrounded her. Pleased to see Jacqueline, Dorr immediately and abruptly stopped on the street.

Dorr said, "Troubled soul always brings you home, child. You are on a journey. Watch out for the gunman; do not go back to New York. He is still looking for you, but do not worry, you be okay. Dorr knows, bless you, bless you my child." Then she headed directly on down the street without another word to Jacqueline, just talking to herself. Jacqueline was sure that others saw Dorr as crazy because she talked to herself, roaming the streets of New Orleans, dressed in bright colors and big hats, but Jacqueline did not think Dorr was crazy, at all. How in the hell did she know Jacqueline had been to New York? Long ago, Jacqueline quit trying to figure how Dorr always knew about her life. It was clear that Dorr was a seer.

Jacqueline knew who Dorr's gunman was, and considered Dorr a good omen. It was strange how the old woman always crossed Jacqueline's path in New Orleans, and how Dorr always knew something about events in Jacqueline's life. Dorr always seemed to speak words that clearly connected to what was happening in Jacqueline's life, words like "gunman" and "New York." Dorr had no way of knowing anything about Jacqueline, let alone New York.

He was there again. Jacqueline saw him in the distance, and without thinking, she began running with her rolling bag. She almost ran into the path of a streetcar before she realized she was doing it again. Over the years, Jacqueline had seen someone who looked so much like Rose. Whenever she did, she would start running in pursuit. However, she knew Rose was dead and she thought she had learned to control these foolish thoughts. How many times had she chased that ghost? She knew better. Now, after hearing the recordings, hearing his voice, dredging up all of those memories of Rose and seeing him in the hologram, was it to come back to haunt her life – this phantom, this ghost – again? Jacqueline slowed her walk back down; she knew it was not Rose, just her stirred up imagination triggering illusions.

Now she wondered just how far this journey would lead her, as she headed back to the airport. She mailed the packages with the book and key to Marie at the post office in Louis Armstrong airport on her way to board a plane for Tampa International. Jacqueline had already mailed the letter; she had put it in a mailbox on the street before leaving the French Quarter. It was late in the evening when Jacqueline settled in for the short flight.

On the plane, she tried to relax for what was ahead. She missed reading her book, *Aristotle on Ethics*, and decided that when she had time, she would pick up another copy. Unable to sleep on the plane, the phantom on the street still haunting her, she began going over the next steps of her plan. Jacqueline had decided to stay at a Tampa hotel to contact Meier Finch. She wanted to be on familiar ground when she met Finch, in case he would come to her. However, she did not want him coming to her home, even though she planned to sell that house. Adel Youssef, the man from Hamas or Hezbollah, showing up at her door after the burglary made that decision for her. If Meier Finch was not involved in the burglary, she certainly did not want to give him the opportunity to enter her house. She remembered Rose telling her on the tape, "Be very careful and think through everything you do."

The plane landed about midnight in Tampa. Rolling her small case behind her, she stopped at a newsstand. Rose had said on the tape that when she met with Meier Finch to have a copy of *The New York Times* where he could see it. Jacqueline took a cab to the Renaissance Hotel at International Plaza. She knew that the hotel was a five-minute ride from the airport. She checked into a room with a view of the front of the hotel. She had already decided that she did not want to make the call to Meier Finch from her home, so she thought a hotel was the best plan.

Struggling to remember all of the instructions on the tape for her meeting with Meier Finch, she settled into her room exhausted, and immediately fell asleep. Rose came to her in the night. His face was clear and his eyes were pure as they stood together one more time beneath the waterfall. She could feel his hands gently touching her face. "My love, the road ahead is long, watch out for the gunman and you will be fine." Jacqueline felt at peace when she awoke from her sleep. She remembered the kindness in his face and the same message that Dorr had for her in New Orleans, "Watch out for the gunman."

It was strange how she clearly understood the warning, yet she had no fear. Jacqueline laid there for a few minutes trying to recall more of her dream. She knew that Rose, the man she loved, had come into her dream as the man before the madness, but she did not expect to recall any more. Slowly she pulled herself up from her bed of dreams. She turned on the hologram for company and made a pot of coffee. She knew it was odd to want to see the hologram; after all, it was not really Rose at all. She could never enjoy Rose's company again. Still, the hologram gave her comfort, and looking at Rose's image would give her the strength she needed to do what was yet to come.

It was time to make the call to the telephone number on the tape, the number of Meier Finch. Jacqueline recognized the area code as one for the Washington, D.C. area, but she knew that meant nothing. Finch could be anywhere in the world. She had followed the instructions Rose had given her from the grave. She wondered what Finch's reaction would be to her call. Hell, would he even answer the telephone? If he answered, she knew he would be interested in talking to the one person who had heard Rose's recordings.

Carefully, she dialed the telephone number. The second ring had barely finished, before a baritone voice answered. Jacqueline said, "Meier Finch, please." The commanding voice replied, "Who is this? Why are you calling?" "My name is Jacqueline Rosenberg, and I have the recordings of Solomon Rosenberg. I would like to meet with you." This was what Rose had told her to say. Without any questions and barely any hesitation, the voice requested, "May I have your address please?" Although the voice had a distinct accent, she could not identify where he was from.

Jacqueline carefully repeated her hotel address and room number. "It will take me some time to get to Tampa. I will be there tomorrow at 4 PM. Please wait for me if I am a few minutes late." Then the telephone line went dead. Jacqueline was terrified. She had started the plan in motion with that call to Meier Finch. She thought, "Now he knows for sure that I have the tapes."

Jacqueline realized that her hand was trembling as she hung up the telephone. However, she remembered Rose's words on the tape. "You must contact Meier Finch and get trained. You will need to go with him, until you can take care of yourself." Meier was interested in the tapes. That was clear from his immediate response to her request to see him. She had begun the journey and there was no turning back.

Jacqueline finished her morning coffee. Finally, she turned off the hologram and put on her swimsuit for a day of rest at the hotel swimming pool. The pool was almost empty of guests and that suited her perfectly. She ordered some lunch and a cocktail poolside, as she read *The New York Times*. Relaxing in the chaise lounge by the pool, she wondered what Meier would say tomorrow when she approached him about the bonds and training.

Well, at least Rose was right; Meier was interested in talking to her about the tapes. Now that Jacqueline had heard a sample of the recordings, she was even more afraid for her life. However, she could see no other way out. Youssef's unexpected visit and the burglary at her home made it clear that she could not be a passive participant in this. People were going to come after the recordings and documents Rose had left behind.

Meier Finch came alone the next day to Jacqueline's hotel, as far as she could tell. Arriving at three fifty in the afternoon, he was timely. She saw the limousine arrive from her hotel window and a driver opening the back door. Jacqueline was shaking as she saw a man much older than she expected, maybe seventy-five or more. He wore an English style suit, a gray fedora hat, and walked slowly with a cane. His slow movement did not dispel her fear. She knew that Meier Finch was a dangerous man. Jacqueline was not going to underestimate his power.

She watched from her window as he approached the front of the hotel, alone. The driver stepped back into the limousine. Jacqueline's heart was pounding as she saw him enter the main entrance of the hotel. Quickly, she looked around her hotel room to see that everything was where she wanted it to be for the meeting. After a few minutes, the knock came at the door to her suite. She opened the door and the man immediately addressed her, "Jacqueline Rosenberg?" "Yes." "Meier Finch," he said calmly as he walked into her room.

"It is a pleasure to meet you, Mr. Finch. Please have a seat. May I offer you a cup of coffee? In a very firm voice he said, "This is not a social call. I did not fly 5700 miles for coffee. Where are the tapes?" Alarmed by his harsh demeanor, Jacqueline immediately turned, picked up her micro-cassette recorder from under the Times newspaper lying on the table and turned it on. She had carefully started the tape at the part containing the Geneva meeting, Finch's name, and C Street. After only a couple of minutes Mr. Finch said "Turn it off. What do you want?"

She explained what Rose had told her to request, and Finch agreed without hesitation. Then he asked for all of the tapes. Jacqueline explained that Rose had instructed her to keep the tapes. Mr. Finch asked where the tapes were, and she told him that they were safely out of the country. She did not think that Meier Finch completely believed her statement about where the tapes were, but he seemed to accept his role in taking care of her. He asked only a few more questions. "Have you told anyone else about the recordings or C Street?" Jacqueline thought for a minute then replied, "No, I have just left instructions in case of my unnatural demise. As well, Rose installed a second trigger. I do not know who holds that set of recordings. It would be released were I to die and my death was suspicious in any way."

Meier Finch asked for the tapes again but Jacqueline refused, and told him she had placed them in a secure place that no one would find unless something unnatural happened to her. Finch asked, "How many recordings are there? Are there any documents?" Jacqueline was not about to be too specific, so she said, "There are more than 25 tapes and many documents." He continued to press her. "What is on the other tapes?" She told him only, "Mr. Finch, the other recordings are much more detailed than this one." He asked, "What do you plan to do with them?" She said, "I plan to keep them secure. If there is any sign that I died an untimely death, a contingency plan ensures that no one can stop the release of the recordings and documents. I just want the bonds, to be trained to protect myself, and to be left alone."

Mr. Finch's demeanor changed from the bully who entered the room to a more fatherly one at that point, as he informed her that she would receive both the Israeli Zion Bonds and training. He would provide a monthly income from what he called "The Geneva Trust." Mr. Finch told her, "Money will be directly deposited monthly in a bank of your choice, and you will receive training in Israel to protect yourself. We will commence the deposits and your training immediately." He never told her the amount of money or the length of time she would be gone. Jacqueline did not ask; she had no choice now that the wheels were in motion.

Finch then said, "I am an old man Jacqueline, and I do not want these tapes released as long as I am alive. I will honor my part of the agreement with the monthly payments and training. I will also arrange for a lump sum payment to be deposited into your account upon my death. I expect you to honor your part of this agreement by keeping the recordings and documents secure and undisclosed. I would prefer that you destroy them." Jacqueline responded, "I will consider your request, Mr. Finch. But I know that Rose also set an independent contingency trigger, although I don't know who holds the switch. So my safety is very important to you."

"Jacqueline, you learned well from Rose. Believe me, your safety is very important to me and you have nothing to fear. However, if those recordings are released, either by you or by the trigger, I cannot be responsible for what happens to you. We knew that an additional set of these recordings existed, and that Rose had arranged for an immediate release of that set if you were harmed. Rose made that clear in a letter to me delivered by Günter. We were unsure about the supporting documents until now. Do you know who has the other set?" She told him, "As I said, absolutely not, but I'm grateful to Rose for that trigger."

He smiled a fatherly, yet grim smile, saying, "I already knew the answer to that question. For your own protection, Rose would not have told you. Jacqueline, you belong to Mossad now; we will not harm you. We will train, protect, and pay you. That is our part of the bargain. I believe from what I know of your character that you will not harm us. That is your part of our agreement. Everything Rose said on those recordings could be just the ramblings of a man gone mad. Even if any of the information on the tapes is true, what happened was for the betterment of America.

"This is my only warning to you – do not release anything and secure it well. You would be a dead woman if anything comes out about C Street. I would not be able to protect you, even if I wanted to, at that point. Do you understand?" Jacqueline nodded. "I understand, and I will never release anything. Everything is secure, Mr. Finch. You have my word."

She thought to herself, "What Rose recorded on those tapes is true and the documents prove it. Meier Finch knows that it is all true." However, she did not argue the point with him. Jacqueline was not sure what the future would bring concerning the material she held, but she wanted to convince Meier that she would never release anything. It was clear to her that he believed she would not. Rose had recorded most of the tapes before his retirement and she believed every word on them. She was careful to show no emotion.

Meier Finch assured Jacqueline that he would handle everything, and that her travel would begin in the next few days. He told her that he would deliver written instructions to her at the hotel, the day before her journey would begin. She remembered Rose's words on the tape, "Trust no one completely." Therefore, with that thought in mind, she agreed to be ready to travel.

"Mr. Finch, would you like my bank account information?" "No. Just choose a bank and a new account and identity will be established." "I want to use Chase Bank in Manhattan, the Fort Washington Avenue Branch at the Presbyterian Hospital." Finch nodded once. "It will be handled." "Thank you, Mr. Finch." "Call me Meier – we will be spending a lot of time together." "Thank you, Meier." As he began walking toward the door, Finch told her, "I will be staying at my home on C Street in Washington for the next few days, in case you need anything. Do you still have the number you called to reach me?" "Yes." "Use that number if you need anything. Be advised, I will be very generous with you, financially. Do not get any other ideas about the information you have. Trying to use it or release it would be signing your death warrant. As long as you honor your agreement with me, I can assure your safety." They said goodbye at her hotel door.

Jacqueline replayed their meeting over in her mind after Finch left. She realized that Rose told her to put that newspaper in plain view as a subtle threat to Meier. It worked. She watched Meier's eyes as he saw her pull the tape recorder from below the Times. She knew at that moment that Meier Finch was going to give her what she wanted. Jacqueline thought that it was not very good for a Mossad agent to give away fear in his eyes, but he was getting old and he had a lot to fear. She was pleased with her performance – Rose would have been proud of her. She had remembered to tell Meier that there were fewer than the true number of tapes, and she had revealed the existence of the documents, as Rose instructed.

Rose was right when he said that Meier would ask her to give the recordings to him. She did exactly as Rose had instructed her to do on the first tape, and it worked. However, she was relieved that Rose had made a duplicate set of tapes and given them to someone else to protect her from assassination. Now it made sense why he left the letter for Günter and wanted her to tell Meier that she knew about Rose's contingency plan. She had no idea who he would have trusted with a trigger. It was probably some lawyer who had no clue what he was holding in his possession. Jacqueline did not care; Rose had insured her safety.

Sitting back on the sofa, she pushed the button on the fob. "Hello Jackal." She said "Mossad." The hologram responded, "Mossad is the Hebrew word for institute or institution." Jacqueline thought that was appropriate; they all belong in institutions!

The hologram went on, "Mossad has many bedfellows, under many names: Metsada, Kidon, Bayonet, Aman, Shin Bet, and so forth. Even before the creation of Israel, a precursor to the Mossad existed to subvert British quotas on Jewish immigration to Palestine, which was then controlled by the British. The current State of Israel declared its independence just after World War II ended. The fledgling government soon needed an agency to coordinate and improve cooperation between its existing security services, so Mossad became an official agency of the Israeli government the next year.

"What started as an agency for coordination has morphed into much more than that today. The Mossad is responsible for intelligence collection and covert operations, including paramilitary activities. It is one of the main entities in the Israeli intelligence community, along with Aman – military intelligence, and Shin Bet – internal security, but Mossad's director reports directly to the Prime Minister. Meier is the brother of a previous director of Mossad.

"The largest department of the Mossad is Collections. This department is tasked with many aspects of developing and conducting espionage overseas. Employees in the Collections Department operate under a variety of covers, including diplomatic and unofficial. Their field intelligence officers, called Katsas, are similar to case officers of the CIA.

"The Political Action and Liaison Department is responsible for working both with allied foreign intelligence services, and with nations that have no normal diplomatic relations with Israel. Mossad, unique in its covert intelligence gathering beyond Israel's borders, is designed to prevent development of non-conventional weapons by enemies of Israel, to prevent terrorist acts against Israel and Israelis abroad, and to bring endangered Jews home from other countries, like Dietmar Slusser, who you will meet one day. We develop and maintain Special diplomatic relations and other covert operations. Most of all we carry out political and operational intelligence operations and enforcement.

"The Institute for Intelligence and Special Operations, Metsada, known as Kidon or Bayonet, is an unorthodox Zionist organization. Metsada is involved in and is responsible for assassinations, paramilitary operations, sabotage, psychological warfare, propaganda, and deception activities. Also, the Mossad has a Research Department, tasked with intelligence production, and a Technology Department, concerned with the development of tools for Mossad activities.

"Jackal, as a Jew, I was born to be Mossad, and I always have been a Katsa of Metsada. I have trained all over the world. I served as a CIA agent in a special unit, since America's and Israel's interests are parallel."

The voice stopped. Jacqueline now had a base of information on Mossad and Meier Finch. Now she was beginning to understand who Rose really was – maybe. However, she knew what she had to do. And waiting for instructions was next. She would follow the path left for her. One thing she was beginning to understand is that all paths lead to the men of C Street.

The following day, Jacqueline relaxed, enjoying the Florida sunshine and the amenities of the hotel again, while she waited for the instructions from Meier. She went to her house and picked up a few things, stopped by her bank, checked her post office box, and contacted a real estate agent to list the house, as final business tasks. She visited the Salvador Dali Museum to see the Morse collection. Then she dined al fresco, at one of her favorite restaurants in downtown Saint Petersburg. Ordering a grilled Portobello mushroom appetizer and glass of wine, she watched the boats coming and going on the bay.

Jacqueline did not know how long she would be gone. She wanted to tie up any loose ends and enjoy the Florida life for a little longer. She sat on the restaurant's deck, sipping wine, watching the boats on Tampa Bay, and reading her mail. She expected it would be a long time before she returned. She hoped that she had made the right decision, and prayed she would make it back alive.

She made a telephone call to one of the disposable cell phones Marie kept for emergencies. While she sat on the deck, Jacqueline explained some of what had happened and then calmed her daughter. Marie was not happy about her mother going to Israel. Jacqueline explained enough to let Marie know that Jacqueline would be safe and where she was going. But not everything – Jacqueline performed a delicate balancing act between reassuring her daughter and giving enough information to protect Marie and herself without endangering Marie by giving her too much information.

Jacqueline wanted to enjoy the sunset one more time, so with thoughts of Rose as he was before the madness, she began to enjoy her final sunset in America, at least for a while. It lasted for only a few minutes, but the raging ball of fire at sunset was as beautiful as she had ever seen. Jacqueline did not know how long it would be but, God willing, she would make it home to see the sunset again.

The next day, Jacqueline came back to the Renaissance Hotel from a shopping trip to find a message at her hotel. It was from a courier stating that a package would be delivered the next day at 2 PM. She decided to go to the airport, have a quiet dinner at the rotating restaurant on the top floor of the Airport Marriott, then return to her hotel to get a good night's rest. Maybe if she were lucky, Rose would come again in the night and fill her dreams.

She could hear the piano music playing as she stepped from the elevator. The restaurant was quiet and she asked for a table at the window to see the view of the airport, the city, and the water. The restaurant's rotation provided continuously changing vistas. She wondered what danger was ahead and hoped that she was doing the right thing following the instructions on the tapes. Jacqueline had no idea what this turn of events would bring, and she was scared. She quickly changed her thoughts to keep her tears from streaming down in public.

Mark – that is what she would think about to distract her mind! Suddenly she felt a smile come over her face.

She wondered if he accepted what she said in his office about not being the same Jacqueline that he had met in San Francisco. The more she thought about Mark Steinberg being her lover when she was a young flower child, the more she smiled. All the time that Rose and she talked about Mark and the tapes, neither of them had any idea that Jacqueline and Mark had met, let alone that they had been involved in a wild sex orgy in an opium den. She began to relax as she finished her dinner while enjoying the ever-changing views of Tampa Bay. With a buzz from the wine, she took a cab back to her hotel for a good night's rest.

Half-drunk from the wine and sad with loneliness, she entered her hotel room. She sat and thought about Mark – she could not get him out of her mind. She recalled their long strolls on Fisherman's Wharf and the time they spent together in the park. Finally, she decided that a soak would be what she needed before she went to bed. She dimmed the lights in the bath and stepped into the Jacuzzi tub full of bubbling hot fragrant water. Her mind was racing with thoughts of Mark and her memories of that long-ago opium den. She lit a cigarette, and her body relaxed while her mind was awash in pleasant memories.

Alone in the warmth of the water, she pampered her body with her own gentle touch. Jacqueline felt her sudden smile as she reached her wet orgasm, inspired by her thoughts of Mark, the man she had left behind again. Satisfied by her memory-inspired release, she stepped from the Jacuzzi and slipped the warm terry robe around her body. Then she saw her smile reflecting in the mirror.

Within minutes, she was fast asleep in the middle of the king sized bed without another thought of what was to come.

Sid wanted to know more about Meier. "You said that Meier walked with a cane. Do you have any idea why he used the cane?" Jacqueline told her, "Meier had a severe limp. Considering what was happening in the hotel room, I didn't ask him about it then. Later on, I found out that he suffered an injury in the '67 Arab-Israeli war. He was not supposed to have ever walked again after that, but Meier was too strong to let an injury rule his life."

"Jacqueline, can you tell me how you felt when you first met Meier in your hotel room?" "Sid, I was nearly paralyzed with fear when he first came in. But after he tried to intimidate me and I started the tape, I became very calm. I knew then that I had tremendous power over him, or he wouldn't have tried that. When he heard the tape, I saw a glimmer of fear in his eyes, but only for a moment. I half expected that he would kill me right then, but I knew that if he did, his dirty secrets would come out. That was the thought that kept me going."

"Jacqueline, you look tired. Do you want to rest for a while?" Jacqueline was tired, but she knew that she had to continue. Sid needed to hear it all….

Chapter Seven
Tel Aviv

THE COURIER arrived the following day, as promised, with the documents. Included in the package was a new passport in the name of Michelle Lerner with Jacqueline's picture, and a dossier about her new identity for her to memorize and then destroy. The picture of Jacqueline on her new passport was one that she had never seen before. Jacqueline knew it had to be from surveillance photos taken unbeknownst to her, and found that petrifying. She had no idea someone had photographed her, but it was a photo of her and it was recent.

Also included in the package were a plane ticket from Tampa nonstop to LAX and a separate ticket from LAX nonstop to Tel Aviv. The package also contained five thousand dollars in cash. The tickets were for round trip airfare, with an open-ended return date. She would travel to the Middle East under a false passport and would undergo the training that she had requested. Where she would go in Israel she had no idea, but she knew who would train her – Mossad.

When Rose said, "Get trained," she never expected that it would take her to Israel. Jacqueline had mixed emotions about going to the Middle East. However, Rose had made it perfectly clear on the tapes that she must go with Meier Finch for training. Well, the plans were in motion and she could not back out. Jacqueline found the idea of training in Israel scary, but exciting, intriguing. It was strange, she almost felt secure with what was about to happen. She hoped that her sixth sense was working correctly.

Jacqueline boarded a plane the following day for Israel. Her first ticket took her from Tampa to LAX. Her tickets required a plane change in Los Angeles. She got off the plane at LAX and to her surprise, Meier Finch was waiting at the gate. They walked slowly together through the airport as she told him, "The dossier did not say anything about you meeting me." "Neither did it say that there would be two Mossad agents on the plane from Tampa with you, Jacqueline. We wanted to make sure that no one was following you. I will be with you from here and I want to assure you that you are safe. Just concentrate on your training – you have nothing to fear from us." Jacqueline did not know if Meier's little speech made her feel better or worse. Either way she was in this for the long haul.

She felt relieved not to be traveling to Israel alone, but Rose's words played in her head, "Trust no one completely, not even Meier Finch." Jacqueline had not realized that there were two men following her from Florida. That was a rude awakening to her. It was safe to assume that the agents had followed her ever since Meier left her hotel room. It disturbed her that she had not spotted them at all, and that she had no idea they were on the plane.

The agents must have taken the surveillance photo that was now on her passport. They walked together to an empty gate, and Meier opened the door for them to board. She walked with him down the long vacant corridor onto an empty plane. "What about my ticket, do you need it?" "No, you do not need a ticket for this plane, the ticket was sent as cover only; there is no such plane leaving here today."

After they had boarded the plane, Meier asked, "Would you care for anything to drink?" The plane was already backing away from the gate. "Do you have any Grand Marnier aboard?" Meier moved slowly on his pearl handled cane to a panel. He paused as he pushed the panel open to reveal a cabinet filled with liquor bottles. Meier poured her a drink from a bottle that she recognized as Centennial Edition Grand Marnier. After pouring a generous portion, he passed the crystal snifter to Jacqueline and sat down just before the plane began to accelerate on the runway.

"Jacqueline, you have been made privy to the dark side of our work. I want to tell you some of the good Rose did for our countries before we begin this journey together. I believe the insight will prove a balance for you. Rose was a very complicated man; however, his complicated mind made him capable of handling all that America and Israel have faced in the last few decades. I remember when he saw the first crate in Iran that was stamped 'Death to America' in Arabic script. It was when we were faced with the beginning of the Iranian Nuclear Project. Rose located three crates of semi-enriched uranium being transported and scheduled to be transported. In less than four days, he arranged the interception of all that uranium.

"Rose was assigned to Cairo after Anwar Sadat was murdered by the radical group al-Ikhwan al-Muslimeen, also known as the Muslim Brotherhood. That murder was an attempt to destabilize the achievements in the peace accord between Israel and Egypt. It was Rose who helped us stabilize Egyptian-Israeli relations in the aftermath. He could ferret out an explosive terrorist ring simply by walking the streets, listening and watching the people; he could tell who was conspiring. During the weeks that followed Anwar's murder, Rose uncovered seven attacks in their planning stages, saving countless lives by his instincts. His explosive work took out many in that Muslim Brotherhood organization in the following months. I only wish we had him in Cairo before the murder of Anwar!

"Rose spent time in Russia and had a long relationship with Sakharov. Rose slipped into Gorky to get intelligence information from Sakharov. Over the years, Rose brought to America many defecting KGB agents. He was so effective that his name was on KGB Chairman Uri Andropov's hit list, yet Rose would return to Russia when needed. As well, he safely arranged passage to America for defecting scientists from China and Iran. I hope you will be able to see some balance in his work. Rose was involved in covert operations in Iran, Iraq,

Afghanistan, Egypt, Saudi Arabia, China and Vietnam, just to name a few places. He was the best operative that we ever had, and he possessed language skills that were unbelievable.

"At the end of the last Iranian mission, Rose took an extended leave. He liked the tropics and we assumed he would relax at some resort for a few months. We thought nothing about that; he was long overdue for a rest. He was checking in with me from 'Club Med.' The next I knew, he was practicing law in Florida. When I paid him a visit there, he told me he was out of the intelligence business for good. However, I knew if we needed him that he would have to return, that was the rule. He signed on for life. I really thought he would come to his senses and be back.

"We were surprised, but found it a harmless phase; it happens often with these kinds of agents. Until he married you! When I confronted him about that complication, he advised me of the tapes and unnatural death trigger for the information's release and threw me out of his law office. I was not sure he was telling the truth, but we let him go for a while. We figured he would not do us or himself any harm by releasing information immediately. At least that gave us time to evaluate the situation.

"Then he called me in Israel and told me he would return after a year or so, that he just needed a sabbatical and practicing law in that little town was a perfect one. That conversation with Rose made us feel better. I told him to take his time. He assured me that you knew nothing about his past. I was not sure what I would need to do, so we monitored him with Günter.

"Before I could make a decision on eliminating the problem, the two of you disappeared, flying to New York. We thought that you might have left the country. You had no credit card activity after that first day in New York. That threw us for a loop. It was just before you left the hospital in New York that we were able to locate him. Once we did, we sent Günter to visit Rose. When we learned his condition, we figured our problem would be solved when he died of natural causes.

"But he surprised us all. He didn't die in New York, he returned to Florida and went wild – he was even seeing a psychiatrist. That is when we sent Günter to Florida to evaluate the situation and bug the house. Before we knew it, all hell broke loose, Rose tried to kill you, then he fled again, and so did you! Günter found you on the mountain and kept an eye out for Rose to show up. Then Rose died in Europe two days before we located him there.

"When I received Rose's final letter after he died, he included a serial number from one document he stole from the operations. I knew then he was not kidding. By this time, we could not trace every place he had been before he arrived in Florida, and we had no idea who held that release trigger. There can be no doubt – Rose was good."

"Meier, the reason you had trouble finding us is that we left for the hospital in New York the same night Rose received the diagnosis of terminal lung cancer in Florida. We left quickly, and without telling anyone. Even his office thought he was on vacation, and we only told the office after we left. Günter would have thought we were in for the night as usual while we were really packing for New York. We took a late night flight. I guess if you want to hide out, a hospital is a perfect place."

"Yes, Jacqueline, the hospital turned out to be an obstacle for us; it took many weeks to locate the two of you in that New York hospital. However, leave it to Rose to live through that massive treatment. The next we knew, he was in Florida again and seeing a damn psychiatrist! That is when I really panicked. We stopped that. You cannot have a Mossad Agent seeing a shrink. Rose knew that was unacceptable, but he did it anyway. Dr. Pillar's death became a necessity, as we had no idea of the information Rose had given him." Jacqueline knew at that moment that Rose had been right. The CIA or Mossad had killed Dr. Pillar, not a hit and run accident.

"By this time, we knew Rose was completely out of control. We thought Dr. Pillar's death would constrain Rose some. I received word that Rose had died shortly after, so I was unsure if Dr. Pillar's death did any good. I was sad about my friend Rose, and I did consider him a friend as well as an agent. But I was relieved that he had died. Rose had left us few options. We had no choice but to order that he be eliminated. His death from natural causes allowed us to cancel that order.

"Then the final letter made it clear. You had the tapes he recorded and the evidence, and a trigger was set to protect you. The CIA, Mossad, and B6 are organizations of dead men walking if those tapes get out, so your well-being became very important to us.

"It seems Rose stayed one step ahead of us throughout his cancer. After the psychotic episode at your home, he fled by car. That really threw us for a while. Then we picked up his trail at LAX a few weeks after he departed for London. By the time we located him in London, he had moved on to Paris. By the time we found him in Paris, he had already died of the cancer a few days before our arrival, at a medical facility at l'Université Pierre et Marie Curie. He had ordered direct cremation, and chose to be buried in the Père Lachaise Cemetery. It is a huge Catholic cemetery in eastern Paris. That is especially surprising for a Jew!

"Rose knew he had to flee; he knew that we would be after him. He was the best we had until he became our worst nightmare. I was relieved that he had died of the cancer. No one wanted to eliminate Rose. However, had he survived his illness, his death was still inevitable."

"Unlike you, Meier, I'm not happy he lost his battle with cancer! I feel the pain of Rose's death every day. He should have lived to be old with me!" "I understand. I am sorry for your loss and the loss of my lifelong friend. Jacqueline, I do not mean to sound so harsh, but I'm telling you the reality of being part of C Street, B6, and Mossad. Rose's planning saved the lives of you and your daughter. They would have come for his family next, just to tie up loose ends. This is not a pretty business. Those tapes tied the hands of those who had voted for his termination."

Jacqueline nodded as she said, "I understand what you are saying. But I want to know – how did you vote?"

Meier shook his head. "Be grateful that things worked out the way they did and with how well you are protected. I do not want anything to happen to you – I like you.

"I may never know what information he left behind, unless you turn over the tapes. That second trigger for release was Rose's ace in the hole, as they say. If he had lived and we could get to him, we would have gotten the information by using you and Marie, or possibly by other means. However, with Rose dead and you not knowing who holds the secondary trigger, we have no choice but to follow Rose's plans for you. Rose set the stage by giving you the information, but he closed the play by setting the unknown trigger. I must say it is some of his best work. He was a genius, you know!"

"Yes, I do. Meier, I really don't know who has the trigger that Rose left to protect me." Meier nodded. "I know you do not. Rose would not have told you. Rose was too smart for that. Your ignorance is your insurance. He was protecting you from the grave, and he did a damn good job.

"I assume that you have listened to all of the tapes. The big picture is that much of our work saved us all from a nuclear war, and likely from another world war as well, at least for now. Only some of our work do I regret. However, when our work is viewed piecemeal, like on the tapes, I realize it looks quite different.

"I am tired now. We will not have any stewardesses aboard, so if you want anything, just let me know." He handed Jacqueline some material to read saying, "You are incredibly inexperienced in spy craft. Hopefully, when you leave our training you will know when someone is following you, and you will be able to protect yourself from physical threats if need be. Study these documents. We do not want to waste any time; you have a lot to learn." Jacqueline read for a while and then fell fast asleep on the plane. It had been a long day.

Meier's voice woke her, "We will be landing in Tel Aviv soon." Jacqueline stared out the window as she wondered what was ahead. From the window of the plane, she could see the indigo blue water of the Mediterranean Sea giving way to land below. The plane landed at Ben-Gurion Tel Aviv Airport. It looked like any large American airport, with its duty free shops, restaurants, a train station inside the airport, and signs boasting that it handled 5000 to 7500 flights a month. The airport was under heavy guard; Israeli soldiers with Uzis were all around. Meier walked Jacqueline briskly, a security detail behind and another in front of them, through one corridor and to a waiting car.

The car drove through the modern city of Tel Aviv, through the suburbs and into the countryside, which was a clear reminder that she was in a desert, on foreign soil. Meier slept as the driver headed what seemed to be southeast, through small towns and vast desert land. After maybe forty-five minutes, the car stopped. Jacqueline saw a complex of buildings made of marble and block on the lower half and beautiful onyx and blue glass on the floors above with a circular glass top. It was the Ministry of Foreign Affairs (MFA) in Kiryat Ben-Gurion, in Jerusalem.

Meier escorted her into a lovely suite in the back part of the MFA. "The clothing and everything else you will need is in the suite. I have taken the liberty of having tomorrow's clothes laid out, so you will have an idea of what to wear. If you need anything at all, please call extension 12. Get some rest. Your training will commence tomorrow. Please go with any instructors who come for you. Everything has been arranged; you will receive the most intense one-on-one instruction ever given outside the training center at Herzylia." As the door closed, Jacqueline felt relieved that the trip was over and she had arrived.

Israel was far more modern than she had expected, and she felt reasonably safe. She looked over at her expected attire for the next day: khakis, t-shirts and military boots. This gave her an idea of what to expect. She desperately wanted to turn on the 3D hologram of Rose for comfort. However, she knew that would be too risky while she was inside MFA. She assumed Meier had the room wired with surveillance. Trust no one completely.

Although she did not know exactly what lay ahead, she felt surprisingly comfortable inside the beautiful building of the MFA. She looked out her window at the city, only to realize it did not appear that different from cities in America. People were moving around the cement courtyard, talking and conducting business. All seemed quite normal, here in the Middle East.

Suddenly, an explosion and the sound of sirens filled the air. Within moments, there was a knock at her door.

She rushed over and opened the door. Meier could see the distress on her face. "Everything is okay, Jacqueline – there has been another car bombing. You are in the Middle East and although you are very safe in this compound, this kind of thing is likely to occur once or twice a week."

"Thank you, Meier. I'm fine, but I must admit that I was startled. Do you know what happened?" Meier shrugged. "No more than I told you. I am in the next suite at extension 12 if you need anything." He closed the door and Jacqueline walked back to the window. She could see smoke in the distance and commotion far away, but nothing more.

Over the next months, Jacqueline learned the art of self-defense at the Israeli Ministry of Foreign Affairs. She received an education in the art of disguise, secretive travel, memory association, deception and escape. They taught her martial arts – something they called Krav Maga. She learned strategies, weapons, explosives, and they even gave her driving lessons for escape by car. In the deserts of Israel, she learned to maneuver a car through stone and wood barricades in the dead of the night, while armed soldiers were attacking the car. With bright lights flashing into her moving car, soldiers banged on the car's windows and yelled as she maneuvered through stones, bushes, and barricades in the desert.

Within the MFA training camp on the grounds where she was living, Jacqueline attended class alone with one or more Midrasha instructors. She even learned to use common household ingredients as materials to make explosives. She spent weeks learning the art of deceit, memorization of lies about a cover identity, and the use of medications like succinylcholine, a muscle relaxer, to weaken a target, or even to kill. Meier personally gave Jacqueline an insulin kit, ready to go with succinylcholine as well as numerous pieces of deadly jewelry. How to use currency and diamonds as funding in transit was among her lessons. Her training on surveillance and spotting surveillance were intensive.

She finished her training on the gun range, shooting with 99% center mass accuracy. Simply stated, it meant that out of every hundred shots she fired, ninety-nine shots would kill and one would scare the victim to death. However, at close range, she would not miss. She was trained for a close kill, and how to make a silencer out of anything. She was taught that the first choice was to kill and make it look like suicide, and that her last resort was to set a charge of explosives and get the hell out.

Jacqueline also learned the Code of Mossad, "Everything cannot be explained by the laws of the natural world. See what you cannot see; hear what you cannot hear." She was mastering, truly mastering, self-defense and survival in a world that she hoped she would never get to know. Meier Finch was keeping his word.

Jacqueline had become Michelle Lerner, a guest of the Ministry of Foreign Affairs. She rarely saw Meier, except on a few occasions when she attended a couple of black tie dinner parties as Meier's companion. Her clothes for each dinner were compliments of Meier Finch and she was introduced as Michelle Lerner.

Finch's taste in clothing was not as good as Rose's had been. She still remembered the black evening gown Rose had surprised her with before she attended the State Department dinner. Still, the clothes were lovely and they seemed to be an appropriate style for the Middle East. Following each event with Meier, he would question Jacqueline on her knowledge and observations of the guests at the party. Even evenings out were training exercises!

As far as she knew, Meier had told no one who Jacqueline was or why she was there. No one at the MFA or at the dinners asked her any questions about her background. Jacqueline assumed these were planned events as part of her training. Not even the five experts who trained her in the different areas of defense asked any questions. They all seemed to have complete instructions on what they were and were not to do. She was very busy for eight to twelve hours a day, six days a week, with classroom lessons or hands-on training.

On Saturdays, she relaxed but she rarely left the compound. By then, she was so tired that she would just soak her muscles, sore from the martial arts training, or sleep all day. She really had no interest in leaving the compound, as the bombing and the sirens had not stopped since she arrived.

On her last trip outside the compound with Meier, their car was pursued in a chase though the streets, shot at, and their armed security detail killed the perpetrators. That was when she first realized that Meier traveled in armored vehicles, and she understood why they had a security detail. Jacqueline's plan was to make it out of Israel alive and well trained. Staying inside the compound seemed to be her best course of action.

The Middle East in the last ten years had seen the election of a new Palestinian leader to replace the deceased Yasser Arafat, and peace between the Israelis and Palestinians was no closer. Israel's width runs from the Mediterranean Sea to the Dead Sea, a distance of only about seventy-five miles. The country is a combination of mountains and plains with lush land and desert not far apart. The cities are a montage of ancient architecture and modern development; burqa-clothed women on the Palestinian side of the border and Versace dresses on the Israeli side.

Religion and politics have always been intertwined. Islam's basic tenets are laudable. It is as much a religion of peace as any other. For 1400 years, Islam gave women the right to work, the right to inherit, and their freedom. Like most modern religions, Islam is now being misused for political reasons. Some Islamic groups are misinterpreting religious rules to reinforce women's lesser value in society by restricting women's right to inherit, prohibiting them from working, and even placing burqas on them. Islam is even being used as justification for unprovoked attacks on others based on prejudice.

In America, there is a similar attempt to seize control of political power by the Christian religious right, by convenient interpretation of the Bible and exertion of religious influence to weaken American's civil rights and engender fear, prejudice, and hatred. In the recent past, political and financial gain seems to be driving all religions, rather than being byproducts of constructive religious freedom. More men have been killed in the name of God than in any other name.

That constant threat of violence to Israel means that the country is always on high alert. The Israeli Air Force is on guard at all times. Twenty-four hours a day, they keep their fighter jets running with pilots strapped into their seats inside the planes, on eight-hour shifts, ready to defend Israel. Knowing this did make Jacqueline feel safer from foreign attack. However, nothing could make her feel safe from the civil war between the Israelis and Palestinians. During the last weeks of her stay, a group based in Lebanon had kidnapped two Israeli soldiers. A full-blown war had started, with bombers blowing up the Northern part of Gaza. The commotion among the Mossad was fierce; they were sending out agents on retaliation missions.

The country had a strange magnetic beauty to Jacqueline, with its golden, sun-covered sands of the desert. The people were kind, hard working, educated and good, but the country was in constant uproar, due to acts of violence. Arab suicide bombers were blowing up targets at random. The Jews had taken a vast desert, turned it into a state of plenty, and they were not willing to give up the land. Jacqueline did not want to remain exposed to the violence of the Israeli-Arab war any longer.

She had been in Israel for months while receiving intense training to become a killing machine. Jacqueline did not plan on working as a killer for Mossad, so she decided to leave the Middle East. Besides, she had not seen Marie in months! Jacqueline was able to keep Marie calm with telephone calls, but it was clear that Marie did not like Jacqueline being in the Middle East.

It only took a simple request to Meier Finch for her to leave the Ministry of Foreign Affairs behind, the same way she had arrived, through LAX. "Only you can decide when you leave us; we could train you for years. However, I think you can take care of yourself now, which was our goal. If you would like to stay with us here, you are welcome. You have shown great promise in your training. I have observed your progress – all of your training has been videotaped for my review. Your ability to make appropriate decisions quickly is beyond superior.

"You could be an asset to Mossad now, even with the training you have received. I must say, I hand-picked the best instructors from the training center for you, and your progress has been stellar. If you completed the course at the Mossad training center at Herzylia, you would be a force to be reckoned with. If you change your mind and want additional training, just call me and I will arrange it – either here or there. In another year or two, you could serve us well."

"No thank you, Meier. I'm ready to go home." Meier smiled. "Then you will leave tomorrow. If we need you, I will contact you. You said that you want to travel again and that you wanted to return to work. We will arrange for you to join the Israeli Diamond Market in the United States. You have your tool case, protection devices, passports, driver licenses, credit cards, your diplomatic immunity code, my private number and your code name. Guard these items well." Jacqueline nodded. "Yes, I understand. But I do have a question. Who picked my code name?" Meier smiled, and said, "I did." She responded, "I'm not surprised, Meier." Grinning ear-to-ear, Meier told her, "Well, there will always be 2 Roses for me."

At a time when tourists were having trouble getting out of Israel and Lebanon, all Jacqueline had to do was tell Meier that she was ready to leave. On her way to the airport, she thought about the last thing Meier had said to her as she was getting in the limousine. She had been taken aback by Meier's words. He had said, "If we need you, I will contact you." Jacqueline had uttered no response, for she certainly did not plan to become an assassin for Mossad.

She boarded a private plane back though LAX, with no security checks, and she was home in the United States. Jacqueline had decided to visit with Marie in California. They spent a few weeks catching up and she taught Marie some of what she had learned in Israel's Ministry of Foreign Affairs. She began working in the diamond industry in America, but in a traveling position for Israeli diamond merchants. Jacqueline had the comfort of knowing that she had the training to take care of herself now. Meier had made all the arrangements for her to travel and work if and whenever she wanted in the market. However, she went to Israel as one woman and returned as a very different one.

Sid stood and walked around the living room. "Jacqueline, weren't you scared of Meier and going to Tel Aviv?" Jacqueline stretched as she responded. "Sid, I was actually more petrified of Meier on the plane than I was of the thought of going to Israel. He was almost too calm. It was the kind of calm where I could not tell if he had accepted the role of my protector or because he was going to kill me. Landing in Israel was actually a relief. By the time I arrived at MFA I was a little more trusting. I must admit, the thought of Meier having me killed in a training exercise did cross my mind. But it did not take too long before I realized his plan was to honor our agreement."

"How did you make it through that training? I think I would have collapsed after the first day, and you did it for months!" "Sid, I did what was necessary. I was there to learn how to survive, so I was really motivated. After I left Israel, I decided to follow Meier's advice and return to the diamond market, but this time working with Israeli dealers – but before I did anything else I had a lot of catching up to do with Marie. Then I went back to work...."

Chapter Eight
Diamond Market

AFTER RETURNING to America, on the very first night in her hotel, Jacqueline turned on the hologram and simply began speaking phrases into the microphone. In addition to hearing and seeing Rose, she hoped he would provide more information on what she had been through in the last months. She had to admit, it was mostly to see Rose's face and hear his voice again. Jacqueline was trying to decide what she should do with the information she promised Meier she would never release.

It became clear to her she needed time to absorb all that had happened before she made any more decisions. After a month's rest, she began traveling in the United States nearly every week. She truly loved it. From San Francisco, Dallas, New Orleans, Memphis, New York, and Connecticut to Atlanta, she was home.

There were no bombs exploding in the streets, no sirens responding to the injured or dead from suicide bombers in America, at least not on a daily basis yet. America was not without turmoil – Jacqueline had watched the 9/11 bombing of the World Trade Center with horror before she left for Israel. Now she had seen the daily violence in the Middle East.

Jacqueline was determined to block the tapes and all that went with them from her mind. Although she would find herself chasing a ghost from time to time, when someone reminding her of Rose would cross her path. After a few foolish chases, she had learned, he was gone and it was simply her mind playing vicious games.

She had accepted the job that Meier had arranged, to keep herself occupied. It was much better work than the traveling position she had years ago. The new job allowed nearly constant travel, which she loved. She made many acquaintances among the women who worked for her, but none of them knew what she had been though in her life, and none of them knew her real name.

With its constant dinners out and travel, Jacqueline's career in the diamond market had become a profitable and comfortable way of life. Her nights were spent alone with Rose's 3D image for comfort. She was making very good money – considerably more than she spent, even though she was living lavishly. Of course, she did not need to make money at her job to survive. Deposits appeared on her bank statement every month from the Israel Zion Bonds. They were timely and were simply listed on her bank statements as, "The Geneva Trust." Life once again was becoming peaceful for her.

From listening to the music of Bourbon Street, to visiting the museums of New York, to eating in the finest restaurants America had to offer, she was content with the single life thrust upon her. Jacqueline's heart was alone, but she had accepted that her fate was to love only Rose. At least, she could face the world knowing that she could protect herself. That gave her some peace of mind.

At first, America seemed so free to Jacqueline after the Middle East, but soon she was feeling the changing political climate. Jacqueline had found her time at the Ministry of Foreign Affairs very regimented. During her first few months back in the States, she had found her free spirit again. But she quickly realized that America's government had been on an ultra-conservative swing that showed no signs of stopping.

The government had become so conservative that spying on American people by the U.S. government had become common everyday news. Most recently, the news had reported that the President again ordered the wiretapping of American citizens' telephones without a court order, under the "Patriot Act." The government in America had become so radical that even the most conservative of the right wing began fiercely objecting to the administration's acts.

Jacqueline could barely believe that the "Patriot Act" had garnered so much popular support and that it was being renewed regularly! She wondered if people realized that they were giving away huge blocks of their rights in the name of "national security." Ben Franklin once said, "A man who gives up freedom for security deserves neither."

Rose had told her long ago that his work on C Street had succumbed to a group who called themselves CWP before he left Washington, and Tape 35 had given her many more details about the group. These were not religious people, but persons who used religion as a way to control the masses.

The members of CWP cared only about their profit. Concern about what was best for America never entered their minds. They engineered U.S. attacks on oil-rich countries in the name of security and freedom. Then their private companies obtained government contracts for security and construction to support war efforts. Some of the electrical work they did on our troops' living quarters was so shabby that our men and women were electrocuted by turning on water taps in the barracks.

Government and White House officials were the officers and stockholders of companies receiving billions of dollars in government contracts. Those same officials were personally paid millions of dollars as executives and shareholders. It was all compliments of the C Street complex and CWP.

The American people were being lied to about the oil-rich countries having weapons of mass destruction, and had been convinced that they needed to pay for the war from tax money. War is profitable – the question is only who profits and who pays. This was all going on while the same people were running the biggest casino pyramid fraud in history, Wall Street. Investment firms were creating stocks that had no value or guarantees and selling them as though they were fully protected investments.

The result was a collapse. It included the housing market, jobs, the general economy, bank failures, and a massive stock market collapse that wiped out most of the retirement funds of working Americans. Hence, the politicians of C Street nearly caused the collapse of the American and world economy. CWP's domination of

America came about because of B6 losing control of the very power it had created with the internet. One group was really no better than the other. America needed major change, a people's president, and a government for the people. It was something Jacqueline had not seen in decades.

Jacqueline was glad that she was traveling, so she did not have time to follow the politics in America. She knew that if she followed politics closely that it would drive her crazy. Besides, she figured that her travel and training made her less likely to be spied upon, and more likely to detect it if it did happen. She just wanted to forget what she knew about the American government, but she would never be able to do that. It was as though each day of her life had to begin with a decision to escape from the reality of everything she knew.

Jacqueline was finding some peace in books and travel. She loved to work, and every city was different and exciting. An avid people-watcher, she would try to spend some time in every city at local establishments. She found little time to think about how lonely she was, or even to think about Rose's tapes once she began her day. Jacqueline found that meeting her daughter at various locations around the country was a great advantage of her work. Marie always enjoyed coming to the different cities and spending time with her. Marie also loved to turn on the hologram; she missed Rose too. Between working, visiting with Marie, and a wild affair now and then, Jacqueline's life felt somewhat complete. Loving Rose had been so intense that she could never love another man, nor did she want to.

She often thought about trying to locate Maxwell, her lover of long ago, but she did not feel it would be fair to go to him now. After all, she had left him waiting for her at the hotel. While she was seeing Maxwell, she dated and fell in love with Rose. She walked away from Maxwell without another word, and married Rose. Nevertheless, Jacqueline could still feel the excitement that Max had always brought when they made love. She could see in her mind's eye lying on the balcony overlooking Washington making love, stoned until dawn.

However, she left him flat for Rose. She could not ask him to take what was left of her after Rose was gone. Maybe Max was too good a friend to go to him. Besides, the last she knew, he was living in Brazil. Maybe one day she would gather the courage to find him. Even if it turned out that he was married, she would be happy for him. Although she never wanted to love another man after Rose, Max could definitely satisfy her sexual desires. Jacqueline recognized, even with her adventurous experiences, that great lovers are rare.

Jacqueline could still recall the colors of the chaise lounge that sat on Maxwell's balcony in Washington D.C. She was sitting naked in that chair when he gave her the diamond necklace that she still wore. That day, he took her on a trip to the Orient by rubbing her body with opium oil, freshly delivered from China. The memories of the time she had spent with Max were wonderful, but she had given up her infatuation with him because of her love for

Rose. Now Max's life had gone on somewhere in Brazil and Rose was gone.

Peace of mind in her solitude was all that Jacqueline felt she could ask. Being alone assured her that she would never again be hurt. No one could ever get close enough to touch her heart again; she understood that and accepted it. Nevertheless, she was sure the right man could find the sexual woman inside her. For her it would be lust, not love. After Rose, that was all she had to offer.

When she returned from Israel, Jacqueline lived life in the fast lane. Her life was traveling, cocktails, and dancing throughout the country. In casino towns, she would gamble until dawn, then work all the next day. In beach resort towns, she would stay in town for a few days after a show and relax on the beach. In the major cities, she would tour museums, go to bookstores, and shop for fine clothing. In the market, she would buy diamonds that she found to be exceptionally good deals. Life had gone on for Jacqueline; she was living alone, but she was not lonely. She was a very different woman – more intense, more cautious, after Israel.

Jacqueline had been living in hotels around the United States, and sold her home in Florida. Sometimes, she would travel to her loft apartment in the French Quarter of New Orleans. She loved that small apartment, hidden from the street, across from the Acme restaurant. The apartment's entrance from the street opened onto an old brick courtyard complete with a T-shaped swimming pool. The courtyard was quiet, private; it was separated from the street by a twelve-foot brick wall topped with rolled, barbed wire.

The only entrance to the courtyard was a wrought iron gate decorated with French-inspired patterns. Despite her love for her loft in New Orleans, she was traveling so much that she did not get there nearly as often as she would have liked. Every time she returned, she rediscovered what she loved about the parish. No matter what her mood, she could always find something to do. She could always find a party in the French Quarter, but if she wanted to relax alone, her loft was her sanctuary. Every now and then, she would stop in for a day or two, just as she had before her trip to Israel.

On one of her trips to New Orleans, she decided to put the name Jacqueline Rose to rest. She went to her safety deposit box and locked away all of the documents in that name. From that point on, she would only be Michelle Lerner. She could not risk being identified as Jacqueline Rosenberg.

She was training women to become wholesalers for the Israeli diamond market at trade shows. Meier Finch had made this arrangement, and it was a perfect job for her. Vendors would travel in circuits around the county, and even internationally. The shows were not open to the public, only to others in the trade. Customers at the shows were retailers who would resell the goods to the public in stores. The shows normally ran from Thursday until Sunday, but a few lasted a week or more. On any given weekend, there would be about one hundred different shows going on across the country.

Vendors would show up to sell their wares in beautiful, large, air-conditioned convention centers in major cities around the United States. The giant rooms would be marked off into aisles. Each aisle had lines of booths. The booths numbered in excess of fifteen hundred per show. Then over a seventy-two hour period, under the watchful eyes of armed security forces, forklift drivers would bring in shrink-wrapped pallets. Guards walked ahead of and beside each forklift, and there was always another on each lift, giving instructions to the driver about the delivery of the jewelry and diamonds to the designated booth.

Each pallet held millions of dollars worth of gems and jewelry. Dealers waited impatiently for their pallets to arrive. Then, while the vendor's employees stood watch, the security guards and the dealers would unload the pallets and verify the inventory. The employees would then open metal boxes full of jewelry and place jewelry into display cases as directed by the dealer. The dealers had already installed display cases that they rented from the show promoters. Everybody in the market had an angle for making money. Once the contents were secure, the dealers and their employees would hang their signs and put out samples of their merchandise. Usually, the dealers would only show some of their merchandise, while more of their gems and jewelry remained in locked boxes until needed.

The gates would open promptly at 10 AM, to a throng of select commercial buyers wearing security tags. Vendors and buyers would negotiate the purchases of diamonds until 3 PM, for three or four days in a row. Small sales of merchandise, merchandise with a value of twenty thousand dollars or less, were completed at the booths. Some buyers paid by credit card, but most paid cash. For larger sales, rooms had been reserved, and the negotiations would go on behind closed doors. There, briefcases filled with cash were exchanged for small bags of diamonds and other gemstones.

Within two hours after the close of a show, security guards would pick up unsold merchandise and ship it to the dealer's next show by armed transport. Within three hours, the convention centers would be empty again. The dealers would board planes with their false-bottom briefcases full of cash, and head to the next show. The vendors would vary from show to show; not every vendor was at every show, but Jacqueline would run across the same vendors a few times a year. This lifestyle was a perfect existence for her. Nobody really knew much about anyone else in this underground world. They just passed one another as acquaintances from venue-to-venue around the country, nodding their hellos, barely knowing one another's first names.

No one knew who Jacqueline actually was or where she had come from. In this life of traveling from show to show, no one really cared much about anything except how well this show was doing and where the next lucrative show would be. Jacqueline told people that her life's tale was a story of a quiet mid-west upbringing, marriage, divorce and single motherhood. She told them nothing else. In this world of traveling from show to show, everyone was from somewhere else and no one asked too many questions.

Some of the women Jacqueline traveled with had become her closest friends. Lisa was a thirty-nine year old blonde. She had married young, and had a daughter almost of legal age. Recently divorced, she was one of the wildest women on Jacqueline's crew. She was always laughing, carrying on, and chasing men. During one show in New York, she had stayed out all night. When she returned to the booth the next morning, she looked like she had a terrible hangover, but she was excited and bubbly.

"Last night I fulfilled my fantasy. I found two soldiers and had a ménage à trois! I did my duty for my country!" Jacqueline asked Lisa if she enjoyed living out her fantasy. "Well, I can't complain, but let me tell you, it was a lot of work! Although I must admit I enjoyed having one man licking my breasts and kissing me, while the other was satisfying me in other ways."

Lisa was a good worker and she was vivacious. Jacqueline had accepted that all of the single women who worked for her were looking for husbands. However, Jacqueline would enjoy their company at dinner or for drinks, and then return to her hotel alone. She knew that she could let these women get only so close. Jacqueline's life had been so different, and none of them could ever really know who she was.

Nevertheless, Jacqueline did use her Israeli training to keep all of the women safe from the dangers of the cities. In every hotel room, her .38 pistol was under her pillow at night. However, she could not save the women from themselves and from their lust for the men who were readily available. Sometimes things did work out; at least they did for one of Jacqueline's girls.

Jacqueline had quite a shock one day, when Lisa announced that she had found the right man, and he had asked her to marry him. Jacqueline thought that no one man could possibly satisfy Lisa's desires. Lisa married a neurosurgeon and the last Jacqueline knew, Lisa was living happily in Connecticut.

Jacqueline was not prepared to share her past with anyone, or even settle down in one place. She feared that someone might recognize her as Mrs. Solomon Rosenberg. She continued to use the primary name that Meier Finch had given her – Michelle Lerner – for that very reason. The gypsy existence of good hotels, fine restaurants, and choosing where she went next suited her needs just fine. When she wanted time off, Jacqueline would just pick a place and visit it until her next show. Marie would meet her in different cities when she could. She was finishing her degree in computer science overseas and writing code freelance for German companies.

Marie was now divorced, however. Jacqueline never forgot watching the door at the wedding for her only daughter, fearing that Rose would arrive in a crazed, manic phase. Sometimes in her nightmares, Jacqueline could see her bipolar husband, gone mad on drugs and sin, coming at her through the crack in the bedroom door with a ten-inch knife, or she would hear the tapes he had left behind playing in her head. It was strange when she turned on the hologram. Rose's eyes were those of the kind, gentle man she had married and not the crazed psychotic from whom she had fled. She blocked the bad memories as fast as they came by keeping herself busy.

In the underground world of the diamond shows, Jacqueline was a person of no importance, and she loved it. After a while, she had become moderately comfortable with the idea that no one from her past would ever stumble into that subculture. She felt as safe as possible considering her history. However, her .38 had its coil cut back for rapid fire, just in case. To Jacqueline, all that had happened before was just a nightmare that reoccurred, giving her no peace.

One Saturday late in August, while she was working at a show in San Francisco, Garrett Johnson approached her at her booth. He was a large, imposing man with a Boston accent. She had noticed him working in the market, and had said hello to him at a few shows around the country from time to time, as a social grace. They were barely even acquaintances, so she was surprised when he began chatting.

"Michelle, how are you? I wanted to let you know that I made plans to take a trip to Costa Rica, leaving from San Francisco, three days after this show finishes. There are a number of people going from the market but I'm going to have to cancel since I didn't make much money at the last few shows." Garrett went on to tell her that he had paid in full for his trip and, "I'm willing to sell it to you for ten cents on the dollar, just so I don't take a total loss." Since Jacqueline did not know Garrett well, she asked to see the travel plans. The computer printout clearly stated that the trip was twenty-one days at a four star hotel in San José, Costa Rica and round-trip airfare.

Jacqueline, who had learned to trust no one, questioned Garrett. "Why are you offering this trip to me?" "Well, you seem very nice and everyone on the diamond circuit knows that you make good money. I need cash for the trip package today. By the next show, it will be too late." "How can the tickets and hotel be transferred to my name?" Garrett told her, "I will call my travel agent and have her make the change. She can e-mail the new reservations to me. You will have it today, and you will leave this coming Wednesday. Do you want it?"

Jacqueline thought about taking a six thousand dollar trip for six hundred dollars. It only took her a minute to decide. "Sure," she replied, "Get my name on the papers and have the agent e-mail the confirmation. Then I will pay you. I can take the time off. That was six hundred, right?" "That's right, six hundred dollars cash, and the trip is yours." "Thank you, Garrett. It's a deal." Garrett asked her full name, and she responded, "Michelle Lerner."

Jacqueline knew that she more than needed a long vacation. It had been a long time since she had even thought about stopping to relax. A day or so at a time was just not enough. Even though she loved her job, she needed to stay in one place for more than a few days. And the nightmares were becoming less frequent, so she thought she might be able to truly relax for the first time in what felt like years.

Central America sounded like the ideal place to get away from everything, and what a deal! She had become a workaholic and wondered why it had not occurred to her long ago to see the rest of the world. Jacqueline had not been out of the country since her trip to Israel, and that certainly was not a vacation. Well, she knew that this vacation was just what she needed, even if she had not realized it until Garrett walked up to her booth. She continued her work at the booth, while thinking about the glorious adventure to the Caribbean Sea and the mountains of Costa Rica.

Jacqueline could feel the excitement running through her body as she thought more and more about visiting the rain forests of Costa Rica. However, she wanted to make sure the arrangements that Garrett had promised were true. She decided to pick up her cell phone and call the hotel listed on the original travel papers. She spoke with a desk clerk by the name of Santo, who confirmed the room reservation, the expected date of arrival, and told Jacqueline that the travel agent had just called to change the reservation to her pseudonym, Michelle Lerner.

It looked like she really was getting a Caribbean vacation at a great price! She called her office and explained that she would need a few shows off, because she was taking a long vacation. That would give her more than thirty days. Jacqueline's thinking was that she would need a week or so to recover when she returned. Her office staff was surprised and excited, since everyone thought "Michelle" worked too hard and should take some time off. The ticket confirmation came by e-mail within the hour, and she paid Garrett six hundred dollars in cash, as he had requested.

As the final day of the show came, Jacqueline was ecstatic about the trip. She gave the last instructions to the women of her crew and said her final goodbyes for a month or so. Jacqueline had decided that she would travel with the clothes she had at the Edwardian Hotel, where she had stayed for this show, and shop for new clothes in Costa Rica. Knowing that she could not carry her weapon out of the country, she packed her gun in the inventory going to the warehouse and notified her company that she would pick it up on her return.

She decided that she would go to the local bookstore that night, to get maps and a Spanish translation book. Jacqueline could speak only remnants of her third grade Spanish and really didn't know much about Costa Rica, but she knew that she would find out soon. She was flying right out of San Francisco International Airport and she would have three days to rest and prepare for the trip.

Jacqueline's daughter Marie was now living mostly in Paris and planned a complete move from the United States in the next year. Jacqueline was very happy that she had decided to settle out of the country. She had felt that after Rose, it would be safer for Marie to live overseas. The plan had been in motion for over a year, and she would be living full-time in Paris by the winter. Soon, Marie would have no real connection to the United States but Jacqueline, and Jacqueline's time in the States was limited, as well. Jacqueline had already decided that she would be moving to Europe soon.

However, Marie was in the States now and planning to meet her in San Francisco after the show to visit with each other for a day. Jacqueline could tell her about the vacation plans that very night. Marie was to meet Jacqueline at her favorite seafood restaurant in San Francisco, "Castaneda's Wharf" on Jefferson Street. Jacqueline purchased every map of Costa Rica in the bookstore and headed to the restaurant early. The breeze was warm as she walked the Grotto pier she had always loved. The aged wood and modern cement paved the way for people to walk far out over God's water to view the glory of San Francisco Bay.

When Jacqueline arrived at "Castaneda's," Antonio, the owner, greeted her at the door with, "Jacqueline, so good to see you! Is Marie coming?" Excited, she told him that she was expected shortly. Here, she could not use her pseudonym; Antonio had known her immediately. Antonio went straight to the kitchen to have the chef prepare something special for Marie. Jacqueline laughed as she sat at a window table with a spectacular view of the Fisherman's Wharf.

The restaurant's design was a combination of old cherry and cedar woods, lit by candles in small cut glass holders on fine white linen tablecloths. Windows surrounded two sides of the building so that the restaurant's customers could clearly see the beauty of San Francisco Bay. Servers in black tuxedos attended to one's every desire. No cigarette went unlit, no glass ever emptied, and no waiter was ever in the way. This was a truly elegant restaurant, yet nothing felt stuffy; it was a comfortable atmosphere.

Jacqueline ordered a Grand Marnier, and Antonio delivered pâté and sour dough bread to tide her over until Marie arrived. A full moon beautifully lighted the night, as Jacqueline watched the tide with white capped waves roll in and crash against the rocks near the shore of the bay. Jacqueline's mind drifted back out with the waves, as she thought about vacationing in Costa Rica. She felt foolish that she had not taken off more time over the past year.

If Garrett had not come to her booth with the offer of a discount vacation, she would have just gone on to the next show. Relaxing days had been so few and far between in her life that she had simply forgotten how it felt. There was really no excuse. She had gone from an adventurous hippie to a prosperous yuppie and did not even see it happening. When she returned from Costa Rica, she felt she would revisit the thought of working; she didn't need the income, and maybe it was time for her to travel and see the world.

However, something was missing from her life. It was something she could never have again – love. With deep sadness at the reality of her lonely heart, she began reading the maps of Costa Rica. She was trying to hide her loneliness and to get an idea of where Costa Rica really was, when Marie walked into the restaurant. Marie looked even more radiant than she did two months ago, when she had visited Jacqueline in Los Angeles.

With her Hepburn-like face, porcelain skin and lion's mane of thick, dark brown, curly hair, Marie stood out in a crowd. Jacqueline saw her enter the restaurant, her rose red lips casting a smile that lit the room. Her voice cracked as she called out, "Momma," while moving through the dining room with the ease of a dancer and the pace of a racer, heading directly to Jacqueline's table. Jacqueline's heart jumped with happiness at the sight of Marie. By now, she was used to Jacqueline's traveling job, and they both treasured these dinners.

They sat down just as Antonio came out of the kitchen with a special olive pâté for Marie. He said, "Marie, it is so good to see you! When I saw your momma, I knew you were not far away. This is for you," as he sat down the pâté. "Okay little princess, what would you like?" "Maybe I will have a red wine, Antonio. Something dry, please. Surprise me." Marie was excited that they were again back at Castaneda's together. When Jacqueline said that she was going to go to Costa Rica, Marie was surprised but excited about her mom's vacation. "Mom, what brought this about?" "I just need a vacation." "Well, I agree with that, but this seems sudden." Marie was a little skeptical about new things. "Yes, it is sudden, but I got a great deal on the ticket."

"Oh, that makes sense, then. Will you put me in your suitcase? Go have a wonderful time – you need a vacation, Mom." "Thank you, Marie. I have copied my itinerary for you. Now, let's enjoy dinner." Jacqueline gave Marie the information about her hotel, and promised to call her on Friday. That would give Jacqueline time to clear customs and settle into her hotel in San Jose. They enjoyed cocktails and a wonderful dinner of lobster bisque with San Francisco sour dough bread, followed by lobster tails and chocolate desserts made with local chocolate from Ghirardelli.

Late in the evening, they took the Number 30 Stockton trolley car up to Chinatown. It brought back many wonderful memories for Jacqueline. She and Marie used to ride this car when Marie was a child. Jacqueline pointed to a store along the trolley route. "Many years ago, that store had a pink stuffed elephant displayed in the window and I jumped off this very trolley car to buy you that toy when you were four years old." Marie told her, "Mom, I remember that pink elephant! It was my favorite!" They could not believe the store was still there.

The night air was wonderful through the open cable car windows. These were the best months of weather that San Francisco had to offer. The city lights flickered as the sounds and smells came into the open-air trolley. Marie and Jacqueline did a little shopping for her trip, purchasing a few silk Chinese summer dresses. They enjoyed the colors of Chinatown. Its lights shined in red, green, pink, and gold splendor. In the daytime, Chinatown was packed full of people, street vendors, and clutter. Chinatown was so much prettier at night.

On Monday, Jacqueline and Marie left the hotel for a day trip to the Palace of Fine Arts. The "Exploratorium" was built in 1925 in honor of the discovery of the Pacific Ocean and the completion of the Panama Canal. This massive science, art, and human perception museum was housed in a six-sided rotunda of carved marble and cement. It was truly captivating.

Jacqueline first saw the museum when Marie was both a child and a very ill patient in the Hospital of Mercy. The museum building had been easily visible from Marie's hospital room. As soon as she remembered that the Exploratorium was near the hospital, Marie insisted, "Mom, I want to go see the hospital again." She remembered her time as a patient, and took every opportunity to cheer up ailing kids.

Well, to say the least, Jacqueline knew that was what Marie really wanted to do with her afternoon, so they spent the remainder of the day playing with the ill children at the Hospital of Mercy. It was a fine way for them to spend the day together before Jacqueline put her daughter on a plane for Paris.

That evening, Marie left San Francisco for her home in Paris. Even though she was always sad to see her go, Jacqueline was also happy any time she put Marie on a plane departing from the United States. After the years of Rose and the CIA, she wanted Marie out of America. Marie knew too much, and Jacqueline feared for her safety in the U.S.

On Tuesday, Jacqueline returned to the Fisherman's Wharf area alone. She spent the morning shopping, and then headed to the Cannery for lunch. The building was just as she remembered it. It stood several stories tall, surrounding a brick courtyard. After grabbing a salad and a glass of wine, she walked to a picnic table in the courtyard. Belly dancers were performing on the outside stage. The sun was beating down as Jacqueline enjoyed watching the people and dancers.

After a few minutes, Jacqueline found herself in conversation with a young man named Stephen, who was visiting San Francisco from the Isle of Capri. He was tall, maybe six feet two, with dark hair and thick glasses. Jacqueline found Stephen charming. She talked for a while with him about the business he was working on in the States

In their idle conversation, she had picked up a stock tip on his company. It was called "Dome," and it was based in Capri. An internet company from San Francisco was buying Stephen's company. He was the liaison in advance of closing the deal. Stephen told her that the whole thing was being kept very quiet, to keep Dome's current customers from getting nervous. Jacqueline recognized the name of the purchasing internet company, and suspected that Stephen's company was probably a low dollar stock company.

Playing her hunch, Jacqueline left about 2 PM and took a cab to a brokerage house downtown. She was right. The stock was not expensive, so she bought a few hundred shares of stock in Dome. She would watch the market, and wait to see if her instincts about the stock tip were right. It seemed like a nice investment to make just before she left for Costa Rica.

Jacqueline sat alone that night, re-reading Camus's "The Stranger," in an Italian restaurant called Nicholas's Inn, near the Edwardian Hotel. Nicholas's Inn was an old restaurant that had remained in the founder's family for generations. Sitting alone at a back corner table, Jacqueline was completely lost in the ambiance of the historical restaurant where she and Rose had once dined. A white lace tablecloth covered the Italian floral linen cloth below. A lone candleholder of pink Depression glass lit the table. The chairs were made of mahogany, and upholstered with royal blue basket-weave leather. The immaculate care of them over the years was obvious; nevertheless, they were slightly worn from age.

Seventy-five year old murals of the Italian countryside covered the walls. Beams of walnut supported the ceiling, and Jacqueline supposed, supported the walls, as well. The table looked directly at a long curved mahogany bar with a black leather cushioned rail.

Wrought iron divided the back of the bar from the rest of the restaurant. Huge collector bottles of Chianti and rare Italian liqueurs soared from the bar's back counter to within less than a foot from the ceiling beams, lit by the tiffany chandelier in the middle of the bar. The only signs of the modern world were the computerized register and a lone yellow happy face mug filled with candy.

An Italian man who appeared to be in his late sixties entered the restaurant. He was about five feet six, with silvery white hair combed straight back and covering his neck. His entrance caused a stir among the patrons. It seemed that everyone but Jacqueline knew who he was. He wore black slacks, a white silk shirt with its sleeves rolled part way up, and a black and gray plaid silk vest. Jacqueline heard the excitement of the other customers as they called his name. "Nicky, Nicky," rang out from every table and barstool. The man spent time at each table, talking with each of the customers as if they were old friends.

It was clear that he was the owner and that patrons of many years were happy to see him. He was very friendly to everyone. He kissed the hands of the women, and then he would shake the men's hands while patting their backs with his other hand. After making rounds of all the other tables in the restaurant, he approached Jacqueline's. The old man, full of Italian charm, turned, looked at her, and paused at her table. "Don't I know you? You look so familiar to me." "No, I do not think so. I'm just passing through." "I'm Nicky Contadino, and I appreciate your business. Is everything satisfactory?"

"Oh yes, thank you; the food is wonderful. My name is Michelle." "May I ask what are you reading, Michelle?" "It is Albert Camus's novel, *The Stranger*." The old man smiled, saying, "I remember the book title, but I have never read it. I have begun reading more in my retirement years, now that I finally have the time. I have often wondered how writers can keep writing books. Hasn't every story been told?"

Suddenly, the hearty Italian charm evaporated, replaced by quiet introspection. He stood before Jacqueline as simply a man who was interested in ideas and reading. She shook her head. "No, I don't think so. Even though there are only five facts to fiction, it is how the story is told that captivates the reader. I think the next story is just waiting to be told." The man asked, "What is it about *The Stranger* that attracts you?" Jacqueline replied, "I have read this book many times, and I truly appreciate the opening sentence, 'Mother died today or maybe it was yesterday. I don't know.'"

The old man thought a moment, and then said, "I can appreciate those lines, as well. I lost my mother two years ago. That is a powerful opening. May I see the book?" Jacqueline handed the old man the book and just as he began to look at the back cover, they heard the sound of his name being called from new patrons who had entered the restaurant. He hesitated as he tried desperately to flip through the book. Nevertheless, his name came through the air again, "Nicky, Nicky." He slowly put the book back on the table, and said, "Excuse me, please." Jacqueline watched as he walked away, once again putting on the Italian Stallion persona that the customers so wanted to see. She thought to herself that just as she lived under false name, Nicky had to live with a false persona in public.

Early Wednesday morning, Jacqueline checked out of the Edwardian Hotel in San Francisco and headed to the airport for a long-overdue, relaxing vacation in Central America. She was really looking forward to the adventure. The airport was packed with people, security was high, and that meant delays at every turn. She found herself racing for the plane to Costa Rica. As she boarded, Jacqueline began to recognize the faces of a several men seated a few rows behind her on the plane. They were dealers from the diamond market. She remembered Garrett saying that there would be others from the diamond show on this trip.

The travelers from the market were a group of Middle Eastern businessmen. She knew that they were actually dealers in South African diamonds. Her employers, the Israelis, would have nothing to do with them. She said a quick hello and hoped that she would not need to engage in more conversation than that, as she started stowing her luggage in an overhead compartment near her seat, several rows in front of them. They seemed very surprised to see her on the plane. One of the men walked up the aisle and began talking to her. "Michelle, what are you doing on this trip?" Jacqueline was annoyed, but still tried not to create hard feelings. "I'm just trying to get away on vacation for a while." The man's reaction was not what she wanted. "Great! We will party with you." She would have to take a more aggressive position. "I do not think so. I'm here to rest."

As usual with men like him, even mild rejection did not work. "Oh come on, Michelle, you are always telling us no." Fine, she would make it really clear for him and his friends. "Yes, I am, and nothing will change on this trip." She called back to the group, "I suggest you gentlemen enjoy yourselves without me." The men were obviously excited that she was on the plane, and still hopeful. Jacqueline ended the talk with, "Bye, guys. I'm going to sleep." Then she sat in her seat and faced forward.

She could not believe that these men were the other people from the show on the trip. Knowing the amount of violence and human rights abuse in the South African diamond trade, she did not care for them or their ways.

She did not care that they were Arabic, although her employers certainly did. Jacqueline knew men like these all too well. They were always bothering the women and they regularly made sexual passes at her during the shows.

One of the men, a man maybe forty years old, had offered Jacqueline any diamond in his display case if she would sleep with him. That was not more than three months before this trip. She told him, "The last one offered me his entire case. No, thanks." She really did not care for these seedy men. They had no respect for women, and they seemed to feel that women should not be working except toward the gratification of men. That sort of attitude gave her a great distaste for this particular group of diamond dealers.

As she settled in for her trip, she could hear the men behind her talking. Sometimes they would speak in Arabic, and sometimes in English. From what she could make out, it sounded like they were planning to launder some of the cash that they made in the market in Costa Rica by purchasing real estate. Jacqueline knew that there was a tremendous invisible cash flow in the show circuit. She wondered what had she gotten herself into with this trip. Then she decided that they were not her responsibility. After all, this was her vacation. Jacqueline decided that she would simply avoid them if they were at the same hotel. This was not how she planned to start her peaceful vacation to Costa Rica.

She glanced to the seat beside her, as a man began to sit down. He was a good-looking executive in a Brooks Brothers suit, with beautiful gray hair. He smiled as he settled in and began to adjust his seat belt. Jacqueline recognized his smile immediately. Just at the very moment that she recognized the man, he shouted out, "I can't believe it!" "Mark, it has been a long time, again." She became very nervous, but she hid it well. After all, she was traveling as Michelle Lerner, and that was her name as far as the diamond dealers behind them knew. They had never heard her called "Jacqueline," and she certainly did not want them ever to hear that name. With Mark sitting beside her, any conversation they had could be quiet. "Jacqueline, I'm surprised that you recognized me. I have lost some weight." "I see that you have, Mark. You look great!" "Thank you. It is wonderful to see you again!"

Then in a way that was almost charming, he continued to talk. "Jacqueline, I cannot believe it is you. After you left my office, I became sure that you were the young girl I knew in San Francisco. Why did you tell me you had never been here?" "I'm sorry, Mark. I was stunned to see that Rose's old college friend was the man who had taken me to an orgy in an opium den. I never expected that! I just could not deal with seeing you again, and I had to concentrate on our business. I'm so sorry."

"I always thought that if I ever saw you again I would recognize you, no matter how many years had passed. However, you had grown up and were even lovelier than I expected. I could not argue with your response that you had never been to San Francisco. That was clever. I raced from my office to the sidewalk and watched as you pulled away in the taxicab. By then, I knew it was you

169

and you were gone. Suddenly it all made sense. The woman that Rose was so in love with was you! My Jacqueline of so long ago! I finally understood.

"I don't blame you for refusing to see me again after I took you to the opium den. I have always felt bad about that. You had no idea what was coming when I walked you into that den; we were young." "Mark, I was never upset about the canyon. I have often looked back on it with fond memories. However, during that time, my daughter was seriously ill and I simply could not become heavily involved in the Haight Asbury drug culture. It is so strange to see you again."

"Did you find what you were looking for in Rose's package?" "Yes, it really was just personal things." Mark told her, "I can now understand why Rose was so in love with you. I remember how deeply I fell for you during our brief time together in San Francisco. After you left my office in New York, I couldn't believe that I let you get away with telling me that you had never been there. I was caught between handling my legal obligations regarding the package and trying to figure out whether it was really you or not sitting across the desk from me."

They continued to speak of the amazing coincidence of being in San Francisco and then being brought together over twenty years later by their respective relationships to Rose. Mark said, "I'm really surprised that only personal information was in that package. I had no idea what it held, but I thought for sure it had some involvement with Rose's government work." "No, it was just personal mementos and some documents from his law practice."

Now they were traveling to Costa Rica on the same plane, but Jacqueline was becoming uncomfortable with Mark's inquisitive nature. She did not want to discuss that package or Rose with Mark. How could he just happen to be on this flight going to Costa Rica seated next to her? God, this world connected to Rose just would not leave her alone!

Jacqueline really had liked Mark at an earlier time in her life, but more than twenty years later, she did not want to befriend him. She admitted to herself that it was mostly due to his connection to Rose. Mark continuously tried to keep her engaged in conversation. Finally, she told him she was tired and needed to sleep. She laid her head back to rest and closed her eyes, thinking, "He is even more handsome than when he was a young man." She fell fast asleep on the plane, and did not wake until the pilot's landing announcement.

As the plane began its descent, Mark mentioned how beautiful she was sleeping next to him and how his memory of her had never faded. He was trying again to chat with her. "Where are you staying? I want to see you while we are here." She avoided his question. "I'm only going to be visiting for a few days." "What hotel are you staying at?" Jacqueline looked resigned. "I'm staying at The Markus Hotel." Mark looked ecstatic. "I'm staying there too – it's the only decent hotel in San José!"

Jacqueline was beginning to get annoyed by the time they prepared for landing. She really did not come to Costa Rica to rekindle an old flame from an opium den, especially when he was a friend of her deceased husband

and the lawyer who was the keeper of Rose's recordings. This was all too much for Jacqueline to handle.

At that moment, she felt that she had been directed to take this path. Maybe she was headed toward getting some answers. It was just too coincidental that Mark was on this plane. He made yet another effort. "Well, I will see you at the hotel, or we could share a cab?" Jacqueline tried again to cool him off. "Mark, I already have plans for my time in Costa Rica." It was obvious that didn't work when Mark next asked, "Are you seeing anyone?" Jacqueline pretended not hear his question over the noise as they exited the plane. She wanted to think about seeing him again before she made any commitment. Mark was extremely handsome, but whatever feeling there had been between them had ended for her many years ago. Now he was linked to Rose, and she had learned not to trust anything or anyone connected to C Street.

Jacqueline looked out the window of Sid's living room, and realized that the darkness was beginning to give way to the first glimmer of daylight. She had been talking all night. And poor Sid! She must have writer's cramp by now! It was clear that Sid was willing to continue when she asked, "Jacqueline, did Mark tell you any additional information about Rose?" "No, Sid, Mark was just an innocent lawyer – if you can believe that one!" Since Sid was game for more, Jacqueline would give it to her....

Chapter Nine
Costa Rica

THE PLANE was taxiing to the gate when one of the men seated behind Jacqueline asked her if she needed a ride to her hotel. "No thanks; I'm not going straight to the hotel." Then she hurried away from the gate to avoid both the diamond dealers and Mark, who had tried to pick her up on the plane. She really wanted to prevent any problems with the conflict in her names. Jacqueline was quickly ushered to her place in the customs line, only to turn and find Mark right behind her in line, still trying to make conversation.

She was once very attracted to him, a long time ago. However, she was a grown woman now and she did not trust him at all, as soon as she found that he was the guardian of the recordings. Jacqueline did not believe in coincidence, and she did not trust anyone. She was concerned and edgy about the fact that someone who knew both Rose and her was on the flight. It seemed that anonymity evaded her, even on vacation.

The customs center was cold steel and concrete. Massive terminals numbered "un" to "quince," (one to fifteen) were all that could be seen ahead. Each terminal was filled with lines of fifty or more people attempting to enter Costa Rica. Every few minutes, men in light tan khaki uniforms carrying assault rifles would walk up and down the line and pull people out. The noise level was so high that she could barely hear Mark, who was directly behind her, speaking. Suddenly, Mark was no longer there. They had been separated by the crowd.

At the same time, she noticed a man standing near the clearance point of the customs line holding a sign over his head with Jacqueline's pseudonym "Michelle" on it and USA printed below. She waved to the man and he came over to the customs line. "Are you here for me?" The man holding the sign did not speak English and handed her a piece of paper with her full name, "Michelle Lerner" and hotel written beautifully in English. She summoned up nearly all of her newly-learned Spanish and said, "Plegase espera un minuto." The man said "Sí, señora." He turned and walked away, while folding his sign and putting it into his coat pocket. She was surprised that the hotel had sent a car to pick her up. Nevertheless, she was pleased, since she knew no one who lived in Costa Rica. And after all, she was on foreign soil.

After the driver walked away, he stopped and waited near the exit. Just then, Mark walked up behind Jacqueline in the line and asked if he could call her at the hotel for a drink. She said, "That should work out, but I have plans and I'll be very busy while I'm here, so I'll call you." Mark was still unwilling to give up. He said, "I would be happy if you would just have a drink with me for old times. Jacqueline, I really mean it when I tell you that I have thought of you so many times over the years. Are you married? Will you tell me that?" Because of the noise level, Mark had to scream the question. She shook her head and quickly answered, "No Mark, I'm not married."

Just then, the customs official came up the line and began asking each person why he or she were in Costa Rica, how long they were staying, and other standard questions. It occupied them both as the massive crowd continued to move and separated into two different lines. The noise of the people in the customs area was drowning out their conversation anyway, and the Costa Rican officials escorted Mark to another line.

At the same time, another official grabbed a bag from a man in line next to Jacqueline's left and two men in khaki subdued the man. Women and children began screaming in Spanish. The noise just kept getting louder as the line pushed forward. After about fifteen more minutes, Jacqueline cleared customs, without having any further conversation with Mark.

Just as she walked away from the customs line, she saw the driver from the hotel. He took her bags that had now been hand-searched. She was feeling a lot safer with him than she would have felt traveling with the men from the market or with Mark. The driver led her from the airport building to a waiting four-door subcompact car. As she neared the car, she looked back to see that Mark was clearing customs.

She entered the car alone with the driver from the hotel. Jacqueline knew that she was looking forward to seeing Mark again, but she knew she would have to be careful. She decided to tell Mark that she used a different name now. She could tell him that she had it legally changed, because being called Jacqueline, the widow of Solomon Rosenberg, was just too painful. She did not want to admit it to herself, but Jacqueline knew that long ago, she had been falling in love with Mark, and was still attracted to him. Besides, she had to know why he was in Costa Rica. Either way, Jacqueline knew that she would be seeing him.

Even after all these years, she felt the spark immediately when she saw Mark's eyes in his New York office. He was so nice to her in San Francisco when they were young. She remembered the walks along the San Francisco bay, how he listened as she spoke of her ill daughter in the hospital, and the memories of the wild time they had in the opium den.

Jacqueline looked at him again, to confirm that Mark was even more handsome as an older man than he was when he was young. He caught her glance, and she smiled and waved goodbye to him. Maybe she should have seen him again after the opium den in San Francisco, but she was so young and scared during those days in California. She still could not believe that Mark was Rose's college friend, the New York lawyer who had held the tapes of Rose's CIA missions.

Still, she knew that she had been alone too long and wanted to be touched. Jacqueline was convinced that Mark was perfect to be a lover for her in Costa Rica. She knew that no one could get closer than a lover, and she could try to find out information from him. She would kill two birds with one stone. If he were involved with the CIA, she would have it figured out by the time she left

Costa Rica. Either way, Jacqueline intended to have a wonderful time with him.

Jacqueline tried again to speak English to the driver. However, it was clear he did not speak English and she spoke so little Spanish. Becoming a bit unnerved, she rechecked for her translation book as the driver sped off, throwing her head against the seatback of the small car. Within seconds, her eyes looked up to see the radiant mountains, an oasis of lush green around the edge of the dirt road, and coffee plantations dotting the hillside. Jacqueline just wished the driver would slow down the car, so she could enjoy the breath-taking scenery.

Her inability to communicate with the speeding driver meant that she would just have to catch what she could of the view from the car window as they continued up and down the winding dirt road. Out the window, she could see the mountains high in the sky, yet they seemed so close that she could almost touch them. The mountains were the deepest of emerald green, with glorious fields of red and white flowers covering the landscape. Numerous banana trees covered the lower parts of the mountains. She saw that the banana trees had strange blue bags hanging from them, covering the fruit. The name of what appeared to be an American company, DuPont maybe, was in large print on the bags. Enormous butterflies, some the size of birds, and others colored a most iridescent blue, filled the air, flying gently by the mountains. The landscape around her was stunningly beautiful.

However, the car was going too fast for her to make out for sure what the writing on the banana tree bags said, or for her to enjoy the scenery. Jacqueline was becoming more concerned as the driver took the mountainous curves on the narrow road at what appeared to be about 70 miles an hour on the speedometer of the car. She began quickly flipping through her translation book, looking for a way to tell him to slow the car down.

As the driver took the curves faster and faster, Jacqueline was tossing about in the back seat while yelling "slow down, slow down!" She heard a squealing sound. Then, almost in slow motion but with great force, her body thrust forward as the car met a tree with a loud thud. She could feel sudden warmth on her face, then nothing.

She awoke with her head pounding, her vision blurred. She could hear voices, and people were standing above her as she struggled to focus her eyes. At first, she could only see white and steel, but finally she saw a man in his late fifties to early sixties standing over her. He was wearing a white coat with a black object in his pocket and a very concerned look on his face. His hair was thin, gray and long, reaching to his shoulders. He stood about six feet tall, with a strong but thin build. He was speaking perfect English to her with an accent she could not identify. "Where am I?"

The doctor said something to the nurse in Spanish, and she left the room. Then he said, "Michelle, you are going to be fine, you are in Hospital Clinica Biblica." Jacqueline asked, "How do you know my name?" "We found your ID in your purse after the accident." Jacqueline thought for a minute, "Car accident?" "Yes, yes, Michelle, you were in an automobile accident on the way from the airport. You are in San José, Costa Rica. You were knocked unconscious; thankfully you do not appear to be severely hurt."

He took a black object from his pocket and shined the light as he began looking into Jacqueline's eyes. Then he began asking her where she was from, her age, what year it was. She answered his questions one by one, maintaining her cover, and he told her that she was going to be fine. "You have a concussion and a few cuts. You will just need some rest. You were very fortunate."

His concerned looked changed to a most pleasant smile. "Are you in any pain?" She said, "No, I just feel a bit numb." "That is to be expected; we have you on painkillers. You can leave tomorrow if you have someone who can take care of you." She shook her head. "No, I don't know anyone in Costa Rica, but I'll be fine at the hotel." "No, you cannot stay alone; we will transfer you to a rehabilitation center outside San José for a few days. In three or four days it should be safe for you to be on your own."

Jacqueline was in no shape to argue with the doctor. She could barely lift her head. Thanking him, she fell immediately back to sleep. When Jacqueline woke, the doctor told her again that she was being moved to the rehabilitation center. "Doctor, I don't even know your name or where this center is located." "Oh, I'm sorry, I am Doctor Enrique Curran, and the rehabilitation center is about 20 miles away. You will be quite comfortable there. I will see you there shortly."

Jacqueline was bruised, a little nervous, but mostly she was just very sore and tired. She knew that the doctor was right. She was not in any shape to care for herself. The nurse and doctor helped her into a wheelchair and let her know that her personal items would follow. "Doctor Curran, I would like to see my face before I leave the hospital." "Michelle, your face is injured, but you have my assurance you will not be scarred. The nurse will get a mirror for you."

Then he spoke to the nurse in Spanish. The nurse retrieved a mirror from a dresser in the hospital room and held it in front of Jacqueline's face. Jacqueline could see the bruising about her eyes and left cheek. Her jaw was extremely sore, and there were a few stitches in her forehead. She had some bruising on her body, but overall it was not too bad. Jacqueline thanked the nurse and was comfortable that the accident would result in little scarring, if any. Dr. Curran wheeled Jacqueline out into a waiting limousine. "Do not worry, Michelle; I will be along shortly. Just rest when you arrive."

The sun was shining, and the temperature in Costa Rica appeared to be in the eighties. The breeze carried a warm, fragrant, cotton-candy-like scent. Jacqueline knew that her head was still foggy, but she needed to test her mental ability. She remembered being told in Israel that recent memories were the first ones lost in brain trauma, so she needed to recall something that she recently learned. Maybe she could remember something from the travel books about Costa Rica. She began to concentrate on what she had memorized about this land before she left America.

"San José is the capital of Costa Rica. It is a meadow-like valley at an altitude of about three thousand, five hundred feet, and it has a spring-like climate. It is tropically situated about eight degrees above the equator. "Good," she thought, "keep going." Jacqueline knew retrieving this kind of information would assist in triggering her memory, as she had just studied Costa Rica before the she left America. She thought, "Costa Rica is a land bridge that joins North and South America between the Caribbean Sea and the Pacific Ocean. It is a small country of only about twenty-four thousand square miles, about the size of South Carolina." Jacqueline rested her head on the back of the seat, gazed out the window as she pulled information from her memory and played it like a tape in her head.

"The giant volcano Poas dominates the Costa Rican valley and is a constant reminder of an erupting, violent geological history. Legend says that a beautiful young tribal princess fell in love with a handsome prince from a rival tribe. When her father discovered their love, in anger he captured the prince and threw him over the cliff into the volcano. When the princess found out, she moved to the volcano's edge where she bore the prince's child. At birth she tossed the child into the volcano to be near its father, and lived her remaining days in isolation near the edge of Poas." Jacqueline could remember! Maybe her injuries weren't so bad, after all!

Suddenly, the memory of trying to speak to the driver, begging him to slow down, popped into her mind. She quickly got her train of thought off the accident and back on Poas. "It is here at Poas that the volcanic lava joined two continents; the stage was set, for Costa Rica's extraordinary plants, animals and forests. Costa Rica is full of tropical plants with gardens that create hummingbird and butterfly sanctuaries, all in the presence of majestic waterfalls soaring to the sky, with temperatures that cool your skin to the sun. The Sarapiquí Rainforest is in the northeastern Caribbean section of Costa Rica. Well, I guess my brain will be all right."

This country's beauty was why Jacqueline had come to Costa Rica. Suddenly, all she had read about this land in the three days before she left America was before her eyes. She could see the beauty of the mountains in this tropical Eden. The books could only attempt to describe it – it had to be seen! She could understand what all the books and travel guides were trying to relay. The car ride was when Jacqueline got her first real glimpse of Costa Rica. It was clear to Jacqueline that her memory remained intact and that she was not brain damaged.

She tried to ask the driver about the area, but it was clear that he spoke no English. Besides, Jacqueline's jaw was so sore that it hurt to talk. The driver drove slowly for about twenty miles directly north through the mountains. Amidst the mountains was an old, Spanish-style, hillside city high above the road. Jacqueline just laid her head back and enjoyed the stunning view of the mountains and the sky.

The car turned off the road into a long drive, and then stopped at a large iron gate in a fence that surrounded a wooded area. The driver stopped the car and opened the tall, wide metal gate. Jacqueline noticed that the gate was embellished with a large medallion that she could not quite make out. Then the driver stepped back into the driver's seat and continued driving through the gate.

Once the car was through, he stopped and got out to close the gate behind them before continuing though the forest. It seemed that every tree was full of different kinds of noisy birds. Some of them, with long multi-colored beaks, were cawing loudly in the breeze. Before Jacqueline's eyes appeared a waterfall some two hundred feet high, coming out of the side of a mountain.

She wanted so much to ask the driver about the area, but knew it was useless. The jungle-surrounded dirt road led to beautiful, landscaped grounds. Between the mountains and rain forest, carved in fine detail, sat a picturesque estate landscaped with white orchids and Madagascar flowers of red and orange. The flowers stood out against rich emerald foliage, and more iridescent blue butterflies filled the air.

The car came to a stop at a large, beautiful, old, salmon-colored hacienda with stained glass windows, surrounded by manicured grounds. The entire estate stood against a backdrop of the soaring mountain ranges. It was the most beautiful sight that Jacqueline had ever seen. Never before did the description emerald green have such a meaning. Jacqueline had discovered paradise, or in the alternative, she was in a glorious coma from the accident.

She thought, "Well, I could be in a worse place; this rehabilitation center is the most beautiful place I have ever seen. It is no wonder that people recover here. I cannot wait to see the bill for this." A woman in a white uniform came to greet the car, as the driver opened Jacqueline's door. The nurse seemed to have a startled yet cold look on her face as Jacqueline turned toward the open door of the limousine. Jacqueline heard a brisk conversation in Spanish between the driver and the nurse as he brought a wheelchair around to the car door. She did not think her cuts and bruises looked so bad as to cause that kind of reaction!

Together, they helped her into the wheelchair, and the nurse rolled her up to the marble steps. The driver assisted the nurse in lifting the wheelchair up the steps to the entrance. Jacqueline thought it was strange that they did not have a wheelchair ramp at this very fancy rehabilitation center. The nurse and the driver carefully sat the wheelchair down on the grand marble porch, and the nurse continued to roll Jacqueline into a beautiful center lobby, with its coral marble floors and art hanging from every wall.

Everything inside seemed so quiet, "Where are the other patients?" The woman rolling the chair said, "Sólo usted, Curran de doctor estará en casa pronto." "Casa – home, what do you mean, is this his home? Am I the only patient?" Jacqueline had gotten that much from the woman's reply. The nurse said, "Yo no hablo inglés." Okay, Jacqueline got that too. The nurse did not speak English. She continued rolling Jacqueline into an elevator and down a grand wood-paneled hall to a beautiful bedroom with a balcony overlooking a garden.

Dr. Curran arrived within minutes, reassured Jacqueline that she was safe and just needed rest. He helped her to get out of the wheelchair, as she was still feeling sore, and sat her on the edge of the bed. In Spanish, he dismissed the nurse. His hands seemed very warm and tender as they touched her face to see how she was recovering. He began shining the light into her eyes one more time. Smiling, he said, "Ring the bell beside your bed if you want anything, and Carlos or Eva will take care of you."

"Is this your home?" He nodded. "Yes; I wanted to make sure you were in a safe place to stay, where the care will be sufficient for you to have a good recovery." He handed Jacqueline a pill and a glass of water from the nightstand. "This will stop the pain and help you to heal more quickly. Just rest for now, and I will see you later." Then he quickly left the bedroom. Within a few minutes after taking the pill, she had fallen fast asleep. When she awoke, the only light in the room was from the moon and stars shining through the open balcony doors. The night air was gently stirring the white linen curtains inside the French doors. Jacqueline slowly lifted her sore body from the bed and walked toward the bedroom door. As she did, she heard footsteps coming down the hall. She called out, "Who is it?" A male voice responded, "It is Dr. Curran, Michelle. Everything is fine."

As Dr. Curran entered the room, Jacqueline immediately felt relieved and calmed down enough to begin asking questions. "Why am I at your home?" The doctor told her, "I had you brought to my home to recover since you knew no one in San José. I felt you would be more comfortable here. I'm at home most days, so I can check in on you and follow your recovery. We spoke about this earlier. Don't you recall that? Are you having any dizziness?" She told him, "No, I just have a very bad headache." He nodded. "Well, that is to be expected. Carlos, my assistant, will be here if you need anything at all. Dinner is being prepared, if you feel up to joining me."

Jacqueline was simply shocked and most grateful that the doctor had brought her to his home. She thanked him, just as she noticed that her luggage was in the room. "May I clean up? I don't think this hospital gown is suitable. As soon as I'm presentable, I'd love to join you for dinner." Dr. Curran asked, "Do you need any help getting up?" She shook her head. "No, I'm fine, I'm just a little stiff and sore." The doctor insisted that she walk a few steps, so he could assess her gait and balance.

Jacqueline walked toward the doctor, stiff but with apparent ease. "You seem to be doing very well. I have put some pills next to your bed for pain. Take one or two tablets every four hours; you are due for one now. I will see you downstairs." She told him, "Thank you. I'll take the medication, freshen up, and then I'll see you in a few minutes." As he was leaving, the doctor said, "Please pick up the telephone when you are ready to come down. I do not want you to walk down the stairs by yourself yet." Jacqueline agreed. "Thank you, I'll call."

Jacqueline's head was spinning, maybe due to the car accident or maybe because of the amazing medical care in Costa Rica. She thought, "I can't imagine that doctors would be this caring in the U.S." Her head also was throbbing, so she took one pill from the bottle. Within fifteen minutes, she could feel the effect of the medication.

She found herself suddenly intrigued by her first real look at the room since she arrived. It was a grand bedroom suite of sage green and white linens, parquet floors, and beautiful mahogany furniture. On the wall hung three etchings of an old man, all of them signed Picasso, surrounded by sage matting in mahogany frames. The room was simply stunning, with its tapestry-covered furniture and high ceilings.

She found a robe in her luggage, and walked slowly into the bathroom. It was more like a spa; it was huge, with floor-to-ceiling windows housing a glass shower, and to her left was a large marble Jacuzzi. Jacqueline took one look at the Jacuzzi and knew that it was a necessity for her stiff, sore body. She would try the bath instead of taking a shower – besides, she was unsure about standing up long enough to shower anyway. She felt stoned from the painkillers.

Drawing her bath, careful not to get the water too hot, she dimmed the lights before entering the tub. She stepped carefully into the hot, bubbling water. While she reclined in bliss, a most captivating view of the mountains, lit only by the moon and stars, was visible through the windowed wall. As the jets filled the tub higher and higher, she felt the soreness leaving her body. Almost immediately, the pain gave way to a pleasant buzz from the medication, as she rested in the steaming water. The beauty of the Costa Rican night, from her vantage point in the marble and gold Jacuzzi, simply overtook her thoughts.

She was not in pain, and that was a relief. The medication had eased the pain and seemed to have a most wonderful effect, as she viewed the beauty of the land outside the glass. An almost sensual feeling came over Jacqueline, something she had not felt in a very long time. Mountains framed the sky, and Jacqueline tried to count the stars. There were more stars in the sky than she had ever seen, but they seemed not only to twinkle, but to move, as well. Jacqueline realized she was higher than she ever could have imagined from the medication, and was enjoying it.

Time just seemed to slip away. Jacqueline was almost asleep when she heard the doctors' voice outside the bathroom door. "Michelle, are you okay?" Startled by the sudden voice, she quickly answered, "Yes, yes, I decided to soak the soreness out in your Jacuzzi." She had no idea how long she had been soaking in the tub, but realized that the water was still hot. "I hope you don't mind. I'll be down in a minute."

"I am sorry to bother you, but I was concerned about your head. Did you take your medication?" "Yes, I did, and I'm not in much pain, thank you." "We'll make sure that you continue to take it every four hours, as it lowers your blood pressure. It will keep you out of pain, but more importantly, the reduced blood pressure is good for your head injury. It dramatically reduces the chance that you will develop a cerebral aneurism."

The doctor continued, "That is why it is so important for you to take your medication on a regular schedule without missing a dose. Because I care about my patients, I will remind you. Please call when you are ready, and do not try to take the stairs by yourself. Can you get out of the Jacuzzi alone?" She nodded. "Yes, I can, and I will call when I'm ready. I'll just be a few minutes."

As the doctor's voice left the door, Jacqueline slowly lifted her sore body from the Jacuzzi. She could feel the euphoric effect of the medication, rainbows swirling around in her head, when she stood up. It took her two tries to wrap the towel around her, which made her laugh. Finally, she made her way to the bed, sitting down for a minute to stop the spinning. Gathering her composure, she got a long white kimono dress from her luggage. She had purchased it in San Francisco. She steadied herself, and slowly slipped into it.

Combing her long, wet hair while inspecting the bruising on her face, she paused. The bruising was not too severe, and since the only makeup she owned was lipstick, it was impossible to try to cover it up. She knew she could not hold the dryer for her hair, and decided that the wet, bruised look was all she could do for the evening.

She had been relieved at the hospital when she saw how little damage there appeared to be to her face; Jacqueline knew she would heal. It could have been much worse. Suddenly, her memory flashed to the car speeding wildly, just before it hit the tree head-on. It was a wonder that she had survived the crash. She walked slowly to the telephone and picked it up. Carlos answered. "I'm dressed, now." "Sí Señora."

Jacqueline hung up the telephone, taking one last look in the mirror at her bruises. Within seconds, she saw that it was not Carlos, but the doctor who was at the door. "Dr. Curran, please forgive me. I couldn't hold the dryer for my hair." "You look beautiful, Michelle." "Let me get my shoes, and I'll be ready." "Michelle, you do not need shoes, you look like you belong to this land."

As she exited the bedroom with the doctor for dinner, she realized that the beauty of his very old hacienda was simply astounding. She had so many questions for Dr. Curran. They walked into the landing at the top of the U-shaped double staircase with its carved mahogany railing, as the doctor pointed out the art on the walls while naming some of his paintings. She could now appreciate the beauty of the art that she had seen on the way into the hacienda. However, it was more amazing than she even realized. Dr. Curran's collection would be the envy of some museums.

A gray cloth covered one large painting. It caught her attention because she could not see the painting underneath. All of the other pieces were very old oil paintings or prints. Every one appeared to be very expensive. Jacqueline recognized paintings by Dali, Picasso, Monet, and Renoir. "Dr. Curran, the art is stunning!" "I have been collecting for many years, Michelle. Let's take the elevator."

"I'm fine, I can take the stairs." "Are you sure you want to take the stairs?" "I will be careful. Besides, I want the exercise." He took her arm and pulled her close to him. It was the first time she felt the heat of his body next to hers. He cautiously guided her down the mahogany stairs to the coral marble foyer at the bottom. The doctors' arms were strong, and she liked his touch.

She realized that her body was tingling with sexual arousal at his very touch. What a pleasant surprise! It was an uncontrollable chemical reaction between them; she recognized it immediately, like an old friend.

"Dr. Curran, I want to thank you for bringing me to your home. It is more than kind of you. Thank you, again." "It is my pleasure, Michelle." "Your home is beautiful, and the oil paintings on the walls are simply unbelievable. I noticed a painting covered with cloth, the one hanging in direct view from the top of the staircase. Why do you have it covered, doctor?" "I'm having some conservation work done on that piece."

Jacqueline thought she noticed a slight sharp tone when the doctor responded to her question, but maybe it was just the medication playing with her mind. "Do you live here alone?" "Yes, I lost my wife many years ago." Jacqueline nodded sympathetically, and said, "I'm sorry." Dr. Curran told her, "It has been a very long time, and time is supposed to heal all. Nevertheless, I still miss her. It seems like just yesterday she walked down that very same staircase to me."

They walked, Jacqueline on the doctor's arm, through the halls of mahogany and cedar. Artwork covered the walls, and furnishings of carved wood displayed Ming style vases and crystal bowls. Her eyes remained in constant motion, for there was something beautiful to see everywhere she looked. Entering the dining room, she saw a mahogany table, beautifully inlaid with different woods. Eight chairs surrounded the table. It was set with a beautiful array of crystal, silver flatware, and bone china trimmed in emerald green.

"Michelle, would you care for a drink?" Jacqueline told him, "You are the doctor. If you think it would be okay for me to have a drink, I would love one." Dr. Curran asked, "Would Grand Marnier be okay?" She was stunned at the coincidence. He was offering her favorite drink to her! "That would be wonderful, thank you."

The doctor went on to tell Jacqueline, "I do not know if you have ever tasted it before, but in America you can only get the orange Grand Marnier. In Costa Rica we serve Cordon Jaune Grand Marnier, which is actually clear." "I have only had the orange, and it is my drink of choice." "Good. If you like the orange-colored liqueur, I believe that you will enjoy the Cordon Jaune. It is less sweet, and tastes more of fresh fruit. Dinner will be ready in half an hour. Would you care to relax on the veranda? The night is beautiful."

He picked up the bottle and two snifters, and they walked together and sat in two overstuffed chairs on the veranda in the warm night air. Stars filled the sky, and Jacqueline could hear the wild animals in the night. Dr. Curran stood and lit a few sconces, which cast a golden glow engulfing the entire area.

"May I use your telephone to call my daughter?" As he began pouring their drinks, he answered, "There is one by your bed; feel free to use it anytime. Would you like me to call Carlos? I can have him bring a telephone to you now." Jacqueline nodded. "Yes, please. Marie, my daughter, will be beside herself with worry. What day is it?" "Today is Friday. You have a daughter?" "Yes, she is grown, but we are still very close."

The doctor said something in Spanish into an intercom, and Carlos came onto the veranda with the telephone. Jacqueline knew that Marie would be worried if she didn't call as promised. A quick call to Marie and some fast explaining brought comfort to both. After the call, Jacqueline could relax and enjoy the night air. "Do you normally bring patients to you home to recover, Dr. Curran?" "No, Michelle. You are the first. I knew that you were in this country alone, and you seemed so helpless lying there in that hospital bed. Besides, you remind me of someone I once knew."

"Who is that?" "My wife. She was beautiful, like you, with olive skin and long dark hair." Jacqueline was surprised. "Thank you, Dr. Curran. Do you have any children?" "No, I do not. Do you play chess, Michelle?" She replied, "A little." "Well, maybe we can play after dinner. I'm not very good myself. I read books all the time on the great chess masters and moves, but I just do not seem to get any better." This man was a complete stranger to Jacqueline, but she sensed that she had met him before. Although his face was not one she remembered, his mannerisms seemed very familiar.

Jacqueline asked, "Where is the bathroom?" "Are you feeling okay, Michelle?" "Oh yes, I feel fine." Dr. Curran pointed and said, "You will find a bathroom on the left." Jacqueline sat her drink on the table and began to rise from her chair; the doctor was quickly on his feet. "I will show you." As they walked inside, she could not shake the feeling of familiarity with him. Carlos came into the hall to tell them, "Dinner is served."

"Go ahead Dr. Curran, I'll be right along," as she walked into a bathroom of spectacular size with gold faucets and high ceilings. The house had been restored, but with all of the most modern amenities. That suited her just fine; she loved the look of old and the convenience of modern luxuries. She took a final look at the beauty of the room as she washed her hands in a sink of mosaic tile, and dried them on towels with the initials EC monogrammed in gold.

Then she walked back out the door into the hall, only to find the doctor was waiting for her. He gently took her arm, escorting her to the dining room. "Dr. Curran, this medicine is making me euphoric." "It is okay, Michelle. The medication will allow you to heal more rapidly." He pulled out Jacqueline's chair and seated her at one end of the table, then seated himself at the other end. They enjoyed a wonderful dinner of fish and fruit with a dozen different ceviches. They talked as they ate, while Eva served dinner in complete silence.

Jacqueline was full of questions for Dr. Curran. "Where are you from?" He answered, "I was born here in Costa Rica." She wanted to know more about him.

"Have you ever been to the United States?" His response was, "Yes, I studied at Harvard for a few years and I have traveled through most of the United States. Eventually, I returned home to Costa Rica to practice medicine." Jacqueline was interested, and asked, "How long did you study at Harvard?" The doctor told her, "I was there for four years in the early seventies."

Jacqueline was trying to put out of her mind the familiarity she felt with Dr. Curran, because she knew she had never met him before. She could not have possibly met him when he was in the U.S. When he was in Massachusetts, she was in California. "How is the driver of the car doing?" "I'm sorry, Michelle; I had hoped that you would not ask right away. He died at the hospital." "Oh how terrible!" "Yes, and we were all amazed that you were not more severely injured." Jacqueline said, "Oh, I'm so sorry for that man." Dr. Curran told her, "Yes, it is sad, but you were very fortunate. You were very, very lucky. Now, I do not want you to think any more about the accident. You need to rest and recover."

Sid stirred in her chair. "Jacqueline, it sounds like you were lucky to survive that crash. How are you doing now – do you feel any effects from your injuries?" Jacqueline told her that she was fine, but she still had a little scarring on her forehead. "How about pouring us another cup of coffee, Sid? I think that you will need it when you hear more about Dr. Curran...."

Chapter Ten
Enrique Curran

NEAR THE end of dinner, Dr. Curran inquired, "Michelle, do you like books?" Jacqueline smiled. "Oh yes, very much. I'm an avid reader." "Then I must show you my library after dinner. Feel free to use it while you are here." Jacqueline nodded, but said, "Thank you, however, I'm feeling much better. Maybe I can go to my hotel and get out of your hair tomorrow."

Dr. Curran was adamant. "No, no; you are not ready to leave. You need to rest for a few more days. I want to make sure you do not have any complications from this head injury. I do not want you to be alone yet. It is just as a precaution. Besides, you are not in my way. This big old house felt empty until you arrived. Carlos and Eva are my house servants, and they will take care of anything you need." Jacqueline smiled. "Thank you for all of your help, doctor." Dr. Curran smiled gently at her, and said, "Call me Enrique." "Thank you, Enrique."

They continued enjoying cocktails, mint chocolate chip ice cream with banana chips, and conversation late into the evening. Jacqueline was quite stoned from the pain medication and alcohol, when Enrique offered her a tour of the hacienda. She noted the manner in which Enrique spoke, and it reminded her of Rose. Suddenly the most uncomfortable feeling overcame Jacqueline. Enrique reminded her too much of Rose.

They continued to tour his home as he described the massive house with its seven bedrooms, eight bathrooms, three balconies and a pool. He mentioned a formal garden, and that the hacienda sat on ten acres of land in the middle of the mountains of Costa Rica. To Jacqueline, the art in every room was magnificent, with each room having a different artistic theme. Some rooms displayed only portraits, while the art in other rooms was dedicated entirely to waterfalls or landscapes.

Arched double French doors extending more than ten feet high led them into the library. Jacqueline immediately noticed a collection of Spy prints on one wall. It was the series of Spy prints depicting doctors. "I love Spy." Dr. Curran asked, "Are you familiar with his work?" "Oh yes, for many years." One print of an old doctor had a note written on it. It was obviously a notation to a printer at Vanity Fair Magazine, and it read, "Don't forget to make the flesh red." "That is an original, isn't it Enrique?"

"Most of my art work is original, Michelle." Then the sheer magnitude of Dr. Curran's collection of books caught her attention. Bookcases full of books went from floor to ceiling. The cases covered nearly every wall, with a wooden ladder on a brass rail that rolled for easy access to the top shelves. It was the most massive personal collection of books that she had ever seen.

Jacqueline just smiled, feeling intoxicated from the presence of all of the books. She was now sure that the medications intensified her emotions. "I will enjoy this room much more tomorrow, but I'm getting very tired now." The library had simply taken her breath away, and she wanted to be rested to enjoy this room. "Of course, you are tired." Enrique took her arm and walked with her into the hall, pushing the button for the elevator.

"I think you have walked enough tonight. Please promise me that you will not take the stairs without me." "I promise." They took the elevator to the second floor, and arm in arm, Enrique walked Jacqueline to her room. "If you desire anything, anything at all, just push the intercom button on the telephone, and Carlos or Eva will answer. They will gladly attend to your medical or personal needs. Do not forget to take your medication, and get a good night's rest. Would you like Eva to help you undress?" "No, I'm fine, thank you." "Good night, Michelle, sleep well." "Good night, Enrique."

Jacqueline's first thought was to sit down on the bed and to call Marie again. Marie was glad that her mother had called her back, because she was curious about Dr. Curran. "I'm glad to hear you are safe with the doctor, but tell me, what does he look like?" Jacqueline with a laugh said, "Calm down, Marie. Yes, he is handsome, but you should quit trying to fix me up with every man who wanders into my life. I'll call you in a few days. I just wanted to make sure you know that I'm fine." Jacqueline minimized her injuries to lessen Marie's concern. She thought that waiting to tell the story of her car accident would make the tale of her Costa Rica trip even more exciting to Marie, once Jacqueline was safely home.

"Well Mom, then don't get too close to the doctor. After all, you told me you were thinking about looking up Maxwell when you got back to the States." Jacqueline laughing, said, "What? Do you think I can't handle two men in my life? Don't worry; I'll keep a respectful distance!" Marie was giggling when she said, "Enjoy your vacation." "I will; I love you, Marie." "Love you too, mom. Now have fun. Remember you are on vacation, so enjoy it!" "I will." Jacqueline could rest now. She was feeling no pain from her head injury as the medication had taken care of that, but she took the medication again as prescribed. She was euphoric, and ready for a peaceful rest in the home of a most kindly man, Enrique Curran. Maybe she would have pleasant wet dreams with thoughts of Enrique or Maxwell, or both!

The warm breeze blowing through the open balcony doors stirred the white linen curtains, causing a soft rustling noise as the curtains blew through the open doorway. Jacqueline again thought of how much Enrique reminded her of Rose. It was his rise from the table, his manner of speaking, his love of chess and books. Her mind became lost in the happier days with Rose. As tears of loneliness for a love lost filled her eyes, Jacqueline fell fast asleep to ease the hurt inside.

The morning sun broke through the large French doors; Jacqueline awoke rested but stiff, and with a headache. Quickly, she took the medication by her bed. Then she slipped into the Jacuzzi to ease the soreness again. Shortly, she began to feel euphoric from the medication. She rested in the hot jets; her mind filled with thoughts of Enrique, and realized she was getting excited. "What a wonderful feeling," she thought. Slowly, she dressed for breakfast with the doctor and walked to the staircase as her eyes again caught the draped painting.

Then she saw Enrique at the bottom of the staircase, waiting. "Good morning, Michelle. Did you rest well?" "Oh yes, Enrique; I had a wonderful night's sleep, after I spoke with my daughter again." "Oh, very good, Eva has breakfast ready." Jacqueline headed down the stairs, as Dr. Curran headed up. "Wait, I do not want you to fall! Remember, you promised not to take these stairs alone," as he reached his hand out to Jacqueline and guided her to the bottom of the stairs. She told him, "I'm sorry. I will call down from now on."

Enrique escorted her to the dining room. "Michelle, you look lovely this morning. I take it you are feeling a little more comfortable?" Jacqueline told him, "Thank you, yes, I'm feeling much better." Enrique pulled out the chair at the end of the table and gently seated Jacqueline in the same chair where she had sat at dinner the night before, and he again sat at the other end of the long table. Eva gave her that strange cold look which Jacqueline had noticed when she first arrived at the hacienda, as Eva served a breakfast of Eggs Sardou and fresh fruit in silence.

Jacqueline took a drink of her coffee, "Enrique, my coffee tastes a little strange." He called Eva and spoke to her abruptly in Spanish. Eva removed the coffee from in front of Jacqueline. Enrique apologized, "Michelle, I am so sorry. It appears that Eva has served you what I drink, half coffee and half tea. Eva is bringing your coffee." Enrique continued by saying how happy he was that she was feeling better and more relaxed.

"Michelle, I know that you came here for a vacation, and I want you to know that Carlos is at your disposal to drive you around in a few days, when you are feeling better. However, when you feel up to it, I would be pleased to show you my country. That way I will know that you are safe. I just want to watch your head injury closely for a few more days."

"Thank you, Enrique, but I will be returning to the hotel today. I have been enough of a burden." Enrique said, "I am saddened to hear that. Your companionship has been wonderful in this big old house. You have been anything but a burden. Since I lost my wife, I have lived in this house alone. Having you to care for has been a pleasure. Have you contacted the hotel to see if they still have your room?" "Oh, Enrique! I did not even think of that!" Enrique rang for Eva to bring a telephone and the number to the Markus Hotel.

As they waited, Jacqueline asked what he would recommend that she visit while she was in Costa Rica. "There are wonderful waterfalls, rainforests, volcanoes and butterfly ranches here." Eva entered with the telephone and the hotel clerk on the line. Enrique instructed her to give the telephone to Jacqueline.

To Jacqueline's surprise, the room was re-booked when she did not show within twenty-four hours of her reservation, and nothing was available. She asked about other hotels in the area and Santo, the desk manager, informed her that there was only one major hotel in San José. As she hung up the telephone, she looked at Enrique. "I guess I had better call the airport. My hotel room has been filled, and no other rooms are available."

"Don't be silly, Michelle! I am honored to have you as my houseguest. You have come a very long way from America to see Costa Rica. Please accept my hospitality." "Thank you, Enrique. I do not know how long I will stay, but I'm grateful for your kindness." Jacqueline could barely look at the man across the table without her mind flashing back to Rose. Until she arrived in Costa Rica, the memories of him had remained somewhat buried. Enrique's words and actions were beginning to be a constant reminder of Rose.

As they finished breakfast, Enrique suggested they revisit the library that had so intrigued Jacqueline the night before. He took her arm and escorted her down the hallway. She was even more amazed at the grandness and beauty of the room. Enrique sat down behind an immaculately clean mahogany desk with its crystal accessories and a lone laptop computer in the middle, saying, "I have a little work to do." "Well, then let me get out of your way, Enrique." "No, please stay. Enjoy the books. I think that you will find that the chairs are extremely comfortable. I spent many years designing this library for comfort. This is really the only room of my house for which I carefully picked each item."

Jacqueline began looking on the shelves and could not resist climbing the rolling ladder of wood and brass, even though her head was spinning from the medication. Enrique called out, "Be careful! Remember, you have a head injury. By the way, did you take your medication this morning?" "Yes I did, and it's still giving me a euphoric feeling." "That is to be expected Michelle; the side effects are mild, aren't they?" "Yes, I just feel a little high." "Well that is okay, and the medication will assist your head injury in healing more quickly."

He told her, "However, I want you to be careful walking and climbing while you are on that medication. It will take the pain away, but it will also fool you into feeling like you can climb a ladder!" "I will be careful, and I'll only go up a couple of steps," as she continued climbing the ladder. Jacqueline looked at the books for a very long time.

She could not be sure if it was because she was stoned, but all of the books reminded her of the books in Rose's library. Then one book caught her eye. It was "The Kingdom of God and Peace Essays," by Tolstoy. Slowly, she took the little gray book down and felt its burlap cover. It looked just like a copy of the book that she had once owned and loved to read over and over.

Then she backed slowly down the ladder and sat quietly in a large, overstuffed burgundy leather chair. Opening the cover ever so gently, she saw a signature inside that read, "A long time passing... A gift from Jack Kennedy, 1960." Her book certainly did not have a dedication from JFK! Very gently, she touched his signature, as she thought fondly of the man who had signed the book.

She experienced the feeling of inner strength once again that the book had always given. If anything, this copy, signed by JFK, made the emotion greater. She assumed her favorite reading position, with her feet tucked under her dress as she had done so many times before in her life, and began the pleasure of reading. Jacqueline had once dreamed of becoming a writer, but the years had slipped by and her life had taken her in other directions.

Minutes became hours, before she looked up at the desk and saw Enrique watching her read. "Michelle, you have been so content reading Tolstoy. I have looked up many times to see your deep concentration. You look beautiful and peaceful seated there, as though you belong in that chair. Of all the books in this library, I always wonder which one someone will choose. Have you ever read Tolstoy before?" Jacqueline told him, "Yes, this is my favorite of all of Tolstoy's works. It is an essay that he wrote and then later revised and included in *War and Peace*."

"You are an amazing woman. Eva will have lunch ready in few minutes. We can eat, and then if you feel up to it, I will take you out to see the city." "Enrique, I would love it! I'm feeling fine. There is really no reason for your concern." Enrique rang Carlos and told him that he would need the car after lunch. Slowly they walked, arm in arm, down the grand hall to the dining room. "Enrique, I feel as though I have known you for a long time." With a chuckle, Enrique replied, "Well, maybe we met in another life."

Lunch was prepared, and Jacqueline's medication was on a gold plate next to her water glass. "Don't forget to take your medication," Enrique said as he seated her at the dining table. She took the medication as Eva filled Jacqueline's soup bowl from a tureen of blue and white Chelsea china. She was still getting the feeling that Eva did not like her, although Eva had said nothing to make that clear. Her expressionless silence bothered Jacqueline.

The soup was a wonderful wild mushroom in a yellow cream sauce, like a thin hollandaise. The taste was exquisite. Next was a marinated salad of fresh vegetables and sugared walnuts. Jacqueline enjoyed lunch and put thoughts of Eva's disapproval out of her mind. Maybe she had a thing for the doctor and just did not like another woman in her house. However, this was not Eva's house, and Enrique said Eva was just an employee.

Enrique seemed a little more talkative over lunch. "Tell me about you," Enrique asked. Jacqueline was not sure how much she wanted to reveal about her past. "As I told you, I have a grown daughter, Marie, who is the light of my life. I was married and my husband died very young. I work in the wholesale diamond market in the States and that is how I ended up coming to Costa Rica. It is a vacation from the chaos of my everyday life. Tell me about yourself, Enrique."

"As I said, I was born in Costa Rica. However, I was educated in Switzerland and did my last years of education at Harvard in America. A two-year residency followed Harvard, at Johns Hopkins University. As soon as I could, I returned to Costa Rica. I have traveled the world, but about ten years ago, I realized that I'd seen all that I wanted to see. I never want to leave my homeland again."

"Never is a long time, Enrique." "Yes, but I'm sure I never want to leave this land again. I have everything in Costa Rica that I want. The land is beautiful, the people are kind, and my money was made a long time ago. Therefore, I never want to leave again. My home is my sanctuary.

"I am retired and I work only one day a week at the hospital. In fact, I was not scheduled to be at the hospital on the day of your accident, but I had a board meeting that day. When I saw you come in from the ambulance, I felt as though I had seen you before. I could not tell until they cleaned your face if I knew you or not. Then I just decided to take over your care. The nurses searched your belongings from the car and you seemed so alone in Costa Rica. I waited by your bed all night just looking at your face. I still feel as though I have seen you before. Michelle, do we have any connection? Might you have been at Harvard or Johns Hopkins?"

Jacqueline laughed. "No, I've never been to either place." "Well, Michelle, I guess it is just your resemblance to my wife. Are you feeling up to going for a ride?" "Yes, just let me change my clothes." Enrique walked Jacqueline to her room, where she said, "I'll change and be right down." He reminded her to use the elevator. Jacqueline quickly slipped into an ivory summer dress and sandals. Then she opened her purse to see that nothing had been disturbed when the hospital searched it for her identification. Something Enrique said brought that precaution to her attention. Everything was fine; no one had discovered the secondary compartment in the purse. As she took one final look in the mirror she thought, "I hope this outfit pleases the doctor."

His gray long hair and thin body were quite appealing, and she knew she was feeling aroused by him. In fact, this sudden feeling of sexual attraction was a surprise, as few men could cause that reaction. Then she thought that she had better just keep this on a friendly level, although she could see something in his blue eyes that told her he was interested in knowing her better. She knew what was attracting her to him was his similarity to Rose.

Jacqueline quickly put thoughts of Rose out of her mind and rushed down the staircase to meet Enrique. He came running to meet her on the stairs. "Be careful darling, you might fall from the medication!" "I'm sorry, Enrique. You're right, I feel like I could fly. I did mean to take the elevator, I just forgot." He asked, "Are you feeling any other side effects to the medication that I'm giving you?" "No," she replied, thinking to herself, "...not unless sudden sexual arousal is a side effect!"

It had been a long time since Jacqueline had felt that spontaneous warmth within her body from the mere sight of a man. Something in her had died with Rose and even though she was feeling these emotions, she knew that it was not love. With Rose, Jacqueline had been a woman of uninhibited sexual arousal. In the years since his death, her sexual encounters had been few and they did not have the impact of arousal for someone she loved.

Carlos opened the door of the limousine and they settled into the back. Carlos drove up the dirt road leading off the estate. The car stopped after about twenty miles at a large outdoor market filled with bright colors reflecting in the Costa Rican sun. Wonderful smells filled the air. She knew that it was the medication intensifying her senses, and Jacqueline was enjoying the mental rush. After all, everything begins in the mind. Enrique reached his hand to Jacqueline and as he helped her out of the car, he extended his arm to steady her walk. Her mind flashed for a moment on how Rose would gently guide her step on long walks together.

They walked through the marketplace filled with colorful items, as Jacqueline blocked her thoughts of Rose. She concentrated her focus on the colors, smells, and sounds of the market. Suddenly Jacqueline saw something that she knew she must take back to America – a Panama hat! She tried on more than a few and finally Enrique said, "That is the one; it looks wonderful on you."

Jacqueline asked, "How much money American," to the man running the street shop. She had not had time to convert any money to Colons, the Costa Rican currency, since her arrival. The man in his colorful Poncho and Panama hat replied, "Seven dollars American." She reached in her purse and paid the small cost. As they continued through the market, Jacqueline told Enrique that she needed to convert some dollars to Colons. He told her, "Do not be concerned about Colons; they love American dollars in Costa Rica. The price should be about fifty five percent less with American money."

Wearing her Panama hat, she twirled in the street for Enrique, as they continued to walk the shops of the street market. The locals seemed so pleasant and a number of them were obviously familiar with Dr. Curran. The children were wonderful and, unlike in some third world countries, they were not panhandling on the streets. And they appeared healthy. After about twenty minutes, they returned to the car, as Enrique was showing concern about Jacqueline overdoing. Carlos drove them north to a boat ramp.

"Let's take the tour boat up the river for a while. It runs all the way to Nicaragua, but we will just ride for a little while and Carlos will pick us up. I want you to see the river – it is beautiful." Enrique purchased two passes and they boarded the long, aluminum flat-bottom boat. Enrique said something to the captain in Spanish, as he sat Jacqueline down on the low metal seat.

"The boat captain will make a stop about an hour up the river where Carlos is picking us up." As the boat moved north, up the river, Enrique pointed out the animals and the countryside to Jacqueline. "If we took the full tour, we would almost cross into Nicaragua by boat. The country is beautiful and the people are kind, but you must watch out for the drug lords. They control the countryside, and they do not like it when people get too close to their crops or labs."

"They are growing fields of coco and manufacturing it into cocaine for export to the United States. The CIA has an arrangement that allows a certain amount to flow in to America, as long as the drug lords cooperate with the

United States government. This has been going on for more than fifty years." Jacqueline cringed internally at the letters CIA, but she knew that Enrique had no idea of her past. "Enrique, why does the CIA have such an arrangement?"

"The profit margin is so high on illegal drugs that the United States keeps all drugs illegal, just like alcohol was illegal during prohibition. The American government profits in many ways. That includes the RICO, or Racketeering Influence Corrupt Organization act, through the seizure and the sale of American citizens' property when they are arrested for using the drugs that are imported with the American government's assistance. That is why the prisons are overflowing in America. San Quentin receives over two thousand new inmates a month, mostly on drug related charges. Eighty percent of all the prisoners in the United States prison system are there because of drug-related activity. I'm amazed that your country arrests and incarcerates people even for the use of cannabis."

The boat made a stop where a road ran parallel to the river. Jacqueline could see the black limousine waiting for them, as Enrique helped her up the small riverbank. The sun was starting to set over the mountains, and Enrique asked her if she would like to see the nightlife. "That sounds wonderful. I could use a drink." "Are you sure you are not too tired?" "No I'm fine, just sore." As they walked to the car, Jacqueline was becoming more intrigued with Enrique. Inside the limousine, he handed her the medication he had prescribed and a bottle of water, while he spoke in Spanish to Carlos. She took the pill even though she realized that the one major side effect was that she was becoming more aroused with each dosage.

Slowly Carlos drove the winding mountain roads. "Is it making you nervous to be in a car after the accident?" "No, I'm very comfortable riding with you, and Carlos is a wonderful driver. Not like the crazy cab driver going 70 around the curves." "We wondered how fast the car was going when you went off the road." "Enrique, the last thing I remember was the speedometer reading about 70 and then waking up to you, very sore and with quite a headache."

"Well, you were very fortunate. You have a concussion and a few cuts and bruises, but you are going to be fine. I am so glad you are staying with me; I would never have forgiven myself if something had happened to you." She gently told him, "Enrique, I'm not your responsibility." He smiled. "I took on your care at the hospital because I saw something special in your face that afternoon. I want to be responsible for your safety." "Thank you for all your care. Now, let's relax and you can tell me more about Costa Rica."

As she rested in the back of Enrique's limousine, he began to tell Jacqueline of his land. "Michelle, Costa Rica's economy is based on tourism, agriculture, electronics exports, and of course, drugs. Poverty has been substantially reduced over the past twenty-five years; yet it remains a problem. Foreign investors in the land, money laundering, and the problem of drugs spilling over from Columbia and Nicaragua are problems that continue to increase. The Costa Rican government continues to grapple with its own problems of massive corruption.

"Costa Rica is currently preparing to participate in the U.S. Central American Free Trade Agreement, which should result in economic reform and eliminate some corruption. Hopefully, it will improve the social, political and investment climates. We accept our role as a transportation crossroads for cocaine and heroin from South and Central America. That will not ever completely disappear – it's too lucrative. The illicit production of cannabis is in small, scattered plots, mostly. However, domestic cocaine consumption is rising, especially crack cocaine. Crack is also seeing a surge in America.

"I personally have never understood why people were not happy with the herbal drugs such as cannabis, which unless abused, can afford benefits medically. And for the most part, herbal drugs are much safer than alcohol. Have you ever heard of any of these drugs Michelle?" "Yes, I have tried cannabis and even opium once a very long time ago. The medication gives me the same euphoric feeling as opium." "Michelle, that effect is because the medication has an opiate base. But in your case, it is being used medicinally and not abused. There is a difference between the two."

"I agree, Enrique. Use of cannabis is even illegal for medical patients, who can benefit from its anti-nausea effect. Besides, it is far less dangerous than alcohol. The Indians used it as a way to relax into their minds. I have tried it, and it is fine. It's not something I care to have every day, but now and then, sure. Drugs like heroin are a different story. They should be regulated, although the scientific community should be able to study their medical use. America simply has too many unnecessary laws. It causes more problems than good."

"We agree on many things, Michelle. To most who visit here, Costa Rica appears to be a Central American success story with over one hundred years of freestanding democracy. Although this country claims that it is a democracy, military control over everyone exists as a regular part of day-to-day travel out of the city. The American government has made this country a haven for their CIA covert operations."

Jacqueline's heart skipped a beat when she heard Enrique's words. She had felt free up until the moment he said, "CIA covert operations." Suddenly, the long buried nightmare of fleeing from the CIA, her knowledge of their covert operations, and nearly having died at their hands – it all came rushing back to Jacqueline. She was chilled to the marrow, but she spoke not a word as Enrique continued his story of Costa Rica.

"Michelle, Costa Rica is both tropical and subtropical, bordered by the Caribbean Sea on the east and the Pacific Ocean on the west. Nicaragua is to the north, and Panama is to the south. Our coastal plains are separated by intensely treacherous mountain ranges that include over a hundred volcanic cones, many of which are still major active volcanoes. Clouds of steam hide most of the volcanoes. I will show them to you.

213

"Michelle, let me tell you of my perfect day in Costa Rica: it is a warm spring day, cloudless, and a breeze fills the air. I am lying stoned and naked on a slab of sun-warmed granite projecting out above a cool, mist-filled tropical waterfall hidden deep in a canyon. Layer upon layer of magnificent greenery softens the intensity of the hot sun, burning brilliantly in a sky the color of our Caribbean blue water, with rays of light flickering in the water below.

"The only sounds I hear are the never-ending lullaby of the cascading water, and the occasional shriek of a passing monkey swinging effortlessly from branch to branch, or the sound of a bird cawing high in the trees. I rest with only a slender connection to the real world. I have only seen this place alone, but I dream of going there with the one I love in my arms. Costa Rica is a waterfall and hot spring haven, and a lover's nirvana."

"My God, Enrique that is the most beautiful description I've ever heard! I guess we all dream of finding the right one to share such a world. I once had that with my husband, and nothing will take those memories from me."

"Michelle, at one time I would have said that Rincon de la Vieja was Costa Rica's hidden utopia. But now, I regret to say, the secret of this hidden paradise is long out to the world. When I built my home, I chose its location because it was similar to the Ricon area.

"However, Rincon de la Vieja is a must-see. It is buried deep in the slopes of a double volcano; the area consists of cloud-filled forests, colorful birds, crystal clear lakes, hardened volcanic rock, and boiling mud pots of mineral baths. It also has secluded hot springs for the sensual bather, and of course, a number of glorious waterfalls."

Enrique continued, "Places such as these exist all throughout Costa Rica if you know where to find them. Tomorrow, I will show you the countryside if you are feeling well enough." Jacqueline said, "I'm feeling fine; I cannot wait to see the country." "Then tomorrow, we will explore together."

The limousine turned up a foggy side road. Puzzled, Jacqueline asked Enrique, "What is all the fog?" "You will see in a minute." The car came to a stop and Carlos opened Enrique's door first, and then Jacqueline's. Enrique was waiting with his hand stretched out for her as she exited into the fog-filled air.

The atmosphere was almost that of the most dark and foggy London night. Moisture filled the air. Enrique took her arm as he walked her through the fog to the rail at the edge of a cliff. "These, Michelle, are active volcanoes." As far as Jacqueline could see, there were hot moist clouds filling the air. She could hear a gurgling noise coming up from the clouds below her feet.

"Is it safe here, Enrique?" "These volcanoes have not erupted in forty years. I would not want my house built on this land, but it is fine for a visit." Jacqueline could smell a pleasant burning scent coming up through the clouds below. She reached on the ground and picked up a rock. "This is beautiful, Enrique. What is it?" "That is volcano rock."

"Oh, it's wonderful! I will keep it as a souvenir of Costa Rica." "No Michelle, what is created in Costa Rica by nature is supposed to stay here. As a matter of fact, you could be arrested for trying to remove this from the country." Jacqueline put the rock back down and they walked to the rail's observation point to see a spectacular little eruption of smoke and fog. It was as though they were in heaven, far above the clouds, looking down.

As they returned to the car, Jacqueline heard a loud cracking noise, and at the same time she felt the pressure of Enrique pushing her into the open limousine door. His body followed her inside. Carlos looked directly into Jacqueline's eyes with concern, and then sped away from the fog. Stunned, Jacqueline asked, "Was that a gun shot?"

Obviously alarmed, Enrique and Carlos conversed in rapid, high-pitched Spanish. After a few minutes of driving, Enrique responded to her question. "I don't think so, but Costa Rica is dangerous, and maybe a drug lord did not like us at that location." Jacqueline sat quietly in the seat, as her heart slowed back to a normal beat. She was positive that it had been a gunshot. However, she said no more. Enrique had warned her that this was drug trafficking country.

"Michelle, you have had enough excitement for the day. We need to return home, so you can rest." They arrived back to Enrique's home and Eva prepared a late dinner for them, but Enrique came into the dining room a few minutes late. Jacqueline had heard Enrique and Carlos speaking loudly in Spanish in the library. Enrique joined her at the table. She ate very little, although the food was wonderful, as usual. "Michelle, you are not eating. Are you feeling all right?" "Yes, I'm just a little tired."

Enrique walked Jacqueline to her room and gave her medication, as he looked tenderly at her resting on the bed. "If you need anything, don't hesitate to call. Do not be concerned about today; I do not think it was a gunshot. It was probably just a fire cracker to warn us that we should leave the area." "Goodnight, Enrique. Thank you for taking such good care of me." He told her, "Michelle, it is my pleasure. Good night." Within minutes, Jacqueline was fast asleep, and she only woke when Enrique was at her bedside giving her the medication again. She slept until late the following morning.

It was fully daylight. The sunshine was pouring in Sid's window. "Jacqueline, Dr. Curran sounds like a real charmer. But it also sounds like he liked to play with opiates." "Sid, that's just the beginning of the story of Dr. Curran and Costa Rica. You may want to withhold judgment until I finish." "All right, I'll wait for the whole story before I decide about him. But I'm hungry! Would you like a sweet roll?"

They took a break to eat, and then, sipping her coffee, Jacqueline returned Sid to her task of writing the rest of the tale of Costa Rica and Dr. Enrique Curran....

Chapter Eleven
The Seduction

STIRRING AWAKE to the breeze coming in the balcony doors, Jacqueline slipped into her robe and walked through the doors onto the sundeck. The view was of spectacular forestland surrounding the house, and she was captivated by it. Her groggy observation of the colorful land was broken by a light knock at the open bedroom door. "Hello, sleepy." "Good morning, Enrique. Thank you for everything; I slept wonderfully." "Are you still sore?" "Yes, I'm still a bit sore." Enrique gestured and said, "Please come with me."

Enrique took Jacqueline's arm at the bedroom door and walked her down the hall to a room at the end. "I want you to go soak. Eva has taken care of everything for you, including your medication. It's on the counter, so don't forget to take it." "My God, Enrique, you have been so kind. Thank you."

She walked into a cedar room filled with fragrant steaming air and a large bubbling Jacuzzi. On the counter was a gold trimmed plate with her medication and a glass of water on a tray next to it. Next to the water was a crystal champagne glass filled with orange juice. She took the medication and then sipped the juice, discovering to her pleasure the taste of champagne. Jacqueline marveled at the beauty of the cedar-walled sauna with its huge glass windows twelve feet tall, as she sipped the cool mimosa.

Within seconds, her robe fell to the floor, and she stood naked below the radiating heat of the ceiling lamp. She realized that steam was coming out of the walls. Slowly she and her mimosa slipped into the Jacuzzi. She began soaking her sore body in the steaming hot water with jets of bubbles bursting against her skin. The view through the massive windows surrounding the tub overlooked a part of the forest area she had not seen on the property. Trees soared to the sky, and long-beaked toucans of black, red, green and orange sat on their branches. Occasionally a monkey would swing from tree to tree. The toucans seemed completely unconcerned about the monkeys' fun. It was as if they had lived in the forest together forever, and they had.

After about thirty minutes of resting in this paradise, a knock came at the door, and Eva entered the sauna. She quietly laid a towel, slippers, and robe on a warming stove for Jacqueline. Surprised, Jacqueline thanked her as Eva removed Jacqueline's old robe and quickly left without a word. Although she was always polite, for some reason Eva seemed very uncomfortable around Jacqueline. Maybe Jacqueline really did resemble Enrique's deceased wife. Eva had probably known her, and perhaps she did not accept other women around Enrique.

After Eva left, Jacqueline slowly lifted her body out of the water, only to realize that she was a little dizzy. But she was no longer as sore. She took one last look at the forest as she slowly dried her body. When the towel rubbed across the nipple of her breast, she felt a sensation of arousal immediately. Surprised, she smiled as she slipped into the warm robe and slippers. The heat from the robe against her body made her moist. She knew that it must be the combination of medication, environment and Enrique causing this excitement. She was now finding these sudden periods of arousal quite pleasant and somewhat amusing.

As she walked back to her room, she saw Enrique coming up the stairs. "Well little one, how are you feeling now?" "Wonderful, Enrique, I'm hardly sore at all! But I think this medication is having some real side effects." "What are they, Michelle?" "My head is not clear. I feel a little stoned and, I would say, maybe lightheaded." Enrique laughed, "The medication you are taking is an opiate, but those side effects are not anything to worry about. People pay a lot of money to feel that effect. Are you hungry?"

Jacqueline realized that she was starved. "I'm famished." Enrique grinned at her. "Well, brunch is almost ready. Would you like to have some help getting dressed?" "No thank you, I can do it." "Well, if you are feeling light-headed, I could send Eva up." Jacqueline told him, "I'm fine." "Michelle, if you like, we could have our dinner served on my boat." "You have a boat, Enrique?" "Yes, Michelle. Just dress comfortably. After we have brunch, we will spend the afternoon relaxing here, and then we'll go to the boat for dinner."

A few minutes later, Enrique returned to accompany Jacqueline down the stairs. After they had a sumptuous brunch, they wandered around the property, with Enrique describing the plants and animals. Afterwards, she rested on the veranda for a while. Enrique announced that dinner was almost ready, and that it was time to go to the boat. They walked to the limousine as the sun was setting, and Carlos drove them to a secluded dock. The only boat was a catamaran yacht about sixty feet long. Carlos prepared to serve the dinner on the deck below the stars. Jacqueline again noticed Carlos looking directly into her eyes as if he were trying to tell her something, but he said nothing.

Enrique poured champagne and guided Jacqueline on a tour of the three-stateroom yacht. The boat appeared to be mostly mahogany inside and it was decorated in the most elegant of nautical designs, with all of the amenities of a fine home. Jacqueline and Enrique dined on deck, overlooking the blue Caribbean beneath the stars. They feasted on portobello mushrooms over lettuce with roasted red peppers and feta cheese, drizzled with an aged balsamic vinaigrette reduction. Perfectly grilled sea scallops circled the plate.

Enrique was charming as he spoke of love and the ease of life in Costa Rica. Carlos cleared the dishes as Enrique spoke to him in Spanish. Carlos quickly finished and left in the limousine. "Where is Carlos going?" "I thought we would stay here, and tomorrow take the boat out. Since we will not go far, I can handle the boat alone. The cabins are quite comfortable." "What a wonderful idea Enrique, but I don't have any other clothes." "I had Eva pack a few things, and Carlos put them in the master stateroom for you. I will take one of the other staterooms. They are all very comfortable."

"I don't want to put you out of your room! I will take one of the other rooms." Enrique shook his head. "I already had your luggage put in the master bedroom. You don't want me to have to move it, do you?" Jacqueline, moved again by his hospitality, simply said, "Thank you, Enrique." He refilled their champagne glasses and told her to feel free to slip into the robe in her stateroom and get comfortable for a relaxing evening on the boat, while he prepared dessert. Jacqueline walked to her stateroom and sure enough, a lovely white terry robe marked with the monogram EC was waiting. She slipped into the robe and slippers, brushed her hair, and touched up her lipstick before returning to the deck.

Slowly she strolled back up to the deck and could see candles burning, with light flickering on the deck. She looked forward, and noticed a trampoline with small holes in it stretched between the bows. "What is the trampoline for?" "It stabilizes the boat by keeping the hulls gliding through the water – but you can rest in the sun tomorrow on the trampoline, and the spray from below will cool your body."

An array of fresh fruit and cheese surrounding another bottle of champagne was on the table between the two deck chairs. Enrique took Jacqueline's hand as he seated her into a deck chair. The temperature was a spectacular seventy-five degrees. A gentle breeze was blowing lightly, visible in the fire of the candles. Enrique gently lifted Jacqueline's legs and placed an ottoman under her feet. Then he handed her the nightly dose of medication. "Enrique, this medication is really having some side effects, and the euphoria is becoming much stronger. I hope that I'm not acting strangely."

"No Michelle, you need to relax, and that euphoric feeling allows the nerves to your brain to relax and heal. Don't be concerned." "But I feel my senses are so over-stimulated." "Can you describe how you feel, Michelle?" "Well, I don't know exactly how, but every emotion, smell, taste and sound is intensified, and I feel no inhibitions." He told her, "That may not be the medication. Maybe you are just happy and relaxed." "Maybe," she said, not wanting to tell him that she was completely sexually aroused.

Enrique sat back in his chair and began to talk. "Costa Rica is different from the United States. Here, we are more relaxed and free. In Costa Rica, sexuality is considered a wonderful thing, and it is much freer. As well, the simple moderate use of drugs such as cannabis or opiates is the norm. For example, you could remove your robe and truly enjoy the night air without any restriction. I would not bother you. I would enjoy seeing the beauty of you relaxing." "I don't know if I would feel comfortable, Enrique." "If you decide you would like to, as I said, I would not seduce you. But I would enjoy watching you."

Jacqueline changed the subject. She began asking Enrique about his life. She knew she was getting higher from the medication and the champagne; Enrique's every suggestion was arousing to her body. "Have you ever been involved in politics, Enrique?" Enrique became very adamant. "Absolutely not!" Then he began to speak of the corruption of all governments. He said he had spent a large portion of his life studying the workings of the governments of America and other countries.

"I'm convinced that every government is a money-making structure for the rich, at the expense of the poor. The war America started in Afghanistan after the bombing in New York was retaliation against an entire country for the actions of a few. When it was clear that America could not gain control over Afghanistan, the warmongering shifted to Iraq. Despite what was said, the war in Iraq was not to prevent the spread of weapons of mass destruction or to stop terrorism in America. It was an excuse for Texas oilmen to gain control over oil-rich land in the Middle East. The result was leaving American, British, and other soldiers in the middle of a civil war in Iraq.

"Now, many of the countries of the Middle East and Asia are either in civil war or on its brink, and the proliferation of weapons in those countries means that Israel needs to massively increase its military presence and weapons cache just to defend itself." Jacqueline listened intently as this obviously brilliant man spoke of the abuse of power and its worldwide implications.

As she began to tire, Enrique helped her back to her stateroom. He turned down the covers and removed her robe, gently placing Jacqueline in bed. Enrique kissed her goodnight on the cheek and closed the door as he left. Jacqueline was very high and her body was hot with desire as she removed the sheet to feel the breeze coming through the open porthole. She relaxed and rubbed her hands across her breasts in the beautiful night air then fell fast asleep.

Morning came late, and Jacqueline woke sore but smiling at the thought of Enrique putting her to bed the night before. He had been so tender and caring. She stepped into the shower and dressed back in her robe and slippers. Slowly, a little stiff, she walked up the mahogany stairs to the deck. Enrique had prepared breakfast when he heard Jacqueline in the shower. By the time she got to the table, food was awaiting her.

The morning was warm and sunny, and they relaxed over a simple breakfast of scrambled eggs and fruit. The coffee was simply wonderful and Enrique had her medication next to her cup. Jacqueline finished eating as Enrique was cleaning the dishes from the deck. He suggested that she relax on the trampoline. Giving her a mimosa and setting the bottle of champagne next to her on the deck, he told her, "I'm going to take the boat out; just relax."

Jacqueline heard the engines start and before she knew it, they were pulling away from the dock and moving out into the bluest water she had ever seen. The sun was hot and the sea mist spit up a slightly cooling breeze through the holes of the trampoline. It only took a short time to move from the shore into clear indigo blue water that stretched as far as she could see.

After about half an hour, she heard the engines stop, and Enrique came back to the deck wearing only a small bathing suit. His chest was firm and his body long, lean and tanned. His smile was beautiful as he stood enjoying the blue water all around them.

"Michelle, let me welcome you to the Caribbean." "Enrique, it is the most beautiful water I have ever seen, so blue, clear, and clean. Not too long ago, our water in the American Gulf of Mexico was heavily contaminated by an oil leak from a pipeline. It caused massive environmental damage." Enrique replied, "I heard about that leak. I cannot understand why a country like America is so dependent on oil for energy. The technology for solar, geothermal, and wind energy production already exists, and those natural resources are plentiful."

Enrique poured himself a glass of champagne and sat down in the chair next to the trampoline where Jacqueline was reclining in her robe. She lay back, enjoying the view and the privacy, with not another boat in sight.

Jacqueline opened her robe to bare her legs to the sun. Then she untied her robe and opened it wide so her entire body could bake in the sun, and she would provide Enrique a visual feast. "I see you are feeling the freedom of my land, Michelle." Enrique smiled as he rested his head back and closed his eyes. They rested on the deck in the sun for hours, with barely a word spoken.

"Michelle you had better roll over; the Caribbean sun is very strong." "Thank you." She rolled over, removing the rest of her robe. "Would you like me to rub oil on you? "Yes, please." Enrique's hands were like fine silk

226

as he lay on the deck rubbing the oil on her legs, then up to her buttocks and back.

Jacqueline was so aroused, but said nothing about wanting more when he stopped and returned to his chair in the sun. She fell fast asleep and awoke to a lunch prepared by Enrique. Jacqueline rolled her stoned, hazy, hot body over and asked Enrique for her robe. "You don't need it to eat lunch." She sat up naked as Enrique helped her into a chair and she dined on the fruit, cheese and wine Enrique had prepared.

His eyes seemed pleased as he watched her eating, naked, the sweat dripping from her nipples. "Your brown body is luscious and the color of the pineapple against your red lips is like a fine oil painting." "Enrique, I feel so euphoric and content. I can't believe how safe and comfortable I feel with you on this boat."

"I'm pleased, Michelle; you are becoming a native." "Enrique, I feel no inhibitions." He could have made love to her there, but he did not try. She finished her lunch and then returned to the trampoline. Enrique came over and began rubbing oil on her breasts. She wanted his kiss. He just continued to rub the oil deep into her body and even though she could feel the moisture as his hand rubbed the oil between her legs, she just closed her eyes and said nothing.

Enrique attracted and aroused Jacqueline, but she was unsure if she wanted to become involved with him physically. He would always remind her of Rose, which was his attraction. His mannerisms reminded her so much of Rose in the earlier years. However, those memories brought back thoughts of the bad years and the terrible sadness of losing Rose. Jacqueline knew that she could not be around Enrique without those terrible memories coming back to cause her pain.

She was asleep in the sun when she heard the engine start and the boat began to cruise slowly to shore. Enrique came up to the deck and handed Jacqueline her robe. "We will be ashore soon, and Carlos will be picking us up." She slipped into her robe and left the deck to dress. Carlos was waiting when they arrived at the shore. The ride home was quiet and Jacqueline wondered why Enrique had not tried to make love to her, even if she was not sure that she wanted it to happen.

As soon as they arrived back at the hacienda, Jacqueline told Enrique she needed a bath. He suggested, "Why don't you soak in the Jacuzzi and I will bring you a cocktail. I was wondering if, after dinner, you would like to go out for a drink in the city?" "That sounds wonderful." "Do you need any help in bathing? I can send Eva up." Jacqueline told him, "No, I will be fine."

As Jacqueline entered the room and closed the door, she laughed aloud. When Enrique offered her help, she thought he was offering to help her, not to send Eva! She knew if Enrique helped her, she would not be able to keep her hands off him. She was hot! Her body was so stimulated from Enrique rubbing the oil on her that his touch was the only thing she desired.

It had been a long time since she had truly experienced that longing feeling. She slipped into the Jacuzzi just as Enrique came in and handed her the medication and a bottle of water, followed by a Grand Marnier. He told her she looked beautiful in the water and then asked that she call when she was ready to get out. Jacqueline lay in the water looking out and sipping her drink, wondering what Enrique was thinking. Did he want her? Maybe he was just not interested, or maybe he was gay.

Jacqueline took a long luxurious soak in the Jacuzzi. After she bathed, she looked through her clothes, freshly pressed and hanging in the closet, and found her red silk dress and heels. She looked in the mirror and thought the outfit was a bit wild and that she should change. Then she looked again and decided that it fit her aroused mood and hoped it would please Enrique. Her nipples were slightly visible through the silk dress. She turned to look at the back of the dress in the mirror and saw the outline of her panties. Without hesitation, she slipped her silk panties off and looked into the mirror again. "Perfect," she thought. A dress and heels was all that she would wear. After all, Enrique said she should feel completely free in Costa Rica.

Jacqueline picked up the telephone and dialed zero. Carlos answered and said "Apenas un minuto." Enrique picked up the telephone, "Are you ready, dear?" "Yes." "I'm on my way; don't try the stairs by yourself." Jacqueline finished putting on her lipstick just as she heard Enrique coming up the stairs. "My God, Michelle, you look stunning in red with your Caribbean tan!" He took her arm at the top of the stairs and laid his hand on top of hers with a gentle pat. Slowly he walked her down the stairs and into the dining room. He pulled out the chair at the opposite end of the table.

"I must say it again Michelle, you look absolutely stunning. Red is a wonderful color against your olive skin and dark hair. You are a beautiful woman." "Thank you." Eva came into the room and filled Jacqueline's soup bowl with lobster bisque. Her attitude had not changed. She still seemed cold, with never a smile or word.

The late evening breeze was cooling the still-hot evening air; Jacqueline could feel the breeze as it came through the open balcony doors, entering the low v-neck of the silk dress, cooling her breasts. It seemed the medication was still intensifying Jacqueline's senses. Her lips and tongue were attuned to every nuance of the texture and taste of the bisque.

She told Enrique again about the effects of the medication she was feeling, but not about the intense sexual arousal she felt. However, she doubted that he could miss it – her erect nipples were pushing out a full half inch against the thin red silk. He again assured her not to be concerned about the effects of the medication, just to use caution while walking and to let the staff help her if she needed anything.

Just then, Carlos came into the room and announced something to Enrique in Spanish that included the English name, "Doctor Stanley Letterbaugh," and the only Spanish word she could make out, "biblioteca." She knew that meant "library." Enrique seemed flustered and rose quickly, excusing himself and heading straight for the library. Jacqueline waited at the table while Eva cleared the dishes in her usual silence.

Alone in the dining room, she could hear voices coming from the library. She could not tell what was being said, but she could clearly tell that it was a heated conversation. After about fifteen minutes, she took her wine and walked slowly past the library. She tried to see in, but the door was closed, so she continued to the veranda.

She waited there for about another half hour before Enrique returned. He seemed calm as he said, "Michelle, I am so sorry. It was just hospital business." "Oh. Do you need to cancel our outing, or would your business associate like to join us?" Enrique shook his head as he said, "No, no, he has already left. Now let's forget about business and enjoy our evening." Jacqueline was more than a little curious about this Doctor Stanley Letterbaugh, but she just let it drop.

Enrique rang for Carlos to bring the car, and this time Carlos brought a black Mercedes convertible. Enrique drove. The sun was beginning to set, and in Jacqueline's altered vision, colors burst like diamonds from the sky. The countryside seemed to be a vision of mountains and forests. Flowers decorated the hills, and the only flat land seemed to be Enrique's property. Jacqueline was now sure that Enrique's home had been carved from the center of the mountains. She really could not be sure if the hues of Costa Rica were as brilliant as she thought, or if the medication was intensifying her perception of the colors of the land.

Jacqueline heard the sound of salsa music drifting into the open car. "Listen, Enrique," she said with great excitement in her voice. "I hear it, Michelle." The closer they came to the city circle, the louder and clearer the music became. It was so filled with life. "Do you salsa dance?" "No, Enrique – actually, it's been a long time since I danced at all."

"Well, maybe you will allow me to show you a little. Not too much, though. I am still concerned about your head." "Oh Enrique, I would love that!" They continued to drive around the roundabout that surrounded a stone fountain. "Oh look, there is the Markus Inn, where I was to stay." "Yes, it is a wonderful hotel Michelle, and after we go to the salsa club, I will show it to you. I belong to their private club."

The car pulled to a stop in front of a three-story adobe building. The adobe walls were an almost-pink color, and the doors were wide open. A young valet, who barely looked fifteen, took the car. The music was pouring out of the building. Jacqueline could see the patrons in fast movement on the dance floor. As they entered, the door attendant welcomed Enrique. It was clear that they knew one another.

The doorman quickly moved a table from beside the door to the inside of the filled bar, lit a candle, and placed it on the table. "Bienvenida, Señora," the gentleman said. "Hello, I'm Michelle." Enrique immediately interrupted, "He does not speak English," and then he spoke to the man in Spanish. The man hurried away, and Jacqueline stood with her gaze directed at people in full motion on the dance floor. In bright colored clothes, their hips were swinging, and they were joining hands from time to time, all to the beat of salsa music.

The man returned with two snifters of clear Grand Marnier and a bottle of water. Enrique handed Jacqueline another pill and the water bottle. She took the medication and sat down at the small round table with its red candle burning in the center. A young girl came to the table selling flowers from a basket filled with many different kinds and colors. Enrique quickly took a rose from her basket and paid the girl.

He handed the rose to Jacqueline. She was surprised that from all the different flowers in the girl's basket, Enrique had chosen a yellow rose. Her mind immediately went back to the first flower that Rose had ever bought her, a yellow rose that lasted for eight days. Enrique's similarities to Rose were troubling, yet intriguing. She felt like she was on an emotional rollercoaster.

The club was three stories high inside, and people were dancing on the balconies of every floor. Some were watching over the balcony rails as the lights flickered off the dance floor below in magnificent shades of gold, red, blue, purple, and green. Jacqueline could hardly hear Enrique speaking over the salsa music. However, when Enrique rose to his feet and stretched his strong hand out, she knew what he wanted.

"I don't know how to salsa." "Don't worry, we will start slowly." As they entered the dance floor, Jacqueline could feel the beat of the music running through her body. Enrique took Jacqueline's hand and guided her into his arms. She felt the chemistry immediately, that feeling of stimulation, and she knew the eternal dance had begun. Jacqueline clearly realized Enrique's smooth seduction, and she was enjoying it.

Her body began to follow Enrique's lead and the salsa came naturally. When the music stopped, he walked her back to the table. She was a little light headed and breathless. "Very well done, Michelle! You must have Latin blood. But that is more than enough dancing for you tonight." They finished their drinks, unable to hear each other over the music.

Leaving the bar, the Markus Inn was to their left. Enrique collected his keys from the valet, but left the car parked where it was, right beside the salsa club. The breeze from the night air was flowing through Jacqueline's clothes, cooling her from dancing and arousing her at the same time. They walked the cobblestone street that surrounded the fountain in the town square. Jacqueline was enjoying the freedom of Costa Rica – she felt as free as the butterflies in the air.

Most of the buildings were small businesses, one after another. Jacqueline could tell by the names of some that they were obviously American-owned or American-influenced. Enrique took her arm; she was feeling the medication and the alcohol was hitting her. They walked past the Markus Inn attendant, who greeted Enrique with a smile as he opened the door to what was obviously the most luxurious hotel in town.

The inn was very nice with a small marble foyer. Nevertheless, the foyer was not as impressive as the one at

Enrique's hacienda. Most of the buildings in that area of San José were made of adobe but this building was marble, and it was among the nicest in the city. They walked through a hall to large double doors at the back. They were marked, "Private – Members Only." Enrique opened the door with a key card and escorted Jacqueline though. The largest solid white marble swimming pool that she had ever seen was before her eyes. "It is beautiful!"

She could smell the plant life all around; some of them were twenty feet tall inside the enclosed marble and glass pool area. The flowers and plants emitted a remarkable fragrance, intensified by Jacqueline's opiate medication. "Come this way, Michelle. I have a surprise for you." As they walked across the enormous deck toward the back, just past the gorgeous pool, she saw a full sauna area with a small Roman-style bath. The bath was surrounded by pillars of black marble supporting a glass ceiling that formed a dome. Through the dome was a display of the Costa Rican sky.

The spectacular beauty of this gigantic oasis of tranquility captivated Jacqueline. She had never seen such a well-hidden manmade structure. Nothing like this existed in any of the fine hotels where she had stayed. Enrique was watching her face, and it was obvious he was enjoying seeing her awe-struck.

He smiled and said, "I thought this would help to soothe the soreness from your body. The lobby of this hotel is modest, and only members have access to this part of the hotel. It was originally built around 1920 and has seen many grand renovations, enlargements and improvements."

"Enrique, this is the most beautiful spa I have ever seen! I've never seen anything like it! It is so peaceful. Are we the only ones here? Look, look, you can see the moon and stars through the ceiling!" Before Enrique could even answer Jacqueline's question, a large, well-built, olive-skinned Latin young man with long black hair pulled back in a ponytail and a beautiful young Latin woman with long, wavy, dark hair came through a door from the dry sauna room. Both were dressed in white linen and greeted Enrique in Spanish.

The man welcomed Dr. Curran in Spanish and addressed Jacqueline, "Señora, bienvenida." "Michelle, their names are Ramón and Cielo, and they will be giving you a massage tonight. They do not speak English, but they will guide you through your evening at the spa." "Enrique, I'm not sure about this; I'm pretty high." "Do not worry, Michelle. Life is far more relaxed in Costa Rica. They will take good care of you. You can go with them, and I will go to the bar for a drink. They will help keep the soreness from getting any worse."

Ramón and Cielo escorted Jacqueline to the dressing room. Inside, it was decorated with furnishings of white linen and terrycloth. Ramón waited at the door with his arms crossed in front of his chest, while Cielo guided Jacqueline to the back of the dressing room. Cielo sat her down in a chair covered in white terrycloth, then removed Jacqueline's heels and placed warm slippers on her feet. Then Cielo unzipped Jacqueline's dress and held a white terry robe for her to put on. Jacqueline stood up and let her red dress fall to the floor. She reached for the robe, but Cielo held it open and slipped the warm robe around her.

Cielo straightened the robe around Jacqueline's shoulders. As Jacqueline was reaching for the belt to tie the robe, Cielo's hands touched Jacqueline's, and the masseuse completed even this most simple task for her comfort. Cielo hung the red dress on a padded hanger and placed her heels on a shelf. Then she took Jacqueline's hand and walked her into a hot sauna room to a table covered in the same terrycloth.

The room was lit with candlelight, soft music was playing, and the smell of flowers filled the air. Cielo pulled a stool from below the table and motioned for Jacqueline to step up and recline on the table. She took the step up and rested her back on the warm, comfortable table. Jacqueline watched as Cielo soaked her soft dark hands with oil and began rubbing Jacqueline's feet. Completely stoned, she found her warm oil foot massage heavenly.

Jacqueline was sinking deeply into a trance when she felt Cielo untying her robe. Cielo placed a warm towel over the middle of Jacqueline's body as she removed the robe. The room was so warm and moisture filled the air. Jacqueline could feel the hot oil dripping from her feet. Her mind was lost in complete euphoria. She had no reservations about the enjoyment that was being provided; she was determined to lose all of her inhibitions and just seize the moment.

The heat of the room, the music, and the flickering candlelight raised Jacqueline's opiate high to an even greater level, as she viewed the stars shining through the glass ceiling. Before her eyes was the constellation Cool Sack. Never before had she seen such a spectacular sky. Jacqueline's head was spinning, yet she felt completely relaxed even though she saw Ramón approaching the table.

He smiled tenderly, and she had no fear as he placed his oil soaked hands upon one of her legs while Cielo continued rubbing the other. Cielo and Ramón rubbed in absolute harmony. It was as though their hands were in complete sync, touching each muscle of each leg at the same time.

Jacqueline's eyes opened to stars above the glass ceiling of the candle-lit room. At that moment, she saw the Southern Cross for the first time, in perfect view in the black starry sky. Her mind was captivated by the unparalleled beauty of the shining cross, as she reveled in the pleasure of their hands on her body.

Splendid sensations were flowing through her mind and body as their hands were moving in tandem. The towel gently fell to the floor. They massaged her shoulders as they had her legs, then she felt both of them massaging the oil deep into her breasts. Jacqueline was completely exhilarated by their touch, and she was stoned enough to relax and enjoy it all! She could not have planned a vacation like this if she had tried! She did not know what lay ahead, but she intended to enjoy every sensation to the fullest.

Gently, they rolled her body over while continuing the deep oil massage, applying the slippery, warm oil to her back. She was enraptured! She was filled with feelings that she had never known. The pampering made her feel as if she were a powerful queen from some ancient time. Jacqueline saw Enrique coming into the room, wearing only a towel, and carrying a snifter in his hand.

Her mouth watered at the thought of how delicious he looked. Jacqueline knew what a night this was going to be! For months and months, her body had been untouched by another, and she was ready to delight and be delighted. He stood over Jacqueline and gently stroked her hair while he watched her body being oiled and massaged. Then he sat on a stool at the end of the table so she was facing him.

Enrique stroked the side of her face while looking deeply into Jacqueline's eyes, as Ramón and Cielo continued bathing her body in hot oil. "Enrique, my body feels wonderful and my mind is in a heavenly place that I've never known before." "Michelle, this is just the beginning." He placed his fingers in the snifter and began rubbing the Grand Marnier gently, sensually on her lips repeatedly, as she began sucking on his fingers. She was enjoying the taste, as well as the sensation, of his fingers touching her lips and in her mouth. "Rest, Michelle. You need this."

She could feel two pair of hands in gentle motion on her bottom. Then Ramón's strong hands were rubbing her back. Enrique said something in Spanish and they gently rolled Jacqueline over onto her back again. Jacqueline still felt no inhibitions as she watched the Southern Cross still shining high in the night sky. Ramón and Cielo were attending to her every desire even before she knew what she desired. Her nipples were fully erect and moisture had begun to seep from her body.

They continued to rub the warm oil deep onto her breasts, and Jacqueline relaxed even more as she looked into Enrique's eyes. "Michelle, your body is beautiful and tonight you will feel pure pleasure." Jacqueline closed her eyes at the very moment she felt Enrique's first kiss. His lips were so soft and his tongue was comforting. Her lips, still coated with Grand Marnier, responded without hesitation.

Then her body felt the first sign of being not just moist but internally wet from his kiss. Enrique's hands replaced Ramón's on her breasts as Jacqueline slowly opened her eyes. Cielo and Ramón were rubbing the oil slowly and softly between her legs.

As she became even more aroused, Jacqueline closed her hazy eyes again. Then she felt a sudden wet warm touch, as Enrique bent over the side of the table, placed his lips on her erect nipple, and sucked ever so lightly. Then his tongue traced the silver dollar sized circle of her nipple.

Gradually, Enrique moved down her body and between Jacqueline's separated legs, as the masseur and masseuse continued to massage her feet. Jacqueline was seeping onto Enrique's lips as hands gently rubbed her hot, oily body. She had never had such an experience – it felt like the only reason for existence was pleasure.

Enrique slowly moved back up to her lips; she could feel Ramón's hands slipping away from her feet and then she felt them on her breasts, as Enrique kissed his way back down. As her legs gently parted, Enrique's tongue slid in more deeply. Both of her breasts were being soaked in oil as Ramón's hands continued to rub while Enrique dined. Jacqueline came in snapping orgasms, her body jerking up and down, as her eyes watched Enrique. Cielo's hands, separating the lower part of Jacqueline's legs, made it impossible for her to move as her body continued to seep, uncontrolled, into Enrique's lips.

Then she struggled to move Enrique's lips up to hers. He kissed her and slid himself into her. His body was hot and wet as he slowly slid deeper. Ramón and Cielo were gently rubbing her arms, stretched high above her head. Enrique's hard body melted into Jacqueline's warm wet juice until she came repeatedly, waiting for Enrique to fill her body with a sudden burst. Enrique kissed her lips deeply, "This is just the beginning, Michelle. I want you to have all the pleasures this world can offer. You are mine, forever."

Enrique motioned to Cielo. "They will bathe you now, and I will join you in a few minutes." Cielo gently placed the warmed robe around Jacqueline's shoulders, as she helped her down from the table. Then she walked Jacqueline into the large Roman-styled Jacuzzi bath of hot bubbling water.

Cielo helped Jacqueline into the tub as though she knew how woozy Jacqueline was from the medication and all that had just happened. The water was a hot and wonderful sensation. Cielo, wearing the white linen dress, entered the large bath with Jacqueline. Ramón followed them into the water, as his white pants and shirt clung closely to his hard body. He lifted Jacqueline into his arms, resting her on a warm cement ledge just below the water line, with her head placed on a curved pillow.

Cielo lathered her hands with warm water and soap then gently placed her hands over Jacqueline's breasts as her body rested partly submerged in the water. Slowly and sensually, Cielo began washing all of Jacqueline's body. She was gently rubbing her hands across Jacqueline's breasts, down her body, and between her legs. Jacqueline watched as Cielo's soaked white linen dress became see-through and clung tightly against the dark skin of her thin body.

Enrique came into the water, handing Jacqueline a pill and bottle of water, followed by a snifter. Then he walked back and sat in a chair next to the bath where he had been watching her bathe. "Michelle, things in Costa Rica are much freer sexually than in America. You are just beginning to enjoy the pleasures of our country. I want you to enjoy them forever. Michelle, I believe your life has been one of little joy until this day. Now and forever, you will be my queen and live a life of pleasure and joy."

Enrique continued .to watch as Cielo washed Jacqueline's body with her soapy hands, rubbing every inch in a slow soothing motion. Jacqueline lay on the bench in the hot bubbling water with her eyes closed, sipping from the snifter. She opened her eyes every now and then to see Enrique sipping from his glass and smiling as he watched the slow sensual movement of Cielo bathing Jacqueline.

Cielo washed Jacqueline's hair in a lilac scented shampoo and then Ramón lifted her onto the deck, as Cielo began to dry her body. Then together they slipped Jacqueline back into a warm terry robe. After seating her in a white chaise, Cielo brushed Jacqueline's long hair as Enrique watched with enormous pleasure. Enrique said something in Spanish, and Ramón began rubbing warm oil with the smell of lilacs on Jacqueline's body as she lay on the chaise.

Ramón knelt over Jacqueline as he rubbed the oil into both breasts with a wonderful massaging motion, stopping each time at the tip of her nipples to assure they grew to massive size. His touch was euphoric and Jacqueline did not know which man she wanted inside her body. It appeared that she was getting the pleasure of both, with Cielo as a bonus.

His hands were more stimulating than relaxing. Jacqueline had studied Ramón's water-soaked body as he stood before her, his pants forming a clear picture of his sculptured manhood. He was dark, muscular, and strong. Jacqueline could feel the moisture between her legs as she viewed him kneeling beside her chair, while he massaged the oil into her body.

Enrique asked if they were stimulating her and she replied, "Yes." "That is what I want. I want your body and mind completely stimulated, Michelle." Jacqueline and Enrique were having a complete conversation while both Ramón and Cielo pampered her body from top to bottom. She enjoyed the soaked physique of Ramón bulging in his wet linen pants. It was more than obvious to her that he was enjoying his work.

Enrique spoke again in Spanish and they both left the room. Enrique dropped his towel to reveal his large, hard, thick cock and again slid deeply into Jacqueline as she cried out with pleasure. The oil heated Jacqueline's body as Enrique satisfied her deeper and deeper. Finally, she felt his explosion.

Jacqueline collapsed back into the chaise lounge and Enrique summoned the servants. Ramón carried Jacqueline to the bath and held her, as Cielo bathed and dried her again. Ramón oiled her body again as Enrique watched. Ramón's hands were soft but strong, and Jacqueline became even more intensely aroused by his touch. Enrique walked slowly to Jacqueline as Cielo slipped the robe back across Jacqueline's oily body. Enrique dismissed the servants. "I want to dress you myself." Jacqueline's body was so relaxed that she could barely move.

Slowly, Enrique knelt on the ground in front of Jacqueline as he carefully removed her slippers, toweled the excess oil from her feet, and replaced the slippers with her red high heels. Enrique helped her from the edge of the chaise lounge to her feet. Then he asked Jacqueline to let her robe drop to the floor. She raised her hands to her shoulders and the robe fell to the floor, as she stood before him naked, her skin glowing from the oil.

Jacqueline's nipples still stood out from the skill of Ramón's hands. Enrique rose as he rubbed a different oil in his hands and then onto her still-erect nipples. Her nipples began to tingle like the warmth of a fire, and she became wetter. Enrique took his oil-soaked hands and caused the same fire between her legs. She was dripping from the oil, before him in only her red high heels.

"Michelle, I am in love with you." Then his lips kissed her more deeply. He continued to inspire the flow of warm juice from her body. She placed her hands on his face. "Enrique, enjoy the woman in me, but do not love me." "It is too late Michelle, I already love you." He kissed her as he dried the excess oil and slipped Jacqueline's dress onto her, telling her, "That is all you ever need to wear." Enrique pampered her as though she were the Queen of Egypt.

Enrique kissed her and handed her another drink from the tray brought in by Ramón. "How does your body feel now?" Jacqueline exclaimed, "Satisfied, warm, and wonderful! Enrique, you are full of surprises." He smiled broadly as he said, "Michelle, in our country sexual satisfaction has fewer boundaries than in America. Ménage à trois is more than accepted in Central America. In this case, it was only the satisfying of you by the pleasure of a multitude of hands warming your aching muscles.

"The oil, just like Ramón and Cielo, was only a means to intensify your pleasure as I made love to you. Watching Ramón and Cielo provide stimulation to you, as I viewed your beautiful body soaked in oil, aroused me beyond my wildest imagination. Here in Costa Rica, it is more about feeling and less about what people perceive to be proper. Come with me, Michelle; let's enjoy the rest of the evening!"

"We had better wait until my nipples calm down. They are so hard they are pushing through the thin silk of my dress." "I enjoy seeing your nipples, and I want everyone else to enjoy seeing them, as well." Jacqueline knew she was ripe for this wild sexual Shangri-La.

They followed the completely vacant route back out, through the grand pool area under the stars, to an elevator at the front. The elevator doors closed, and Enrique separated Jacqueline's silk dress, revealing her bare breasts. He began licking her nipples, making them even harder, until the elevator stopped at the twelfth floor. Gently he slipped her breasts back inside her dress, just in time for the doors to open. Jacqueline could hear ringing sounds and see dealers standing on the floor behind gaming tables.

"Enrique, this place is unbelievable," as they took three steps down to the gaming area on a glorious green-carpeted floor. At the back was an iron-barred cashier's cage, and gambling tables filled the room. Dealers in black tuxedos and colorful chips on green felt tables were all she could see. No other customers were in the casino.

"Enrique, I can't believe there is a fully equipped casino up here! I had no idea!" "I didn't think you knew," he said with a laugh. "Oh, I love roulette, and my head is spinning! I need to sit down," as she moved toward the table. They took a seat at the roulette table; the croupier, speaking perfect English, cordially greeted them. A beautiful Spanish woman in a black and white short ruffled cocktail outfit came immediately up and offered them a drink. Enrique ordered drinks as he reached in his pocket and pulled out some Colons. Laying the Costa Rican currency on the table, he told the man running the roulette wheel, "The lady will be playing."

The croupier passed a number of chips across the table as he peered directly at Jacqueline's erect nipples. "Does this game work the same as in America?" "Madam, gaming is universal. Have fun. Besides you cannot lose – Dr. Curran has bought the club for the night." She turned to Enrique and said, "You bought the club for the night?" "Well, I didn't want us to be disturbed in the spa or the casino." Jacqueline kissed Enrique. "Thank you for the most beautiful evening I could have imagined." Enrique smiled and said, "It's not over yet."

The server returned with their drinks and a bottle of water. Enrique removed another pill from his pocket and handed the medication to Jacqueline. She took the pill as she placed her bets on the table. They won some and lost some, at the caprice of the wheel, while sipping golden Grand Marnier. "Enrique, I'm not kidding, this medication really has a wild effect on me." "I know, Michelle, but it is the best medication for head injuries. You really don't mind the effects, do you?" "No, I was just pointing them out. The pills make me feel free, sexually aroused, and full of energy!" "It seemed to me that the medication helped you really enjoy the experience downstairs. I know it intensifies everything. But you will find that you are safe with me, so just enjoy the ride, my dear."

Jacqueline placed another bet as Enrique quietly slipped his hand beneath her dress under the roulette table. She felt the warmth of Enrique stimulating her while she gambled. He gently placed his hand high on the inside of her thigh and slowly slid it down and back. It did not matter that he did not enter her. She was so over-stimulated from the spa and the drugs that she again became moist, her nipples pushing the silk of her dress far away from her breasts.

After about an hour, they returned to the elevator and took it to the fourteenth floor. The door opened and they walked down a hall into some sort of theater and took a seat on a large red sofa. They appeared to be the only people in the place. The window before them showed a gorgeous outline of the mountain range, bathed in the light of the moon. Jacqueline had never seen a theater with a window. Just then, a man dressed all in white came over and brought them the same drinks they were having at the spa and in the casino.

The music was playing a soft Spanish song when three dancers wrapped in silks of red, green and yellow came into the room. They moved to the low stage in front of the window and began to dance. They slowly began removing the layers of silk, one at a time. The show was beautiful, and multicolored silks draped the moonlit stage by the end of the dance.

As the music changed, the performers left the stage. Beautiful quiet music began to play, and Jacqueline and Enrique were alone in the room to sip Grand Marnier and watch the moon gloriously cascading over the mountains through the window. Enrique held her closely, his hand rubbing her breast, brought forth from the red silk dress, until Jacqueline decided to take him again right there.

Sometime in the early morning hours, Jacqueline admitted she was getting tired. They walked slowly, arm-in-arm, as they left the club area and reentered the hotel. A man sat tall behind a grand piano, playing softly in the front foyer of the hotel. "Would you care for a final nightcap or morning refresher?" "That sounds wonderful, Enrique!" Suddenly, Jacqueline found that she was energized again. They sat in two of the high leather chairs that surrounded the piano. Enrique ordered drinks and made a request of the piano man. "Will you play *La Vie En Rose*?"

Jacqueline was shocked by his request. "Why did you have them play *La Vie En Rose*?" As the music began he said, "It is my favorite song. Have you ever heard it, Michelle?" "Yes, I fell in love with my husband to that song." "I am sorry. Does it hurt to hear it?" "No, it just brings back memories." "Yes, it brings back memories of my wife for me as well – I asked her to be my wife while *La Vie En Rose* played."

Jacqueline was feeling that there were just too many coincidences. She had said nothing before about this song playing when Rose asked her to marry him. It was as if she was living the excitement of her life with Rose all over again. However, she knew that Rose was dead and she was seeing and hearing only the dream she wanted. At that moment, she knew it had to be the pills. Was Enrique reading her thoughts? This relationship was getting too serious too fast. Now that Enrique had announced his love for her, Jacqueline was becoming nervous, for she knew that this could not last forever. In the next few days, she would leave Costa Rica and Enrique behind, but she would have wonderful memories.

They listened in complete silence while the piano man played. After finishing their drinks and thanking the piano player, they began the walk back to the car. Enrique drove slowly down the empty road, turning off onto a smaller road then pulling the car to the side. Enrique took Jacqueline's hand to help her out as he walked her to the back of the car. His lips were hot with kisses, intensified beneath the morning sky. Slowly he lifted her red silk dress, brushing his hands on her skin as the silk moved higher.

Jacqueline was so aroused and anticipated what was to come next. He gently turned her body, as he laid her over the back of the shiny black Mercedes. She could hear his zipper as he placed his hand in the middle of her back. With great force, he applied himself as she screamed in pleasure, calling out in the morning air, "More, more, more!"

He helped her back into the car; she laid her head on his lap as he drove. Enrique took Jacqueline's hand in his and placed it into her lips inside her red silk dress. He began to caress her with her hand. As she took over, he took his hand away, slid it into the long V of her dress, and toyed with her nipples. They continued to caress her as she came over and over again and passed out in his lap. The next thing she knew, Carlos was lifting her in his arms and carrying her to bed. Enrique sat on the edge of the bed with a pill and bottle of water. She raised her head slowly and took the pill. Enrique undressed her and placed the covers part way up on her body. Then he kissed her deeply and stroked her nipples with his tongue. Jacqueline was almost asleep when she heard Enrique say, "I love you."

"Jacqueline, I need a coffee break. I'm getting too hot to think! Besides, my hand is cramping from taking notes." Jacqueline laughed. "I understand – I've been watching you taking notes, and even with shorthand, your hand has been flying! I need a minute too." Sid left the room for coffee and she spoke from the kitchen. "I agree with you Jacqueline, there are similarities to Rose, but Enrique does seem like a man who knows how to treat a woman!"

When Sid returned with coffee, Jacqueline said, "Is your hand better? Are you ready to write some more? Because my story isn't over, it's just beginning. There's a lot more to tell...."

Chapter Twelve
Strange Familiarity

MORNING CAME early in the afternoon for Jacqueline. She woke, foggy-headed from her drug and alcohol fueled sexual adventures. She was wobbly, and walked slowly into the shower, its floor-to-ceiling window facing the private courtyard. It was a much smaller garden than the others that she had seen on the property. Completely enclosed by tropical plants for privacy, it was the most beautiful of all of the views.

She turned on the shower and sat on its marble bench, looking out the window, as the water drops beat gently down on her body. She slowly closed her eyes, as her mind played *La Vie En Rose*. Enrique was so charming and so similar to Rose, with his perfect manners and wild sexual appetite for pleasure.

When he held her in his arms on the dance floor, there was no denying her arousal. By the end of the evening, she had sampled the delights that he had to offer, while he aroused her body in a way she had not felt since Rose. Jacqueline's mind was lost in thoughts of the enchanted evening, as her hands so naturally slid to the breasts that Enrique had licked as she fell asleep. She was playing with her hard, erect nipples and the feeling of the water between her legs began to arouse her more. Slowly, she laid her head back against the marble wall and opened her eyes wide to the tropical garden with memories running though her head of Ramón.

After only a few minutes, her eyes closed, and she had brought herself to orgasm. Jacqueline knew the medication was making her highly aroused. It was not missed on her that it took drugs for Enrique to take her to the same level of arousal that she had found in Rose's mere existence.

Stepping out of the shower, she saw the satisfied smile radiating on her face in the mirror. She wondered if Enrique would notice her intensified glow at brunch. She had not felt true sexual arousal since her life with Rose, like when they made love under the waterfall in Jamaica. Still, Enrique and the drugs did make her feel alive again.

She finished dressing in white linen and heels. Again, Jacqueline chose to put nothing under her semi-sheer dress made of only two thin layers. She knew the dress was completely see-though, given the right lighting. Here in Costa Rica, she did not care. She was in a tropical paradise of sexual freedom.

Then she took her medication and slowly placed wine-colored lipstick on her lips. She was ready for whatever this day with Enrique had to bring. Even though she knew this relationship would not last, she could feel the intensity of her sexual arousal by Enrique, and she was going to enjoy him while she was in Costa Rica.

Jacqueline could see Enrique walking toward the bottom of the staircase. She wondered if he would see the orgasmic glow on her face. Then as she reached the middle of the staircase she heard his voice; "Michelle, you look even more radiant this afternoon. Last night must have been what you needed." "Enrique, last night was exactly what I needed, thank you."

Enrique told her, "Michelle, I have wanted you since the moment that I first laid my eyes on you." His words sounded so familiar. She smiled as she spoke, "Thank you, Enrique. I slept wonderfully after the evening you filled with surprises for me, and I woke in a most euphoric mood." His hand reached out to her as she neared the final stair. Arm-in-arm, they walked toward the dining area one more time. It seemed as though they had made this walk a million times, yet they had only known each other for a few days. Suddenly, Enrique turned and pulled Jacqueline into his arms near the library entrance.

Within seconds, he had turned the corner into the library, closed the door, pushed the few crystal pieces to the back of his desk and placed Jacqueline on the edge. He began ravishing her body, slipping his hands and tongue around the edges of her dress and beneath the white linen. She was in full orgasm in moments.

The emotions in Jacqueline were flying wildly. She knew that Enrique aroused her and that she was feeling more sexual desire and freedom than she had known in years. She could not believe that she was feeling that long-forgotten emotion – passion. She wanted to feel his complete touch, his body inside of her at every moment.

She knew it with his first touch, and the feeling had only intensified with the evening of pleasure he had provided. Now on his desk, she was snapping in multiple orgasms. This was a feeling long ago hidden inside her.

Nevertheless, she knew it was his similarity to Rose that was sending her mind into lost feelings of desire. Enrique was falling in love, and Jacqueline was merely lusting.

Jacqueline stumbled with weak legs from the power of her orgasms, as Enrique brought her to her feet. He guided her into the adjoining powder room, and in a few minutes she came out, her dress straightened for brunch. They walked slowly in to the dining room. This time, Enrique seated Jacqueline next to his side at the table, as they enjoyed the afternoon brunch.

The servants moved around without a word as Enrique and Jacqueline talked more deeply than before. Enrique asked if she truly loved her husband who had died. She responded, "More than you could know. No human being should ever love another with that intensity. No one could ever replace that love. That is why I told you, Enrique, enjoy my body and my passion – but do not fall in love with me. When Rose died, my ability to love died with him."

Enrique spoke of his deceased wife and said he also thought he could never love again. Jacqueline asked her name, and Enrique replied, "I prefer not to speak her name, it is still too painful. However, I now know I am capable of loving again. I discovered that it was possible when you came into my life. I love you. I want you for the rest of my life. We can have a wonderful life together in Costa Rica."

Just then, Carlos walked in to deliver a package to Enrique. Again, she heard the name Stanley Letterbaugh, when Carlos was describing the package to Enrique.

Enrique opened it at the table. At first, his face seemed surprised as he looked inside the package with deep concentration for a minute. Then slowly he pulled a chess clock out of the package. Jacqueline was stunned. "My God, it's the same kind of clock Rose used!" "Really," replied Enrique, "Well, it is the best." Enrique pulled out a magazine that was also in the package.

Jacqueline could see some writing on the magazine in black marker, but she could not make out what it said. Then Enrique reached into his shirt pocket and pulled out his glasses. It was the first time she had seen him wear glasses. They were the same wire rims Rose wore, but Jacqueline said nothing. She truly believed that the similarities were just her imagination. She had once loved Rose so much, and now she was feeling the same kind of emotion again. However, it was her memory of Rose that was the inspiration behind the feelings, and not her love for Enrique.

This relationship was just an emotional end-run, because Jacqueline knew Enrique would always just be a reminder of both the good and the bad in Rose. Enrique summoned Carlos and spoke to him in Spanish as Carlos took the box away. Enrique slightly stumbled with his words as he said, "I'm glad that arrived. I have been expecting it."

Jacqueline got the feeling that the package had upset him. She wondered what the writing said. She simply had too many emotions stirring inside her, but she stored away the name Stanley Letterbaugh. That was something her training in Israel had taught her – file information away, because you never know when it can become important.

Suddenly, all the memories of Rose's tapes began coming back. How long did she think she could bury the thought of what Rose and B6 had created? She had been traveling and working to forget, and now she was using drugs and sex that to stop the reality of B6 and the CWP. Her brain began to run wild.

Maybe Israel was a dream, and Rose's tapes never existed. However, she knew better. Moreover, she knew that while she hid B6 from her mind, the computer takeover of America by C Street was really happening. She could not stop the thoughts, and she was becoming more upset with each one. Jacqueline knew she needed to be alone and calm her mind.

Enrique suggested that they go on another trip after they ate. "Enrique, I'm feeling a little tired. Maybe we could have our outing later, if you don't mind." He told her, "That will be fine, Michelle. Are you sure you are okay?" "Yes, I think I'll just relax on the balcony in my room and read." Enrique asked, "May I join you?" "I would enjoy that." She really felt that she needed to be alone; she was beginning to feel a little smothered by his attention. Still, she agreed for her host to join her on the balcony.

She had walked downstairs with her body hot for Enrique and he had pleasured her immediately. Then, just as suddenly, his similarities to Rose had spoiled the moment. "I will change my clothes and be right out," Enrique said. As Jacqueline began to rise from the table,

Enrique rose from his chair and softly guided her out of hers.

Jacqueline changed into her swimsuit and sat in a chaise lounge overlooking the gardens of her room. Her mind was spinning from the emotional turmoil she was feeling from Enrique. Now suddenly all of Rose's tapes had come rushing back. All of the murder, conspiracy, and espionage were playing like a broken record inside her mind and she could not stop it! Her thoughts were racing and tumbling from topic to topic.

She was attracted to Enrique, but at the same time, she knew that she was reliving her love for someone else through his passion. All of the similarities to Rose bothered her mind but they inspired her body. Even though this was her vacation, she could not get the man Stanley Letterbaugh off her mind. Enrique had not appeared happy when Letterbaugh first arrived and they met in the library, nor when the package arrived today. That package's appearance had triggered the nightmarish memories that Jacqueline had been pushing to the back of her mind.

Enrique joined Jacqueline on the balcony and he began speaking of his city of San José and of all the things that they would be able to see that evening. Jacqueline wanted anything to take her mind from her dark thoughts of the CIA. Listening to Enrique talk was helping her to concentrate on what he was saying and not what the CIA was doing in America. Of course, Enrique could have had no idea what was traveling through her mind at warp speed. He had no idea what Rose had connected her to in the States.

Enrique gave Jacqueline a quick orientation about the geography surrounding his home and the countryside beyond. Then he asked her if she would mind if he spoke freely. "Please do." "Michelle, when I first saw you, I knew that I wanted to know you. You did not only look helpless in the hospital, you were the most radiantly beautiful woman I had seen since my wife. I was immediately attracted to you. Last night was just the beginning of what I want for us. I want to provide you with unending days and nights of pleasure, with anything your mind or body wants."

"Enrique, when I first met you, I was immediately attracted. The more I knew you, the more I realized that I was attracted to your similarities to my deceased husband. That would haunt us both forever. Please, we need to keep this relationship as one of friendship with wonderful lovemaking, for the best interests of us both. I won't be staying here forever; it would be too painful for me, because you would always remind me of my husband." "Michelle, let's not make that decision now. Are you feeling up to going out now?" Jacqueline told him, "No, let's wait until tomorrow. I'm enjoying just resting." Enrique smiled, saying, "You rest, and I will be right back. If you like, you can sunbathe naked. It is far more soothing. The servants will not disturb you." Enrique left through the balcony doors.

Jacqueline smiled with the thought that she would enjoy bathing naked in the sun. She knew where this was going, and she wanted him physically. Mostly she wanted him to take her mind away from the thoughts of the CIA. Jacqueline knew she would not stay in Costa Rica and she had told him. She also knew that being with Enrique would constantly remind her of all the bad that had happened in her life with Rose, and those memories would destroy any possibility of a peaceful life for them.

As she laid thinking on the balcony, she slowly removed her swim top and gently rubbed the sore muscles of her breasts. Feeling the sun on her nipples was magnificent! Before she knew it, she was laying completely naked with the sun heating her body. The breeze was just enough to keep her cooled. She was almost asleep when Enrique came back through the balcony door.

He sat down next to her chair and his first words were, "I want to see you right there for the rest of my life, just like you are now." Then Enrique handed her a new medication. "I have just taken the other medication and I'm not in pain. I'm just very high." Enrique explained that this one would work with the other medication. She took the yellow pill and rested her head back in the chaise. Anything was better than having her mind hear Rose's voice on the tapes describing the horrible plans that he had helped to implement. Suddenly, she felt like the warmth of the sun beating down on her body was intensifying.

Enrique kissed her deeply as he cupped her breasts in his hands. Her mind and body became his at that moment. No longer were thoughts of the tapes racing through her mind. She knew it had to be the medications causing the massive sexual arousal that she had been experiencing. However, it was what she needed to stop the pain of her mind at that moment. Suddenly, she could smell the flowers' fragrance all around her; the smell filled her mind with pleasure as Enrique was filling her body with euphoric sensations.

Enrique was kissing her deeply, making her body warm and wet as she came from his kiss. Sweat was beginning to pour from her brow. "Enrique, your kiss is making me wet." "Oh, Michelle, I have waited for your love." His lips slid gently onto her breasts as his wild passion for her fueled him. His tongue circled the nipples of her breasts. At the same time, she began to see a rainbow of colors appear before her eyes. Then slowly he kissed her body as his head moved lower and lower. The colors were spinning in her head, as the effect of the new medication had taken over her mind. She was in orgasmic spasms even before his body found its way into hers.

Again, she could feel the snap of her body in orgasm as rings of color flashed faster around her head, the sweat continued to pour from her body. Jacqueline could not believe that she was capable of such continuous arousal. She could barely move her body, except to snap in orgasm. Snap she did, repeatedly, as if her body were electrically charged.

When her body became so sensitive it was untouchable, Enrique sat next to her chaise lounge on the brick floor and reached for the Grand Marnier. "No more Enrique! I'm perfectly high right now." "Michelle, our life will be wonderful together. We have no need to leave Costa Rica ever. I love you Michelle. I feel as though I have loved you forever." "Enrique, this is moving too fast! We knew that we wanted each other and nothing was going to stop this from happening. However, it is our love for two other people seducing us. We are both looking for them in each other." Enrique gently disagreed with her. He said, "No, Michelle, we will be fine, we will learn to live with the memories. Our memories will only enhance our love for each other."

Enrique poured the Grand Marnier onto her breast and began licking it off as the alcohol provided a tingling sensation. The spinning colors of gold and red continued to intensify. Jacqueline's mind was floating in a field of color between orgasms. Enrique's voice was like an echo. His lips were like fire against her nipples.

She was trying to tell him that this was not forever; it could not be, but Enrique was not listening. "Enrique, I see my dead husband when I see you. I will always see him when I look at you, and that will not change. We cannot create a life together based on old memories. Please understand – I lust for you, but I will never love again. We must accept that our time together is limited. I'll be going back to the States in a few days; I think that is best."

Enrique stood straight up as his entire expression changed. She saw anger on his face for the first time as he walked through the balcony doors. Jacqueline was so high she could care less if he was angry. Besides, she knew that she was right. So she sat alone on the balcony watching the drug-induced colors and thinking. Until Enrique came in to her world, the thoughts of Rose remained buried. Now her mind only found peace while in orgasm. Nothing but painful memories filled her. The more she saw the similarities to Rose in Enrique, the more the memories flooded back.

Enrique came back to the balcony a few minutes later and told Jacqueline, "I understand your feelings. Let's go enjoy Costa Rica." The anger had subsided and he seemed to understand the limit of their relationship. "That sounds like a wonderful idea, Enrique. I'll dress." Jacqueline felt each drop hit her body as she showered, barely able to stand while preparing for a beautiful evening in San José. Nevertheless, she knew that she had to leave in the next few days. However, right now, she was so high and she intended on enjoying the evening.

This similarity to Rose would drive her mad if she stayed. However, she knew she would not stay, as she slipped back into her white linen dress and walked to the staircase to see Enrique waiting at the bottom. "Be careful! Wait, I'm coming up." Jacqueline did not object, as she was dizzy from the medication and each stair appeared to be a different color floating in air.

When Carlos brought the car Enrique informed him that it would not be necessary for him to drive and that they would be returning late. As they pulled away in the car, Enrique handed Jacqueline another yellow pill. "There is a water bottle in the car door pocket." Jacqueline murmured, "Thank you, Enrique," as she reached for the bottle and took her pill.

Sid chuckled and said, "Jacqueline, I need some pills like that! How much does it cost to fly to Costa Rica? That seems like the perfect spot for my next vacation! Does Enrique have a brother who might be looking for a new perfect someone? I think I could volunteer for that duty!

"Actually, I think I'll settle for an aspirin, instead of any of Enrique's special pills. I have a sneaking suspicion that I'm not done writing. My hand is throbbing, but so are some of my other parts! One of those pills would only make me more distracted, I'm afraid. Besides, I'm a little hungry. I've heard that sex gives you an appetite. Do you want a snack?"

Jacqueline laughed aloud, shaking her head at Sid. "Sid, as far as I know, Enrique has no brothers – sorry! As for food, Sid, I'll have a little something. You need to keep up your strength, and I guess I do, too. You'll hear more of my story about my trip to Costa Rica in a few minutes. You may change your mind about that vacation, but maybe not. I assure you, the men there really are quite something."

As Sid returned with a plate of canapés, she noticed Jacqueline looking out the window with a sad faraway look. They ate as Sid rested her writing hand a bit. Then with a smile and a deep breath, Jacqueline began speaking....

Chapter Thirteen
Love's Return

AS THEY drove the mountain road, Enrique turned to Jacqueline. "Would you like some cannabis?" He reached into the console of the car and pulled out a freshly rolled joint. As she lit it, he said, "This is one of the many reasons I love living in Costa Rica. We are freer here in many ways than you are in the United States. Over the years, America has slowly taken away the hard-won rights of the American people. Your freedom of speech is disappearing. The government has America's young men and women overseas dying for oil. Your government has entered your bedrooms and boardrooms for its own profit." Jacqueline was so stoned that his words made no impression.

Enrique began pulling her closer to him. Stoned, she slid happily over to him. He laid his arm around her, gently fondling her breast from beneath the white linen of her dress. Jacqueline took in the breathtaking mountains and laughed with Enrique as they talked of the effects of medication and pot. "Did you enjoy the spa last night?" "Enrique, it was one of the most amazing experiences of my life."

Enrique slowed the car to a stop, at a powerful waterfall cascading down from the green hillside two hundred feet above. As he was helping Jacqueline out of the car, her white dress separated in front. "Oh Michelle, you have nothing below again! What a delightful way to spend the day." "Well, I had a feeling you might enjoy it."

Together they walked slowly toward the water. "I purchased this land many years ago and vowed never to sell it. I knew one day I would be here with you, the woman I love." Jacqueline was feeling as though Enrique had forgotten all she had said. "Enrique, I have not loved since Rose and I will never love again. I'm leaving Costa Rica in a few days." "Michelle, I understand that you are not going to stay. Before you go, there is something I want to tell you."

Jacqueline could barely focus on the waterfall. The colors were quickly multiplying and flickering off the water. It was the drugs. The new medication was making her hallucinate. They continued to walk closer and closer to the waterfall. It was surrounded by Golden Shower Cassia trees covered with rich yellow flowers. "This is one of the most beautiful flowering trees in the world. Look over there – blooming from between the wet rocks is the legendary Papaver Somniferum, or opium poppy, in colors of white and crimson." Jacqueline was so high that she was mumbling as she struggled to say, "What did you want to tell me?"

There was silence for a moment before Enrique spoke. "Some years ago, I had to make some very hard choices. My work for the CIA forced me to make these choices." Jacqueline's head reared back and her mind began to swim when the letters "CIA" coming from Enrique's mouth snapped her out of her daze and back to reality. Her fear from simply hearing those letters made her almost straight, even in her opiate-intensified state.

Enrique continued, "You see, after cancer I lost my mind, my love, and most of my memory. As my memory began to return, I realized that I had been a CIA assassin. I wanted no more of that life. Therefore, I caused the uproar with you for your protection and let the CIA take me to a secret facility for care in solitude, while they decided what to do with me. I assume that my memories were so well entrenched that they were unable to get the information even under sodium pentothal. Thanks to my training, I was immune to the drug. They also knew I had set a trigger; it was the way I set the trigger that saved me. With no ability to force information from me, and the danger of triggering the release of evidence if they made a mistake, they had to cooperate.

"However, the chemotherapy and pain medications I was given did damage my memory some. Years ago, we discovered agents repeatedly exposed to sodium pentothal during long-term operations were immune to the effects of it. So with my memory loss, there was a danger of my giving them the wrong trigger. So if they acted incorrectly in reliance on my information, they would trigger the release. After about a year of recovery, they decided that with the information I had hidden away, they could not kill me. Hence, they offered me a new face, a new identity, and money. They performed extensive plastic surgery to alter my face and my fingerprints.

"Although I did not regain all of my memory, my memory of you returned shortly after the last surgery." "No," Jacqueline said in a screeching voice that echoed through the ridges of the waterfall, "You're not my husband!" "Yes, Jacqueline I am, it is me. Do you remember when I gave you my college pin outside our bedroom window? It's me."

Jacqueline began to flee toward the waterfall, slipping on the damp stones. Enrique chased her, trying to calm her by calling out repeatedly, "It's me, Jacqueline; it's me! Remember our home with all the books, the dinners out, the law firm, and all the shopping we did for Marie at Christmas? I don't have all of my memory, but it is really me." Enrique caught up to her and pulled Jacqueline into his arms. They both fell to the ground.

His lips pressed hard against Jacqueline's face. Tears were streaming down her face as she struggled to get away from the nightmare. She wanted to believe him, to be with him and at the same time, to flee from him. He rolled Jacqueline on the grass next to the fall, holding her tightly in his arms, saying, "Remember the fun we had in Jamaica?"

Jacqueline was beginning to calm down. She was unsure if it was because she wanted to believe he was Rose, or if it was because of the reality of the danger that she faced. Jacqueline immediately turned and kissed him passionately. He kissed her deeply with his warm soft lips and lit the fire. Within seconds, he had separated the linen dress from her body and was wildly tearing off his own clothes.

His tongue was warm and wet like the mist from the fall. She began to come as the sun baked her body. She cried out his name. "Rose, it is you – loving me again!" "Yes, Jacqueline, I'm Rose, and nothing will ever separate us again." At that moment, she had her first orgasm from complete passion in many years. Her mind was calling for her body to respond to her husband and it did so more strongly than she knew was possible. Then one after another, the orgasms came in rapid succession as her body twitched in spasms.

She felt as though they were in Jamaica again. Rose was alive and she was in his arms. Jacqueline felt the fire that she thought was dead. Slowly, she turned to accept her husband's body into her lips. Then suddenly she stopped as her mind reached warp speed. "Enrique-Rose, stop I need to catch my breath." Enrique immediately stopped, "Jacqueline, are you all right?" "Yes, I just need to catch my breath! You have taken my breath away, Rose.

"Do you have another joint?" Puzzled by her sudden reaction, he quickly pulled a joint from the pocket of his torn shirt lying on the ground. Jacqueline inhaled the smoke deeply. Then they began making love repeatedly until Enrique was completely satisfied.

They put their partially torn clothes back on and walked slowly to the car. Enrique did not stop talking the entire way back to the hacienda. "I had to tell you, Jacqueline. I could not live without you. I could not let you leave Costa Rica." She listened as he talked, taking in every word. "Our life together will be wonderful here.

I will let the servants go on vacation for a month so we can have the entire house to ourselves and make love in every inch of it. We will have the life we were planning when cancer first came into our lives."

As they entered the house, Enrique suddenly noticed that he had been doing all of the talking. "Jacqueline, are you okay?" "No, Enrique – Rose, I'm simply stunned!" "I understand. It was a lot for me to take in as well. When I first looked in the mirror in Bethesda, I did not recognize myself. However, you will need to call me Enrique to keep up the appearances here in Costa Rica. I love you, Jacqueline! Our life will be wonderful together."

He quickly lifted her into his arms and carried her into the elevator, then to his bed. "Enrique, I need a bath after making love on the ground." "Of course, take a bath, and I'll get us some champagne. Relax for a while." Jacqueline walked in and turned on the water in the Jacuzzi full force. Then she quietly closed the door; as she slipped into the water, she began to sob.

She knew this was not Rose, but who was he? Why was he doing this? He read the same books, liked the same artists, and wore the same glasses. He even seemed to know the most private information about Jacqueline and Rose's life together. He had the same old school gentlemanly manners. She slipped completely under the water to wash the tears away. No matter why or who he was, Jacqueline knew that she must not let him find out that she knew he was not Rose. After all, she was in the middle of Costa Rica, at least 20 miles from anywhere.

She had nowhere to turn. Whoever he was, he must be CIA.

As she was finishing her bath, she heard three or four popping sounds. She dried herself and looked out toward the balcony. She decided it must have been the monkeys making noise. She returned to the bedroom and looked at her face in the mirror to see if Enrique would be able to tell she had been crying. Fortunately, the color of her sun-bronzed skin hid the marks from her tears. Steeling her nerves, she wrapped a fresh towel around herself and rested on the bed, knowing what it would take to survive him. She fell asleep.

When she woke, Enrique was drinking champagne on the balcony. "Come out," he called to her. She walked out onto the balcony knowing what was to come, and knowing that Enrique was not Rose. Her mind quickly accepted that she would have to be available at his whim until she could get away from this madman. Whoever Enrique was, he had gone to great lengths to set Jacqueline up. He had to be insane, vicious, or more likely both. However, she knew one thing for sure; he was not her dead husband.

Jacqueline sat down in the chair next to Enrique and he immediately stood up. I gave the servants a month off, so we have the house to ourselves. He removed her towel. Then on his knees, he began kissing her lips and breasts. Jacqueline's thoughts raced in anger, "Go ahead and enjoy yourself, because your time is limited. You are not my husband!" Just then, she realized who Enrique had to be. The chocolate chip ice cream with banana chips and half coffee and half tea! She knew! She spoke not a word as her mind lit up like a firecracker. She suddenly realized who was doing this.

It all made sense to her. Just then, he separated her legs and began attempting to bring her to orgasm. However, he had killed even that fire with his trickery. Jacqueline looked down and realized she liked his head between her legs; that way she did not have to see his deceitful eyes.

Enrique pulled Jacqueline to her feet and took her into his bed. Then his body entered hers and he delighted in her for hours as he vowed his love. Jacqueline swore her undying love, in an Emmy award winning performance. He was enjoying pleasing himself and she was thinking, "Take my body – you will never have my heart." How in the hell would she get away from him? No two minds were ever farther apart than theirs were at that moment. Finally, he laid back, lit a cigarette and passed it to Jacqueline. Then he lit one for himself.

"Jacqueline, I'm so glad I came here as a retired doctor. The CIA had to give me over a year of medical training and set me up in a life of luxury in this third-world country to get rid of me. I have decided to stop working at the hospital. Even one day a week is too much for us to be apart. Nevertheless, I will have to go in and handle my full retirement properly. I don't want to be away from you ever again.

"By the way, what did you do with my tapes?" "What tapes Rose, I mean Enrique?" Jacqueline was name-dropping just so he would continue to think that she believed he was Rose. "Didn't I tell you about the tapes I recorded?" "No, you didn't." "Never mind, I just thought I told you." Jacqueline knew there was no way she was going to acknowledge anything about those tapes, especially to him.

"You realize of course that I sent Garrett to you with the ticket to Costa Rica?" "Yes, Enrique, I assumed you did. Who is Garrett?" "Just some fool I contacted through the Internet once I found you on the show circuit. I spared no time or expense in getting the tickets to you. Garrett tried to keep the money without buying the ticket and arranging for you to take it. It took three months for him to communicate with you. I was getting extremely agitated. Finally, with a little persuasion, he finished the job. However, he will not be enjoying the money that I paid him."

She asked, "Why didn't you just send Günter after me?" Without a hint of hesitation Enrique replied, "Jacqueline, Günter was killed in South Africa a few years ago. Sadly, he died in an explosion. Didn't you know? I assumed that you had heard about it." Jacqueline told him, "No, I have had no contact with him since I was told that you were dead."

"I had it all planned. When you arrived in Costa Rica, you were to be taken to the hotel. I planned to bump into you there and meet you. I could not believe it when you came in the ambulance! What had I done? Then I realized the driver caused the accident, not me. Well, to say the least, his care was not as good as yours." Jacqueline cringed as she wondered what this CIA monster had done to that driver and the poor fool Garrett. Neither of these people had any idea who they were involved with. "You know that I will always protect you, Jacqueline. We will be safe here in Costa Rica."

Jacqueline knew better than most what CIA operatives are capable of doing. She could see this "doctor" being able to walk into the driver's treatment room and inject him with a lethal dose of something, and then go for lunch. As for Garrett, Enrique would probably have just entered him on someone's hit list. Garrett would never have seen it coming.

She knew from Rose what the government was capable of doing. Jacqueline remembered the days when she could not stop Rose from speaking of Astrolite, the explosive that he used many times to destroy human lives in the name of America. She thought again about how the young college girl had died by accident when Rose, on behalf of the CIA, blew up a target in Ireland. How he had told her that the compound was still in its experimental stages and that the explosion was a little larger than they expected. She recalled the look on Rose's face as he told her – how upset he was by the death of an innocent.

Jacqueline almost understood how these operatives lose their minds after years of deceit and murder. However, she could not understand why this was happening; she had lived through enough when Rose lost his mind.

"Enrique, how much do you remember about our life?" "Jacqueline, I told you some. I don't remember

274

everything – the treatment took that away from me. You do know it is me, right?" "Of course I do, Rose!" "Remember, call me Enrique." "I will." "Well, my memory is very sparse and I want us to make all new memories, so let's just go forward and not look back, Jacqueline." That statement told Jacqueline that Enrique was not too sure of the things he had memorized about her life with Rose.

She knew Enrique-Rose would never let her go; he had gone to a lot of trouble to get her to Costa Rica. Enrique handed Jacqueline a glass of champagne. She smiled as she thought to herself, "Well, at least this will numb me from what is really happening." While Enrique sat, rubbing her body with some new cream, Jacqueline drank the glass of champagne and immediately her head was spinning. She no longer cared what was about to happen.

Enrique repeatedly took what did not truly belong to him – Jacqueline's body. She found no pleasure, but plenty of disgust for this man, this creature that would do the things that he had done. Finally, she fell fast asleep just to stop him. When she awoke, Enrique was standing over her dressed in his white hospital attire. "I need to go out for a little while, but I will be right back." He handed her two of the pills and a glass of water. He stood there as she placed the pills in her mouth and took a drink.

Then he kissed her forehead and told her, "I love you." Jacqueline kissed him deeply, "Hurry back darling." "Jacqueline, I noticed that your eyes are a little dilated. Do not get out of bed while I'm gone. You have been doing too much and you need to stay in bed." "Okay honey, I'll stay in bed." After Enrique left the room, Jacqueline removed what was left of the pills from her mouth. She hid behind the drapes and waited until she could see the Mercedes going up the road. She went straight to her purse, only to realize that her passport was gone. At least her driver's license, in the name of Michelle Lerner, was still there. Apparently, Enrique somehow missed it. When she checked the purse's secret compartment, it was empty. All of her backup documents were gone too! That just confirmed what she already knew. Enrique was CIA. He knew just where to look, and he got everything! At least he had left the hologram behind. She had to get out of here, so she would need to figure something out, hopefully with the help of Rose's hologram.

She had said nothing to him of her knowledge that he was not Rose, and she was sure that he could be only one person. Only one person might know enough of the details of Jacqueline's life with Rose. She quickly ran into the bathroom and threw up. Then she climbed into the shower to wash him off her. She let the water beat down on her, to help lessen the mental fog she had been living in for days.

Jacqueline turned on the hologram, "Need to explode house in Costa Rica, kill someone inside." Rose's response was, "Use the gas line in the house." Next, "Need to escape on foot from Costa Rica to California." Rose responded, "Use any mode of transit to avoid exhaustion, and claim to be a Peace Corps volunteer to avoid detection." She began plotting her way out of the mess. Rose had programmed everything he could into that device.

One thing was for sure – she could not call Meier Finch for help until she was out of Costa Rica. He would never give the approval for what she needed to do. If she did not contact Meier directly, he would not be able to prevent what she was about to do. By leaving him out until after it was over, he could not stop her. He would simply have to deal with what Jacqueline had done, once he found out.

Finally, a little more alert from the shower, she picked up the telephone and called Marie. "Marie, it's Mom. There is a problem. The boys are back! I need your help. Just listen. Get a pen and paper. Do you have it?" "I'm listening Mom, what's up?" "Agency troubles, Marie, so please follow these instructions carefully. Go to our safety deposit box as soon as you can get there. You will find money. Get cash. Take twenty grand, mostly hundred dollar bills and a few twenties. That way it doesn't take up as much room. Get your extra passport and matching driver's license that I keep in the box. Leave the box open but empty it, and move all of the other contents – the recordings, money, documents, and anything else, to another box at a different bank in your name.

"Place the money, ID, and passport in your purse bottom; it will not register on any scanner at customs. Do not use the replacement passport; just keep it in your purse. Bring your passport, ID, and the money to me.

"We'll meet at the largest hotel in the city of Tijuana, Mexico in seven days. If you have any trouble figuring out which one is the largest, just go to the biggest hotels and ask. I don't know what the name of the hotel will be, but I'm trying to fix a meeting point. If we are both in Tijuana, we will find each other. Keep that extra passport on you at all times. I'll be there on the seventeenth. No matter what anyone tells you, do not worry. Just be at the hotel on that date.

"If I'm more than three days late to the meeting point, I'm in trouble. Call Meier Finch – you have his number, and tell him I'm traveling from Costa Rica through Nicaragua, up the Rio Ulùa near Guatemala headed by land to Mexico. Do this only if I'm seventy-two hours late. It will not matter if Meier knows then."

"Mom, are you okay?" Jacqueline reassured Marie, "I'm fine. We have survived these people before. I know what I have to do and I know that you will follow my instructions. Travel alone. Tell no one else. Don't try to reach me or contact me before our scheduled meeting at the hotel. Can you do this?" Marie replied, "Of course. I'm calm, and I know you will get to me in Tijuana. Don't worry, I have the instructions, just meet me in Mexico." "I will, Marie. I love you." "I love you too, Mom. I'll be waiting for you."

Jacqueline hung up the telephone and sat down in the chair on the balcony, as tears began to form in her eyes. This was no time to feel sorry for herself! She hastily wiped the tears from her eyes as contempt replaced her sadness. "How dare him, bringing this kind of pain into my life!" She began formulating her plan for getting out of the hacienda and across the land without Enrique following. Jacqueline was sure he would pursue her to the end of the earth, given the chance.

All that training in Israel was going to pay off. Jacqueline knew she came out of Israel a different woman. Physically, she was deadly to those who wished her harm; mentally she was a Bayonet soldier, never to be defeated in battle. Size should not matter, for there is a weapon formed of strength of mind and body that is undefeatable. They were no longer fooling with the weak little girl of so many years ago! Now she was Mossad and trained to kill. However, she was not carrying an Uzi or even her .38 revolver. Besides, whatever she did must look like an accident. First, she would have to figure out how to get off his land, and that was at least a mile or two in any direction.

Jacqueline's mind flashed back to something Rose had told her on the tapes. "If you look carefully enough, you can tell when the identity of someone you know has been changed by surgery." There was no doubt that this man was not Rose. Jacqueline knew who he had to be, and she believed that she could outsmart him. However, she also knew that she had to leave no trace of herself or her wrongdoing when she left. Just then, she saw the dust flying in the air as the Mercedes came down the dirt road. Jacqueline quickly slipped back in bed and pretended to be asleep from the medication.

She heard Enrique coming up the stairs, so she stayed perfectly still, feigning sleep, hoping he would leave her alone. He came to the door and paused for a few seconds then left. Jacqueline was relieved. She could continue thinking about how she would get to Marie and keep this SOB from ever finding her again. The servants were gone for months; she would not have been able to rely on them for help anyway.

She laid there thinking for about an hour. Then she heard Enrique coming up the steps again. He stood next to the bed and she could hear him pouring water from the pitcher. "Jacqueline," he said in a low voice. She pretended to stir awake. Enrique handed her another pill and she took this one. She did not want him to realize that she was not taking the pills.

Enrique then picked her up and carried her to the balcony. Placing her gently in the chaise lounge without her clothes, he stood back at the balcony rail looking at her naked body. Then he began walking back and forth, talking while he paced. But he was not wringing his hands, and Rose had always wrung his hands when he was nervous.

"Did you rest while I was gone?" "Yes, I did. You know, two of those pills really put me out." "Good. Your eyes look fine now. I will have to go to the hospital tomorrow for a board meeting to formally tender my resignation." "Are you sure you want to resign?" "Oh yes, I plan to spend every waking moment with you forever." The words sent a chill up her spine. Then he pulled a chair up to Jacqueline, who was sitting naked in the chaise lounge, and he began to kiss her feet and stroke her legs.

The palms of his hands moved softly up the inside of her legs, gently spreading them. She knew what was about to come and wrapped her head around the unenviable. She was prepared to give him the fucking performance of a lifetime. Enrique removed a jar of oil from the medical bag that he had carried onto the balcony and began rubbing oil on her body. The oil had a clearly floral scent, but she could not identify what flower she smelled.

Her nipples became immediately erect, yet numb at the same time, just like the night before. His hands cupped her breast as he rubbed the oil. Speaking softly, he told her how much he loved her. "I have waited for you to be my wife again, and now I will have you forever." Jacqueline just kept her eyes closed as long as possible. He rubbed the oil all over her body and either the medication or the oil had her completely hot and tingling.

Then he began rubbing Grand Marnier on her lips again and kissing her deeply. His hands, wet with the oil, slipped between her legs. The warm sensation there began making her wetter. Either the pills were stronger or the oil had some mental effect, for Jacqueline could feel her body responding though she did not want his touch. It was as though her body had a mind of its own; a mind that refused to recognize Enrique for what he was. Suddenly, she could barely make out his words, although he was talking obsessively.

Jacqueline's muscles felt paralyzed. She was unable to lift her arms. Then she felt another orgasm pouring from her body. Enrique laid the chaise lounge all the way back. The sudden movements of the chair's back made Jacqueline feel as if she were falling. Her head was spinning as she felt Enrique lifting first one of her arms over her head and then the other. Her legs began to separate and she could see red on her ankle.

Unable to speak although she tried, Jacqueline realized that he had tied her body to the chair. She felt him kissing her and licking the oil from her body. She was unable to move, paralyzed in sick pleasure. Jacqueline began to make out his words. He was saying, "Promise you will never leave me." Then he made her body wet again. "Promise me." Jacqueline knew, as drugged as she was, what she needed to say and found her voice. "Rose, I promise I'll never leave you. We are together forever." She knew that was what he wanted to hear and she was in no position to argue. She was going to make him believe that she was his for eternity.

Jacqueline's mind switched on as she began the game for her life. "Oh Rose," she mumbled, "My husband, I love you." Again, he kissed her lips and continued down her body. He placed his lips on her as she seeped, and she cried out, "Rose, I love you." She could see the pleasure that he was getting by having total control of her and hearing her promise of eternal love. Enrique slid his body inside her strapped-down legs and took his pleasure repeatedly. When he had exhausted himself, he untied her and carried her to the bed. He gave her another pill, but this one she did not swallow. She had to get some of the drugs out of her system!

"I will bring dinner up to you, Jacqueline. Do not get out of bed." It was clear in Enrique's voice that this was an order and not a request. When he returned with a tray of pears and cheese, Jacqueline suggested that she take a bath. "I'll run the water for you." His tone had changed, and Jacqueline knew she would have to outsmart him fast to get away. She could hear the water running as Enrique came out and lifted her from the bed.

Placing her into the bath, he began to wash her body but his touch was no longer tender. There was a complete change in his personality as he bent over the bath and kissed Jacqueline. Raising his lips from hers, he slapped her face with the back of his hand. She felt sudden pain racing though her body.

"That my dear, is for failing to provide above average orgasms when I was stimulating your body." Wow, Jacqueline did not see that coming! She immediately apologized, while telling him how much she loved him and that she was so happy he was alive. He pulled her wet body to his and lifted her from the bath. Then he carried her to the bed and dried her body.

Enrique reached for the radio beside the bed and turned the music on low. He slipped Jacqueline's feet to the edge of the bed and into her red high heels. After he helped her to stand, he lowered himself into the chair beside the bed. "Dance for me!" His tone was that her compliance was presupposed, so Jacqueline began dancing to please. "Down on your knees, in front of me." She went to her knees and he pushed her head down into his naked lap.

Jacqueline knew what Enrique was going to take. As her lips touched his erect body, her mind fled far away to the Statue of David in Florence, Italy. She immediately began thinking about the wondrous awe of the male anatomy. How beautifully soft yet firm, sculpted, tucked between the round balls of human existence. Jacqueline had found a way to take her mind to visions of splendor elsewhere.

Enrique pulled her head to his face and lifted her body, bending her over the side of the bed as he slid inside and began slow, deep strokes. His hands were rubbing the roundness of her cheeks, spreading them ever so slightly with each deeper stroke. Jacqueline's body slipped into the orgasm with full intensity. She was so wet and warm that she wanted more, pure and unadulterated.

When he was completely satisfied, she was suddenly thrust forward on the bed with a painful smack on her soft bottom. Enrique rolled Jacqueline over and then he slapped her face again. It all came within seconds. "Just remember – you are mine and you will do what I want! You will do as I say and now I want you to sleep. I will let you know when I want you again." Jacqueline pulled the covers over her body as Enrique walked to the veranda. She knew she was in even more trouble than she could have imagined. His violence came out of nowhere. It was scary, even from a CIA assassin.

She passed out, only to be awakened as Enrique was tying her arms again. "Enrique, please don't tie my hands. I can't touch you." Enrique slapped her face again. Then he tied her other arm without a word and restrained her feet at the bottom of the bed. She knew better than to resist; there was no way to fight him with all of her limbs restrained. "I want you to get used to it. Whenever I leave, this is how you will wait for my return."

Then he left the room. Jacqueline realized when she pulled on the thick red cloth that it became tighter. She knew that she would have to win his trust. Then her eyes caught a glimpse of a letter opener with a jagged edge on the desk across from the bed. She realized that she would have to get that letter opener once he had freed her again, so that the next time he left the house she would be prepared.

Enrique returned a short time later and untied her legs and arms. "Jacqueline, I am so sorry, but I can't let you leave me." "Rose, I will stay with you forever. I'm your wife." "Oh Jacqueline, I love you." Then he began again, this time making gentle passionate love. Jacqueline found that she was nauseated by his touch. She knew that her only hope was to convince him otherwise.

When he finished, Enrique went down to the kitchen to get some champagne without tying her, and Jacqueline immediately tiptoed over and grabbed the serrated letter opener. She placed it in her pillowcase as she climbed back into bed. Enrique returned with champagne and water for Jacqueline's medication. He appeared to be his old charming self again, and Jacqueline took the pill as instructed this time. She was not going to do anything to alarm or agitate him. She knew that he had to go to the hospital the next day.

As the evening ended, Jacqueline was free to walk around the room, with Enrique treating her like a queen again. She was stoned, and she believed that he was increasing or changing the medication. They spent an evening drinking champagne and eating from the fruit and cheese tray. Jacqueline decided to eat a lot to absorb some of the drugs and alcohol from her body. Enrique spoke endlessly of the plans he had for their life.

Jacqueline knew when Enrique no longer could make love, and asked if she could take a bath. Given permission, she walked in and started to close the door. In a sharp voice, Enrique told her, "Don't close the door. I never want you out of my sight!" She ran a bath and washed him off her, feeling disgust, but careful not to show it, in case he was watching. After soaping and scalding her body in the hot water, she put on her robe and returned to his bed. He held her so tightly that night that she could hardly move, and she wondered what horror was yet to come.

Jacqueline's exhaustion finally forced her to fall asleep in the early morning hours, but Enrique standing over her in his hospital attire had caused her to wake abruptly. He kissed her and said, "I have to tie you now." "I understand, but please darling, don't make them too tight, so I can roll over and fall back asleep until you get home." Enrique handed her the pill. "I will not make them too tight."

Jacqueline appeared to take the pill with a drink of water, but let it slip back into the deep red glass. Then he loosely bound her again, naked on top of the covers. He began kissing her as he removed his hospital pants and forced himself inside her only slightly separated tied legs. With her arms bound, he held her face to his and told her, "If you try to leave me, you will never get out of Costa Rica alive. I will kill you."

"Enrique, I never want to leave Costa Rica, now that you're alive." Then he began kissing her and exploded inside her bound body. When he was done, he dressed as if nothing had happened and told her he would come back as soon as possible, and that he would never have to leave her again. He apologized repeatedly for leaving her tied. "Just this one more time – I promise," then he left the room and headed down the stairs. Jacqueline lay perfectly quiet, listening for the car to make some noise. After about five minutes that seemed like hours, she heard the car leaving.

Jacqueline had positioned the open end of the pillowcase very near her loosely tied right arm. Holding the hard metal letter opener tightly in her mouth through the pillowcase, she pushed it to her hand. It only took a few minutes to free herself. Jacqueline had practiced freeing herself from being bound to a bed during her training in Israel. The practice had worked.

She had already decided that there was no need to cover her tracks any more. She knew that it was only a matter of time until he killed her in one of his rages. So, one of them would die when Enrique returned. She had every intention of making sure it was him.

She walked into the hallway with the letter opener in her hand. The house was completely silent. There was not even the tick of a clock. It dawned on Jacqueline that she had only seen one clock in the hacienda – the chess clock. How strange that she had not noticed it before.

Then her eyes once again saw the cloth-covered painting at the top of the stairs. Jacqueline ran back to the balcony to be sure that the Mercedes was still gone. She ran back to the covered painting. She was determined to see what was under the cloth, but she could not reach it. She grabbed a cane that she had noticed in her room and walked back to the edge of the landing, where she could reach the painting. Jacqueline jumped and hooked the cane into the cover three times, but she could not remove the cloth.

Giving up on uncovering the painting, she started back to the bedroom in complete frustration. Suddenly, she heard something hit the floor. She turned quickly, seeing the uncovered painting for the first time. It was a painting of her, but she was about twenty years younger! She remembered the picture that must have been the inspiration for the oil painting.

The picture came up missing from Rose's hospital room years ago. She walked closer so she could see the plaque below the painting. It read Mrs. Günter Lehman! She had no doubt it was Günter who had first posed as Dr. Enrique Curran and then as Rose. He had set her up to get her to Costa Rica and lied about being Rose in a desperate attempt to win her love and keep her there.

She suddenly realized that the cane had a latch on the handle. Opening the latch, she discovered the handle was a .22 automatic handgun, and it was loaded. Ecstatic at her discovery, she ran naked down to the library and began going through the desk. Prying the lock open on the desk with the letter opener, she found a file folder inside with her name on it. It contained, among other things, notes on her life with Rose.

Pictures of Jacqueline had been carefully cut from old photographs of Jacqueline and Rose together. She found the chess magazine from Mr. Letterbaugh with the note written in marker. The note read, "You are a dead man!" She also found the picture of her that had disappeared from Rose's hospital room.

Notes about events in her recent life were on a yellow legal pad. That pad had a section called "Garrett." It consisted of line after line of angry memos about Garrett not completing his assignment. The final note with Garrett's name read, "Completed" and the word "Exterminated," in large red letters, was the last entry under his name. A document that appeared to be a Costa Rican marriage license application was in the file as well, with Jacqueline Rosenberg and Enrique Curran's names as the applicants.

Günter was obsessed with her. Rose had been right; his old friend would kill to have Jacqueline as his wife. Nevertheless, this was complete insanity. Then she thought again about the identity changes Rose had spoken about on the tapes. Enrique-Günter intended on keeping her in Costa Rica any way that he could. If she left, he would find her, just as he had on the mountaintop and again after Rose died. He had been watching her all along.

Everything was suddenly clear. In a split second, she knew that Enrique meant what he had said. He did not intend to let her leave his house or Costa Rica alive. She knew that she needed to stick with her prior decision. One of them had to die. She knew what she needed to do. If they were both alive, this man would follow her to the ends of the earth for the rest of her life. Jacqueline's training clicked in. She raced back to the bedroom, and pulled her remaining driver's license from her purse.

Jacqueline walked into the bathroom, lit a candle, and proceeded to burn the edges of her license. Then she rinsed it off to cool the plastic and patted it dry before placing it in the back pocket of her jeans while she dressed. She placed the lighter in her front pocket. Jacqueline put everything of importance in her backpack including her money, jewelry, and her purse. She decided to forget the clothes. She packed just a few shirts and pairs of jeans. She knew that her money and jewelry would serve as transit currency on her journey to Mexico, and her backpack needed to be light enough for her to carry it easily.

She thought for only a moment – maybe she should wait for his return and use the bracelet given to her at Mossad to kill him. However, she did not want anything turning up in an autopsy, not even venom, for that would immediately tell Mossad that she was responsible. Jacqueline had no idea if Günter was connected to Mossad or simply a federal agent, FBI, CIA, or some other combination of letters. Nor did she want to get close enough to him again to find out. She had taken her limit from this man. No, she knew that it had to look like an accident, without a trace of foul play.

Jacqueline looked drained, and she said, "Sid, that was a really tough time for me. I think I need a break." "I understand, Jacqueline. And to think I was envying you your relationship with Enrique! Günter turned out to be one dangerous man." "Yes, Sid, it was hard for me to believe this was the same man who ate meals at our table and who used to give Marie a ride to school when she was young. He had planned to take over Rose's life and his wife."

"Jacqueline, would you like to go for a walk? A change of scenery would be good for you." "Lord, no! I can't risk being recognized. I'll always be in danger now. When I leave this apartment, I'll be headed out of the country!" Laughing, Jacqueline said, "Sid, you're stuck with me for the duration." Sid looked out the window nervously. "It's all right, Sid. I'm sure you're perfectly safe, but I'm not – at least, not if I'm seen. Of course, the sooner we're done, the sooner I can be gone, and the sooner you'll be sure that you're safe." Sid shook her head and smiled. "Well, how about a jog around the living room, then?" "No, Sid, let's just keep going. You need to hear about the rest of my time in Costa Rica..."

Chapter Fourteen
Self Preservation

JACQUELINE WAS ready for this son of a bitch's apocalypse. Günter Lehman, also known as Dr. Enrique Curran, was going to leave God's green earth and Jacqueline was going to be the cause of the cosmic cataclysm that destroyed him. This could be Jacqueline's Armageddon, but she was ready for the fight. She remembered Rose's words, "Go get trained." Jacqueline wondered if Rose knew that Meier would have her trained so well in Israel. Well, she was about to put her education to the test. If she failed, she would be the dead one.

Jacqueline finished dressing in her jeans and walking shoes for this unknown journey through the jungles and rainforests of Central America. She took her backpack filled with valuables, the cane, her Panama hat, and her sunglasses. She grabbed the candle from the dresser. She ran back to the library and turned on Enrique's laptop computer. When the password window came up, Jacqueline only had to take one guess to get into the computer. The word she typed was "Günter." She went straight to an English language search engine, and began printing maps of the land and rivers between San Jose, Costa Rica and Tijuana, Mexico. Then she quickly accessed the Peace Corps website and copied their logo to an image-editing program that Günter had loaded on the computer. The next thing she did was open a web page to an internet translator. She knew she would need it.

Within minutes, she had created official-looking documents that read "Peace Corps Transit Papers" with Marie's name. Jacqueline printed signs that read "Peace Corps – Ride Please" in English and "El paseo del Cuerpo de Paz por favor" in Spanish. She knew with more time, she could have made better forgeries, but she believed the documents she had hastily created would work. Quickly, she removed the hard drive from the laptop and placed it in her backpack. Jacqueline had no idea how long she had before Günter returned from the hospital, but she was sure that this was her last chance for escape.

She put the documents, the signs that she had created, and a compass and small flashlight from Günter's desk into her backpack. Then she quickly headed out of the library. Suddenly she stopped, turned and went back into the library. Jacqueline quickly scaled the ladder to the top bookshelf and retrieved the Tolstoy book. Placing the book into her backpack, she headed straight into the kitchen, which Eva had left immaculately clean.

All of the appliances were high-end professional models, as she expected. The stove was a freestanding gas one, and it was far enough away from the wall that she could easily reach the gas connection. Good. The stove was fed by a large propane tank on the back porch of the kitchen. Jacqueline unplugged the power cord for the stove, to disable any safety shut-off valves or alarms, and to avoid accidentally igniting a burner with the stove's electric ignition. She removed the unlit candle from her pack and placed it on the counter next to the stove.

In the pantry, she found a pair of pliers and loosened the gas line after shutting off the supply valve at the fitting. She easily turned the supply valve with her fingers, so she placed the pliers back in the pantry. When she was putting the pliers back, she saw a piece of cheesecloth. She grabbed it, and wrapped it around the candle, so that a corner of the cloth was touching the wick. It looked like her plan would work.

Leaving the hacienda through the back door of the kitchen, she walked to the surprisingly sanitary garage directly behind the hacienda. There she found a group of bicycles. Jacqueline was relieved to discover them; she would not have to flee on foot into the jungle. She took one of the bicycles and quickly checked to make sure its tires were inflated. Then she began to roll it out of the garage.

Suddenly, she noticed a pool of blood coming from below a tarp near the garage door. She lifted the edge of the tarp slowly, revealing a woman's body in a white uniform on top of a male body. It was Carlos and Eva; both servants were dead. She dropped the tarp and headed out of the garage, hiding the bicycle in the trees outside the door of the kitchen, and laid her backpack down on the ground next to the bicycle. Going nervously back into the house with the cane in her hand, she made one last call to Marie.

"Hello honey, I'm on my way to you in Mexico."
"Mom, I've already made the air reservations, and the

largest hotel in Tijuana is the Grand Hotel Tijuana." "Thanks, Marie – that information will help me." "Mom, can't I just come to you?"

"No, Marie. We must do it this way, and no matter what you hear, I'm alive, so just meet me at the hotel. My Customs form has your phone number, so if the police or any government agencies contact you and say that I'm dead, sound devastated, ask a few questions about what happened, then act hysterical and get off the phone. Just know I'm alive and I'll meet you in Mexico. I love you Marie – I'll see you at the Grand Hotel Tijuana on the seventeenth. Order me a drink." "I love you Mom." "I love you too – don't worry." Jacqueline hung up the phone, praying that her plan would work.

Without an ounce of remorse for what she was about to do, Jacqueline stood next to the balcony door in the upstairs bedroom and watched for the dust of the Günter's Mercedes returning. The realization that Günter had already killed Eva and Carlos reconfirmed everything she already knew about him. She began going over the details of her plan in her mind. Günter would enter from the front door and the kitchen was in the back. When Jacqueline saw the car coming down the dirt road, she would walk slowly down the staircase and to the kitchen. That would give just about enough time for Günter to drive up to the house. Repeatedly, she went through the details as time passed, wondering what she had forgotten.

Out of nowhere, the car began coming down the road, sending up a rooster tail of dust. It was only 9 AM, much earlier than she had expected! Jacqueline darted down the staircase into the kitchen, tossed her driver's license on the floor, and turned the valve on the gas supply line.

She could not hear him, but she stood next to the candle holding her breath. She reached into her pocket for the lighter. Just at that very moment, she heard Günter enter the front door. She lit the wick of the candle and the cloth began to light. As it did, she ran!

She raced out the back door to the bicycle she had hidden in the trees. Picking up her backpack, Jacqueline suddenly felt a sharp pain as she scraped her arm on the thorn of a rose bush while mounting the bicycle and strapping on her backpack. Ignoring the pain, she began to ride as fast as she could. She heard nothing. She was frantic, and thought, "Damn, not enough gas built up! It didn't blow!" She could feel the fear of Günter catching her, and she peddled even faster.

Suddenly a blast came that shook the ground below her, followed by another and then another. Jacqueline kept her eyes on the road ahead and did not look back until the blasts had stopped for a while. When she finally looked back, she saw a massive ball of fire 100 feet tall, raging flames spewing red and orange, where the hacienda and the garage had been! It was clear that what little remained was fully involved in the fire.

She turned her eyes back to the road and peddled even faster, and then heard another blast and another. The first fire truck that Jacqueline saw was at least a half hour later, and it must have been over five miles from Enrique's estate. She slowed down as the fire truck passed her. It was heading toward the hacienda.

After the fire truck had gone by, Jacqueline took the only fork in the road that she felt sure was correct. She pulled to the side of the road and took the maps out of her backpack. She glanced at them, looking for the route to the river. She needed to figure her way out to the boat ramp where she had started the riverboat tour with the man she thought to be Dr. Curran. She knew immediately where she was, so Jacqueline just kept peddling the bike as fast as she could. Another fire truck passed her.

Just as she was feeling that she could peddle no more, she saw the riverboat ramp ahead. Jacqueline parked the bike in a rack with all of the others, hoping some kid would steal it. Quietly, she purchased her passage and six bottles of water for her backpack, and then she boarded the flat bottom boat with several other people. Taking the nearest seat she could find on the metal boat, she sat quietly waiting, staring out at the jungle to her left. It seemed like forever before the boat began to move on the river and finally begin the trip north up the Rio San José out of Costa Rica.

As the boat began moving slowly up the river, Jacqueline knew she would get to Marie. Nothing was left of the hacienda, and her driver's license was all that was left of her at the fire if it survived the massive explosions. She had carefully burned the edges in hopes that the authorities would believe her dead as well. However, with the size and the number of explosions she had caused, it was possible that her license had not survived the blaze. She would just have to wait and see. There was nothing more she could do now.

With her Panama hat, dark sunglasses, cane, and backpack full of money and jewelry, she sat on the long shallow metal boat filled with tourists headed up the river to Nicaragua. She was nobody again. As the boat slowly motored up the river, Jacqueline realized that she could no longer find beauty and pleasure in the sight and sounds of Costa Rica. Reaching into her backpack, she placed the bracelet Meier had given her on her wrist; she did not know what lay ahead. The only defense she had for the jungle escape was the gun in the cane handle, poison in the bracelet, and her training.

Her mind was racing. Günter had manipulated her trip to Costa Rica, and had undergone all that surgery to hide his identity. He had Garrett assassinated, had killed his servants, and probably the cab driver, too. She could not help but wonder why he was so obsessed with her, who fired the shot at the volcano, and who sent the package to Günter that contained the clock and the death threat.

Günter thought she would love him once he got her to Costa Rica. He expected the kind of love she felt for Rose. He thought that he would be able to make her love him without telling her who he was. Finally, as a last resort, he claimed to be Rose to keep her from leaving. His sudden violent behavior made Jacqueline wonder if being bipolar was a criterion to be a CIA assassin or if it was a result of the work. Rose had told her Günter was FBI, but he seemed more like a CIA nut to her.

Jacqueline's thoughts went to when she knew Günter back in the days of Rose. He had always been very attentive to Jacqueline and Marie. Rose had made a few remarks about his best friend being in love with his wife. Jacqueline had always taken those remarks in stride. He was Rose's friend and college roommate, so she always treated him with great kindness, but she was never attracted to him, ever. All those years she thought Rose was kidding about Günter being in love with her – Rose obviously knew.

Jacqueline may have believed for a moment at the waterfall, in her drug-induced daze, that Günter was Rose – he had miraculously returned to her from the dead. She was so vulnerable in wanting Rose to be alive, for him to be the way he was so many years ago, before cancer and drugs destroyed his mind. What kind of madness could cause Günter to go to such extremes for the love of a woman? However, when she truly gave herself to Günter, it only took a matter of minutes for Jacqueline to realize he was not her flower, her Rose, back from the dead. Not even the drugs could allow that man to convince her that he was Rose.

It took a while for her to figure out who could have even attempted to fool her into thinking he was Rose. It was not too long before the answer became obvious. Even though she was positive before, if Jacqueline had any doubt about who had tried such a horrible deception, the portrait under the tarp had sealed it.

Jacqueline sat quietly in thought. She heard the boat captain telling the tourists about the animals and plants along the river without really hearing what he was saying. She could see the monkeys hanging from the trees and the crocodiles not more than a foot away from the low bottom of the riverboat. As the crocodiles opened their jaws, she could see the thousands of tiny needles that they had for teeth.

Jacqueline thought, "Do not mess with me today croc, I just blew a place sky high." The reality of what she had just done was setting in. Jacqueline was becoming no better than the assassins that she was fleeing. She had taken the life of another human being with malice and forethought, plain and simple. She had committed the premeditated murder of a federal agent.

However, Jacqueline knew that Günter never intended to let her leave Costa Rica alive. No matter what, if Günter had remained alive, he would pursue her, forever. He had gone to great lengths to get her to Costa Rica. She believed from Günter's statement, "Garrett would not live to spend the money," that Günter had Garrett killed after he sold the tickets to her. However, the killing of Eva and Carlos, his loyal servants, shocked even Jacqueline. Günter planned to hold her hostage forever in his "paradise," and did not plan to leave any witnesses. That is, until he killed her, too. She knew that would have eventually happened. Günter was too unstable and too violent – he would have killed her, either by accident or intentionally.

The notes on the pad seemed to confirm to Jacqueline that Günter had Garrett killed. She knew she would probably never know the answer to that for sure, since she did not know Garrett well. Even though she felt remorse for what she had done, Jacqueline was at peace with her decision to do it; she had exterminated an insane agent, with extreme prejudice.

Thankfully, the boat did not have the same captain as when Enrique had brought Jacqueline part of the way up the river, so she went unnoticed by most. When the guide asked her what she was doing in Costa Rica, she told him she was with the Peace Corps and would be getting off at one of the final stops up the river. He seemed to buy the Peace Corps story completely. That was a good sign to Jacqueline. She had a long road ahead, and that cover story was her best protection.

The boat captain asked, "What happened to your arm?" Jacqueline looked over and realized that she was bleeding. "I scraped it on a thorn. It's fine." Then he advised her, "Be careful if you plan to cross into Nicaragua on your trip. Los Chiles is close to the border. The border areas are dangerous. There are a lot of drugs and violence in Nicaragua, so be careful." "I will be. Thank you."

Jacqueline knew that she would be in danger from the drug lords as well as the American-backed Contras out in the jungle. As dangerous as the borders were ahead, she began to relax as the boat moved farther up the river. For Jacqueline, the journey had just begun and she did not think what was ahead could possibly be more terrifying than what she had left behind.

Late in the evening, at the riverboat stop at Los Chiles, she got off the boat with the other tourists. The guide escorted everyone up the riverbank to a late night feast provided by the tour company. Jacqueline was not hungry, but she did place a few corn muffins in her backpack before slipping away, on foot, into the darkness. She stopped to check her compass.

She was heading north, and the boat captain had confirmed that the border to Nicaragua was nearby. She knew that she needed to head north, not knowing how far she would have to walk. Jacqueline walked for several hours through low brush and trees, resting on and off, checking the compass needle frequently. She walked all night.

To her surprise, just before daybreak, she saw a U.S. military truck on a nearby road. She waved at it, and it stopped. As she first walked toward it, she was a little afraid, until the soldiers immediately assumed she was with the Peace Corps. The driver said "Hello, beautiful, are you with the Peace Corps? Need a ride?" "Hello boys! Yes I am, and I need to get to Honduras." "Hop in, we are going that way. I think the U.S. Government would not mind if we went a little farther. We have to make a few stops, but we can get you to within five miles of the border. That is our maximum range in this hell hole." Jacqueline was relieved, and said, "Thanks, guys." One of the men gave her his seat and jumped in the back of the truck. After a few dozen lies to throw them off track, she fell asleep in the back seat. She woke as the truck arrived at Ocotal, shortly before about noon.

Thanking the soldiers for their kindness and wishing them well, she headed off on her own. She thought, "That has to be the best break I could have gotten; they took me all the way across Nicaragua." Four American young men protecting her for the first 150 miles! She was about five miles from the Honduras border. She got away from the town, from the roads and from the border crossings.

She did not want to risk showing her forged documents if she could avoid it. If she ran into border patrols, she would have no choice, but she wanted to avoid both leaving a trail of her route and the chance that officials would recognize her documents as frauds. She began to walk the mountainous terrain for hours, knowing she had to have crossed into Honduras. Unfortunately, there were no signs marking the land. She continued to walk north for hours through the mountainous rainforest, and avoiding every road.

Exhausted, she stopped next to a secluded mahogany tree near a river. The tree soared 175 feet high, and it was maybe 30 feet around. It was located near the riverbank. Jacqueline rested her aching legs while she ate a muffin from her backpack. She marveled at how beautiful the different trees were.

Some trees she could recognize, such as the African Palm tree. Jacqueline ate, enjoying the sweet muffin like a feast, as she rested her weary legs and drank from the clear water of the river, saving what was left of her bottled water for later. Laying her head on her backpack against the trunk of the mahogany tree, she fell asleep in the shade.

When she woke after only a short nap, she felt that it was safer to keep on the move. She continued hiking the green forest northward, using the river as her guide. It was early evening when she awoke, and she decided to travel through the night. After dark, Jacqueline used her flashlight and the backlight from the compass to travel throughout the night, resting for only short intervals as she continued north. She was pleased that she had seen so very few people around the area – and all of them at a distance. Although she was very afraid, traveling in the jungle at night, she was far more afraid of what she left behind.

Jacqueline could smell a strong odor of chemicals in the air, getting stronger as she walked north. Knowing that she must be in the drug cartel area, she moved slowly and quietly to assure that she did not run into them. Abruptly she stopped, seeing in the distance five or six men around a smoldering vat. They were far more frightening than the animals in the jungle, which had graciously left her alone.

Jacqueline stayed very still for hours, waiting for them to leave the area before continuing through the rain forest. She never moved from a squatting position for over an hour, until she felt her legs giving out. Watching the men for any sign they heard her, she quietly moved from squatting to sitting on the ground. Jacqueline knew that once she made the move to the ground, she dared not move a muscle for fear she might rustle the brush.

Hours more passed as she remained perfectly still, her body aching from her inability to move. Her position was perfect for watching the men through the trees and brush. Finally, the men left the smoldering vat. She had been in that position for hours and getting up was excruciatingly painful.

Jacqueline continued through the forest after the men had left the cocaine refinery. Soon, she realized her muscles had become weak from staying in one spot for so long. Just as she thought she could go no more, she spotted some wild coca plants along the river. Quickly, she picked a few leaves and began chewing them, hoping for some stamina to keep her going. The taste was sharp, bitter, and green.

She loaded as many of the leaves as she could in her backpack for later. She immediately felt the adrenalin rush to her muscles and was able to continue walking, although her head was no longer clear. The coca leaves kept her going for hours; however, she was starting to slow down. It was not long before Jacqueline was sure she could not go any farther. Just then she saw an outdoor market shack along a roadside, not far from where she was walking.

It was simply a wooden shack selling fruit and candy, with trinkets for the tourists hanging from the tin roof. Jacqueline dusted herself off, walked out of the jungle path, and approached the shack. The locals, speaking broken English, told her that a tour bus was coming and she would be able to catch a ride.

Relieved, Jacqueline purchased a candy bar and a few more bottles of water, and then sat down under a tree near the shack, to wait for the bus. From what she could understand of the locals' English, the bus would be coming soon. To Jacqueline's amazement, within about ten minutes a large transport bus pulled up and stopped. It was like a greyhound bus, and it had a big sign on the front stating "North". The driver said he was headed far northwest toward the border of Guatemala.

Jacqueline climbed aboard as she told the driver her story. "I'm with the Peace Corps. How much will it cost for a ride north?" The driver told her that there would be no charge and invited her to get on the bus. "Thank you. Take me as far north as you are going."

"Okay. That will be the end of my run tonight at the Santa Ana, Santa Bárbara, but you will have to get local transportation to take you to the border. These buses are not allowed to come within five miles of the Guatemala border, and I'm not going quite that far." Jacqueline thought that was perfect, as she did not want to cross at any official borders. She took two seats on the bus. Exhausted, she fell fast asleep.

The driver woke Jacqueline at the Santa Ana bus depot, and she stepped off the bus only to see a few parked buses in the same area. One had its door open. She climbed in, went to the back seat, and fell back to sleep. A driver abruptly woke her with, "What are you doing here?" "I'm with the Peace Corps," she replied, since that story had been working fine. "I'm with the Peace Corps, headed north." "Well I'm not going north, but see that bus parked over there, with the sign reading 'Border?'" "Yes." "The driver has a border pass, ask him for a lift; he's headed north to the border today." "Thank you," as she grabbed her backpack and walked away from the buses.

Jacqueline knew that she needed to cross the border at a non-official location, so she did not want to take the bus that was going to the official border. She headed up the road on foot until she saw a donkey cart loaded with locals coming up the road. Jacqueline held out the sign that she had made before she left the hacienda. It read in English, "Peace Corps" and written below were the Spanish words for "ride, please" – "El paseo del Cuerpo de Paz por favor."

The cart stopped; Jacqueline could not completely communicate with the people, but was able to secure a ride on the cart for a few hours, having no idea where it was going, just kind of northwest. At this point exhaustion was overtaking her, and she was just happy not to be walking. Anything was better than walking through the jungle. Well – almost anything!

When the cart passed through a small town, Jacqueline jumped off, thanking the people in her best Spanish. She walked to the local bus station and went up to a table under an umbrella with items for sale. Immediately, she noticed newspapers for sale.

The headlines were big in the Costa Rican newspaper, and even in Spanish she could tell it said something like "Local Doctor Killed in Accidental Explosion." Her heart stopped when she saw the papers. Jacqueline purchased four newspapers, the Guatemalan newspaper *La Hora*, the Honduran newspaper *Diaro La Prensa*, the Nicaraguan *La Prensa* and the Costa Rican *La Tribuna*.

She needed to know if Günter was dead, because if he were not, he would surely be in hot pursuit. As far as she was concerned, the world was better off without anyone crazy enough to do the things he had done. Jacqueline hoped the Costa Rican officials investigating the fire would find her license and declare her dead before the CIA came snooping around the site of the fire.

She tucked the newspapers in her pack and walked around trying to figure out if she was in Guatemala. Jacqueline noticed a small shack made of aged gray wood with an old metal Miller beer sign near the door in English. Another sign in the window looked very official and as she walked closer, it read "License to sell Alcohol by the Guatemalan Government," in Spanish and English. Yes, she really was in Guatemala! She was making progress, and she wasn't still in Honduras!

She saw a tour bus pulling in, and ran over to board. Showing the driver her Peace Corps pass, she sat down in the very back seat and stared out the window as the bus headed north. After the bus had been moving a few minutes, she removed two of the three newspapers from her bag and placed the Costa Rican paper inside the local *La Hora*. Then she pulled out her translation book and began translating word by word.

There was a photo of the charred remains of the hacienda, with a caption that read, "Accidental Propane Explosion at Casa Inolvidable Alta." The story stated, "Severely injured was Dr. Enrique Curran, a prominent doctor, and three unidentified persons are believed dead." Jacqueline was shocked by the name of the hacienda, "Casa Inolvidable Alta." The first letters spelled CIA! Those were the letters she had been unable to make out on the monogrammed gate when she arrived there! She realized it was a collage of the letters "CIA" in some sort of ornate script, with one letter overlaying the others until it was indistinguishable to most anyone. With all of her training in cryptography, shouldn't she have been able to recognize it?

She had found out enough information for now. Günter was not dead or maybe he was, since the CIA would be controlling the press. Now she knew by the hacienda's name that Günter was a CIA agent.

Rose had told Jacqueline that Günter was with the FBI. However, the gate was clearly the initials of the CIA. Since she did not believe Rose would have lied about that to her, maybe Günter had changed agencies. He was always trying to move up in the government, so maybe he parlayed his connection with Rose. She placed the papers in her backpack and dozed off for a few minutes.

Jacqueline was asleep when the bus came to a stop deep in the jungle. Suddenly, the overhead lights came on in the bus. Three men in brown khaki military uniforms boarded, wearing sidearms and carrying M16 rifles. The sleeves of their uniforms read, "Policia Nacional Guatemala." They walked the aisle of the bus looking at the passengers. They were expressionless; they said nothing, as they stared at each person's face.

It was clear they were looking for someone and Jacqueline hoped it was not her. She could see a guard shack outside her window to the left of the dirt road. The wooden shack housed M16 machine guns propped up against the opened windows of the ten-by-twelve foot wood guard shack. Jacqueline quietly pushed the cane down the side of the bus seat. In case of arrest, she did not want to be in possession of a loaded .22 from Enrique's hacienda.

Suddenly two of the men in khaki uniforms grabbed a man from the middle of the bus and dragged him off kicking and screaming. The third soldier looked around the bus as he began backing up and stepped off. The door closed, the lights went back off, and the driver continued north with the passengers completely silent. Jacqueline's heartbeat slowly returned to normal, although she wondered about the fate of the man and his chances in this "new democracy." She pulled the cane back out from beside the seat.

When the bus was nearing the most northern point of Guatemala, the driver made a routine roadside stop for food and souvenirs. This was where Jacqueline decided she should part ways with the bus. She did not want the Mexican border patrol to ask for her passport, which she did not have.

She waited and watched as the bus pulled away, then immediately asked an old woman running the souvenir stand, "Do you speak English?" "Un poco – a little." "I am with the Peace Corps and I need a bed for the night." The old woman told her she could sleep in the shack behind the stand. "But no take food you no pay for!" Jacqueline gave her ten dollars American, for food and a bed. The old woman was happy and walked Jacqueline back to the shed, giving her a blanket and candle, saying "Uno night!" "Uno only, no more money," Jacqueline replied.

Jacqueline, exhausted, slept until daybreak. When she woke, the old woman was at her stand again selling her goods. Jacqueline asked, "How far to the Mexican border?" The woman replied, "Alrededor de una hora de caminar hacia el norte – Uno hour," as she held up one finger, pointed to the north, and then imitated walking with two fingers on the palm of the other hand. The old woman handed Jacqueline a bag with a banana, corn bread and a bottle of water inside. Jacqueline knew she could not offer to pay, for safety she had told the old woman that she had no money left. Therefore, she thanked the woman and started up the road.

Seeing the border in the far distance, Jacqueline immediately turned off the road, heading east, to find a place where she could cross without going through the customs checkpoint. After Jacqueline walked for about another hour or so, she saw a man, a woman, and two children walking north. She knew that it must be a safe crossing. She turned back to the north and followed far behind the family.

When the family walking ahead of Jacqueline reached a large eucalyptus tree, soaring 125 feet high, each parent reached down, picked up one child, and started to run. After a few minutes, they put the children down and all continued to walk with ease. Jacqueline followed the families' moves and in a few hours, dead tired, she found a group of trees and decided to stop for a while.

Making herself as comfortable as she could on large palm branches, she settled down to rest. The sun was reflecting off water near the area where she had been sleeping. She had been so tired that she hadn't even noticed the water or heard the sound of the surf! Jacqueline knew immediately from the intensity of the blue water and golden yellow sun that she had fallen asleep near the Pacific Ocean.

One thing she was unsure about was how many days she had been traveling through the jungle. Was it two or three days? She was sure the coca leaves had caused the confusion. However, she was convinced she had only been in the jungle for, at most, four nights. Since she had given herself seventy-two hours leeway after the scheduled meeting time, she felt she would make the destination in plenty of time. Taking out her maps, she discovered that she simply had Mexico left to cross. Although she knew it was a long distance, there were no more border crossings between her and Marie.

No one seemed to be on the stretch of beach she had found. Jacqueline took off her clothes and walked slowly into the warm blue water of the Pacific Ocean. The water was warm against her body and for a few precious minutes, she swam in the sea, forgetting all that was behind and ahead. For a very short time, as her body floated on top and dipped under the water, she was free. Only as she began dressing in her dirty clothes, did the reality of her situation come back.

Strapping her backpack on, she headed north though the beginning of the forest, staying near the water line. Jacqueline walked for hours without seeing another person. However, her legs were becoming weak and she knew that she could not continue on her own. Reaching into her backpack, she took out a few of the coca leaves that she carried in her backpack. Chewing the leaves gave her a burst of energy. However, it made her head spin again.

At least she could no longer feel her legs hurting as she continued. Eventually, she stopped at nightfall in a group of banana trees. In the morning, she woke to sounds coming from a short distance away. Jacqueline headed toward the sound and found a truck loaded with men, women, and children headed north. She grabbed her sign from her pack and held it up. The passengers motioned for her to get onboard.

She threw her backpack on the truck as she jumped aboard. It was wonderful to be off her feet; she rested and rode for hours in silence. The longer she could ride on the back of the truck, the better her progress would be. Finally, the truck stopped and Jacqueline jumped off with a simple "Gracias," having no idea where she was. She continued up the road on foot and found herself looking at a sign that said, "Ometepec, Mexico." Jacqueline knew she was moving across Mexico at a good rate.

Now she just needed to make her way across the rest of Mexico to Tijuana and to the Grand Tijuana Hotel. However, Jacqueline needed some rest. She was exhausted; every muscle in her legs was hurting. She had no desire to use any more of the coca leaves, as she knew they were addicting. Barely able to walk, Jacqueline entered the town of Ometepec, where she spotted a local tour bus going to Acapulco. She purchased a newspaper dated the fifteenth.

Jacqueline was dirty and tired, but it only took a moment for her to decide that Acapulco would be a great place to rest, and to board a bus for Tijuana. She purchased a ticket for the short ride to Acapulco, headed to a place she had never been but had always dreamed of visiting. Of course, she had not planned to see it under these circumstances. As the bus arrived at the beautiful city of Acapulco, she felt for the first time that she was back in civilization.

The city was busy, full of cars and people in the real heartbeat of Acapulco, the main market area known as "Mercado Central." Everywhere she went in Acapulco brought her back to this main street area. The Town Square was in the tranquil part of town called Mango. Rubber trees dotted the area; there was a cathedral at one end of the square, and sidewalk cafés with brightly colored tablecloths lined the street.

Talk of the legendary daring feats performed by the La Quebrada cliff divers filled the city on that day. The divers scaled a high cliff in swimsuits and prayed at a shrine before they made their dives. The young divers would dive from a lower cliff and the more experienced dove from the higher. Each diver was trying to outdo the diver before.

Magnificent beaches and never-ending nightlife surrounded the town square. Jacqueline would have loved to participate in the sensually infused nightlife. Nonetheless, she wanted rest and to stay low-key while in Acapulco. She was unsure if Günter had survived his injuries and there was no way for her to find out right now, if ever. That was a scary thought, even though she was sure Günter died in that explosion. It was so massive that she did not see how he could have survived. She knew she could never trust what was said in print about the accident, not with the CIA involved.

If she tried to call the hospitals, Jacqueline knew that she would set off alarms. It was a risk she could not afford. If Günter were dead, as she suspected, she had no idea how long before Meier Finch would find out. Nor could Jacqueline tell what his reaction would be to her involvement. "Well, time tells all," she thought.

After walking the city for a while, she quietly took a room in a small motel. At the desk, the clerk told her it was 75 pesos and she told him that she was meeting her Peace Corps sponsor and only had 20 American dollars. He told her that was good. She knew that she was being overcharged in the conversion, but she was too tired to haggle. Jacqueline left the man at the front desk with the impression that she was broke, for her own safety.

The room was small but clean, with a good luck blessing above the door. She took a long semi-warm bath, as the water was not too hot in this one star hotel. With no soap, she bathed as best she could, re-dressed for the following day, and fell fast asleep in her clothes. Around noon the next day, she heard a knock and a voice saying, "Check out, check out." Jacqueline opened the door and the sun blinded her eyes. She told the motel clerk, "Gracias, Señor. Apenas uno minuto." The desk clerk waited at the motel room door while she put on her shoes, and grabbed her backpack and cane.

Jacqueline began walking the main street area and stopped at a local restaurant street stand on Avenida Costera Miguel Alemán. She struggled to find change in her jeans pocket to pay for a tamale. She wanted everyone to think she was broke. Jacqueline continued her walk on the street to the Zócalo, eating her tamale.

To her right as she faced the town square, was the glorious cathedral, Catedral de Nuestra Senora de la Soledad, and to her left were the outside cafés. She continued through the square as she came upon a beautiful gigantic resort called the BreakFree Acapulco Resort. At that moment, she decided that she would stay one more day. She could use the rest, not to mention lots of hot water and some soap. Jacqueline figured that she could go unnoticed in a resort this large. Besides, she did not want to hang around Tijuana waiting for Marie. At this point, Jacqueline was clearly going to arrive tomorrow.

Walking up to the desk, she heard the clerk speaking perfectly clear English, to Jacqueline's relief. She told him the same story about the Peace Corps and took a room for seventy-five American dollars. When she asked about food, the host told her they had restaurants and stores on the premises. Jacqueline wanted to go unnoticed, so she chose one of the stores.

Quickly purchasing bread, cheese, a bottle of wine with a screw cap, and maps of the area, she walked to her room. As she entered the room on the third story, before her eyes appeared the most captivating view out the open balcony doors, and a sudden calm came over Jacqueline. She was tired and still felt dirty from the lack of soap

316

when she bathed at the small motel. However, she did feel safer than in the jungle.

Tossing her pack on the floor next to the beautiful cream-colored bedspread, she sat her supplies on the counter and headed straight to the shower, then to the open veranda. The air was fresh and a mild breeze caught her hair and cooled her neck from the heat of the ninety-degree temperature. Her eyes focused on the view of crescent-shaped Acapulco Bay, framed by the verdant mountains that plunged into glittering sapphire water. The view gave Jacqueline a feeling of peace she had not known since her arrival in Central America.

Jacqueline opened the wine, and then took her cheese and bread from the counter out to the veranda. Sitting back in a chair, she relaxed, enjoying the beauty of Acapulco Bay. She realized that she could relax for one more day and then she had to make her way across the rest of Mexico. Her mind wondered at how she had been able to travel through the forest and jungles of Costa Rica, Nicaragua, Honduras, and Guatemala without any trouble, and with just a few bug bites. She was amazed.

It was a lot of luck, like spotting the men at the chemical vat before they spotted her near their cocaine processing area. Then she thought back to all the training she had received in Israel, and knew that she had applied everything they taught her without even thinking about it. Maybe it was both luck and skill, but Rose's advice for her to get training had saved her life.

Jacqueline opened the travel brochures, and to her relief, most were in both English and Spanish. She

317

discovered that a bus left every day at 6 AM for Tijuana. Finishing her wine and bread, she climbed into a hot bath with soap, and then set a wake-up call for 5 AM. After resting for a day and a quick morning shower, it was time for her to go. She really wished she could have seen more of Acapulco than just the view from the balcony. However, she felt it was safer to stay low key, hidden inside the room.

At least when she saw Marie she would not look completely exhausted. She still had some healing cuts on her face from the accident, but the last of the stitches in her head had fallen out on the trip through the jungle. She was thin and tanned. "Overall, I'm not in such bad shape for the hell I've been through in the last ten days," she thought as she looked in the mirror.

Jacqueline walked slowly to the bus station, less than a block away, enjoying the early morning sights and sounds of Acapulco. A slight breeze stirred the air, and the temperature seemed cool – in the low eighties. After the jungle heat in the high nineties, it was quite a relief. She asked the ticket master about the arrival time and cost in American dollars for the bus to Tijuana. "Bus arrives in 15 minutes, twenty American Dollars."

Jacqueline told him she would have to see if she still had twenty dollars, and walked into the station bathroom. She took some more money from her backpack and put it in her front pocket. Then she went back and purchased a ticket to Tijuana, appearing to scrape for ones and fives to pay the fare. She had enough for a ticket and a cup of coffee in her pocket. In a few minutes, the bus arrived and she began the long ride across Mexico. Jacqueline knew she would be in Tijuana by late afternoon and that was perfect timing to meet Marie.

There was one thing that Jacqueline could depend on; Marie would be at the meeting location. She was hoping to stay in Mexico a day or two. However, she would have to tell Marie that she was not planning to go back to the U.S. to live. Jacqueline planned to enter America through Mexico and head straight for LAX to board a plane for London. She would settle there for the time being. Marie had lived through having to hide out from the CIA, and Jacqueline knew Marie would understand her need to live outside of the States. Besides, Marie was living in Paris most of the time, so in a way this would work out better for both of them. It would be a much shorter trip for them to be together than to commute from the United States.

As the bus pulled in to Tijuana about 3:30 PM on the seventeenth, Jacqueline could see the Grand Hotel Tijuana sign through the bus window. Relieved, she smiled as she saw the glass tower, nearly twenty stories high, reflecting in the sunlight. It was a heavenly sight for Jacqueline. Walking toward the hotel, she saw Marie sitting at one the outside café tables that were covered with red and white floral cloths.

It only took a few seconds for Marie to see Jacqueline walking toward the hotel. Jacqueline watched as Marie nearly tipped her chair over standing up, when she saw Jacqueline coming. However, she immediately slowed down to keep from drawing attention to her mother, and walked slowly toward Jacqueline.

Marie reached Jacqueline in minutes and her first words were, "Momma, I knew you would make it," as she took Jacqueline's arm. "I called my recorder at home this morning and there was a message from the Costa Rican police that there had been an accident. When I called back, they said you died in an explosion. I took the information and pretended to be in shock. But I didn't tell them anything. I knew you were okay, you had to be okay, and by the way you look like hell!" Marie had said it all with barely a breath. "Well kiddo, you should have seen what I looked like before I spent last night at a resort in Acapulco!" "Acapulco! I'm jealous, Mom! Really, you look great."

Jacqueline could see that Marie had been through hell for the last few days, not knowing for sure that her mother was safe or even alive. This was one thing Jacqueline held Rose accountable for, the pain he had caused Marie with worry over his CIA involvement. It had been part of their lives since she was only eleven years old.

They walked arm-in-arm back to the table, and ordered Jacqueline a Grand Marnier and cup of coffee. "I took a suite; are you tired Mom? Are you okay? You really do look like hell." Marie reached to touch her mother's bruised face. "I'm fine, just exhausted. Let's take our drinks and go to the room."

As they walked into the hotel elevator, Marie said, "Mom, the police call scared the hell out of me, even though you warned me." "I'm sorry, Marie, but I had no choice." "Mom, I know that it must have been bad." Jacqueline said, "Order some food from room service and

I will tell you what happened." Jacqueline pulled the newspaper out and asked Marie, who was fluent in Spanish, to read the article.

The look on Marie's face was one of complete horror. "Who is Dr. Curran and who is the unidentified tourist who died?" Jacqueline told her, "Marie, Dr. Curran *is or was* Günter Lehman. As you can see, the article says that he was severely injured. There was no way I could check to see if he was alive without leaving a trail."

"What the hell?" Jacqueline laughed, saying, "I'm the unidentified tourist." Marie paced with paper in hand, "Günter Lehman!" "Yes, Marie, it was Günter – the CIA gave him extensive plastic surgery and put him out to pasture in Costa Rica, probably when his life's work began attacking his mind." "Mom, do they just think that they can train these men to live a life of deceit, drugs, and murder with no long-term effects?" "Marie, I believe they fully understand the damage, and the CIA's solution is extermination, or if necessary because of information they have secreted away, expatriation onto some foreign soil. I don't know what power he had over the CIA to set him up in Costa Rica, but Günter had developed some kind of mad obsession with me. I think it started during the years that Rose was still alive."

"Mom, I remember Rose saying that Günter was crazy about you on more than one occasion." "Well, Rose was right; Günter hired a man to sell me cheap tickets in order to get me to Costa Rica, probably after looking for me for years. You know that old saying, if it appears to be too good to be true it probably is. When I would not agree to stay with Dr. Curran forever in Costa Rica, as a last ditch effort he tried to convince me that he was Rose!"

"Doesn't he know Rose is dead?" They talked through the night. Marie, with her analytical mind, wanted to know how Jacqueline had gotten away. "Marie, you don't need to know any more than you do. Let's just say my Middle East training came in handy." Marie asked, "How did you make your way from Costa Rica to Mexico?" Jacqueline told her, "I rode a bicycle off the estate as I heard the explosions, and boarded a riverboat headed out of the country. Disguised as a Peace Corps volunteer, I walked and hitched a ride with American soldiers. After that I walked more, rode in a donkey cart, slept in the back of a truck, and cruised in tour buses, until I reached you."

"Wow! That is really ingenious, mother!" Marie agreed that Jacqueline had no choice but to do what she had done to get away. Nevertheless, Marie had to ask the question, "What caused the explosion?" Marie looked at her mother. Jacqueline calmly answered, "I tried to blow Günter sky high, and I think I succeeded. I have no regrets, except that I did not see his body. That is something I was taught in Israel. Confirm the kill – no one is dead until you see the body." "Mother, if that explosion was that big, no one could survive. You're sure he entered the house, right?" "Yes, he was inside and he has to be dead. I don't like what I had to do, but he was a nut!" "Mother, that bastard would have killed you, so you had no choice. I know that. But you will have to tell me how you did it." "Okay, but later. I'm still wrapping my head around what I had to do." "I understand, mother; I can wait."

Marie could not believe Günter Lehman tried to pass himself off as Rose. "How did you know?" "Well there were a lot of signs that he was not Rose, other than the fact that Rose is dead. I was his wife and I know his touch. However, the thing that really clued me in was Günter's eating and drinking habits. Günter drank half coffee and half tea in a cup, and ate potato chips in chocolate mint ice cream. So did Dr. Curran, except he used banana chips in the ice cream.

"Just before I left the hacienda, I found that Günter had a complete file on me. Among other things, I found that photograph stolen from Rose's hospital room years ago. I accessed Enrique's computer by guessing the password, 'Günter.' He had a portrait of me hanging behind a tarp and the plaque below read, 'Mrs. Günter Lehman.' The portrait was clearly made from that stolen photo. All of that confirmed any questions I had about 'Dr. Curran.' He was one sick man! The day before I fled, he was becoming violent." Marie asked, "Did he hurt you?" "Not as bad as I hurt him when I left!"

As they talked that evening, Marie gave Jacqueline the duplicate passport she was carrying. The picture of Marie was a little young, but Marie's startling resemblance to Jacqueline when this passport was created should allow it to work. "Thank you for bringing it. I assure you that I will keep a better eye on my false bottom purse and passports from here on. I let my guard down; this was to be just a relaxing vacation.

"Marie, you can stay in Mexico for a day or two, right?" "Yes, we can stay together a day or two, and then we'll head home." Jacqueline shook her head. "Well, not exactly; I'm going from here to London on this passport. I can't stay in the States now." Marie was concerned. "I understand. I was worried about that happening. Mother, will our connection to Rose make our lives forever filled with turmoil?"

"I'm afraid to say it may. I thought that we were safe when Rose died, then again, when I learned to protect myself by accepting training in Israel. This came out of nowhere. Yes, I'm afraid this turmoil may be our destiny. I'm making a reservation tomorrow. I'll leave Los Angeles Saturday on a late night flight to London, and I'll settle there for now. I have enough money to last a few years, and Israel will cover anything else I need."

"Oh, Mom, that reminds me, I have your money. Also, I stopped by the post office box for you after I opened a new safe deposit box. That was on the day I left to come here. This envelope was inside, so I brought it with me. I knew it was from Meier Finch. His envelopes to you always have an Israeli return address." "Really! That is a surprise." Jacqueline opened the envelope Meier had sent to her post office box. Inside, she found five thousand dollars in cash and a numbered account at the Lloyds TSB Private Banking LTD, 39 Threadneedle Street, London England. The letter said, "Your bonds are being placed there on deposit for you. Access the account immediately after you arrive in London, so I will know you are safe. Once you access the account, the bank will give you a safety deposit key. Inside you will find what you need. "

"Meier knows what has happened! News travels fast to him. I'm sure there will be a new name and passport waiting for me at Lloyds. Anytime you come in, they do that – they change your identity. I will get rid of your duplicate passport once I get to London. I wonder how Meier guessed I would want to come into London. I suppose our minds think alike. I guess what I thought would be the next logical safe location to disappear for a while was Mossad's idea, too."

"Mother, I'll wait a little while, then research by computer the newspapers, hospital, and morgue records to see if Günter is dead." Jacqueline shook her head. "It won't do any good. The CIA will decide what to publish. If they want him to appear dead, he will. If they want him to appear alive, they will release that. I'm afraid we will never know for sure. However, I saw the explosion and I know that he was inside the hacienda when it exploded. I believe the son of a bitch is dead. Marie, I blew that place sky high."

Jacqueline continued, "Besides, you are going to need to put all your computer skills to use soon. We will talk about it in a few weeks. I know too much." "Mom, you listened to Rose's recordings, didn't you?" "Yes I did Marie, and they were worse than I could have imagined. We'll talk about them later – let's just get this part of the hell behind us first."

They spent a day enjoying Mexico, speaking on and off about what had happen in Costa Rica, and they made plans for Marie to cross the border on Friday. Jacqueline would wait until Saturday, since her passport was a duplicate of Marie's. It was clear to both of them that it was too dangerous for both to try the border crossing on the same day. Jacqueline insisted that Marie go first. Jacqueline wanted Marie safe in the States before Jacqueline attempted to cross the border. As they said goodbye at the hotel on Friday, Marie agreed to pick Jacqueline up on the U.S. side of the border the next day at 12:30.

She slept peacefully Friday night after Marie had safely crossed the border back to the U.S. The next morning, Jacqueline unloaded the .22 in the handle of the cane and threw the bullets away. That way, if someone discovered the cane at the border, she would claim it was a souvenir. Then she stood in line wearing her Panama hat and sunglasses.

As Jacqueline approached the border guard, she handed him the passport with Marie's name and picture. Then she doffed her hat and flippantly said to the border guard, "I'm home! Did you miss me?" The guard, taken aback by her chutzpah, handed her passport back after barely a glance at it and said, "You are obviously American; you can go through." Jacqueline breathed a sigh of relief. It was easier than she could have hoped.

Jacqueline could see Marie standing in front of a rental car. She walked slowly toward her, got in the car, and they drove away. Marie shouted, "Mom, it worked!" "Yes it did, thanks to you!" They laughed as they stopped for dinner in San Diego.

Jacqueline explained to Marie everything that had happened in Costa Rica. They both agreed that Jacqueline should stay out of America, possibly forever. "I'll feel safer out of the country. Besides, it gives you a great reason to expedite your move to Paris. Are you enjoying your part-time life in Paris?" "Oh, I love Paris; I'm spending most of my time there now. I will be a full-time resident in France by the end of the year." "Keep the California home until the end of the year, Marie." "Sure, Mom. I'm in no rush to sell."

As they arrived at LAX, Marie asked Jacqueline what made her absolutely sure that Dr. Curran was not Rose. "Mom, what was the one thing that gave you absolutely no doubt, even before you saw the painting?" Jacqueline knew Marie needed peace of mind that Rose was not living in Costa Rica as Dr. Curran. Jacqueline whispered in Marie's ear, "With all of the plastic surgery Günter had, he forgot one little thing – circumcision!" Marie started giggling, and said, "That's too much information Mom, but I sure can understand why you were so positive!"

Jacqueline told Sid, "I should have asked you for another drink before I told you about all of this!" Sid looked at Jacqueline; she looked worn out. "Jacqueline, I can see why you needed a drink, but you look like you need a break more. I cannot believe how you survived the jungle. I would have been scared out of my mind!" "No Sid, I don't think you would have been. You see, when the fear level is that high, it disappears. You run on adrenaline. At least that is how it was for me. I think the only time I really felt fear was at the drug vats, then I took control of it by staying still and waiting them out. I did not want to kill them, but I was prepared to do that if I needed to."

Sid asked her, "How far away were they? How many of them were there?" Jacqueline told her, "I really don't know how many of them there were. There were quite a few, and they were coming and going and moving around, so I couldn't really count – especially in the dark. They were close enough that I could hear them when they were talking, but they were too far away for me to understand anything they were saying – especially since I'm sure they were speaking Spanish. I am glad that I didn't have to fight them, but I would have done anything necessary to survive."

Sid looked into Jacqueline's eyes at that moment, and she realized that Jacqueline was a very different woman. She was different from the young girl Sid met in San Francisco, different from the woman she ran across in New York, and different from the widow Sid visited in New Orleans. Jacqueline was so much stronger than any of those women. Sid thought that she liked this Jacqueline better than ever. She understood that Jacqueline took no prisoners in life, but was not looking for the battle.

Sid asked, "Would you like that drink now?" "I'm more than ready. We are getting closer to the end of the story, but there is still a lot that you need to know...."

Chapter Fifteen
Conscious Mind

LLOYDS PRIVATE Banking on Threadneedle Street was Jacqueline's first destination in London. She accessed her numbered account, picking up the box key. Within minutes, she had her new identification. Next, she decided to find a few hostels to rotate living in while she looked for a more permanent residence in London. This would also keep her out of sight for a while, as she made sure no one was looking for her.

She could tell from Meier's correspondence that he knew what had happened in Costa Rica, and that Jacqueline was involved. However, he did not seem very upset with her. At least, he was helping her. Although she was tempted to call, she decided against it. When Meier wanted to tell her what he knew, he would contact her. Jacqueline had learned that Meier talked little; he just took care of things. His sources of information reached all around the world and he knew everything fast. She guessed that he did not like Günter either!

Jacqueline settled in the borough of Tower Hamlets in the heart of the East End of London. It was rich in history and not very far from the City of London. The borough is a vibrant mix of old and new, an eclectic community filled with galleries, bookstores, and unique culture, with its own lifestyle and character. Tower Hamlets takes its name from the historical connection between the Tower of London and the hamlets that surrounded it. Jacqueline found a flat after a few weeks. It was located on the Isle of Dogs in a luxurious high rise called Mulberry, and it offered a view of the bright shining beacon light atop Canary Wharf Tower, England's tallest building.

Movie stars from America also adopted this area in London. Jacqueline's high-rise was located at the "U bend" on the River Thames, and centrally located for access to London. Tower Hamlets was once the home of characters such as Captain Cook and Queen Victoria.

In addition, it was where the legendary Jack the Ripper stalked and murdered five or more women of London. Jacqueline figured he was long dead now, so Jack did not worry her much. People from all over the world had settled in the chic area without fear of Jack's return, so that made it a wonderful place for her to blend into the crowd.

Jacqueline spent many of her days in London on the grounds near the British Museum. Since 1753, this museum has been free to the public. It is a massive stone structure with mammoth pillars, and it has been the people's favorite on Museum Mile. It is the central meeting spot for the modern groups of London. It houses some of the greatest collections of human cultural history, from real-life legends to iconic objects such as the earliest known image of Christ. The museum houses rare exhibits such as the one hundred views of Mount Fuji and the history of Cleopatra.

Jacqueline felt the rain coming, and hurried in from the museum grounds to the Orange Door Club, a revival of a sixties poets' corner. It was located on Great Russell Street in the heart of Museum Mile near the British Museum. The large orange entrance door was directly off the sidewalk leading to the museum, and it sent patrons down into a cellar. The club, from the historic boulders that formed its walls to its old brick floor, was as rich in architecture as the walls of the museum. When Jacqueline entered it was late in the afternoon, and the smoke-filled jazz club was busy.

The club was owned by Klaus Reiter, the young son of a family long involved with the museums of England. Klaus was of German ancestry and stood six feet three, but he weighed barely enough to keep the wind from blowing him away. Klaus was a good-looking man who possessed enormous spirit. He was both highly intelligent and highly animated. The club was his twenty-first birthday gift from his father, and Klaus was now thirty-five. Over the past few months, he and Jacqueline had become fast friends.

Klaus had taken to Jacqueline and her to him, on the first day they met. He had introduced Jacqueline, now living under the name Leslie Carter, to all his friends. He invited her to social gatherings around London. Despite the age difference, they had become dear friends. However, she felt dishonest – he did not even know her real name.

Early on, Klaus had invited her to join a book group with readers of ancient philosophy. The members of the group were all from the club. The eclectic group of drug-using people from England, Germany, France, and Italy was a joy. A few of them, like some people in America, abused drugs. However, most just smoked a little pot and drank some wine. Finding friends in London seemed to come naturally to Jacqueline, although she felt that she was betraying those very friendships by posing as Leslie Carter. Jacqueline knew that she could not reveal who she was, and the dishonesty with her new friends made her uncomfortable.

To prevent people from asking questions, she had decided to start working; Klaus found her a position at the British Museum as an assistant in the archive department. Jacqueline received a promotion within a month to a position on the Reading Room Research Team. Her research team was preparing for the movement of the national collections of printed books, manuscripts, and journals to the British Library. Jacqueline loved the work – she spent most of her time alone in the basement of the museum going over old books and documents.

Filling the arched corridors were long hand-carved wooden tables used for workspace and art that had remained hidden from public view. One painting, a giant lone chess piece with a background of a jail and an evil eye, caught Jacqueline's attention repeatedly. It reminded her that she still was not at peace. Her loner's existence kept Jacqueline secreted from the travelers to the museum and limited the chances that someone from America would recognize her. Nevertheless, lying about who she was and why she was in London, deceiving all of the people who had shown her such kindness, haunted her a bit.

Jacqueline knew that telling just one person who she was and why she left the States could cost her life. She felt that she couldn't trust anyone. She could never find peace with the knowledge that she left America, her home, without revealing what the government was doing or attempting to stop it. Jacqueline felt caught and alone as her anger for her government, the American Government, mounted.

Rose had left Jacqueline with information that could save lives and make a deteriorating America great once again. However, she really did not know how to use the information. She was not as smart as Rose, and afraid that she would use the information in the wrong way. Rose had done a great deal of damage in the name of country. He left the recordings and materials for her to correct some of his wrongs.

However, Jacqueline knew she could do more damage than good if she did not think very carefully about how she would handle this information. Most days, she just wished she had never picked up the boxes. But if she had not retrieved Rose's recordings and other material, she would not have the highly classified information about the powers that controlled America. Nor would she ever have seen her old San Francisco lover Mark again.

Even as Jacqueline settled into her new home in England, she found that the thirty-five recordings continued to play repeatedly in her mind. Maybe that was why she had waited so long to retrieve and listen to them.

She thought that the pain of hearing Rose's voice would stay with her once she had heard the tapes. Jacqueline had no idea it would be the horror his words revealed that would continue to haunt her.

The government-sanctioned conspiracies, murders, deceit, and bombings were all on tapes, documented in microfilm, and on CDs. Many of the recordings deeply troubled her, but one tape never left her mind, especially as she watched the presidential campaigning in America.

One that Rose recorded shortly before his death about the meeting of six men in Geneva stated, "The CIA was spinning a total web of control over the United States." At the time of that meeting, the possibility of controlling presidential elections seemed to be far away, but the members of B6 believed it to be possible with new technology on the horizon. The CIA knew the technology was being created in the computer industry.

The most surprising part to Jacqueline was that it crossed all party lines. It was not about the Democrats or the Republications. It was about a few powerful men located on C Street in Washington, working through the CIA. They would hold and control the presidency of the United States of America. Those in charge of B6 claimed it was a preemptive strike against someone controlling the American vote, but Rose saw though that bullshit.

Predicted on the recording was that in the future, American voters would be casting presidential votes in the states by computer ballot. That would be the day C Street and the CIA could use computers to access and control the major electoral states at the very end of Election Day.

The candidate C Street chose would be president. This is what B6's code for a "preventative measure" was really creating.

It was a perfect plan; if things were going the way C Street wanted and its candidate was ahead, the men would need to do nothing. But if the C Street candidate of choice was losing, the CIA would hijack the computers of the remaining states and put C Street's man into the office of President of the United States. The same method could control run-off and primary elections.

That day had come. The States had begun paperless, computerized on-line transmission of votes over the last years. Jacqueline knew that computer technology was being used for vote counting, that the CLIPP code had been in place for a long time, and that the CLIPP code probably had been used.

This would mean that no matter what the American people wanted, the CIA could make the election appear close but the candidate C Street chose would always win. Therefore, the CIA and the five founding families would remain in power throughout the future of America. Rose had said, "They are controlling the oil by war, the people by fear, and the power by trickery." That recording never left Jacqueline's mind, she knew that the CIA really planned to seize control of America forever.

Jacqueline tried to escape from the recordings that she had heard. Now trained to protect herself and living out of the country, why should she care? Nevertheless, she did care. It was only a matter of time until she would have to do something. Jacqueline was an American. She was sure that the CIA had been able to execute this plan and was now controlling the American vote.

She knew the tone of America was freedom and yet elected to the Presidency of the United States of America were the most conservative of candidates. Every four years on Election Day, the race would be close at the last minute. It happened repeatedly. According to Rose's recording, this was the most important part, so no one could prove any tampering. Once the election was over, there would be a few voices of dissent. The government would investigate themselves, and – what a surprise – find no wrongdoing.

Slowly, as in Nazi Germany, the rights of the American people were being taken away by the government's powerful elite. In this case, it was the CIA. State laws were being overtaken by federal legislation. American prisons were filled to capacity, with more under construction. All of this was done to house American people who had become the victims of the religious right moral laws installed by the CIA, implemented by C Street in Washington, and controlled by the Presidency.

Each President was re-elected to a second term, and the government was considering changing the law so a president could serve more than two terms. That would make C Street's control over America even easier. The Patriot Act had taken away civil liberties one by one, under the guise of protection from terrorists, after the 9/11 attacks on the World Trade Center in New York.

The purpose of the Patriot Act was to allow government the free use of wiretaps on the American people, along with warrantless searches on U.S. citizens. It also allowed imprisonment of "suspected terrorists," without the benefit of legal counsel. Under the guise of "Homeland Security," they passed this law. At the same time, illegal aliens were crossing the borders of Mexico and Canada in order to provide cheap labor to the oil refineries, crop fields, and sweatshops.

The prison population was overflowing in America from ever-toughening prohibitions on drug use, and even possessing a bumper sticker objecting to the government's control could get the FBI at your door. Rose predicted everything on Tape 35. Rose helped to develop the plans when he was a CIA think-tank assassin for B6. The government had created the computers, the code, and the internet in America. The American people advanced the computers and codes, until the CIA could take complete control of the country through the work of great American entrepreneurs.

Now Jacqueline was older, but still a believer in peace and personal freedom, just as she was in her hippie days of Haight Ashbury. Everything in her cringed as she watched the American government imprison its people – there were nearly seven million in prison, on parole, or probation. The government instilled fear in the people and controlled the Electoral College.

It was all clear to her when the State of Ohio, a blue-leaning swing state near the town where Jacqueline grew up, at the very last minute of the election, shifted to Republican. She had first begun to question elections when they had the same events in Florida four years before. She was convinced, when Ohio was suddenly called Republican. As a result, the election installed for another four years the most conservative of Presidents, a right wing Texas oilman. It was clear to her that C Street had used the code created by B6 to manipulate that election.

Jacqueline was sure that Ohioans would not vote for an incumbent who wanted to privatize social security until it could die an unnatural death. She truly believed that the President pushed privatized social security so the government would not have to pay back the money that was taken from the people's social security fund to run their oil wars. She knew that blue-collar states would never have voted for anyone who planned to wipe out Social Security. They were the workers who paid to have that fund when they retired. Nonetheless, that President was re-elected for a second term.

Jacqueline knew from press reports that the same President had gone to war after 9/11 by convincing the people that there was an immediate threat from "Weapons of Mass Destruction." No weapons of mass destruction were ever found, and there was some proof in the press that the whole thing was a ploy to invade oil-rich Iraq. Jacqueline was sure he had managed to take over the oil wells of Iraq by using American soldiers to seize and protect them. It was a Texas oilman's dream – an entire military to control oil wells.

In Jacqueline's mind, the continuous guarding of Iraq's oil wells to maintain control of them cost soldiers' lives daily. Gas prices in America had soared, while the

President depleted America's strategic oil reserves mandated by federal law. Once the strategic reserves were reduced, Jacqueline understood that America, the world's largest oil consumer, was at the mercy of countries and companies that stood to profit hugely by producing and importing it.

Most recently, the Middle East had blown up in civil war again. She concluded that the destabilization was the direct result of the terrorists believing that America's occupation of Iraq was because of the oil reserves. Jacqueline thought that as long as American forces were active in the Middle East, the Muslim extremists believed that they were being stopped from their planned Muslim takeover of Israel. She knew from her time in Israel that the extremists' assessment was incorrect, as the military of Israel could protect itself even without America.

Jacqueline knew that the President had pushed legislation through Congress that had given tax breaks to those whose income was in the top two percent of America's population. She realized that the average business owner, doctor, lawyer, or factory worker was paying for tax breaks for the billionaires. She had decided that residing in the White House was an extreme, self-serving "Christian" leader; every time Jacqueline saw the President's smirk on television, her body chilled. This President was so far to the right that he made the standard right wing seem left.

Jacqueline had decided that the American government had managed to convince religious people that it was serving them, when the reality was the religious were being controlled for the profit of the politicians and the powerful. A few religious people had begun to discover what she knew to be the truth, and spoke out about it to the news media. She was convinced that others had made the connection, but were using their knowledge to move up the political ladder. They were pretending to be God-fearing men and women of politics; however, they were as dirty as they come. She had read reports that they were getting busted using political contributions for new wardrobes, mistresses, and more.

Jacqueline spent her days seeing the sights of London and working underground in the museum. All the while, thoughts of Rose's recordings churned in her mind. She spent long nights deciding first, that she must do something, and second, what she would do. She could not be sure that if she turned the recordings and documents over to the Times, it would publish them. The Times might squash them instead. The first thing she decided was that the information was not safe for the long term in that safety deposit box. It was time for her to make a decision about where to put Rose's information so it would remain safe, but in a place she could access it to protect herself from the government.

Jacqueline took a quick trip to the States, landing at LAX, where Marie met her. Together they headed to the safety deposit box Marie had opened according to Jacqueline's instructions. They retrieved the recordings and material, and took it to a hotel where Jacqueline could listen again to the tape of instructions Rose had left for her. She had decided that she wanted to duplicate everything twice. After listening again to the instructions, she placed one copy of everything back in a new bank box in Los Angeles and then returned to London with the original and one copy. Jacqueline took the original documents to the office of a respected solicitor, and gave him five thousand pounds sterling to hold the sealed envelopes. She instructed him to turn the unopened envelopes over to her daughter in the event of Jacqueline's death. If both were deceased, the evidence was to be delivered to *The New York Times*. He was hesitant to agree without knowing what was inside the packages, however her money talked, and he ultimately consented. Jacqueline opened another safety deposit box in London for her remaining copy of the material.

Jacqueline was headed back to the States. She arranged with Marie to meet her at the Coachella Resort in the Palms Desert in a few days. It was the resort where Rose had instructed her to stay. Hopefully, that would give Jacqueline time to accomplish what she needed to do. She left London under the passport that the Israeli government had provided. Her entry into the States would be under a new assumed name, and she would head straight to the Palms Desert for answers. The location was not far from her daughter's home in California. Jacqueline knew that Marie's house had sold, and Marie would soon be living in Paris full-time. This seemed like the best time to act. When the work was completed, both she and Marie would be living safely outside America. However, they would need to rent a base of operations and purchase plenty of computer power.

Jacqueline hoped Marie would be able to look for the necessary computer equipment while she found a place in the desert for them to work. Nothing about creating a location for their work would be easy or cheap. However, she saw no other way. A house in the desert outfitted with computer systems seemed the only solution. Anyway, she needed to follow a map Rose had left before she made any more decisions and she would need to talk with Marie. The resort would be a perfect place to discuss the possibilities going forward.

Checking into the Coachella Resort in the desert, Jacqueline rented a car and drove west on Highway 1-10, as the tape had instructed. With her GPS, she found the hand-drawn map from Rose's package easy to follow. The map gave detailed degree and decimal coordinates – Latitude/Longitude: +33° 55' 44.78", -116° 37' 29.86"; Decimal: 33.929106, -116.624961. Rose's directions had been very specific, including her estimated time of departure for this trip. The directions he gave made for a circuitous route, but she realized that she could easily spot anyone following her because the roads she took were not heavily traveled.

It was nearly sunset when she found the windmill that Rose wanted her to locate. It was one of more than four thousand. She was all alone in the middle of nowhere, and she was hot and tired. However, she was also more than a little curious why Rose would have sent her to this deserted location, with 4000 plus windmills, to locate a single one with a small key in her hand. There was not a house or shack within hundreds of yards. She thought for sure she would find a building. Confirming that no one was around, she got out of the car and began just looking around.

It was a stunning sight, looking up at the windmills – they were huge, snow white, towering 140 feet tall, with blades a half of a football field wide. Although the map had brought her directly to this windmill, the rest of Rose's instructions were cryptic. It was clear he was hiding something in the area; however, even on the tape he was afraid to leave too much information, in case someone else got to the instructions first. Jacqueline looked all around her again – not a soul was in sight, and she had no idea what she should do next. The tape had said, "Once you arrive, look around, no one should be in that area, locate the key tab, turn the key in the lock at sunset and then look north."

Looking all over the area, Jacqueline was confused until the light suddenly reflected off a small flat metal tab about five feet from the bottom of the windmill. Grabbing a knife from her purse, she popped off the tab, discovering a key hole. She looked up as the sun was falling below the horizon. She placed the key in the lock and turned, and a metal plate lowered, exposing an electronic scanner with a voice that said "Retinal Scan Activated." Jacqueline could not believe what she was hearing! Quickly, she looked around the area; it was clear she was in the middle of nowhere. Placing her eyes to the scan, she heard the words "Authorized. Welcome Jackal, you have three minutes to enter," and the scanner disappeared as quickly as it had appeared. Stunned as she heard a groaning noise to the north of the windmill, Jacqueline quickly turned to see a large ramp opening up from between two other windmills, about 1000 feet away. Without any thought, she stepped back into her car and drove down the ramp, nervous as she heard it close behind her car.

The ramp ended inside a large room filled with military trucks, forklifts, and pallets. She stepped out of her car. With the ramp closed behind her, she was becoming a little alarmed. Suddenly, a voice appeared throughout the underground room, "Computer access is granted; welcome to C Street, main door opened." To Jacqueline's surprise, a man in a white lab coat was standing inside the room. He was in his seventies, tall, white-haired and handsome. Jacqueline entered slowly, suddenly overwhelmed by the flashing lights of a mainframe computer system that lined the walls. In a very thick German accent, the man said, "Welcome, Jacqueline, I have been waiting for you. Welcome to C Street. I am the gatekeeper." Jacqueline was puzzled. "The gatekeeper to what, and how do you know my name?"

"I am the gatekeeper to this C Street facility. Rose told me your name. I'm Dietmar Slusser. Don't be alarmed. Let me show you around. I am the architect who built the facility for Rose." His face was clearly not threatening to Jacqueline, so she walked in amazement with Dietmar around the underground space. "The facility is over one hundred and fifty thousand square feet. Rose wanted it to be larger than four football fields. It is powered by the windmills above ground; these are windmills we installed upon completion of the initial construction in the mid-1970s. We have an unlimited supply of electricity, and we are completely off the grid. No one monitors our electricity – there is no meter for our use. The only meters are for the surplus that is sold.

"The computers are up to date, with the most advanced technology I can find in the world. We have monitored security of the outside area, living quarters for twelve persons – including two Scandinavian recliners, Rose's favorite, and a full kitchen. Since I am the only one in this area, we have plenty of room."

Dietmar grinned. "I was watching you outside on one of the monitors." "Well, you could have helped me enter!" "Yes, however, I was testing the time it would take to locate this place and enter, even with complete instructions and the key. I picked up your car on the monitors as you made your last turn. I do not have an opportunity to test these things since Rose is gone." "The place is amazing, Dietmar, and all powered from the windmills above! It's pure genius." Dietmar looked pleased, and said, "Thank you. The construction was my work, built to Rose's specifications." "So you knew Rose?" "Yes, he was my friend and he arranged all the funding for my research, which he allowed me to carry out from this facility, in exchange for being the gatekeeper." "What kind of work is that?" "My research is with technology and robotics."

"Well, this is a perfect place for solitary work, Dietmar." "Yes it is wonderful, and I am accomplishing a great deal." Jacqueline asked, "When did you last see Rose?" "About six weeks before I read of his death. He knew it was close and he wanted to make sure I would keep everything up to date and wait for you. Will it be all right if I continue being your gatekeeper?" She smiled, "Of course it will! How much is your salary?" "I was paid years ago, for a lifetime of gate keeping."

Jacqueline suddenly remembered the computer chess game Rose was building at home long before he became ill. He had a retinal scanner of their eyes to begin playing the game, and this same voice announced one player's moves. Rose had planned all of this; it was his contingency. He just died before he could finish the job. All programmed for her eyes to activate! It was brilliant. She still needed time to complete a plan to use the power of the recordings to stop the computer hijacking of America, but this place might just make it possible for her to finish what Rose started.

"Now that I'm here, Dietmar, what am I supposed to do?" Seeming very distressed at her words he said, "I do not know; I'm just the gatekeeper!" Jacqueline smiled, saying, "It's a good thing I have the key. I know the purpose." The man looked relieved. "That is good. That made me concerned; my primary assignment was to keep the facility fully up to date and operational to Rose's specifications. I have no idea about the purpose for the facility, or what it was designed to do.

"Jacqueline, there is a room I would like you to see. Please come with me. I have not entered Rose's private study. For this room, Rose had me develop the technology and he installed it. Then he installed the updates I had created for the system on his final return to C Street. This room requires your or Rose's eye scan." "I understand, but I would like to become familiar with other parts of the facility before I enter the study."

Jacqueline spent the next few days with Dietmar, becoming familiar with him and the equipment. Dietmar did not mention Rose's study again. Jacqueline had decided she would prefer to wait until Marie was at the facility. She was not sure she wanted to enter a room Dietmar could not enter without someone else around. "Trust no one completely."

Dietmar's information and the C Street Underground facility let Jacqueline know it was possible to stop the code that Rose has created. "I will be heading out to pick up my daughter Marie, and will be back in three days. Do you need anything?" Dietmar smiled. "I would like a few newspapers. I am only able to read them online, and I would like to hold one in my hands." Jacqueline asked, "Is there anything else?" He suggested, "Perhaps some fresh fruit; I rarely leave this facility. I did not want you to arrive while I was away. Now I will feel free to leave a little more often, but not too much. I love it here. This is where my life's work has been created."

"I will see you in a few days, Dietmar." Before she left, Jacqueline did tell Dietmar that she was using the name Leslie Carter for security reasons. She could not afford to have Dietmar telephone for her at the resort or elsewhere, and ask for Jacqueline. She had decided that at least she could trust him with that information. After leaving the facility, she returned to the resort for a few more days.

Marie had been surprised when Jacqueline decided to return to the States so quickly from London, but Marie was planning to meet her at the resort. Jacqueline was excited that many of the problems had been solved by her trip to C Street Underground. She knew that Marie would love the facility and Dietmar. The desert was secluded, a perfect place to live undetected, until Jacqueline could return to London. She wanted to come up with a plan before she told Marie exactly what Rose had left behind.

Within an hour of Marie's arrival at the resort, Jacqueline was ready to tell Marie about the facility. "Let's take a walk and find a private seating area. We need to discuss something." "Sure, Mom. Let's go." Jacqueline decided it was time to tell Marie about everything, the CIA plan Rose described on his recording, B6, C Street, and the other things. Marie, who had long ago begun to despise American politics, was shocked by the information about the code Rose had helped to create.

Jacqueline knew that she needed everyone's skills – Marie's, Dietmar's – as well as her own, to complete this operation, even with the set-up and information Rose had left. Jacqueline played part of Rose's recording for Marie. Marie heard the truth in Rose's own voice, just as Jacqueline had when she heard the recording for the first time.

Jacqueline insisted that they just relax for a few days at the resort. She wanted to make sure no one was watching or following, before she took Marie out to the C

Street Underground location. Marie wanted to go see the place immediately and meet this Dietmar, but they both knew it was wise to wait. "Marie, there is a room at the facility that only I can enter with a retinal scan. I waited to enter it until we return together. I want us both armed, until we get a good read on Dietmar." Marie agreed. "That makes sense to me. While you're in the room, I'll occupy Dietmar and watch your back." Jacqueline nodded and said, "He seems like he's trustworthy – Rose obviously trusted him, but..." Marie chimed in with, "I know, trust but verify." Jacqueline laughed. "That's exactly what I was going to say! 'You have learned well Grasshopper,' to quote Master Po!" After a few days of talking, relaxing and observing, they set off together for the windmills.

This time, Dietmar launched the ramp for them from inside C Street Underground. "Thank you, Dietmar, this is...." Dietmar interrupted with, "Marie. I know so much about you. You turned out to be beautiful, but that is no surprise." "Well, thank you." Marie, stunned by the scope of the operation Rose had left behind, connected with Dietmar right away. Immediately, she began asking questions and studying the computer system with Dietmar.

Jacqueline excused herself to review Rose's documents, tapes, CDs and microfilm, saying, "Dietmar, I'm going to give myself a tour, while you two talk." He responded, "Of course, Jacqueline." She headed down the long corridor, toward the secured area. Within seconds, she was inside Rose's study.

The area consisted of about two thousand square feet of shelves with guns, other weapons, file cabinets, a wall safe, a Scandinavian chair and ottoman, a computer with wall-sized monitors, a photo of Rose and Jacqueline taken in Jamaica, and a black journal on the table next to the chair. It was clear Rose had built this room just for her and her protection.

She turned on the monitor and saw Dietmar and Marie talking away in the other room. Both were heavily engaged in a conversation about the computer systems. Jacqueline had full audio and video surveillance as well as microphone contact with the inside and outside of the facility from this area.

Jacqueline called out, "Hello, Marie and Dietmar. I'm inside the secure area, and I'll be in here for a while reading." "Very good Jacqueline; you are inside." "Yes, Dietmar, I will be out shortly. Marie, do you need anything?" "No, Mom I'm fine." "Dietmar, do you have an intercom or microphone to call me in this area?"

"Yes, I do." "Will you please show Marie how to use it?" "It is the button right here," as he touched a button next to where they were standing. "These buttons are located on panels throughout the facility." Jacqueline watched as Marie tested her ability to communicate with her mother from the main area of the facility to the study. After she was sure Marie had it, Jacqueline said, "Great, now I'm going to do some reading and I'll be out later. This facility is so large I just wanted to make sure you two could reach me." Jacqueline sat in the room, reading Rose's journal. It looked to be full of information, but some of it was in code, so she would have to figure out what it said.

After only about ten minutes of reading and pondering, she recognized a code that Rose had embedded in his journal. Pulling out a piece of paper, she tried deciphering the code with the old Caesar substitution cipher, which simply moves the letter down the alphabet and replaces it with another. After several tries, she tried shifting three letters. Sure enough, she was right. Jacqueline finished the decipher table and followed the instructions Rose had written. "Flip the switch under the desk, pull the third book on the second shelf out, then move the photo of Christ the Redeemer on the wall to the left, and push the button behind it."

Immediately, a hologram of Rose appeared, talking as though he were there with her to guide her on the journey. She listened to it carefully and played it repeatedly, as she searched for more information and also to enjoy his company once again.

Rose had carefully designed the hologram to avoid giving too much information, in case someone else discovered it. However, it served as a guide to anyone who truly knew Rose. He was fascinated with codes and had taught Jacqueline many. When he wanted to say something in the hologram that no one else would understand, the code he used was one that he had devised using Jacqueline's name. It was a complicated code without the name key. Jacqueline knew it. He used several codes in the journal, but all were codes he had taught Jacqueline.

After reading and listening to the hologram for a while, she realized that if she was to trust anyone, Dietmar was the man Rose had chosen for her. The words in the hologram and in the journal made it clear that Rose trusted Dietmar. She contacted Marie and Dietmar by intercom in the main area of the facility, "Marie, Dietmar, would you please come back to this area?" When they arrived, Jacqueline was at the door and invited them in to see the area. "I have not been in this area since the facility was built. I created the computer, but Rose installed it and updated it. He did everything in this room by himself."

Jacqueline was not surprised and said, "As you can see, this room was meant for our protection. Rose told me in his journal that you are to be trusted completely, and you have the information we need about this computer system, so you can help us, if you will. Rose also left this for us. Don't be alarmed, it is a hologram of Rose." Jacqueline flipped the switch. Marie watched in amazement at the clarity of Rose's image in the room. Dietmar's response was, "My hologram works! I designed holograms for Rose, but I never saw one after he programmed the information into it." They then listened intently to what Rose had to say.

"I will give you the same loyalty I gave Rose, the loyalty that kept me here waiting for you." Jacqueline smiled and said, "Thank you." Dietmar went on, "I have already answered many questions Marie has asked. As well, just for your information, I advised Marie she does have access to the CIA computers. What you do with that access is not my concern. I was just to advise you of your access and assist in anything you need."

"Marie, what have you found out about the computers in this facility?" "They are the most up-to-date and powerful computers that I have ever seen, Mom. Also, Rose left us a back door to the CIA computers, passwords and codes. The coded messages he left will take a while to break, if I can. I should be able to do it by using the computer system. Dietmar is a wealth of knowledge, and he might be willing to help me in that area." Jacqueline chuckled, saying, "That's my Rose! However, don't worry about any coded documents he left." Jacqueline handed Marie a piece of paper with the code she had just deciphered, "This might be the code you are looking for." "Good going, Mom! That will save me a lot of time!"

Jacqueline turned to Dietmar. "Dietmar, please update this room's system." Dietmar had anticipated her request. "Jacqueline, I have a new system ready to move into this room. I expected that it would need one. While you were gone, I got everything ready. I also have some special screens to put up. Give me a few hours."

That night, Dietmar and Marie accessed the CIA and Pentagon computers to see if CLIPP, the program that could automatically manipulate the vote, had been installed. Jacqueline was leaning over Marie's shoulder, hoping the code did not exist. "Mom, the CLIPP code is installed, and it's been used before." Jacqueline was visibly upset. "I can see." That was not the news Jacqueline wanted to hear, but it was what she expected. "Marie, back out and wipe your log entry, fast!"

"Already done and out, Mom. We aren't going to need to do updating. This technology is so advanced, we're in good shape. Next, we'll start writing the code. I don't know how long it will take. Once we get the code written, it's just a matter of making our work untraceable. The system is designed so that making the code launch untraceable will be relatively easy." Jacqueline knew that she could be no help to them – what they were doing was out of her league. "Well, I'll let you two get to work. I'm going to get out of your hair and return to the study."

As Jacqueline was heading toward the study, she called back, "Dietmar, what is that wonderful smell?" Dietmar looked pleased. "I have dinner in the oven; we will call you when it is ready. I'm looking forward to having companionship for dinner. I am a good cook, but I have not cooked for anyone else in a long time." Jacqueline and Marie, as one, said, "Excellent!"

Jacqueline returned to Rose's secure study room. Something was bothering her, but she could not put her finger on it. Looking up at the six wall screens Dietmar had placed in the room, she linked up to satellites and began scanning public cameras, worldwide. For hours, she watched the world. Unbeknownst to them, she invaded people's privacy, watching from below the ground in the US. She went to London, Rome, Jamaica, Brazil, and Canada. Washington, D.C., in particular, was of interest, as well as the Cayman Islands, Paris, and more.

She did not really know what she expected to see, but she was looking, watching, and studying the world. With only a break for dinner and conversation, she watched well into the morning hours. Then, night after night, she continued to watch. She was missing something out there, despite all she had learned about B6 and the CIA, the NSA, the FBI, the CWP, and C Street from the journals, computers, CDs, documents, tapes, and holograms. There was something else. Something Rose wanted her to know, but he was afraid to say it, even to encode it, in anything. Jacqueline could not put her finger on it, but she knew she was missing something.

Over the next months, Marie began work on the code. No one was more adept at the process of code writing than Marie – computers had become her life's work. Her hobby was building them and her work was writing computer code for them. Now she had Dietmar to build computers and help her with the code. For the next months, they worked at creating the computer program.

During those months, they ate, drank and laughed at stories of Rose. Dietmar was a wonderful cook, and it did not take long to understand why he had agreed to monitor C Street Underground for Rose. The place was simply amazing. Dietmar had worked in Oakridge as a young man after emigrating to the U.S. from Germany, and later he worked for NASA. Rose had provided Dietmar with many of his opportunities in the sixties. Dietmar's options were limited in the fifties due to McCarthy. He had been with Rose for many years. Dietmar had no family and wanted to continue to serve Rose.

During one trip to Russia in the seventies, the Russian government arrested Dietmar, believing if he were held long enough, that he would provide technological information. Rose was assigned to eliminate Dietmar while he was imprisoned in Russia. Instead, Rose paid off the guards at the stockade where Dietmar was being held in Siberia, then smuggled him out of Russia. That is when C Street Underground was in the earliest phase of construction. Dietmar never re-entered the radar of America or any other country after Rose sneaked him out of Russia. As far as the world knew, Dietmar was dead, and C Street Underground became his home.

He was a man happy in his solitude. He had been watching the outside world on monitors, leaving only rarely for equipment and supplies that came from a military drop by MAGTFTC/MCAGCC Twentynine Palms, California. Sailors would fill computerized requisitions at the supply center at CNIC Naval Weapons Station in Earle, New Jersey, and ship supplies to the Twentynine Palms Marine Base. Year after year, pallets arrived at the base but were never unloaded at Twentynine Palms. Instead, they were dropped off at a specified longitude and latitude in the desert at a specified time. Deliveries to the desert were made shortly before dark, and the soldiers would leave without waiting for anyone to pick up the supplies. They were trained to ask no questions, but merely to unthinkingly follow their orders.

That was how C Street worked. It was simple, as everybody in the military understands. It was all about everyone being on a need-to-know basis, following orders and asking no questions. It was so much a part of Twentynine Palms, the Marine's premier training base.

356

Soldiers would come and go from the base. New soldiers would deliver the pallets as directed. It was beautiful. The Q clearance for these shipments was so high that no one on either of the bases had the authority to question the orders. Their only concern was timely delivery.

Supplies simply arrived from the New Jersey base to the Palm Springs base. There, they were assigned out for distribution the same day at a specific time and to a particular place. When all the ground and air space was clear on the C Street monitors and dark had just set in over the desert, Dietmar would drive out in his military truck, unload his forklift, load the truck, and drive back underground. Over all the years and after scores of drop-offs, no one knew where the supplies were going or asked why they were doing what they did. It was brilliant planning.

Jacqueline stayed low-key. She traveled between her expatriate home in London and the C Street Underground headquarters in the Palm Springs desert. She tried to stay in London as much as possible; she certainly did not want to draw attention with too much international travel. Marie never left C Street Underground during that time. As a precautionary measure, Jacqueline and Marie only communicated in person at the C Street Underground about the code.

If the code was ready, it would probably take some last-minute interference on election night to see that the CIA and CWP did not change the American majority's vote. If that was what it took to return America to the people, Jacqueline had decided that she could not sit by and be guilty of the crime of silence. She was coming for the men of C Street. She would do it from an underground facility built with their funds; one that they did not even know existed.

Jacqueline feared that she was getting her daughter in too deeply, but it was her country, too. If they did not fight now they would lose America forever. Dietmar and Marie worked relentlessly writing the code. It was clear that they did not need Jacqueline's skills; they were so far above her technologically. Marie had promised never to use her skills for hacking, but now she was building the arsenal for just that purpose.

This code would put to the test the skills of both mother and daughter. After months of work, the program was ready – the wheels were in motion. Only time would tell. Marie went home to Paris for a well-deserved rest before the launch. Jacqueline returned to London, wanting to stay out of the States as much as possible. If anyone was looking for Jacqueline, she wanted them to track her to London and not to the Palms Desert. She preferred to face her enemy head-on if necessary, but far away from her underground headquarters.

Sid looked up from her writing pad. "Jacqueline, you must be starving! I've been a terrible host – it's been hours since I fed you anything! How about if we take a break for a few minutes, and I'll fix us some sandwiches? I have to keep your strength up! Otherwise, I'll never hear how this ends!" Jacqueline agreed that she was a little hungry, so Sid got up and headed to the kitchen to prepare the food.

As she was making sandwiches, Sid asked, "Did you feel secure when you were in the C Street Underground? Weren't you claustrophobic?" Jacqueline, laughing, said, "Are you kidding? The place is huge!" Turning more serious, she continued, "I never felt like I was closed in, and the lighting made it seem like I was in a big warehouse and office complex. It was easy to forget that we were buried way under the ground.

"As for security, the facility itself was very secure, so I never felt any concern while I was actually in there. My concern was entering and leaving. Every time the ramp opened, C Street Underground was completely exposed and vulnerable. It was visible to aircraft, subject to satellite imaging, and it could be seen by passersby. There was nothing around but windmills, so passersby were few and far between. That's why we always came and went either at sunset or when it was dark. Still, with infrared technology, our heat signature would be visible even at night, if the ramp was open. So, yes, it always made me nervous when I was entering or leaving C Street Underground. Thankfully, we were never detected."

Jacqueline told Sid, "I needed to go to London before I did anything else. There were loose ends to tie up. I'm going to get some more coffee before I go on. Do you want some more?" Sid, eating her last bite, nodded emphatically. Jacqueline went to the kitchen and poured coffee for both of them. When she returned, she and Sid settled in for another session. As Sid picked up her pen, Jacqueline told Sid, "Even that trip to London had some twists and turns. Let me tell you about it...."

Claudette Walker

Chapter Sixteen
London Revisited

While on a relaxing walking tour of London's historic Docklands and Canary Wharf, Jacqueline slipped on the steps of a wine shop, twisting her ankle. A man walking behind caught her fall. As she looked up, she realized that she was in the arms of Mark Steinberg, her old lover. However, after she discovered he was the one who held Rose's tapes, and then him appearing next to her on the plane to Costa Rica, Jacqueline was certainly not happy to see him in London, especially considering what she was conspiring to do.

Mark seemed as surprised as Jacqueline. He loudly said, "Jacqueline, I can't believe it! It's you!" There was no use denying who she was this time. She was just glad that she was alone. "Mark, it's so nice to see you. How are you?" "Wonderful, Jacqueline! I looked all over Costa Rica trying to find you." "Oh, I was just there for few days on business, and I ended up staying with friends in the countryside. My God, Mark, what are you doing in London?" Jacqueline was more than a little curious about the reason for Mark being in England. He told her, "I came to London on business, and then I'm vacationing for a few days."

Mark seemed far less inquisitive than he was the last time, when they met on the plane to Costa Rica. They chatted for a few minutes. He was tentative, almost shy this time, as he asked if he could buy her dinner and a drink to ease the ankle pain from her fall. Jacqueline could not believe that the man who just happened to be there to catch her fall on the step was Rose's old friend and her old lover.

Now Mark was in London, and that was just too much coincidence for her. She decided very quickly to accept his invitation. She needed to know if this was really just a chance meeting, or if he was involved with the CIA or some other organization. Something like this was the very reason she had returned to England. If anyone was looking for her, she wanted to face them in London. Her entire life in London was under her forged passport in the name of Leslie Carter, but Mark knew her real name. That made him a danger to Jacqueline and everything she was working to accomplish.

Wanting to whisk him away before they ran into someone in London who knew Jacqueline as Leslie Carter, she quickly agreed to dinner. After asking him if he liked French food, she suggested they take the Barbican Tube to Le Café du Marche. She told him, "Someone said it has good French food, and it's a very short walk from the tube station," as she pointed to her foot. At least that would get them out of Thames Hamlet where someone might see them and call her Leslie. Mark seemed thrilled that Jacqueline accepted his dinner invitation.

They hurried to catch the tube and there was little time for conversation. That gave Jacqueline a few minutes to think of what she was going to tell Mark. She knew she was not going to tell him that she lived in London. As they sat down, breathless from the quick dash to make the tube, Mark's questions began.

"How is your ankle feeling?" Jacqueline chuckled. "Pretty good, I guess – I just ran for the tube on it!" She knew the questions she dreaded were coming sooner or later. "So, Jacqueline, do you live in London?" "Oh no, Mark. I'm just visiting, too." "Oh, how long are you here?" Jacqueline said, "Just two more days – it has been a wonderful trip."

She did not like lying to Mark, but she liked the coincidence of him showing up in London even less. "What about you, Mark?" "I'm just vacationing for a few days after being here on business." This was worrisome to Jacqueline, although she did not let it show. "Aren't you still a lawyer in New York? What kind of business brings you to England?" "Our law firm is merging with an international firm. Rose and I both studied international law, you know."

Jacqueline wondered what the answer to her next question would be. "Exactly what kind of law do you practice?" "I'm a commercial transactions lawyer in the Wall Street financial district." Well, that was not what she expected to hear. "We are merging with Dewey, Cheatham and Howe, a well-known firm in London. How about you, Jacqueline, what do you do?" Jacqueline decided that a truthful answer would be good for her soul, even if it wasn't completely true. "I work in the diamond market."

As the tube train neared the stop, there was a man asking for directions. Thankfully, that interrupted their conversation. They both assured the man that they were not local and could not help him. Then the door to the tube train opened, and after asking directions themselves, they headed quickly down the damp street to Le Café du Marche. The host seated them next to a window when Mark told the maitre d', "The Dewey, Cheatham and Howe law firm recommended we try this restaurant." Jacqueline was surprised as Mark told her, "Some of my business associates told me to say that whenever I want a good table in London. It has worked every time."

Jacqueline laughed as Mark ordered a bottle of wine, and they began to review the menu. The French food looked wonderful, as the waiters served the tables around them. The waiter took their orders and then Mark's questions began again. "So, you work in the diamond market?" Jacqueline had resigned herself to lying to Mark. "Yes, in the States. I'm just here on a vacation, and it's over way too soon." Just then, the waiter brought the pâté and touched up their wine glasses.

As he took a sip of his wine, Mark said, "It is unbelievable running into to you here in London, of all places. I am completely shocked, Jacqueline! I really did look all over Costa Rica for you. However, there was no Jacqueline Rosenberg registered at the hotel in Costa Rica." She really did not want to talk about Costa Rica, but maybe it was better than discussing her being in London. "I was registered under a corporate account."

As he took another sip, Mark nodded. "I considered that possibility, but I knew the hotel would provide no assistance. Most of the details of my days in San Francisco are a blur, but I remembered your maiden name. However, that was of no help. I remember so much about our San Francisco days. It seems like yesterday.

"I was so nervous on the plane to Costa Rica. I must have sounded like a schmuck. I had convinced myself when you refused to see me after the opium den that you hated me. Then I saw you again in my office. When you pretended not to know me, I was devastated. However, I felt that you might have been embarrassed by our youthful activity and did not want anything to do with me.

"Seeing you sitting across from me in my office stirred up all those old feelings again. Then I saw you on the plane, and I was determined to get some time to ask for forgiveness. Then when I could not find you in Costa Rica, I was sure that you really did hate me, but you were just too nice to say it on the plane. I could not find any information about you at the hotel.

"I was sure that I would never see you again after Costa Rica, but you lingered on my mind. All I had was this picture of you in my mind and then you seemed gone forever. Your slip on that step today was a blessing for me. God, I just cannot believe it is you! I had begun to think that I had gone crazy and just made you up in my mind." Jacqueline was beginning to relax, but not too much. "So it seems you have done well, becoming a named partner in New York and heading up an international firm merger as well. That's all very impressive."

"Well, sometimes it is a good thing and sometimes it's a bad one. I have been very successful. What I mean about sometimes being bad – being a named partner, I have no time for anything but work. That is why I pushed for this merger; I'm over the practice of law. I want completely out. That is still true, even though in the last few years, I have begun taking more time for myself. But I have had no luck with women. I suppose that is because I lost the only woman who ever really interested me three times – in San Francisco, New York and Costa Rica." Jacqueline smiled.

Mark continued, "I stopped playing with drugs after I took you to that opium den in San Francisco. I fell in love with you in San Francisco, and I was devastated when you wouldn't see me after that night in the den. I knew that you hated me, and I knew that you had every right to despise me. You taught me a great lesson, Jacqueline – a lesson about myself. It made me examine where my life was going and how I was treating other people. I grew up the day you refused to see me again. I focused on my career and becoming a better person."

"I never hated you, Mark. I had a great time in the opium den. I'm glad that we experienced it together. However, I simply could not get involved with the drug culture in San Francisco. I had too much to risk with Marie being ill." "How is your daughter, Jacqueline?" "She is well, and college educated." Mark smiled. "That is so good to hear. Where does she live?" Jacqueline did not want to answer this question truthfully. "She lives in Venice, Italy." Jacqueline figured that would be far enough from Paris to protect Marie.

Then she remembered her training, and began storing the lies that she was telling Mark in a separate part of her brain for instant recall. She pictured a drawer in her mind, and she began putting the untruths she was telling Mark in the drawer so she could open it up when she needed to keep track of her cover story.

Jacqueline knew she needed to find out more about Mark. "Mark, would you excuse me for a minute?" Mark rose, as she got up from the table and walked to the women's room. She quickly dialed Marie and asked her to check Mark out. Jacqueline gave her Mark's full name, the name of his firm, the firm he claimed to be with in London, and she told Marie that he had graduated Columbia Law School with Rose.

She also told Marie that he had lived in New York and San Francisco in the late sixties and seventies, that he had practiced in New York for a long time, that he was a senior partner in his New York firm, and that he was in Costa Rica at the same time as Jacqueline. "Well, Mom, it will be a few hours. As soon as I can, I'll call you back. I'm still in Paris, so I can't use the other computer system to check." Jacqueline said, "I understand your search will be limited, but just check what you can on your own. It's not that important." Marie chuckled and said, "I can find out plenty without using the mainframe. It will just take a little more time"

Walking back to the table, Jacqueline hoped that Mark would come up clean. However, to be honest, what were the chances? She did not have that kind of luck with men. She knew that she could not get a full background check on him. For that kind of information, she would have to contact Meier Finch or let Marie access the CIA computers. If Jacqueline did contact Meier and Mark was an innocent man, Meier would likely figure out that Mark was the one who had held Rose's evidence. Meier Finch was a strange man.

Meier had never questioned Jacqueline about what had happened in Costa Rica, although he did once say, "It was too bad to hear about Günter's death, but it had to be." Jacqueline gave no response to his remark. He also told her to make sure that whatever she was doing, no recording or publicity came out with her voice or picture, since Jacqueline Rosenberg and Michelle Lerner were both dead.

All things considered, Meier had been a good friend to Jacqueline. At least he kept his part of the bargain. Nevertheless, Rose's words on the tape played in her mind; "Trust no one completely." Now, she would just have to wait and see what information Marie could find about Mark. One thing Jacqueline could rely on was that Marie would be thorough.

Even if Mark did check out, she knew at best that all she could have would be a fling. Jacqueline could not risk telling him more about her or the recordings that he had held for so long. So, unfortunately, no more of a relationship was possible with Mark. She knew that she would have to lie about everything, or he would be able to track her down later if he wanted. As she approached the table, Mark rose from his chair and said, "Jacqueline, you are as beautiful as you were in your teens."

Jacqueline laughed as he held her chair for her. "Thank you Mark – you are very kind, but you must need new glasses!" She sat back down to the table and they talked as the hours passed. Jacqueline only drank a little wine, so she could keep her senses while she waited for Marie's call. Nevertheless, she truly enjoyed the evening and conversation with Mark.

Just as they were finishing their wine, her cell phone rang. She excused herself from the table and walked to the lobby of the restaurant. It was Marie, and she told Jacqueline, "Mom, Mark appears to be clean. He's a successful lawyer. He is one of the Fortune 500 names! Everything you said about him checks out." Jacqueline felt relieved, but on the other hand, this information created a new set of problems. "Thank you, dear. I just wanted to make sure he was not Jack the Ripper." "Mom, I know what you were looking for, but he appears to have no connection with Rose after law school. Still, be careful, because with this guy's money, he is probably a real Romeo. I'm flying to LA tomorrow. Love you, bye." Jacqueline, still chuckling, walked back to the table.

They left the restaurant arm–in–arm on a slow walk through the damp streets of London. Mark's beautiful eyes and striking thin physique aroused Jacqueline just as they had so many years ago. Since she saw Mark in New York, he had lost a great deal of weight and looked wonderful. His wit was charming. He made her laugh all though dinner with his wonderful sense of humor. Before she knew it, she was in his arms on the bridge near the Grosvenor Hotel where he was staying. Mark's kiss was deep and hot. Jacqueline knew she wanted him, if only for a night. Therefore, she decided to throw caution to the wind. Besides, she could look around his hotel room, on the slight chance that he was not what he seemed to be.

They made their way to his hotel room, and within minutes, they were on the carpet making wild passionate love. Their bodies were seeking pleasure from each other, from one end of the floor to the other. After six or seven hours of sweating, with rug burns from the carpet, they were exhausted, resting on the floor with their heads lying back against the sofa. "Jacqueline, I wanted our first time together again to be one of flowers and romance. But once I was near you, my passion was too much for me."

As the morning broke, they watched the sun come up from the balcony. "Jacqueline, I cannot believe I found you again. Making love to you was more than I dreamed. This was unlike that crazy party in San Francisco. I have regretted all my life walking you into that den. You were so young, and you never expected that opium. I'm truly sorry."

Mark gushed, "I can't wait to return to the States with you. I told my friends in New York about you after Costa Rica, and they were sure that I had gone crazy over a woman I barely knew. My law partners thought that I had taken the grand dive from stress, from the way I talked about you. I never expected to find you in London."

"Mark, I will not be going back to the States for a while. This will be all of the time we have together. I need to leave tomorrow, but I can't tell you where I'm going or make any promise that we will see each other again." Mark was stunned at what he had just heard. "You are married, aren't you Jacqueline?" "No Mark, I'm not married and there is no other man in my life. But my life is extremely complicated. I can't discuss it with you. I just can't!"

"This is crazy, Jacqueline! I lost you in San Francisco because of my own stupidity. When you came to see me in New York, you pretended not to recognize me. In Costa Rica, you slipped through my hands before I could get close to you. Now, after I have fallen head over heels for you again, and I believe you care for me, you are telling me I will never see you again! Jacqueline, I'm retiring, and I can go anywhere with you. This merger is my last official transaction for my firm. Once I've finished this task, I'm free from the practice of law. Just tell me where, and we'll go.

"We can live well – I have plenty of money. I just do not want to lose you again. I don't care about your past; I just want to love you!" "Mark, it is just not that simple. I have to leave and I can't tell you why I'm leaving or where I'm going. You must return to your life – please do not talk about me or use your legal skills to search for me. It could cause me great harm."

"Jacqueline, are you in danger? If you are, I can protect you. It's those damn boxes of Rose's! I'm so in love with you." He held her in his arms tightly.

371

Jacqueline knew the moment she heard his words that she was falling in love with him as well. She felt that deep burning feeling inside.

"Mark, I can't stop to love you. I know that it is possible that I could be yours later, but you must ask no questions. Take the time while I'm gone to think about living outside of America with me." "Jacqueline, I've made plans to retire to the Cayman Islands. Go with me!" "Mark, when are you planning on retiring to the Caymans?" "In November, Jacqueline. I already bought a home there. Please come with me. Marry me."

"Mark, you know nothing about me!" "I don't care, Jacqueline. As crazy, as it seems, I started falling in love with you again while I watched you sleep on that plane to Costa Rica. Then I lost you before I really knew the woman you had become. I have carried that torch since Costa Rica. I now realize that I have carried it since San Francisco. I knew nothing about you, so I could not locate you after Costa Rica. Besides, I was ethically bound by Rose's instructions not to make contact with you. Even if Rose and I had not had an attorney-client relationship, there was something about the way he said it…. I would not even tell my partners your name. I don't want to lose you again.

"Something happened when I sat down next to you on the plane – I knew then that you were my destiny. It was as if a bolt of lightning hit me. All I could think was, 'I love this woman.' Then when I could not find you in Costa Rica, I nearly lost my mind. I returned home to find a bolt of lightning had hit a tree in my yard while I was on the plane with you. I knew then you were the woman I needed and you were gone forever. Now I've found you, held you, loved you, and you are telling me you must go away!"

"Mark, please, you must understand, as you have no other choice. I have to go; I have no choice either. It can be with the hope of being together later, or we can say goodbye now. The choice is yours. I have some very important unfinished work that I must do before I can do anything else. Give me the address in the Caymans, and go forward with your plans. I will come to you in late fall in the Caymans. Then we can see how we feel. But you must not stir any questions up about me in America. Tell no one you found me in London. Trust me when I say this. Even mentioning my name could cause damage. Promise me."

Mark took Jacqueline's arm as they walked to the balcony. His kiss was deep, as his tears moistened her face. "Promise me you will come in the fall. As a lawyer, I have always controlled my life, and I have never been happier than tonight in your arms. Now I have no control. If I have no other choice, I will take you like this. I promise that I will not tell anyone I found you. I don't care what you must do, just come to me in the Islands. Promise me that, Jacqueline."

She hated to do this to him, but she had no other option. "I promise I'll come before the end of December." Mark's eyes were still pleading. "I'll be there from November, waiting for you." They walked to the undisturbed bed, and as they sat on the edge,

Jacqueline pulled Mark to her body. His body was so hard and hot as he entered her. She felt his power inside her body as he slid deeper. Jacqueline was wet with orgasms; Mark's lips were warm and wet as he kissed her, and his hands radiated pure heat on her breasts.

Repeatedly they made love, knowing it would be a long time before they would be in each other's arms again. The emotions were just increasing with every new experience they sought, each orgasm taking them to a higher level. Jacqueline was falling deeply in love, and Mark was beyond the point of no return in his love for her.

Just as she came in another earth-shattering orgasm, he whispered into Jacqueline's ear, "Will you marry me?" Without hesitation she said, "I will come to you in December to hear those words again." As morning became night and night became morning, the time for Jacqueline to leave had come. Mark's eyes filled with tears as he promised not to look for her, and to wait for her to come to him in the Islands.

Jacqueline took the tube home. Tears filled her eyes. She was beginning to love again. Nevertheless, she knew that she needed to complete the work to stop the computer interception of America before she could surrender to love. If Mark still wanted her when she arrived months from now, how could she tell him all of the secrets in the box that he had held? Was he a trap...?

Marie had looked into Mark's past and did not see any involvement with Rose or his work with the CIA. It made sense that he was not involved, because he had held the recordings and evidence for years and never opened the packages. If Mark were CIA, Meier would never have agreed to help her; he would have killed her instead, because he would already have had Rose's evidence. That was right, wasn't it? Lord, Jacqueline really was in love! The emotions were all too much for her, as she took the elevator to her flat.

Noticing the flashing light on her answering machine, she turned the recorder on. She heard Meier's voice and was startled. Her mind was in love, and the past was on the recorder. "Jacqueline, our relationship needs to be finalized. I am ill, and time is growing short. I am becoming too feeble to continue our relationship. Please call me Tuesday at 11AM, your time, to discuss the final distribution." Jacqueline knew she had to make some decisions before she called Meier back.

Jacqueline walked to the bar and poured a Grand Marnier as she headed out to the veranda, just to sit and think. She knew that her work would be finished in the United States in November. After they launched the code, she and Marie would leave America immediately. She just could not think about Mark, or if it was safe to love him. This was a decision she could make later. Jacqueline had some important work to do, and she would have plenty of time to think about Mark after the work was complete.

Tuesday, as instructed, she made the call to Meier. He answered immediately, as usual, "Yes." Jacqueline said, "It's me. I'm so sorry to hear about your health." "Thank you. I need to make a final payment to you, anywhere you want in the world, from the bonds. I will also send three extra sets of passports and other documents for both you and Marie. Where would you like them delivered?" Meier was all business as usual, but his voice was weak.

Jacqueline thought for a moment then said, "Please put the bond money in the Cayman Islands, and deliver the documents to me here in London. Put the money in an account using the name on one of the passports and send the account information with the passports." Meier acknowledged her request, told her the bank he would use, and then said, "Jacqueline, I will not ask you to return the recordings and other evidence. I am far too old and sick to care anymore. Keep them – they will protect you, as you are aware. It has been a pleasure knowing you, Jacqueline. Shalom." Jacqueline found her voice, for she realized she was crying. "Meier, thank you for everything you have done for me. Shalom." Then the telephone line went dead.

Jacqueline hung up the telephone, and wondered what Meier would think if he knew what she was about to do. She could never tell him, but she thought that he would understand why she was doing it. The passports and the account information arrived the next afternoon. Jacqueline boarded a plane at Heathrow for Los Angeles the following day. She called Marie from the airplane, asking Marie to meet the plane.

Jacqueline became nervous in the final week before the launch, with election night only a few weeks away. She asked Marie to move any remaining sensitive documents or equipment she had into C Street

Underground. Of course, Marie had thought ahead and had already swept her home of evidence. There was not a trace of anything involving the code or of Rose left at Marie's home in California. The timing was perfect for Marie to clean out the house, because the closing for the sale of her property was in a week. Everything was already at C Street Underground. She had also been careful to erase her footsteps. Since Jacqueline Rosenberg no longer existed, only Leslie Carter, she felt that they were reasonably safe.

All they wanted to achieve with the code was a fair presidential election, no matter what the results. That was something America had not seen in years. Late one afternoon, Marie left her home in Los Angeles for the last time. She drove north before circling back east to Palm Springs, and then met Jacqueline, who was waiting in C Street Underground. Everything was set to go. However, Jacqueline knew that they could not risk testing the code before they used it. They would have only one opportunity.

She was not sure how Marie had written the final code, but Jacqueline knew what it was to accomplish. She wanted to know more about how it would work, but Marie said, "Just a minute Mom, and I'll explain it." Dietmar started to walk away, but Marie said, "Hang on a sec, Dietmar – you worked on this just as hard as I did, so stick around for the fun!" Marie typed in an order that would activate the code she had written.

Within seconds, the screen lit up red, white and blue, flashing the letters "DLC," which Marie said stood for

"Democracy Launch Complete." Marie giggled and Dietmar smiled as the computers turned themselves off. "You know me Mom; I had to have a little fun at the end!" They waited a few minutes and then rebooted the system of C Street Underground. While they were waiting, Jacqueline asked, "What will the code do, Marie?"

"Actually, we have already done most of it already. Everything is already loaded onto the Pentagon computers. Rose left many possible routes of entry in their system, so I decided to use two different attacks; a time bomb and a Trojan horse. There is a direct attack with a time bomb, and a denial of service attack through the internet with the Trojan. Let me tell you about the time bomb first. As you already know, this computer can directly access the CIA's servers, and access other government computers from there. Well, it actually can directly connect to any U.S. Government computer system without being detected. B6's CLIPP code is actually launched from the Pentagon's servers.

"The secret to the C Street Underground computers is that the computers here are the government's own computer system, programmed at their very core not to tell the rest of the system that they even exist. These servers have access to every government computer, yet no one outside can even tell. There is one big difference. The systems that the government works with are so outdated, it's petrifying. C Street Underground's computers are beyond cutting edge; they are future computers that the government does not even know anyone is capable of having. These computers are far more advanced than anything available, even in the private sector."

Dietmar said, "Excuse me, but there is one thing I must still do," and left the area. Jacqueline looked puzzled, but Marie nodded to Dietmar, and told Jacqueline, "I'll explain in a couple of minutes."

Marie continued, "C Street Underground works sort of like a mother computer system to the government system, telling the child what it can see and cannot see. Rose and Dietmar have built the most amazing system that I have ever seen. It actually tricks the government computers. At first, I even had some trouble figuring out how it all worked. My background in finite mathematics, finite-set theory and combinatorics also served me well. Knowing some formal logic and Boolean algebra was helpful to me in understanding what was really available here, and of course, so was Dietmar! He helped Rose design the whole thing, and Dietmar has continuously updated and upgraded it ever since this system went online.

"Once we entered the Pentagon system, I realized that Rose and Dietmar had established a gateway for me to gain free access to the CLIPP code. Dietmar smiled like a Cheshire cat when he showed me! I could have destroyed B6's code the moment I entered. However, if I did that, the American people would never know a plot was thwarted, so I figured out another way to do it. I know you wanted a signal to the world that something happened. If I just destroy CLIPP now, C Street and the CIA would just create another, more advanced code for the next election, and they might even be able to have it ready for this one. So I created the time bomb instead. The time bomb will activate as soon as CLIPP is started, and it will destroy the code. Until B6's code starts, the time bomb will be idle and untraceable, because it's within the core of the operating system. It's only when their code starts that the time bomb does its thing. When it was used previously, CLIPP became active on election eve, so that's why I'm calling it a time bomb. Even if the CIA doesn't use CLIPP during this election, my code will wipe out their program on November eighth.

"The second method is a Trojan. The Trojan attack will do two things. It is a denial-of-service attack on the Pentagon's DNS path. Over the next few weeks, it will burrow into the government system, waiting for election night. On Election Day, the Trojan will overload the system with repetitive requests, slowing traffic and keeping their code from launching due to the traffic jam in the system. The system should crash within minutes, before B6's code can work. Once the system crashes, part of the Trojan will not allow a reboot for twenty-four hours. The military computers that will work throughout all of this will be the emergency system at Cheyenne Mountain, for military communication and defense.

"Our Trojan will deny the Pentagon computers' access to communication links to everything, including the state voting computers. That will happen as soon as the CLIPP code is activated to intercept the votes. If CLIPP isn't activated, the first incoming votes to the federal computers will trigger the Trojan. That means the federal computers will be unable to send or receive any information because of the traffic we generated. That should crash the system, but just in case, I wrote a piece of the Trojan that will order a shutdown.

"Then, for twenty-four hours, the Pentagon's computers will shut down, because the Trojan will instruct them to do that, even if they don't crash from the overload. At the same time, the state computers will still be transmitting the actual votes. The states will furnish interim results based on percentages of precincts reporting directly to the news media, as the election proceeds. The difference is that the final tabulations of each state's votes will not be conducted by federal computers, but by computers in the respective states. Those results will then be reported to and by the media, instead of the federal numbers.

"The entire time the federal computers are down, the states will be filling the news media with legitimate election results, including final results. The Pentagon computers will be out of the loop. The upshot is that there will be no opportunity for CLIPP to manipulate the numbers before the public becomes aware of the results.

"On reboot of the Pentagon computers, the Trojan will permanently destroy the CLIPP code the CIA wrote to interfere with the incoming popular and electoral votes, the e-mails, all log information, and every other trace of evidence, and then it will destroy itself. It is redundant with the time bomb to the extent that it destroys CLIPP, but I thought that it was a good idea to write that piece into the Trojan, just to be sure that CLIPP doesn't survive.

"The reason that the Trojan is the back-up is that it requires some action from someone else besides me. The Trojan starts by sending e-mails that give pay-grade step raises to some low level employees at the Pentagon. E-mails from OMB to those employees are being sent now. The e-mails say the raises have an effective date of January first. To find out the particulars, the addressee will have to open an attachment to the e-mail. I knew that sort of news would get people's attention, and that anyone who got one wouldn't question the e-mail. Everyone in the government is looking to move up a pay grade. Out of sheer excitement, they will open the attachment and for a little while be very happy, believing they have received a pay raise. When even one of the e-mails is opened, the Trojan is released."

Jacqueline asked, "What about the traceability of the Trojan, Marie?" "Even attempting to track my hacking would call for a combination of research skills, subpoenas, court orders, search warrants, electronic surveillance, and traditional investigative techniques. Once the Pentagon computers shut down, the re-boot destroys the Trojan I sent, the e-mails, their election code, and wipes our log entry.

"Other than that, it will cause no damage. So anyone investigating should just be running in circles, with all roads leading back to the Pentagon computers. There will be years of investigations, but no results. I started with a spoofed IP address, and then I bounced the Trojan e-mails off of five countries and over twenty-five proxy servers, including government computers of some foreign countries. Some of the countries, like China, won't even cooperate with any internet investigations, including one into this Trojan.

"In today's world, a technically savvy thief can steal more with a computer than with a gun. You know that I made a decision never to become a hacker. I've been capable of hacking for many years, but I stuck to my guns until now. Computers control everything: our power delivery, missiles, communications, aviation, military, basic needs, food supply, air traffic, financial services, and more. They store vital information, from medical records and business plans to voting records. Computers are vulnerable to many things, including our deliberate attack. I've heard that tomorrow's terrorist will be able to do more damage with a keyboard than with a bomb.

"So that's how my codes work. Within a minute, our C Street computer will restart, and there will be no trace of either code left here. While we've been talking, Dietmar dropped the portable equipment I used to write the Trojan into Fermi liquid.

We can thank God that the last presidents did not believe in updated technology. Had we had a modern president who understood the value of technology, this could have been a whole lot harder!"

"It will be weeks before we see the results. What we will be looking for on the next election eve are reports that the CIA, the FBI, and the Pentagon are experiencing computer problems that last for only twenty-four hours. I threw in the FBI because the CIA lies about everything, and the Pentagon would be reluctant to disclose problems to avoid making the U.S. look vulnerable to attack. But the FBI system is accessed by all sorts of outsiders, including the courts and other law enforcement agencies. There's no way that shut-downs of all three systems can go unnoticed by the press! We're doing nothing to change the vote of the American people. We're simply stopping anyone else from changing their vote. I did just what you wanted."

Dietmar walked back just as Marie finished. The three sat together as they sipped their drinks, delivered by Dietmar's robot CS2, knowing that they would not know the results for a while. Marie laid her hand on Dietmar's arm and said, "Dietmar, your help has been indispensable in this project." He smiled broadly. "Thank you. I often wondered what the real purpose was for this facility. I am proud to be a part of correcting this injustice. I came to America from Germany as a small boy, during the reign of horror. I understand what damage ultimate power can do. I will remain here at the facility if either of you need me. Please return, even just to visit."

Jacqueline asked him, "Dietmar, are you sure you don't need help down here? Isn't there someone we could bring to you, even if only for help and companionship?" He shook his head, and told her, "No, no, it is too risky, and besides, I have so much work to do. Instead, I will look forward to your return. This equipment around us is my family. It has been that way for many years – and now I have the two of you as my family, too." Jacqueline told him, "We will be back to visit. Besides, there is more to do, if this project succeeds." Marie, feigning outrage, said, "Mom! Ye of little faith, you'll see when it succeeds!" Jacqueline grinned at her, and they all laughed heartily.

Jacqueline reminded her daughter, "Marie, when the code launches on election night, we cannot contact each other. We will talk about it in person when we see each other when we meet on November twentieth." Jacqueline turned to Dietmar. "Dietmar, if you need us, you can locate us. We will be returning to Europe in a week. Marie and I each have some loose ends to tie up." Dietmar smiled, but shook his head. "I will never attempt to locate you. Rose made it very clear. Once you leave the facility, I must not contact you. So, if you receive any messages, they are not from me! I am completely self-contained. However, I will look forward to your return." Jacqueline hugged him, and said, "Thank you so much."

She had no doubt that the code would work. She also believed that it would be completely untraceable, since they had launched so far in advance. When the time came, the very computers that the CIA programmed against democracy would do the work to prevent the computer hijacking of America.

Marie and Jacqueline had planned to settle on the island of St. Kitts. Jacqueline had not told Marie about Mark, or even decided what to do about him. She planned to hire a security team once they settled down. Some members of B6 were still alive; for Jacqueline that meant someone could torture and kill them, first Marie, and then Jacqueline. Her training told her that would be the best way to attempt to gain the information she had and eliminate the problem once they had what they wanted. So, security would be a must. She also planned to have weapons flown from C Street to St. Kitts, to build an arsenal in the new residence. She and Marie had been staying in different locations for that reason. However, they hated being apart so much. Jacqueline could see that her feelings for Mark could pose a problem for the plans of mother and daughter to settle down together.

Sid shook her head. "Goodness! I always knew that Marie was a smart one! Oh, my, it's almost eleven o'clock at night! We've been at it for almost a full day, Jacqueline." Jacqueline said, "Sid, I know that you're exhausted, but we need to keep going if you can manage to last a few more hours. I have to leave early tomorrow morning, so we need to finish by then." Sid was wincing as she tried to work the cramps out of her hand. "Of course I can! Let's forge ahead. I'm convinced that coffee is the cure for everything. Would you like more?"

As Sid brought more coffee for them, she said, "I'm jealous! You fall down and get a man – when I fall down, I get a broken arm! You have any tips on how I can meet such interesting men? Granted, they all end up trying to kill you, but…." Jacqueline laughed out loud. "Sid, even though I meet interesting men, I have trouble holding onto a good one." Sid looked curious and said, "What about Mark? What's the story with him?"

Jacqueline, leaning back in her chair once again, told her old friend, "There's more about Mark, but first I need to tell you some more about London and what led up to my trip to the Caribbean…."

C Street

Chapter Seventeen
Cayman Journey

It was time for Jacqueline and Marie to leave C Street Underground behind. They headed for LAX in separate rental cars, with only one more thing to do. As a precaution, Dietmar had created two scanning devices that erased the GPS memory chips in the rental cars. Stopping for lunch just outside LAX, Marie scanned the GPS systems until they no longer registered any information about where the cars had been. Since Dietmar made the scanners to look like cell phones, even in an x-ray, transporting the devices on the plane would be simple.

Jacqueline and Marie sat at the bar relaxing before their flights. It was the first time Jacqueline really had a chance to tell Marie about Mark. Of course, Marie's reaction was "Bring him to Kitts." However, when Jacqueline explained he owned a house on an island in the Caymans, Marie replied, "Bring him to St. Kitts, and we will get to know each other. Then maybe I could build another home on the island where he lives, if we can buy some land."

Jacqueline kissed Marie good-bye at the airport with the caveat, "Remember, if anyone contacts you, tell them I'm dead and let me know immediately. I will see you at the Plantation Hotel on St. Kitts. I love you." Marie, now curious about Jacqueline's lawyer conquest, said, "Don't forget to bring Mark!" Jacqueline, laughing, told her, "I'm thinking about bringing him."

Jacqueline watched Marie board the plane for Paris. In a few minutes, Jacqueline would be boarding her flight for London. She believed that they had at least provided America with a legitimate election this time. After that, America was on its own. Jacqueline had given enough of herself to her country.

Jacqueline had finally told Marie about her happenstance meeting with Mark in London, and that Mark was waiting for Jacqueline in the islands. Jacqueline had not made her mind up whether she would see Mark when she went to the Cayman Islands. One thing was sure – she would go to the Caymans to pick up the money Meier had deposited in the bank. She wanted some time to pass before she went there, just to let things cool down. She did not need the money right now, and she had no idea if Meier had given her one last monthly payment or if he had been more generous.

Jacqueline spent the balance of her cooling-off period enjoying London. She wanted to move to a tropical climate before the winter, so she wanted to make sure to visit as many sites in London as possible. Once Jacqueline left London again, she did not expect to return. Her lease was just about up, so she planned to close down the apartment. Jacqueline had rented a furnished flat, so moving should be an easy job. She was going to have to decide about trusting Mark, and she needed a little time to make that decision.

Jacqueline purchased a London Rail Pass, which admitted her to most London attractions for a single payment; it also included her travel by public transport via the London buses, tubes and trains. London has one of the best and most extensive underground/subway systems in the world. Jacqueline was determined to get a final look around London and take her mind off Mark. She wanted to see all the stations like Victoria, King's Cross, Waterloo, and Liverpool Street. She could enjoy the museums and architecture while she thought about what to do next.

Her first stop was at Trafalgar Square, built in the early 1800's. The center of the square was in honor of Admiral Horatio Nelson, who destroyed French naval power in battle and secured Britain from invasion. An eighteen-foot statue of Nelson was the centerpiece to the Square. At the base of the column are the massive Landseer Lions.

The National Gallery and the National Portrait Gallery bordered one side of the Square, which was a wonderful place for Jacqueline to sit and enjoy the atmosphere on warm sunny days. The Square was famous for the large number of pigeons that congregate there; Jacqueline fed popcorn to every one of them. Suddenly, she was overcome with enormous guilt for the original art she had destroyed in Costa Rica. Jacqueline tried to put Costa Rica out of her mind by continuing on her journey of London.

Westminster Abby was her next stop, which she thought was one of the architectural masterpieces of the middle ages, in part because it was a timeline of the medieval period – its construction had gone on for centuries. Westminster Abbey also was a huge repository of British history, as the Confessor's Shrine, the tombs of kings, queens, and countless memorials to the famous were all located there.

It had been the setting for every Queen's or King's coronation since 1066. The church was still dedicated to regular worship services by the people of England. Jacqueline wanted to go to the Abby to seek a peaceful moment. Although more spiritual than religious, she walked slowly up the steps, kneeling at the very top. To her surprise, the building did not explode because of her mere presence!

The immense beauty and peace of the church gave Jacqueline a calm feeling. She could understand why God might stop by this architectural wonder, although she had come to believe that the kingdom of God is in individuals and all they do for this world, not just inside a church.

People passed by her as she knelt. Jacqueline's mind drifted to thoughts of Rose, the man who had taught her this philosophy of life. Jacqueline asked the universe to give her wisdom and forgive her for cutting short the life of Günter Lehmann. It was at that moment she realized that although his was the first life she had taken, it might not be the last. Some of the men of B6 were still out there, and she was sure that they were looking for her.

Her mind returned to thoughts of Rose. She was not angry with him for bringing her into this world. When he signed the CIA agreement after law school, he was young.

Even Rose could not have known how that day would change his life forever. Nor could he have predicted his cancer, his mania, and his psychotic episode at a time when the CIA was breathing down his neck. It was his psychosis that ended their life together, shortly before he died. Suddenly, Jacqueline heard a child cry out and it snapped her out of those deep thoughts.

She turned to see a little girl who had fallen and scraped her knee. Her father was picking her up in his loving arms. As Jacqueline raised her body from the steps, her knees felt pain from supporting her weight on the cement. However, her father was not there to hold her with loving arms. She was alone in this world except for Marie. As she walked slowly down the steps, she found solace in her thoughts of Marie.

Jacqueline went on to visit Parliament, which for over nine hundred years had been a paragon of Gothic architecture and the home of the English government. The Parliament is Britain's symbol of its democratic monarchy, as Congress is for America's representative democracy. The building covered an area of eight acres, consisting of eleven hundred rooms and over four miles of passages. The House of Lords resides in the southern end of the building, while the House of Commons occupies the northern end.

Within the Houses of Parliament, there was Westminster Hall, the Crypt Church, the Members' Lobby and the Peers Library. Outside Parliament, the tower containing Big Ben remains the single most recognizable structure in this wondrous, picturesque, riverside city. As she enjoyed the sights, Jacqueline kept wondering if the English government is as corrupt as the American government. She contemplated whether democracy existed at all, or if the world was only being controlled by the powerful.

Jacqueline had to pay a visit to Buckingham Palace. The Queen receives visiting heads of state at the palace, and it is where she holds garden parties and bestows knighthoods and other honors. Foot Guards from the Household Division, in their red tunics and black bearskins, with expressionless faces guard the palace daily.

The Changing of the Guard ceremony was just beginning as Jacqueline approached the Palace. She watched the military procession as, one by one, each soldier was replaced by another. It was strange to see the guards carrying M-16 machine guns instead of the ornamental rifles of the past. However, with the entire world in fear of terrorism, this was not a surprise to her.

Jacqueline traveled on to the British Museum, where she had so enjoyed her time working in the basement. It was a huge neo-classical building consisting of a series of enormous pillars. Those pillars always captivated her eyes, sending them skyward. In earlier centuries, British aristocrats did many globetrotting expeditions, mostly for public relations. And they returned with priceless treasures from all parts of the world. That resulted in the museum's eclectic collection of Egyptian, Greek, and Roman antiquities. Included in the museum's exhibits are the famous Elgin Marbles, a collection of sculptures, inscriptions and architectural artifacts from the Parthenon and other buildings of the Acropolis.

There were also treasures from China, Japan, India, Mesopotamia, and Britain. Jacqueline thought it was remarkable that so much art came from other lands to England in earlier times. Was it by the larcenous acts of governments? Shouldn't Egypt have ownership of its own treasures?

Jacqueline visited St. Paul's Cathedral, one of the most impressive churches in London. It is an Anglican cathedral. The Anglican Church is the largest Protestant faith in England. The cathedral was designed by Sir Christopher Wren to replace old St Paul's, which burned in the Great Fire of London. Wren's design survived the World War II bombings that destroyed most of the surrounding buildings of the city. It is the fourth or fifth cathedral to stand on the site, and with its three-hundred-and-sixty-five foot high dome, it dominated that part of the city. For over two centuries, it was the tallest building in London.

From inside too, Jacqueline found the dome stunning. It was hand-painted, and she found it well worth climbing up to the Whispering Gallery, named because of the way a whisper will echo, for a closer look at the dome. Jacqueline whispered "Rose," and the word echoed like an old friend calling back. The dome suddenly reminded her of Dome, Inc., the stock she bought after meeting the internet guru Stephen in Ghirardelli Square. She had made $175,000 dollars on that $10,000 investment when she sold her stock. She smiled just thinking about it –

financially, the world had treated her well. She wondered what Meier's final payment had been. That could decide how she would live for the remainder of her life.

She laughed it off; she was not ready to leave London yet, not even to find that out. She doubted that it was enough to change the course of her life. She continued to climb higher, to access the stone galleries on the exterior of the cathedral. At the very top is the Golden Gallery, on which Jacqueline found one of the best views in London. She stood looking over the city, wondering what life would bring next. She knew she was falling in love, but love had nearly cost her life before.

The interior of the cathedral was full of fine statues and detail by renaissance artists. The beautiful woodcarvings and ironwork took her mind off Mark. The glorious Byzantine mosaic work was created by Victorian artisans. Although a piece of history, this cathedral, like many other historical places, was still used by the people. Worship services were held several times a day.

Jacqueline visited Madame Tussauds, one of London's most famous landmarks; it had to be the most unusual voyeuristic pleasure house in the world. But the wax statues at Tussauds reminded Jacqueline of the changing faces of the CIA. There it was again! Her mind was back on Mark and the question of whether she would go to him.

She could not escape her feelings for him. Jacqueline decided to skip the horror section, the Chamber of Horrors. She had enough horror in real life in Costa Rica. Her time was limited, so she moved on from Madame

Tussauds to the galaxy in the Planetarium. At least here, she could look at the stars and remember seeing the Southern Cross for the first time. This was the only true good memory of Costa Rica.

She had been able to sleep in the trains between stops, but she was getting tired. Jacqueline needed a rest, and Somerset House, located between the Strand and the River Thames in central London, seemed perfect. There were always concerts, exhibitions, and theatre, so she could just sit for hours.

On the day Jacqueline went to Somerset House, the play on stage was "Don't Look Back," inspired by the myth of Orpheus and Eurydice. The play told the story of a Greek traveling minstrel, who descended into the dark underground inferno in order to retrieve his deceased wife, the beautiful Eurydice. Beelzebub, the devil, decided that Orpheus's music was so lovely that Beelzebub would grant the return of Orpheus's wife, provided Orpheus did not turn around to look at her beauty until they were back inside their marital home. Orpheus forgot the deal with Beelzebub, and in Orpheus's desire to see his wife's beauty, he looked back to see his wife. When he did, his wife descended back into the underground inferno of Beelzebub. The moral of the story was, "Don't look back."

It was a perfect play for Jacqueline! Seated next to her at the theater was a man about six feet tall, with graying brown hair. During the intermission, he asked Jacqueline if he could buy her a beverage. She declined. When the man returned, he introduced himself as a local accountant named Christian Moorehedge. When the play finished, they walked out together. Christian asked if he could take Jacqueline to dinner.

She declined by stating, "Thank you, but I'm engaged." At that moment, Jacqueline decided not to look back on all that had happened, but to go forward. She would go to Mark. She knew she loved him. Jacqueline needed a little more time, but Mark was the man she wanted. She also knew he was less of a risk than meeting some complete stranger. Mark had held Rose's tapes for years – if he wanted them, they were right there. Mark had to be unconnected to the CIA, and he must be absent of malice.

With a smile at her decision to go to Mark soon, she headed on for a visit to the Tate Modern Museum in the evening. Filled with modern and contemporary art, including works by Bacon, Dali, Picasso, and Warhol, the Tate was a visual feast. It had the magnificent complete collection of Dali's Inferno. The collection was a perfect accompaniment to the play she had just seen. On the seventh floor, there was a café with wonderful views of London, especially the view directly over the river to St Paul's Cathedral, where she had been earlier in the day.

Jacqueline took a table near the window and gazed out as she thought about the implications of admitting her love for Mark. She still could not believe that the man who took her to the opium den was a friend of Rose's. The world was feeling very small.

She also decided to see more of the major museums of London before she went to Mark. Maybe she was not completely sure of her decision, or maybe she did not completely trust him. However, she was excited at the prospect of seeing him. She could find all kinds of reasons to justify going. The money was in the Caymans, it would let her check out Mark more, she was in love. Oh hell, she could have gone on all day with reasons. It was clear – she was going.

She toured the Regents Canal, which stretches from Paddington to the River Thames. The route led her back to her apartment on the Isle of Dogs, near Limehouse. She had to pack a few more things for shipment to storage before she turned over the keys to the flat to the real estate agent.

As she was finishing packing for storage, she saw a small painting she had picked up in London. It reminded her of the art she had destroyed in the hacienda in Costa Rica. How strange – she seemed more disturbed by the destruction of the art than the murder of Günter. Maybe it was because the art truly belonged in a museum and would never be there, but the man in hell was where he belonged.

However, she knew that all of the art hanging on the walls in Costa Rica had gone up in flames. She would have to live with constant reminders, not just that she had murdered a federal agent, but that she had destroyed irreplaceable masterpieces that belonged to all of humanity.

Jacqueline began to wonder. At what point would she become no different from the CIA assassins? Well, at least she saved that irreplaceable Tolstoy book, the one signed by Jack Kennedy! Jacqueline had now occupied herself with sightseeing in London, which to some degree kept her mind off the code launch and what she would do about her feelings for Mark.

As she prepared to sleep, she pondered. Trusting Mark could be a grave error, a deadly mistake. Jacqueline knew that she was a sucker for love and she was falling in love with him. She wanted his touch again! It made sense to her that he was just the lawyer that kept some packages as a favor to an old friend. Nevertheless, she knew there was only one way to find out for sure if his affection for her was genuine, or if he had some government affiliation. She would have to go to him and take a carefully planned risk. Jacqueline knew that if Mark was an honorable man, she could be happy again. But she could be placing him in great danger.

Early the next morning, she finished packing her personal items for storage, and then began packing the things she would need in the Cayman Islands. It was time for the truck to pick up her personal belongings for storage. Then she would turn over the keys to the real estate agent and walk away. Jacqueline knew it was time for her to risk it all on love. Well, maybe not everything; before she could risk too much, she would have to know that he really was an honest man.

She had made a reservation using one of her unused passports, in the name Jessica Hollingsworth, on the 9 AM flight to Paris. She would leave Paris on an evening flight to the Cayman Islands. Meier had used this name on one of the passports and on the bank account in the

Caymans. She would be in Paris for only a few hours, and had only one mission in mind. She would open a bank account to prepare for the transfer of funds from the islands, naming Marie as primary beneficiary on the account and the Hospital of Mercy as the contingent beneficiary. Whatever Meier had chosen to make as a final payment would be all she would ever receive from "The Geneva Trust."

At about ten-thirty, she met Marie at a café on Avenue 26 in Paris for breakfast. "Hello, darling." "Mom, I just arrived!" Jacqueline looked at her daughter, and told her, "I want to speak to you about Meier. He is very ill." Marie had never met Meier, but she knew that her mother had affection for him. "I'm sorry to hear that. Is that why we are meeting?" "Not entirely; he is going to make one final payment to me from 'The Geneva Trust,' and we need to open a bank account in Paris." Marie smiled. "Nice! Do you know how much it is?"

Jacqueline told her, "I have no idea. It may be only one more installment of ten thousand dollars; I'm just not sure." "Then why do you want to open the account in Paris?" "In case he is planning to be more generous, I will need an account to move money into. I could use your help. You know the banks here, and I'll need a transatlantic bank." Marie nodded. "Are you going to need me to stay for a few days in Paris? I'll need to change plans, because I'm scheduled to go to Scotland for a week or so." Jacqueline shook her head, and smilingly said, "No Marie, I can reach you in Scotland, if I really need you."

Before noon, they walked into the CIC Banque Transatlantique at 26 Avenue Franklin D Roosevelt. Jacqueline opened an account with a minimal deposit. She opened it under the name of Jessica Hollingsworth, and used Marie's alternate identity as beneficiary. Telling the manager she would be having funds transferred, she took a card with the account information. They wanted to talk and enjoy lunch at a quiet café, before Jacqueline left for the Caymans. Marie suggested Le Ponthieu, which was less than two blocks from the bank. The food was exquisite, and they ate and chatted until it was time for Jacqueline to leave for Charles de Gaulle airport.

Late in the afternoon, "Jessica Hollingsworth" had settled in on a plane for a long flight to the Cayman Islands and to Mark. Once the plane landed on Grand Cayman, she would go to Barclays Bank in Georgetown, establish herself, and verify the account. Meier did not tell how much money he had placed in the account. Jacqueline did not ask, because she knew, in the end, Meier could do whatever he wanted. She only hoped that he was generous with his final payment and it was not just one more installment. She had gotten the impression that this trust account, "The Geneva Trust", had some serious money in it.

Jacqueline arrived at Owen Roberts Airport on Grand Cayman Island about 1:30 PM the following day, after a layover in Miami. She placed her luggage on hold. Then she went straight to the bank, arriving at about two. Jacqueline walked into the bank manager's office, introduced herself as Jessica Hollingsworth as she presented her passport, and asked for a balance on the account. In a matter of minutes, the manager handed her a sheet of paper with the number $131,127,162.21 USD.

Jacqueline remained perfectly calm as she told the manager that she needed to transfer some funds and add a beneficiary to that account. The manager informed her that Marie Rosenberg was listed as the beneficiary when the account was opened. Thinking quickly, Jacqueline told the manger, "Marie is now married, and I need to change her last name.

Even Meier never suspected her name was anything but Marie Rosenberg, and Jacqueline never gave him a reason to search for her daughter. When Jacqueline arrived in Israel, she gave Meier a phone number to call Marie, just in case anything went wrong. It was a throwaway cell phone Jacqueline had given to her.

Jacqueline wanted the Rosenberg name off that account, and replaced it with DuPont, the name Marie had been using since before college. Over the years, no one had realized that her last name had ever been changed. Every legal document had been altered long ago. That was among the best things Rose ever did, and he did it shortly before he died. He changed Marie's identity completely before she left for college.

Carefully, Jacqueline filled out the transfer slip. She transferred one hundred and twenty-eight million and change to her Paris bank account. The manager told her that the transfer would be completed by the close of business, assuring her that he would handle the transfer personally. Then he thanked Jacqueline for her business and said, "I hope that you will choose to remain our customer." She assured him that she would.

Thanking the manager again for his time, Jacqueline left the bank calmly. But she broke into a big smile about two blocks away. Jacqueline and Marie were definitely retired. Those Israeli Zion Bonds paid off big! Now she had some idea what the recordings and evidence were really worth. Jacqueline also wanted to make one last call to Meier to thank him for everything; however, she thought it best to wait a few days before making any more calls to him.

But she had to talk to someone! She called Marie as soon as she left the bank. Marie answered the telephone on the first ring. "Hello darling, I have some news." Jacqueline hardly noticed that when Marie spoke, she sounded worried. "Mom, are you okay?" Jacqueline chirped, "Yes, I'm fine! I have a surprise for you – he was generous. Marie, can you open a Swiss Bank account online?" Marie told her, "Yes, but it will require faxed signatures. May I ask why?" Jacqueline snickered. "He was very generous. Get the documents ready and fax them for my signature. I will fax them back signed. I want you to open a joint account and let me know when it is established. I want to transfer some money to you." Marie started giggling uncontrollably and said, "I got it Mom! Generous!"

Jacqueline told her, "Send me the fax to sign and open the account. Call my cell when you have an account number. When will you get back to Paris from Scotland?" Marie told her, "In just a week, but then I have to go to

Los Angeles for a few days. I need to give a final report to the company I created the software for in Scotland." Jacqueline thought quickly, "Very good – e-mail your itinerary to me. I will meet you at LAX to say goodbye to the States. But please don't take any more contract work that takes you back to the U.S. after this job. I really want this to be the last time we are in the States."

"Okay, Mom. That's not a problem. There are plenty of contractors in Europe who want me. I'll send all the information on some of them today." Jacqueline was smug. "Very good, send it over, but I don't think you need to take any more contract work." Marie sounded surprised when she responded, "Really! Maybe I should rethink signing a contract for more work, at least until I talk with you in person. I'll send my travel schedule to you, and the account info you need. I'll get an account opened up right now. I love you, bye." Marie opened the Swiss account online, and e-mailed the documents for her mother to fax back to the bank. She knew her mother received money monthly from "The Geneva Trust."

Jacqueline spoke to Marie a number of times every week to find out if she had been contacted by the American or Israeli governments. "Not a word from my big brothers," was usually the report. Jacqueline always laughed when Marie gave her that report. She was also relieved every time she heard those words.

She walked straight to a bookstore and purchased a new copy of *The Stranger,* a nice small paperback, and a perfect place to carry account numbers. Then Jacqueline walked to the nearby Hyatt Regency hotel on Seven Mile

Beach and checked in to an ocean suite. She requested that the concierge pick up her luggage at the airport and gave him the baggage claim tickets.

Jacqueline knew that she was not very far from the island where Mark lived. He had told her his address was 1 Island Drive, Island of Peace, Cayman Islands. She expected that it could not be very far away, but she just wanted a little time to think things over before she let him know that she was in the Caymans. Jacqueline decided to rest and to get some needed sleep in her hotel room. Room service, hot baths and sleep filled the next couple of days for her.

Fully rested, Jacqueline located a map of the Cayman Islands and spent the next day sunning. Her mind was constantly thinking about Mark and making the final decision to see him. She decided to rent one of the hotel's mopeds to see the island. Traveling around Grand Cayman on moped was lovely, and she found a boat whose captain would take her to the Isle of Peace, about five miles off Old Man Bay, whenever she was ready.

She decided on the spur of the moment to take the boat captain up on his offer. She would go to the island and look around, but she still had not decided if she would go to Mark's home. She was still a little uncertain about trusting anyone. The water of the Caribbean was a stunning indigo blue. There was a beautiful light breeze to cool the heat of the sun as the boat headed to the Island of Peace.

The boat slowly pulled up to a dock that had only one large vessel tied up. As Jacqueline stepped onto the dock, she asked the driver, "How large is the island?" He replied, "Big enough for Mr. Mark." Jacqueline saw only one large beautiful house. It was atop a steep slope on a highland, surrounded by tropical trees full of birds, far above the beach. She turned to the boat captain and asked, "Will you wait for me, please?" He shook his head as the boat started to move. "Oh no, Mr. Mark will bring you back." Before Jacqueline could say another word, the engine roared and the boat motored away, leaving Jacqueline stranded on the dock, her decision made for her.

Knowing that she had no choice now, she slowly and quietly began the climb to the house on the highland, hoping all the while that Mark was not just another CIA spy. As she approached the top, she saw smoke behind the house, as if someone had been grilling. Before her eyes stood Mark at the top edge of the slope that led to the house. Jacqueline could not get her head around seeing him again.

He had obviously heard the boat and was coming down to check it out. "He looks handsome," Jacqueline thought. She could see him first, but only for a moment, before she came into his view. His smile enlarged almost in slow motion, as he began walking faster and faster. Then he was running down the slope of the hill as she approached.

Before she knew it, his face became only lips pressed against hers. "I have been waiting so long! But I didn't give up hope." They slowly walked arm-in-arm into the massive beach home. Right away, Mark asked Jacqueline if she would care for a drink. "Yes – the usual, please," she said. "I'm sorry Jacqueline – I know that you drink, and I seem to recall that you drank wine or champagne in London. Is that what you usually drink?"

"Anything will be fine," she said with a smile. Mark gestured and said, "Please let me show you our home, if you will just say yes to my question. I bought this island when I made my first five million at age thirty-two. Back then, I didn't have the money to build, so I waited. Every time I made a large fee, I would build more of the house, knowing I would retire here one day." Jacqueline was still a bit overwhelmed. "I guess I misunderstood you when you first told me about the island – I thought you owned land and a house, not the whole island!" Laughing, Mark said, "Well, it is land and a home! But I do own the entire island."

They walked through the open doors of the house; everything in the main room was open to the Caribbean, with views of surrounding water on all sides. Ceiling fans, mounted on the dark wooden beams twenty feet above, were spinning. Breezes from the ocean came from every direction. Mark told her, "It is a very large house, with seven bedrooms and five bathrooms. Every room is open to the fresh air and has a water view. The rocks that make this home came mostly from this island. There are four floors at different levels; I think the views from every room are captivating, and each is a little different. I do own the entire island, so no one can bother us."

"Mark, I would like to go back to the mainland." Mark seemed distraught. "What! Jacqueline, why do you

suddenly want to leave? I want you to stay." Jacqueline
was firm. "No. I'm not comfortable here, and I just want
to leave now." Mark resignedly agreed. "If you want to
go, I will take you." He reached for a boat key that was
hanging on the hook near the door. "I'm so sorry you do
not want to stay." Jacqueline was still firm in her
demand. "Please take me to the mainland now."

They walked in silence to the boat dock; Mark jumped
aboard the boat and started the engine with tears in his
eyes. Jacqueline told him, "Mark, turn the engine off. I
just wanted to make sure that I was free to come and go."
Mark looked shocked, but at the same time, pleased. "Of
course you are – there is a ship-to-shore radio on the boat,
and the keys hang on that hook all the time. As a matter
of fact, take this key – I have a spare." Jacqueline took
the key in her hand. "We even have cell phone service, or
at least we have it some of the time."

They walked slowly back toward the house. The
smile had returned to Mark's face, although his eyes
looked concerned. "Jacqueline, you scared the hell out of
me! I really thought you didn't want to stay." She smiled
ruefully, and said, "No Mark, I just need to know that I'm
free to go. I've spent most of the last years of my life
afraid, and trust is something I can't give easily." Mark,
still a bit shaken, but hopeful again, said, "Trust me,
Jacqueline, I only want to love you and I will never harm
you. However, please don't give me too many of these
tests. I was devastated."

As they arrived back at the house, Jacqueline felt
more relaxed with Mark, who said, "Now, let me give you

that tour of our home." All the furniture in the house was wood or wicker with beautiful cream-colored linen upholstery. Mark showed her every room in the house. At the end of the tour, Jacqueline and Mark sat together on a high balcony overlooking the water; there was a large statute of Buddha sitting on the wide stone rail.

"Mark, I wasn't really sure about coming to the island, so we need to take this slowly." Mark nodded. "I understand. I'm just glad you came. At least you're willing give us a chance. Where is your luggage?" Jacqueline told him, "I left it at a hotel." Mark started to get up as he said, "Well, we can go get it." She waved the suggestion off and said, "Okay, but later though. Let's just visit for a while."

As Mark was again taking his seat, Jacqueline spoke. "So, tell me Mark, what have you been doing over the last few months?" "After I left you in London, I went back to New York, sold my co-op and my other holdings, tied up the loose ends for my retirement, and came straight here. I wanted to be here in case you arrived early. I arrived on the first of October. It's been a long unsure wait." Jacqueline shook her head. "I'm sorry, but my life is very complicated."

"Jacqueline, please promise me that you are not married or otherwise involved." Jacqueline smiled. "Absolutely, I'm not." Mark was becoming ever more hopeful. "Then it is okay for me to believe we can begin a life together?" "Mark, let's go slowly." Mark was disappointed, but not distraught. "I'm sorry; I'm just hoping that this will be forever."

Mark refilled Jacqueline's champagne glass. "If there is another drink you would prefer, the bar is inside. I also have plenty of champagne." Jacqueline walked slowly to the bar inside the main room, and looked at the small bar filled with liquor bottles as Mark followed. Bourbon, gin, vodka, rum, whiskey, champagne and wine, but there was not a bottle of Grand Marnier to be found. She felt relieved. "I'm enjoying the champagne, so I think I will just stick with that," and then she walked back to the balcony.

"So tell me Jacqueline, what have you been doing? Our parting played repeatedly in my mind, and I realized how mysterious it was. I began to wonder how you managed to convince me not to look for you and just wait for you. I did what you asked, but it was difficult not to be curious. Are you in trouble? I'm a lawyer, not a criminal lawyer, but can I help you?"

"Mark, it is more complicated than you could imagine." Mark had a twinkle in his eye. "Try me, Jacqueline, I have a great imagination." She shook her head. "Not yet Mark, give me some time. Let's just enjoy the evening." He smiled gently. "Okay, but eventually you will need to tell me what in the world is scaring you. I want you forever and that can't be built on secrets."

"Mark, what if at some point, I told you about me, but I felt the need to leave some things out for the sake of both of us? If after hearing part of the story you found some understanding, do you think you might be able to live with not knowing some of the details?" It was clear that Mark was taking the questions seriously. He thought

410

C Street

a moment, then said, "I don't know, but the lawyer in me may need to know. Lawyers, especially in my former area of practice, are detail-oriented. But I would be willing to try."

Jacqueline placed her glass on the table and walked over to Mark. Taking his face in her hands, she kissed his soft beautiful lips. Then she asked, "Do you have a shirt I could wear after a shower?" Mark smiled as he walked Jacqueline into his bedroom overlooking the Caribbean Sea. "All of the showers and baths are outside, and you can pick any one you like. You will find everything you need in the closet." He kissed her deeply. "Please, make yourself at home."

She opened the closet to find a peach negligee and a flowered peach silk robe. It was obvious that they were waiting for her arrival. She took a long hot shower in the open air, less than twenty feet from where Mark sat as he watched her water-soaked movements with great pleasure. He knew she was preparing her body to make love to him. Jacqueline was glad he had no clue what alcoholic beverage she preferred. It made her feel a little safer, and that meant she was at least going to feel his body one more time.

Jacqueline was scared, nearly petrified, but she wanted to give Mark a chance. Maybe he was just a great person and he was not involved with the CIA. It made sense to her; if he were involved, he would have turned the tapes over to the government and never have given them to her. She was sure that he had to be an innocent lawyer who was just keeping some packages for an old

411

friend. But what a coincidence! Jacqueline knew she had to give him a chance; she had decided that she did not want to spend the rest of her life alone.

Mark was sitting in the wicker chair near the rail of the balcony, watching as she stepped out from beneath the shower. "You are beautiful, Jacqueline." She draped only the silk robe around her wet body, as Mark said, "I purchased that in New York for you." "Thank you, Mark. It's lovely."

"Come over here and sit down, Jacqueline. I'm sure the sunset will be even more spectacular than usual tonight, just because you're here. I was thinking while you were in the shower, maybe it would help if I told you about me and what I have been doing all the years we were apart." Jacqueline thought so, too. "That is a wonderful idea."

"Well let's start with where we originally met – in San Francisco. I was just out of Columbia law school and clerking for a judge, because I did not know what I wanted to do with my legal career. Besides, the times were so much fun that none of us took our work seriously. I was getting too involved in the Haight Ashbury drug scene when I met you.

"In our nights walking together on the Fisherman's Wharf, I was beginning to fall in love with you, but I knew nothing at that young age about expressing love. I was not old enough or wise enough to express my feelings well. I thought when I took you to that opium den it would be a great experience for us. Boy, was I young and dumb! That night, I destroyed what we had. When you refused to see me after that night in the drug den, I was devastated; but I also grew up that day.

"Jacqueline, I swore that if I were ever lucky enough to love again, I would not abuse that love. I was never lucky again. I straightened my life out; I walked away from the drug scene and focused entirely on my career. Well, not entirely – you stayed on my mind that entire year. I took responsibility for losing you. I knew that I lost you forever by taking you to that opium den. That first year, I didn't even drink, much less use any drugs. Later on, I smoked a little pot, but I never did any other drugs again.

"In later years, while I was running the offices in Hong Kong, I even lost my taste for pot. When I saw all of the drug-addicted people in Hong Kong, it turned me completely off drugs. Even though I knew pot was not addictive, I just lost interest in it. I also think that, due to the pace of my life, I was never able to find the right person and relax enough to enjoy a pot high. As you know, you need to be pretty relaxed to enjoy the buzz.

"Jacqueline, I come from a very well-off family in San Francisco. After law school, family connections landed me that job as a judicial clerk. My uncle was a judge. It was a wonderful opportunity to learn while I decided what I wanted to do with my life. After you refused to see me, I threw myself into work, and found out that I really enjoyed being a lawyer. My abilities honed, I returned to New York and went to work on Wall Street, thanks to a glowing recommendation from my uncle. For what it's worth, he later told me that his recommendation was sincere, and he really wasn't just trying to get rid of me!" Mark chuckled, and so did Jacqueline.

Mark continued, "I made senior partner after securing a very profitable portfolio for a Hollywood director. Over the years, I became the lead partner, as the older lawyers left. The firm grew to over two hundred lawyers with offices in San Francisco, New York and Hong Kong. I managed the Hong Kong office for fifteen years, while also supervising the other offices. I lived in Hong Kong during that time. I made a lot of money during the years that Hong Kong belonged to Great Britain.

"Before Hong Kong was returned under treaty to China in 1997, I sold everything. I probably would have made a lot more if I had kept my holdings. It turns out that China made Hong Kong an exception – capitalism is still embraced there. But I have always been a very conservative investor, and I preferred to take a smaller profit before China took over, rather than risk a huge loss if China decided not to allow Hong Kong its capitalistic independence. Some years after China took over, I moved back to New York from Hong Kong and made the New York office my base right up to my retirement. I never married and dated very little – my business was my life.

"I was in Hong Kong when my old friend Solomon Rosenberg initially contacted me about holding something for him. I could have never imagined that holding those boxes for Rose would bring you back into my life. I've often wondered if Rose knew about us knowing each other in San Francisco." Jacqueline shook her head. "No, I don't think so. Rose knew all about my life, but I did not even recognize your last name when he told me about the boxes you were holding. On the other hand, he was Rose – and who knows what Rose knew."

Mark continued with the most recent events in his life. "About six months before I ran into you in Costa Rica, I completed the construction of this home. Almost immediately after I ran into you in London, I began my retirement from the practice of law. I was already winding things down when I was in England. My retirement date was November 1, but I tied things up early and came directly here to wait for you.

"I never married, I have no children, and I am financially stable. I inherited money from the Crown side of my family, and besides, I earned a small fortune on my own. I have never been in trouble with the law. I have no other secrets, and, in case I forgot to mention it, I want you forever." Mark grinned and concluded with, "I have never loved anyone else, and I can't believe you've come back and are sitting next to me!"

Mark gently lifted Jacqueline to her feet. "I can live with anything you've done, and give you anything you need and everything you want, if I just know how I can help. If it's money, I have plenty." "No Mark, it is not money. However, I have only about ten thousand dollars in my purse, and I gave the proceeds from the sale of my home to my daughter. So I'm far from rich." She kissed him deeply, knowing that when the time was right she would tell him of her money. They walked slowly into his bedroom, and she sat down on the bed. Mark sat down next to her.

The moon was now full and shone brightly through the open doors and windows. Mark kissed her as he laid her gently back onto the bed. His body touched hers and his lips kissed her throughout the night, in wet and wonderful abandon. They explored each other's body in alternating wild and gentle passion. Jacqueline quietly whispered into Mark's ear, "Ask me again" Mark whispered back, "Will you marry me" "Yes!" as they both exploded in orgasm. Just before falling asleep in each other's arms, Mark reached up and pulled a bell rope. A sheer ivory canopy drifted down and surrounded the bed, isolating them from all of their cares and woes – there were only the two of them in the world.

Early the next afternoon, Jacqueline woke to a breakfast of Eggs Benedict and champagne on the veranda, prepared by Mark. He had catered to her every desire – he even had picked fresh tropical flowers and laid them beside her plate for their breakfast. She knew as she looked at Mark over the table. She was in love with him. Their lovemaking had been so passionate, yet so gentle. They were like old souls, rediscovering each other for the first time.

After breakfast, they laid side by side in the hammock, exhausted, enjoying the incoming sea breeze. Then out of nowhere, Jacqueline asked, "Mark, what do you know about the United States Government?" Surprised, Mark responded, "Nothing really, my legal life didn't involve the government, except for the federal law and regulations involving Wall Street and international transactions. Over the years, I have a met a few Senators, but I don't know much about government itself. Why?" Jacqueline had made her decision. "Mark, Rose was involved in many things in the government. Before I can go any farther, I need to spend about an hour going through this house. Is that okay?" Mark, amused, said, "I understand that trust is hard for you, so I am going to sit right here and you can have your way with the house. Turn this place upside down!" Then gently, "When you are finished, I'd like some answers."

Jacqueline was tempted, for half a second, just to tell him everything. Then she thought better of it. "That's fair, Mark. Please forgive me, but 'trust but verify' is one of my mottos." Mark told her again that he had no secrets from her, and he wanted only for her to be satisfied of that. Then he said, "Do your damndest! Rip this place to shreds!" He whistled loudly, and called out, "Let the games begin," as Jacqueline walked away, laughing despite herself.

Sid was laughing too, although the cramps in her hand felt like they were killing her. "Jacqueline, did you really tear his place apart? Mark seems like such a nice man, and he seems to love you so." Jacqueline nodded her head briskly, and told Sid, "Sid, I take no prisoners when it comes to my survival! After I scanned the house, I checked every computer file, every flash drive, and every CD and DVD for anything suspicious. I looked through every book on every shelf. I checked every drawer, every closet, and every piece of clothing in that whole house. When I was done, there wasn't one inch of that house that I hadn't searched! I'll tell you a little more about it when you start taking notes again. Right now, you need to rest that hand!"

Sid told her, "That search really seems like overkill – Mark had never been anything but kind to you, at least since you met up with him again in New York. I understand that you need to be cautious, but...." Jacqueline interrupted her with, "Trust me; the men of C Street seemed nice too. If I was going to take a chance on Mark, I had to do everything in my power and training to make sure I would be safe with him. After all, remember what you thought of Günter when I first told you about Enrique Curran? 'Trust, but verify everything.' That really is one of my mottos – when I'm feeling charitable!"

Sid told her, "Of course, you're right. Günter seemed like Mr. Wonderful at first. I can see why you would have been so careful with Mark. I'm glad he turned out to be a good guy. He is a good guy, isn't he? You deserve to be happy." Jacqueline smiled widely. "Yes, Sid, he really is a good guy. I'll be back in his arms shortly."

Sid said, "Good! Well, before we get back to it, do you want anything to eat or drink?" Jacqueline told her, "Just bring some more coffee, and then I'm ready whenever your hand is steady. Our time together is getting short." Sid stood and said, "Okay, let me get the coffee and I'm going to take some more aspirin, then I'll be all set to go on." When she returned, Jacqueline said, "I was going to tell you about my search of Mark's house...."

Chapter Eighteen
To Trust

JACQUELINE WALKED straight to her purse and removed the special compact Dietmar had made for her at C Street, and then she started to scan for electronic surveillance and listening devices. As she began to scan the room, Mark's face looked stunned. She just smiled and spoke not a word. For the next hour or more, she scanned and searched everything in the house. Then when she was almost finished, she told Mark, "I need the password to your computer." Still shocked, he told her, "San Francisco."

She laughed as she opened the laptop computer and reviewed the files. It was taking her a little longer than she thought, maybe because she could not find anything that involved Rose, Marie, Meier, Israel, Geneva, or the like. Mark stayed on the balcony the entire time, uttering not a word. A little while later, she closed the laptop and returned to the balcony.

She looked closely at Mark and told him, "Rose was in the CIA." Mark's eyes showed only slightly less shock than when she had started her search of the house. He said, "Wow, I never saw that one coming! Or maybe I did wonder in the early years about his Washington work. He never spoke much about his job, and I think maybe that made me wonder." Jacqueline told him, "Yes, it is true, he was in the CIA. The situation is more complicated than you could imagine. Do you understand why I have been so restrained about our relationship? You can take back your marriage proposal."

Mark shook his head while he said, "No, I do not want to take it back. How bad can it be? After all, he's dead." Jacqueline shook her head and said, "It's as bad as it could possibly be. The CIA believes that Rose made recordings of his work before he died." Mark instantly understood the nature of the package he had held for Jacqueline. She could see it in his eyes. Even though he had already figured it out, he needed to confirm it. So he asked, "The information was in the box that I held for Rose, wasn't it?" She nodded, saying simply, "Yes." He said, "I had no idea it was CIA information." She explained, "Yes, the box contained recordings, microfilm, documents, and instructions." Mark told her, "I thought it might be something to do with the government, but I never thought he was CIA. I knew I was holding something important, but I never even imagined that Rose was in bed with the CIA! I thought maybe he was an FBI analyst."

Jacqueline told him, "The problem is that I don't know who to trust. Because of his friend and partner in the government who had some kind of obsession with me, I nearly died in Costa Rica." Mark exclaimed, "Dear God, Jacqueline!" She continued, "No one knows that I'm in the Cayman Islands with you." Mark told her, "Well, your passport will let them know." She asked, "Do you want me to leave?" He was emphatic, "No, I never want you to leave! Get it straight – you are not scaring me away! I'm just trying to find out what we are up against with the CIA. Understand this, Jacqueline – no matter what the problem, we are up against it together now. You aren't alone anymore."

Jacqueline said, "I don't believe that I can be traced here; I came here using a different passport." "Where did you get that?" She told him, "The Israeli government provided it for me." Mark seemed more surprised by every statement she made. "Damn, it just keeps coming."

He asked her, "Where are the recordings now? Never mind; I don't need to know that. Just tell me they are in a safe place." She nodded. "Yes, they're safe." Mark seemed concerned, but more for Jacqueline's safety than his, when he asked, "How sure are you that they don't know you're here?" She chuckled mirthlessly. "I'm pretty damn sure. They think I'm dead." Mark told her, "Jacqueline, I could never have imagined this was the reason you were so secretive. However, as bad as it is, I'm actually glad this is the reason. I was afraid you were married."

Jacqueline said, "Believe me, Mark, this is very complicated and dangerous. I have spent the years afraid, ever since Rose became ill. Just when I think I might have some happiness, something happens." Mark grabbed her hand and gently squeezed it, saying, "Jacqueline, we will be fine. I'm a smart man; I will figure a way out of this." She thought that Mark's naïve assessment was a little frightening. Nevertheless, she believed he meant well, and from the look on his face, she knew he had no idea of the contents of the package he had held for Rose.

Mark stood up. "It's time for a change of pace. Let's go get your luggage from the hotel." As they walked toward the dock, Mark asked Jacqueline, "Do you trust me?" She told him, "Mark, I did not even plan to come to your house. I assumed that there was more than one house on this island. I thought that I could just look around and leave. I'm afraid to trust anyone, but I'm here and trying."

He told her, "Jacqueline, you can trust me with this information; I do not work for or have any connection with the CIA. Think about it – let us assume the packages I held were of interest to the CIA, yet I gave them to you. If I were involved with the CIA, I would have just turned them over to them, or at least opened the packages.

"I think it would be safe to say that if I worked for the CIA, I would have had an obligation to turn the tapes over to them. So, assuming CIA agents have no ethical obligations, unlike lawyers, you would have never gotten the packages." Jacqueline nodded, saying, "Mark, I know. That is why I have come this far. Just give me some time to believe in you."

Mark helped her onto his boat, a Grady-White cabin cruiser. They sped the five or six miles to Grand Cayman, and then took a cab to the hotel. Jacqueline checked out. She told the desk clerk where she had left the rental moped, and then she handed over the keys to it. That way, someone from the hotel would pick it up. They returned to the island together. Both were quiet, thinking their private thoughts.

Once they were back in Mark's house, he told her, "Jacqueline, let's go on with our life here. I can hire security for the island." Mark held her closely in his arms as they stood gazing silently out to sea. Some little piece of Jacqueline felt no fear for the first time in years. They walked slowly into the house and made love on the living room floor for hours.

As the sun was setting, they walked on the secluded beach. Mark told Jacqueline that he would like to be married immediately. They would use whatever name she chose. "No Mark, let's just be together for a while. I want to give you time to see what you are getting yourself into." He told her, "Jacqueline, if anyone from the CIA figures out who and where you are, we'll face it together."

"Mark, I need to make one more trip to the United States in a week. I will only be gone a few days." Mark seemed excited. "Well, I have some final legal business in California that I've been needing to complete. How about this – we could go to the States together." Jacqueline asked, "How long do you think your business will take, Mark?"

"It should just take two days – but I may need a third day to compile some paperwork. That just occurred to me. I want to prepare formal paperwork, so if anything happens to me, this place will be yours as a safe haven. A number of years ago, I set up a corporation in Las Vegas. The corporation purchased and holds title to the island, so no one knows I actually own it." Jacqueline was shocked and moved by his generosity. "Wow, Mark! Thank you." He told her, "I have no one else. My family is long gone. There is no one I would rather see live here, even if it's without me. Just tell me the name to put on the documents." Jacqueline asked, "That is just way too generous! Mark, are you sure?" As he nodded, she told him, "Well, if you are really sure, use the name Jessica Hollingsworth." Mark smiled, saying, "Good! I see that you are beginning to trust me. I think this island is just perfect, except that it needs a woman's touch. Hopefully, you will share my island with me." Jacqueline felt her eyes welling up. "Mark, I want us to be together for a long, long time."

She returned to planning their trip, and said, "I'll need about 48 hours in Florida, so we can fly out together – when I'm finished, I'll meet you in L.A. The only thing is that we need to fly separately. You go directly from here to California. I'm taking the long way as a precaution, going through London to Florida and then I'll meet you in L.A." Mark exclaimed, "That is the long way! I understand the need. I'll get a room at the Beverly Hills Wilshire Hotel." "That would be wonderful, but I want to leave as soon as we're done in the U.S. Marie wants you to come to St. Kitts. She wants to meet you, and she's interested in buying some land from you to build a house." Mark was ecstatic. "You told her about me! You do love me!" "Yes, Mark, I do love you! But Mark, realize that there are many things I'll never tell you." They sat down on the sand overlooking the sea. "Mark, can you live on a need-to-know basis?"

He smiled and said, "Of course I can, because I understand the reason. If I need to know, just tell me, and we will deal with whatever it is together. However, I would prefer you tell me everything eventually. Jacqueline, please let me know if you think that there is the slightest possibility I may need the information. Please don't hold back until the last minute. No matter what it is, promise me that you won't keep me in the dark – I can't help if I don't know what we're up against."

Jacqueline nodded. "I promise I will, Mark." Mark asked, "Will you tell me everything someday?" She thought for a moment, and then said, "We'll see. I would worry about your safety if you knew all of the information." Mark told her, "I'm not worried about me, as long as I have you." Mark asked, "Does Marie know about this mess you're in?" "Like you, she knows some of it." Mark told her, "I do understand your caution; your fears are well founded, considering the enormity of the CIA's reach." Mark kissed her as he laid her gently back into the sand.

Mark held her and said, "I'm glad we are going to travel to the States together. At least I want to be in the same country as you, in case you need my help. Then when you're finished, we can go to Kitts before returning home. Do you think you'll need to make any other trips?" Jacqueline told him, "I don't know. I probably will if Marie decides to live on St. Kitts." Mark asked, "Why would she live on Kitts, when I own this island? After all, you told me that Marie was interested to know if I would sell her some land to build a house."

"Well Mark, we'll talk to her in St. Kitts; we'll work something out. She is all grown up, so she will choose whatever she wants. We've spent too much time apart these last years and we both want that to end." Mark nodded and said, "We have plenty of room on the island, whether she wants to live with us in this house or she chooses to build another. I have no children, and I would love to have your grown daughter as a friend."

Their bodies and minds joined as one as they made quiet love on the beach. Jacqueline opened her heart to love again. They spent the next few days rediscovering each other in peace and happiness.

Mark and Jacqueline sat together on his island, as they watched the results come in on the day of the Presidential election in America. Jacqueline spoke not a word about what she and Marie had done. However, she was secretly reassured when a news report announced that an unidentified source had reported that the CIA was experiencing computer problems. Another newscast stated that FBI officials announced routine maintenance was being conducted on the FBI's mainframe, and access to the computer would be limited for twenty-four to seventy-two hours. Jacqueline and Marie had agreed not to contact each other on election night, so Jacqueline did not expect a call. The news reports meant that Marie would know the code was working.

Mark chortled, "Can you believe that the CIA can't keep their computers working properly, when the FBI's computers are down for maintenance?" Jacqueline chuckled, too, "Mark, I'm shocked; with all the technology available today, you would think that they could keep the computers up and running." Jacqueline listened for a few more minutes, then stood up and turned off the TV. Jacqueline had heard enough; she knew that Marie and Dietmar had succeeded! "Mark, we will hear the results tomorrow. I'd also like to go to Georgetown tomorrow for some newspapers. For now, let's go for a walk on the beach."

Since Jacqueline Rosenberg was dead, she was unable to vote, even by mail. The best she could do was support her candidate, a young Harvard lawyer, with anonymous campaign contributions. She was careful not to contribute more than the legal limit – she wanted an honest election. She believed he was the people's choice.

Over the next few days after the election in America, Jacqueline was at peace. She had found enough information in the newspapers to reinforce her belief that Marie's code had worked. Jacqueline read a headline about a New York newspaper in the local news; the headline read, "Mystery Tape Received – U.S. Election Hijacked For Democracy."

Jacqueline was glad she had arranged for parts of Rose's Tape 35 to be delivered to the New York newspaper, despite risking her life in doing so. She and Marie had decided to release the information about the C Street computer code. They feared that if they merely stopped the CLIPP code, someone would write a new program and take over the country again in the next election cycle. If the people of the world knew that such a plot was conceived within the government and had been executed, they would be alerted to the potential for it to happen again.

The article in the paper reprinted the New York paper's article. The article read:

"Last night, a courier delivered to the office of this newspaper a CD and letter concerning last night's Presidential election. Part of the recording had been erased and although we have been unable to authenticate the recording or the letter attached, circumstances surrounding yesterday's Presidential election and official reaction seem to indicate at least a grain of truth.

"The recording is said to be the work of a CIA agent. The man on the recording claims to be Solomon Rosenberg. The voice states that the recording was made in 1999. We have verified that Solomon Rosenberg was a government appellate lawyer and a member of the Widocqe Society, a think tank. He also is believed to have been connected to the CIA for more than twenty years. Mr. Rosenberg is deceased; he died in Paris.

"We are unable to confirm at this time that the voice on the recording is that of Solomon Rosenberg. The recording states that Solomon Rosenberg was a CIA explosives expert and links him to the Israeli government. It also tells of a conspiracy devised by a consortium of Government agencies to control the vote in America.

"The voice on the recording claims that a CIA meeting was held in Geneva, Switzerland in 1969, and that he was one of the participants in that meeting. The purported purpose of the secret conference was to develop technologies to, one day in the future, convert the

American voters to computerized voting. When that occurred, it would enable hijacking the incoming popular and electoral votes on election night by computerized manipulation of votes. The voice claims that five founding families of the religious right, with headquarters on C Street in Washington, intended to maintain control over the United States of America by insuring the election of puppets controlled by those five families. The recording states that the code had been embedded deeply in the Pentagon computer system, and that it was developed further during the creation of the technological advances in America.

"According to the letter enclosed with the recording, on election night, the CIA, Pentagon, and FBI computers malfunctioned for 24 hours to prevent control of the presidential election by the embedded C Street - CIA computer program. That letter from an unknown source states that C Street's access to the votes of the American people was blocked by a computer code, so that any attempt to manipulate the election results would fail. The letter claims that this process assured that every American vote was counted, possibly for the first time in years.

"We contacted the White House; a White House spokesman denies any such plot exists, and has refused any comment on the recording or the letter. After this reporter attempted to verify the information on the recording with the White House, the FBI and CIA jointly confiscated the package from this newspaper within the hour. This reporter was ordered by the FBI and CIA to print nothing of this story.

"It is the opinion of this reporter that something happened last night to protect democracy in America and assure the people's choice for President of the United States. If this event did take place as alleged, I salute the computer hackers who stopped that code and returned America to its people."

A later edition of another paper carried an updated article that read:

"In a White House news conference, the press secretary stated today that the recording released by the New York newspaper is false. The statement went on to say that the outcome of this election, like all American elections, was the people's choice. The CIA announced that it has repaired its computer problems and reports that there was simply a minor malfunction. The FBI has issued a press release that states that maintenance on its computers has been completed, and that its system is again fully operational. The Joint Chiefs of Staff issued a release denying that any technology-related problems occurred at the Pentagon.

"The CIA today denied any conspiracy in a written statement, and stated that a complete investigation into the source of the recording is under way. The Israeli Prime Minister had no comment on the American election and denied any knowledge of Solomon Rosenberg."

Jacqueline sat with Mark and asked him to read the articles. After he read the first one, he said, "Jacqueline! You turned over the recording to the newspaper, didn't you?" She just smiled and took a sip of her cocktail. Mark already knew the answer to his question.

"Jacqueline, you are as brilliant as you are stunningly beautiful. I am so glad you are going to be my wife. Just remember to let me know if you think that there will be any trouble."

She reassured him, "Mark, I promise you, at the first sign of trouble I'll let you know. For now, just understand that anything I'm leaving out is for your protection. That said, having this recording go public will have repercussions."

The American vote was returned to the people and the only statements from the White House were ones of denial. The news media reported repeatedly that they were unable to authenticate the recording. America ended up with its duly elected people's choice for President, and the CIA again found its path to plausible deniability.

Jacqueline knew this was only the beginning of stopping the corruption coming from C Street. The men of C Street would not give up their power easily, and she suspected that they would give the new President trouble passing any legislation. However, at least he was the people's choice, not the choice of powerful insiders. He had inherited the job of reversing the damage caused by the last President, who was hopefully the last C Street flunky to be in the Oval Office.

She and Mark went back to Grand Cayman again the following day for supplies. Jacqueline sent Mark ahead for the supplies, while she made a final call to Meier. She really felt she owed him an explanation for releasing that recording excerpt, and she wanted to find out his reaction to the recent events.

Jacqueline looked at Sid and told her old friend, "Sid, I need a break and some more coffee before I go into this part of the story." Sid stood, telling her, "Sure thing, Jacqueline. I'll make us a sandwich, too." Jacqueline said, "I get involved in telling the story, and I forget about food." Sid sympathetically said, "This has been such a journey for you, Jacqueline." Jacqueline rested her head in her hands while Sid fixed the coffee and a snack. Sid called out from the kitchen, "If you want another drink, help yourself – and pour me one too." Jacqueline walked to the bar and caught a glimpse of how tired she really looked in the mirror. Sid returned with the coffee and sandwiches. "Okay; where was I, Sid?" Sid reminded her, "You and Mark had gone for supplies."

Jacqueline continued where she had left off. While Mark was gone, Jacqueline sat down at a table at an outside café, and made the phone call to Meier Finch. The telephone rang seven times but there was no answer. Jacqueline thought that was strange, as Meier had always answered this number by the third ring. This time, there was no answer. Meier's failure to pick up his phone unnerved her. She just sat quietly at the café and waited for Mark. Jacqueline's concern about Meier not answering her call intensified the longer she waited. Jacqueline discovered moments later that she had received a video e-mail message from Meier on her telephone.

Meier Finch had turned on his computer camera and recorded events in Tel Aviv and in Washington, then e-mailed the video footage to Jacqueline. She began playing the video.

The video started with Meier turning on his speakerphone in Tel Aviv and dialing. Jacqueline could hear the voice on the other end answer, "Charles Dahl." "This is Meier. I have been questioned about a recording that was released. I need to see you at C Street, at 7 PM tomorrow." The voice on the phone said, "I will be there at 7 PM." The line went dead. The video had a pause then resumed as though it had been shut off for a while.

When the video came back on, it was immediately clear that Meier regretted his decision to contact Charles Dahl. Meier began going though Jacqueline's file at his desk and shredding all the documents, talking periodically into the camera. He said, "After all, Jacqueline, you did not name any names, and you waited until you knew I was dying before releasing anything." Meier looked into his laptop.

"My call to Charles Dahl was a mistake, Jacqueline. I should not have contacted him, but I was irritated after being questioned by the CIA, and I was angry that you released the recording. I am glad that you destroyed the code. I'm sorry I made that call. I will record everything that happens, and try to protect you to my last breath. I will get this recording to you when I am finished, so you will know your enemy. I'm leaving for Washington to meet with Charles now. I will restart the video when he arrives at C Street. Jacqueline, take the money and disappear!"

Before Charles Dahl arrived for the meeting, Meier spoke into the laptop and told Jacqueline, "I have set up the camera in the library at C Street. I expect Charles will be armed. He generally carries a 9 mm Glock in his left coat pocket." Meier held up his cane, and said, "You may recognize this – I showed you one like it." Jacqueline remembered the cane that Meier showed her – it had a gun in the handle.

About then, Meier called out, "Charles, the door is open. Please come into the library." Jacqueline heard a man's voice saying, "Meier, it is good to see you." As the man came into view, she could see that his left hand was in his coat pocket. Meier still had his .22 caliber cane in his hand, helping to steady his walk. Meier took a seat with the laptop recording the room nearby. Not all of the room was in focus, but Meier could be seen. The audio and video were very bad, but Jacqueline struggled to see and hear as much as she could.

"Charles, we have a problem that I have been handling, but as you can see, my time is limited. Congestive heart failure, you know." Charles said, "I'm sorry to hear that, Meier. This is about Solomon's recording that was confiscated?" Meier confirmed Dahl's supposition, saying, "That is part of the reason I asked you here. Solomon Rosenberg died a few years ago, as you already know. What you may not know is that before his death, he recorded information about our work." Dahl asked why Solomon would have done such a thing. Meier replied, "I am not sure whether it was that he had a guilty conscience, or if it was due to all of the medication he was taking. I do not know his motive in doing this."

Dahl exclaimed, "He recorded information about B6? CLIPP is treason!" Meier calmly agreed, "Yes, Charles, it is. The recordings fell into the wrong hands. I was contacted after Solomon's death and heard part of one of the tapes. I can assure you that we would be promptly executed for high treason if the recordings were released. We were all named. I had no other options, so I gave them what they wanted – money from the B6 account." While Meier talked, Charles Dahl paced around the library. He moved in and out of camera range, and when he could be seen, he was either so close to the camera that his head was cut off, or so far away that Jacqueline could not see his face.

Dahl said, "When I saw the press reports, I knew that recording had to have been made by Solomon. But why did you give them the B6 account money?" Meier told him, "Charles, I paid them expecting that no one else would ever have to deal with this issue. It was a shock to find out that Rose had left this information. I had no expectation that anyone had the capability to access our work on CLIPP and sabotage it. I completely underestimated their ability."

Meier continued, "Frankly, I was not terribly unhappy about the sabotage. Once CWP had taken control of our work, I realized how reprehensible our actions had been and how much potential we had created for damage to the world. All of us have been living with the consequences of our work. Now the world economy is precarious at best. We both know that this is related to our work at B6. However, that said, I never expected Rose to keep enough information to get them into the Pentagon code we created.

"Charles, I told you years ago that I would not release that money to anyone, not even to you. My position has always been that the account was an emergency fund once B6's work was completed. The day I heard that Rose had recorded information and stolen documents, I decided that this was exactly the sort of emergency that justified accessing the account. I had no doubt that Rose meant to get those funds to that organization, and I have no regrets about releasing the money."

"Meier, there must have been millions of dollars in that account!" Meier was angry at Charles's reaction; his ire was clear in his tone and in his words. "That is correct, and I controlled it! It is done!" Charles was insistent and asked, "Who did you turn the account over to? Who is it who has these recordings?" It seemed that Meier was determined to lead Dahl astray if he could. "I never knew who it was I dealt with." Dahl continued to press him, "You must have some information!" Meier's demeanor had calmed, and he told Dahl, "Yes, but I am getting old and feeble. I left the file with what little information I have in Israel." Dahl's temper flared and he said, "God damn it – you have never been a stupid man! Who are you trying to protect, old man?"

Flames entered Meier's eyes. "Soon, none of this will matter to me any longer. I must say, they did not release anything until I was dying, so what the hell! For the life of me, I will never understand how they got into the CLIPP code, but they stopped it dead. You must be wary – the remaining members of your team have no idea about the existence of the recordings. I felt that the B6 members would panic. I believed that they would search the blackmailers out and kill them without retrieving the recordings; as you know, none of the other B6 members are stable any longer. Remember, whoever this is did not release any of our names on Solomon's recording – only his name, and he is dead. The blackmailers could have taken all of us down!"

"I chose to cooperate by turning over the money, because I felt I had no choice. I must admit that I am not at all unhappy about the CLIPP code being destroyed. That, my friend, must be a sign of dying; one finds one's moral compass. However, now they have released some information, although neither the names of the agents involved nor any documents were divulged. I felt that I owed it to you to tell you before my death that our project was compromised. I owe you nothing more. The decisions must be yours to make from this point. It is in your hands now.

"I do not know where the recordings are, how many copies exist, or what they will do with the rest of them. I do know that there is a trigger switch that releases at least one set of recordings if you do find the blackmailers and kill them. Over the years I dealt with them, they seemed reasonable and it was only recently that they released anything."

Meier seemed to be doing everything he could to protect Jacqueline. She supposed that Meier must have been extremely angry with her when he called Dahl. At least he had calmed down quickly enough to try to protect her, once he had set the ball in motion.

Dahl said, "You, Meier, have gotten soft in your old age!" Meier told him, "I am under a doctor's care and in my last days of life. What do I care? When I was questioned a few days ago by the CIA, after the recording's release, I claimed no knowledge of B6. I'm too ill to survive long enough to undergo any future questioning. I assure you, it will not be long until someone looks for the rest of B6. You made the choice a long time ago to destroy your identity and live in Brazil. There is no trace of your existence in the Government. As you know, the others are also out of the United States."

Dahl was obviously angry, "What do you expect me to do without the information you conveniently left in Israel? I assume that you want me to eliminate the problem, but you have given me nothing to work with!" Meier told him, "I do not care to live with more deaths on my conscience in the last days of my life. This is your problem now. For what it is worth, I do not believe that you can neutralize the threat. The risk of the release of information is too high. Charles, were I you, I would simply disappear. You have the skills to do so. It no longer matters to me; I'm dead anyway."

Obviously, Meier did not say what Dahl wanted to hear. His tone was getting angrier and angrier. "Why in the hell did you give them the fucking money? Screw the recordings! With that money, no one would ever find me! Do any of the other members of B6 know about these recordings or the money?" Meier was obviously trying to dismiss Dahl, when he said, "No Charles, I decided to tell only you. I made that decision only yesterday. It took everything I had to meet you at my door. I must go back to bed now."

Charles grabbed Meier's cane in a split second. "You are not going anywhere until you tell me who has the money!" Charles began searching Meier's library and found a file on Jacqueline. Jacqueline Rosenberg's name on a file struck him immediately. Charles looked through the file. Meier said, "Charles, I didn't know that old file was still around. Jacqueline died some time ago." "She's alive, isn't she?" Meier told him, "No, she is dead!" "Then it's her daughter." Meier shouted, "No, it is not! Now get out!" Dahl said, "It is her, old man! Jacqueline is the one you have been protecting! I can tell from the dates of your notes; she is alive, not dead in Costa Rica!"

Meier just sat there. It was obvious to Jacqueline that he was too sick to stop Charles. Dahl continued to look though the files in Meier's desk and found Meier's contact information for Jacqueline's daughter, Marie. "I knew you had the information here somewhere! I tried to contact Jacqueline a few years ago. I left a message for her, but the bitch never returned my call. Once I locate Marie, she'll lead me to Jacqueline!"

Charles was making phone calls rapid fire. Meier, sitting helpless, could only try to stop him by saying, "Charles, stop searching – they have nothing to do with this mess. Jacqueline is dead. I have had no contact with her daughter!" Dahl said into the phone, "I see." He quickly dialed another number and, after listening for a moment, said to himself, "Damn, they sold that house!" He ordered, "Search the airports," and hung up the telephone again. With one more call, he ordered airline passenger manifests scanned.

Dahl turned back to Meier. "I have to start the search somewhere. But before I leave, old man, you are going to tell me everything! I have a lot to lose, you son of a bitch – the other members might strike a deal and flip. Besides, either Jacqueline or Marie has the God damn money from the Swiss account!" Meier again tried to divert Dahl. "No, Charles, they do not have the money or the recording. I don't know who it is I have been dealing with – I have heard only a man's voice in the communications from the blackmailers, and that voice gave me an account number for the deposit. We have fought over this money for years. The money is gone!"

Dahl would not be dissuaded. "Your sole control of the account has always been a sore spot with the members of B6. You are the only one who could access that account. I do not believe you. The only reason that I don't think you stole it is that you're dying! Why would you have Jacqueline's file here? It makes sense that Jacqueline has the recordings, since Rose would have left the recordings with his wife."

Next, Dahl called for a plane to meet his men, who were already looking for Jacqueline and Marie. Jacqueline could tell that Dahl was like a tracking dog; he was hot on the trail. Meier said, "You can find them, but you are looking for the wrong people! I would know if I had been dealing with either of them."

Meier angrily struggled to rise from his chair without his cane. Immediately, he slid to the floor, almost in slow motion. Charles walked to Meier and looked down. He stood over Meier's dead body for a few moments before noticing that Meier was clutching something in his hand. Dahl slowly knelt down, and removed the item from Meier's hand – it was a remote control. Just then, he noticed the laptop that had been on the table near Meier's chair the entire time. It was turning itself off. The video ended.

Jacqueline was sure that Meier had shut down the laptop with a remote kill switch in his hand. The laptop would never again start; she had learned about the technique when she trained in Israel. Meier had erased everything in seconds, right before Charles's eyes! Meier had only lived a few minutes after Charles arrived. His voice had been weak. However, Meier lived long enough to tell Charles that the money from C Street was gone from the Swiss account.

She wished she had called Meier sooner – she should have talked to him a couple of days earlier. Over the time since they met in Tampa, she had come to think of him as her friend. If only she had warned him as Rose's recording was being released! Perhaps he would have vented his anger over the phone instead of calling Charles Dahl!

Mark returned to the café with the supplies. Jacqueline immediately told him, "Mark, I just learned something that I think you need to know. I made a call to my contact in Tel Aviv. He is the person who paid me to keep the recordings quiet." "He paid you?" Jacqueline told him, "Yes, but that is a long story. For now, this is what you need to know. He always answers in three rings. Today he didn't answer at all."

Mark nodded and said, "Yes, I can understand your concern, especially since you just released one of Solomon's recordings." Jacqueline confirmed what Mark already knew. "That's right, Mark; I released part of a recording – it was a part that only included Rose's name. I thought I was being clever, but it may have backfired. Anyway, he did not answer my call, but I received this video a few minutes later. It's too dark to see much, but some of the audio is clear. I want you to listen to it. You need to know before you see this that my contact, Meier, is dead. He died while this was being taped."

Mark and Jacqueline listened to the video together. When it was over, Mark said, "Okay, so we know that someone is looking for you. Do you know who Charles is?" Jacqueline told him, "Yes, I know that Charles Dahl is a member of B6. As far as I know, I've never seen him, and I can't get a good enough look at him on the tape to be able to recognize him if I do see him."

Mark told her, "Well, we'll have to figure out who he is, so we can watch for him. Jacqueline, I knew as soon as I heard Solomon's name that you must have been the one who released the information. I just don't know how you shut down the CIA computers. Let's go, I want to get you back to the island. We will just deal with it as it comes."

"Mark, it *is* coming, and it may be a huge firestorm! Maybe we should re-think the trip to L.A." Mark seemed less concerned than Jacqueline. "No, you're traveling under another name, so you should be safe. We'll still meet in L.A., but then we should leave the States immediately." Jacqueline was reassured by Mark's calmness. "I guess it should be okay. I'm meeting Marie for a few hours at LAX. She has to be in L.A., too. My flight arrives shortly before hers departs. As soon as she's safely off the ground, I'll come to the hotel. But we need to be in and out of America fast! Maybe we can safely get away with being in the States for two days, but Marie needs to be in and out – she should stay in the States only a few hours." Mark agreed, and said, "I will rush my legal work – two days tops! I promise! Then we'll meet at the hotel. We will leave America together, immediately!" Jacqueline still looked concerned, but said, "That sounds good."

Mark was curious about the money. He asked, "You were paid? Is that where you got the ten thousand that you had on you when you arrived at the island?" Jacqueline told him, "Kind of, except I dropped a few zero's. I have been paid millions to be quiet." Mark said, "Well, you did not tell me you were rich!" It was time for Mark to hear the whole story. She told him, "Let's go to the beach and talk. There are some things you must know." They walked to a secluded part of the beach, taking a seat in the sand. "Go ahead, Jacqueline; I believed you when you said I needed to know only some things, but I'm sure I need to fill in some gaps now."

"Mark, after I left your office in New York with the packages, I stayed at the Waldorf Astoria for two days. I listened to Rose's recordings, viewed CDs, microfilm, and more. I lied about leaving New York, because I was shocked it was you holding the tapes. I was afraid, and I just could not involve anyone else in this nightmare."

Mark nodded. "I understand. May I ask what you found?" "Well, I found many horrible things that Rose and the government had been involved with – assassinations, plots, coercion, and more deceit that you could imagine. The things Rose left for me included specific dates, times, places, and names.

"I listened to all I could, but on some of them, the volume was low, and the earliest ones were recorded on large cassettes that I could not play. Besides, there was just a limit to how much I wanted to hear. I decided later to attempt to destroy the code that B6 had created. That was after I returned from being abducted in Costa Rica."

Mark looked at her wide-eyed. "You were abducted in Costa Rica? Who abducted you?" She simply told him, "That is a long story for later." Mark asked, "So you were involved in this computer problem the government just had, right?" Jacqueline nodded. "Yes. It's not too late for you, Mark. You can still get out." He gave her hand a squeeze, saying, "No, I am in for the long haul. I love you. But what and how did you do this?" "Well, it's complicated." Mark exclaimed, "No shit! I'm listening."

"Rose left a lot of information on exactly what he had been involved in creating. As you know, both Rose and I were computer savvy. Then I relied on the Government's failure to update its systems during the past few administrations. Those in charge didn't make technology a high priority." Mark asked, "Your daughter went to

MIT, didn't she? Did she help? Forget that question! I didn't ask that! Don't answer." Jacqueline told him, "I will, because it does not matter; I did this, and no one else!"

Jacqueline would never admit that Marie was the creator of the code. Mark did not need to know, and no one else ever would. Mark said, "I am sure that even if you told me how you did what you did, I wouldn't understand. I'm not a techie! So the recording that the newspaper reported as being made by Solomon Rosenberg – that was sent by you?" Jacqueline nodded, and said, "They really did install some kind of code for political gain with the creation of the internet. They began by developing the technology in general, and then released the internet to the public for further development. However, at each step they worked toward a goal of controlling the American vote. Rose sold his soul to the devil at 22 years old, when he signed on with the CIA. Rose was part of a think tank for the American Government. He was a trained assassin for the CIA who also worked with Israel." Mark was incredulous, and said, "Dear God, an assassin! I can't believe that he would do anything to harm someone."

Jacqueline told him, "Well, he was one of America's six elite assassins. To this day, I really do not understand his connection with Israel. He was Mossad, but that's all I know. I believe what I was told when I was in Israel – he worked for the interests of both countries." Mark was shaking his head in shock, as she continued. "There is more. This all began on C Street, in Washington, D.C.

Rose's home and office were there, compliments of the CIA. The house was a gift to him for passing the bar." Mark said, "I was there once – was he really CIA?" Jacqueline nodded and said, "Are you sure you do not want out? You're in pretty deep now, so if I continue, you will not be able to walk away from what I'm telling you."

Mark reassured her. "Jacqueline, I'm no wilting flower! Keep going, because we are in this forever, together. You were in Israel?" "Yes. Rose's last recording gave me a contact – Meier. He's the man who just died. Rose told me to go to Israel to be trained in self-defense, and Meier arranged it. I'm not sure how far I want to go with this."

Mark said, "I won't press you for more now, but I have a couple of questions. Who trained you in Israel?" She shook her head. "I really do not want to talk about that. You just need to know I can protect myself." Mark smiled. "So you could kill me with your bare hands?" Jacqueline smiled, but there was no humor in her smile as she said, "With two fingers, more or less." Mark was excited, and said, "You are Mossad-trained. As a Jew, I'm fascinated by all of this; I have not even made my pilgrimage!" Jacqueline cut him off. "Let's forget this part." Mark obviously really wanted to know, and said, "No way! How long were you there?" She refused to answer him. Instead, she told him, "Ask your next non-Israel question."

Mark got the message. He asked, "Why didn't you turn over the recordings and walk away?" Jacqueline wanted to answer that question. "Well, I never know who I can trust. Without the trigger for automatic release in case of my suspicious death, I would already be dead." "So there is a trigger to protect you?" Jacqueline told Mark, "Yes, there are two, one I arranged, and there's another that Rose arranged before his death – even I don't know the details of that one, so I couldn't stop it even if I wanted to."

Mark avowed no knowledge of the trigger, and told Jacqueline, "I look at you like a delicate flower, yet I have always realized that you are a survivor. If anyone else had told me this story, I would have thought that the person was insane. Still, I always knew those packages were important. I had no idea just how important they were until now!"

Mark and Jacqueline spent another day on the island in peace and quiet. However, she did notice that Mark seemed a little more concerned; he gave her a key to his gun cabinet. Jacqueline called Marie, and still received the "no big brother" response. She warned Marie to be on high alert. The following day, both Jacqueline and Mark left the island. Mark headed straight to California. Jacqueline flew to London on one passport and then to Florida on another, for security. She wanted to leave no trail, with the danger that was looming. She would meet Mark in Beverly Hills when her business with Sid was done.

Jacqueline realized on the plane just how much she loved Mark. She intended to go to Florida only to see Sid and tell her the rest of the story. Then she planned to meet Marie at LAX, before she boarded her flight to Paris en route to St. Kitts. Jacqueline had decided to tell Marie about Meier's death when they met at the airport. After she saw Marie off, she would return to Mark's arms, and together they would travel through London to meet Marie on St. Kitts the following week. Jacqueline had finally found the man she could love. Despite the danger, she was going to live life, but she would get some security for wherever they decided to live.

Jacqueline looked at Sid and told her, "That's where the story ends ... for now. Can you think of any questions that need answering before I go? Quite a while ago, you wanted to know more about Günter. Do you still have questions about him now?" Sid looked through her notes, and told Jacqueline, "I really can't think of anything that you haven't already explained. I see why you made me wait to hear about Gunter – I never would have suspected that he was Enrique! Jacqueline, I can't get over what you've been through since we last saw each other! I'm sure that you have given me more than enough material for another book."

"Now you have the rest of my story. I hope the remaining years of my life will be uneventful and of no interest to anyone. I'm going to do my best to disappear with Marie and Mark at my side. If I stay ahead of B6 for another week, I think we will be okay.

"Do with the information what you feel is right, as long as the story remains disguised as fiction. As before, you will need to change all the locations and the false names that Marie and I used. It's imperative for the safety of all of us. If they know where we were or the any names we used, they might be able to track us. I prepared a list of possible locations and pseudonyms for Marie and me before I came; you can use any of them for the book. We have not been, nor will we be, around any of the places I listed. It's the same with the names. Doing that will increase the chances that we will be safe." Jacqueline handed Sid the list of possible locales and names for her to use in the book.

Sid reassured her old friend that she would handle sensitive information as she had in their first book. She would be very careful not to reveal anyone's true names or any real locations. She told Jacqueline, "As before, I will keep the plot true to the events as they have happened in your life."

Jacqueline tipped the snifter up to her lips one last time, and then placed the empty glass on the table. "It is time for me to go, Sid; will you call a taxi?" Sid turned on her telephone and made the call, as Jacqueline rose to gather her things. Sid broke their silence with one final question, "How do you feel about the path your life has taken?" "It has forever changed me, and I am stronger for the journey. I have no regrets, Sid, not even one – I would do it all again." "Jacqueline, it looks like you will have the opportunity to do it all again – in loving Mark. I wish you well, but please be careful!"

Chapter Nineteen
The Sunset

Sid walked Jacqueline to the door and they embraced for a long time as they waited for the taxicab. "Jacqueline, I have decided the title for the new book. Wherever you are, look on the shelves for C STREET." Jacqueline told her, "I like that title – I'll watch for it. It says it all. Goodbye, Sid."

Sid watched as Jacqueline walked the terra cotta steps to the brick walkway, and toward the taxi. She never looked back. The morning light was breaking, and it cast a red hue on Jacqueline's auburn hair, flowing down her back in the slight breeze off Tampa Bay. Sid had spent the last uninterrupted thirty hours listening to the rest of Jacqueline's story. Amazingly, she was wide-awake and full of energy! She was anxious to begin writing her novel. Her writer's block was gone, and only excitement filled her head.

Sid knew at that moment that nothing in Jacqueline's life was an accident. Jacqueline was a brave woman, never taking herself too seriously, no matter what albatross hung around her neck. She understood her destiny. Sid knew a person like Jacqueline did not just happen, but was an old soul. She seemed to understand more than most that life is a grand tour ticket on the short ride. She lived her life without regrets, took life as it came, recognized that the course of her life was influenced by her choices, and accepted full responsibility for her participation in the journey.

Sid thought that Jacqueline was the kind of woman who makes every other woman see the possibilities of her own life, and who inspires men with passion and desire. Sid considered that maybe it is not the outer beauty of an old soul that we see; maybe it is inner strength and beauty. Maybe that was the secret.

Sid watched Jacqueline from the doorway. As the light of the rising sun lit her way, Jacqueline stepped into the taxicab. The writer in Sid, always in search of a story, hoped that Jacqueline would come again someday in the quiet of the night. Nevertheless, the friend in Sid prayed that she would never hear from Jacqueline again because she had vanished into safe anonymity somewhere in this world. Sid closed the door after the taxi drove out of view.

Right away, Sid went to work – she was so excited about the new book! She was just a few weeks into writing when a call came from an attorney in Tampa, Florida. He told Sid that a package had arrived at his office, and that he was asked to contact her to see if she would pick it up, or if he should send it to her by courier. When Sid asked the name of his client, the lawyer said that his client wished to remain anonymous. Sid thought, "It must be from Jacqueline!" Sid left immediately for his office.

When she arrived, a small box was waiting for her. Sid chose not to open it at the lawyer's office and left immediately. She wanted to go home to open the box, but she was too excited to wait. She pulled her car over onto a scenic overlook as soon as she was off the Howard Frankland Bridge, and opened the box. Inside it was a small music box and a digital recorder. Sid turned the recorder on, and a computerized voice said, "Don't put the Grand Marnier away! Sid knew it was from Jacqueline. Sid listened, as the voice told what had happened after Jacqueline left Sid's home….

Jacqueline could barely wait for the taxi to get to Tampa airport – she was so anxious to get to LAX. She was going there to see Marie off to Paris. Marie would be waiting for her mother at the airport bar in L.A. They only had a few hours to visit before Marie's plane left. Jacqueline wanted to get to Marie as soon as possible, and had timed leaving Sid's home that morning, so that she and Marie would arrive at LAX at the same time. Marie needed to know about Meier's death and about Charles Dahl. Jacqueline was also was ready to tell Marie everything about Mark.

Marie seemed calm but concerned when she heard about Meier and Charles Dahl. Mother and daughter sat together in a dark bar at LAX. Marie, like Jacqueline, was worried, and ready to leave the U.S. They talked until it was almost time for Marie's plane to take off for Paris. Marie was excited about the money. When Jacqueline told Marie about her feelings for Mark, Marie was happy that her mother had found someone to love.

They would all be together in a few days on St. Kitts, and Marie could get to know Mark. On the island, they would all be able to talk more freely. Marie glowed with pride, because the code she had worked so hard to develop was successful. "They may be after us, but they're busted for their C Street work!" However, they chose not to talk too openly at the airport. That conversation would wait for the island.

Jacqueline gave Marie the account number and password to the Paris bank account. "Marie, I want you to electronically transfer fifty million to your Swiss account as soon as you arrive on the ground in Paris." Marie wanted to know where the money really came from. "Marie, it is your tax money. Well, at least some of it is your tax money! I believe some if it came from Israel, too." Jacqueline told Marie that the money was to pay for silence.

Marie questioned it, saying "But you haven't been quiet, Mom." Jacqueline told her, "I've been quiet about the other recordings and the names of the other members of the team. Only Rose's name was released, and I already had the money before I released anything. Besides, don't forget that Jacqueline is dead. By the way, dispose of the throwaway cell phone you have been using before you get on the plane. Start using the second cell phone, just as a precaution." Marie said, "Good idea! I'll toss the phone on the way to the plane."

Marie gave her mother a hug and kiss on the head, saying, "Thanks, Mom." Jacqueline waved goodbye as Marie boarded the plane. She watched as the plane took off, relieved to know that her daughter was on her way to safety outside of the United States. No one even knew Marie's true identity.

Jacqueline hurried out of the terminal, headed for a taxi to take her to the Beverly Hills Wilshire Hotel and into Mark's arms. She had done all that one woman could do, and it was time for her to enjoy loving Mark. She called from the taxi and Mark gave her the room number. She could hear the excitement in his voice when she told him that she was on her way. He told her, "I'll order a bottle of champagne, and the door will be open. I love you, Jacqueline." "I love you, Mark." That was the first time she had said those words with such meaning to any man since Rose.

It felt as though the cab took forever to get to the hotel. Jacqueline raced to the room – she was a woman in love! As she opened the room door, Jacqueline saw Mark on the balcony and headed straight into his arms. He laid his newspaper on the rail and pulled her to him. "I am so glad you are back, Jacqueline. I love you."

His kiss was the kiss of love – warm, deep, and wet. At that moment, Jacqueline knew just how deeply in love she was with Mark. He was so tender and absent of any malice in holding Rose's tapes for her. She knew that Mark was probably the only innocent person in this whole CIA nightmare. Maybe she would marry him and just let the world find the other three members of B6; after all, she had given up enough. She deserved to be happy. Before her stood the possibility for happiness and she was going to seize the opportunity.

"I love you, Mark." The words had barely rolled off her lips, when the heel of her loafer slipped, pulling Mark forward with her as she tried to maintain her balance. Then there was a loud sharp sound as Mark's body became heavy and limp; they both fell to the balcony floor. She could feel warm blood coming from his head. "Mark, Mark!"

She placed her fingers on his neck and there was no pulse – the bullet had gone straight though his head. She checked him again, but he was not breathing. She listened and all was quiet. Slowly, she crawled from under his body and headed for the door of the hotel room. She saw an envelope with her name, so she took it without opening it. Grabbing her purse near the door, she stuffed the envelope inside, and tried to slip the coat over her bloodstained clothes.

Suddenly, her body was grabbed by a man's arms. He was standing at the hotel door. "Jacqueline, are you all right? I heard the shot! I couldn't get here any faster!" Stunned, her only words were, "Mark is dead." The man said, "Let's go! Down the fire stairs," as he pushed her in that direction. They raced together down the stairs. Then they headed directly out the side door of the hotel and straight into the doors of a carelessly parked car.

Jacqueline's head was spinning – Mark was dead and the escape path was cleared for her by Maxwell. Of all the faces on earth at that movement, Maxwell's was the last face she expected to see. They drove slowly but steadily into the Los Angeles traffic. Jacqueline sat looking out the passenger window, dazed. After a short ride, Maxwell pulled the car to a stop and answered a call on his cell phone. Jacqueline was still in shock as she heard his end of the conversation; he said simply, "Clear," and he hung up.

He reached for Jacqueline's shoulder, but she pulled away from his hand. "Jacqueline, it's okay. It's me; it's Max." Jacqueline looked directly into his eyes as she said, "Max, what in the hell are you doing here? What happened to Mark?" He told her, "Jacqueline, I don't know who shot Mark. However, I knew you were both in danger. I picked up your trail in the U.S. I used GPS to ping your daughter's cell phone to get the location. I arrived at LAX just as you were leaving, and I followed you to the hotel. I was on my way to the room when I heard the shot! Meier sent me to help you. He's an old friend."

She asked, "Meier sent you? Why?" "He knew that you were in danger." "Max, who shot Mark?" He told her, "I don't know. He's dead, isn't he, Jacqueline?" She looked at him with a blank stare and said, "Yes, he's dead." "I'm sorry, Jacqueline. I don't know all the answers, but we need to get you some clean clothes. I'll take you to my home in Brazil, and I'll explain more when we get there."

Jacqueline pulled some cleaning wipes from her purse and began cleaning Mark's blood from her skin. Flipping down the visor mirror to check that she had cleaned all the blood from her face and hair, she said, "For now, let's get me some clean clothes. I'll let you know what I'm doing after I get my head straight." He said, "Jacqueline, you must trust me." She cried, "Max, why Mark?" He shook his head, saying, "I don't know!"

The car pulled away from a stop light. Jacqueline asked, "Max, was that shot meant for me?" "Jacqueline, I don't know, but I believe it was. After all, Mark had nothing to do with B6, so there would be no reason to kill him." She was astounded and said, "How do you know about B6?" "Remember, Jacqueline, Rose and I knew each other in Washington. We'll talk about it later. Can you hold it together to go in the store with me and get you some clean clothes?" She told him, "Yes Max – just follow my lead inside. I'll be fine." Max said, "I forgot that you are trained." Max seemed to know a lot about Jacqueline and Meier.

As they entered the door of La Boutique Trop Cher, the sales clerk greeted them like a lion greets fresh meat. Jacqueline told her, "I would like to try on the suit in the window with an ivory tank top. Size four, please." The clerk, very excited at the possibility of a large sale, headed immediately to retrieve the clothes in Jacqueline's size. Then Jacqueline pointed out coordinating shoes and a handbag, and instructed the clerk to bring a pair of size six and a half shoes.

While Jacqueline was entering the dressing room, she told Max, "Darling, just have a seat – I'll be right out." Jacqueline took the clothes from the sales clerk and closed the dressing room door. Slowly, she unbuttoned her coat. The front of her dress, covered in blood, was beginning to turn brown. Quickly, she removed all of her clothing and wiped her skin clean of Mark's blood. She placed the new outfit on, wiped the blood from the handle of her purse and placed it inside the new larger purse, and then stepped outside for Max to see. "Honey, I love this outfit! I want it, okay?"

Max looked at the clerk, "How much is this going to cost me?" The clerk smiled at him and said, "It will be $5900.00 for everything." He didn't bat an eye. "That's fine." The excited clerk headed straight for her register. Jacqueline told her, "Oh, I will need a bag for my old clothes – I want to wear these." The clerk headed toward Jacqueline immediately with a large shopping bag. Jacqueline met her part of the way across the store, and took the bag from her hand. Then she walked back into the dressing room and carefully placed the bloodstained clothes inside the bag, making sure that no blood was left behind in the dressing room.

Max paid the clerk and they left the store with the bag of bloodstained clothes in his hand. Max headed for the airport. "Jacqueline, you need to go with me to Brazil. I do not know who fired that shot or if it was meant for you." She sat quietly thinking in the car. Max did clear a path for escape. "Max, how much do you know about Meier's and my relationship? He told her, "Jacqueline, I know about the tapes and the money." She was instantly wary. "What do you want from me, Max?" He told her, "Jacqueline you must trust me. I'm the same man you knew a long time ago, and I am trying to help you."

That statement seemed to make sense; under the circumstances, she had little choice but to believe him. "Okay, I will go with you, but I have a lot of questions."

"Let me get us on a flight, and then we will talk. Do you still have the spare passport Meier gave you?" Surprised, Jacqueline reached into the false bottom of her inner purse. "Yes." "Jacqueline, use that at the airport. I know you were Mossad trained – you can handle this." Max knew too much for Jacqueline's comfort.

Max pulled the car to a stop near a dumpster behind an office building, and told her to discard the bag of bloodstained clothes. Then they pulled back into traffic, headed for the airport. As they arrived at the terminal, Max double-parked the car and gave the valet a hundred dollar bill. Max said that he was late for his flight, and asked him to have the rental car company pick the car up. The valet, his eyes gleaming from the hundred dollar tip, was more than happy to accommodate.

Then they headed separately to the American Airlines counter. Jacqueline took one of the unused passports secreted in the false bottom of her purse, in the name of Lilith Cartwright, and purchased her ticket on the midnight flight to Rio. Maxwell presented identification separately, as an Air Marshall. When Maxwell was finished, they met in a corridor of the terminal. They had only a few hours to wait.

Entering the Encounter Seven Restaurant, they were seated near a window. The restaurant was quiet, and Max ordered two snifters of Grand Marnier. He said to Jacqueline, "I was pretty sure you could use a drink. Let's order, and then we can talk." They placed their order; Jacqueline was ready to unload questions on Max as soon as the waiter walked away.

"Max, what do you mean Meier sent you?" Part of Jacqueline wanted to flee at that moment. Max told her, "I received a call from Meier a few days ago. He said you needed help. He told me he was quite ill and needed to see me immediately. I had no idea it was about you." She asked, "How do you know about my relationship with Meier?" He said, "Jacqueline, we were all involved in the same thing in Washington. When Meier contacted me, he had no idea that I knew Rose's wife when he asked me to help you. I never told him I knew you."

The hostess interrupted the conversation as she seated more guests at the table next to Jacqueline and Maxwell. "Jacqueline, we will talk in Brazil. Let's just finish our dinner and go." It was clear to both of them that it was not safe to talk in the restaurant. Jacqueline would just have to wait for the answers to her questions. The reality of Mark's death was sinking in – she had no appetite, so she simply finished her drink.

Jacqueline began fishing for information, "Max, I owe you an apology for leaving you at the hotel so many years ago." He shook his head, and said, "You don't owe me an apology for anything, Jacqueline. Once I realized you were dating Rose in Florida, I called him immediately. We made a gentlemen's agreement – over time you would choose one of us. When that time came, the other one would walk away."

Max continued, "I was surprised that Meier did not know I had dated you when he called, but it seemed clear to me when I met with him that he had no idea about our past together. However, now that I think of it, I'm not sure whether he knew or not. After all, he called me and not another of my partners. He told me in the short time we were together that he had become very fond of you, so maybe he did know. If so, he knew that I would protect you. But he didn't say one way or the other. Let's get some rest on the plane; we will have plenty of time to catch up at my house in Brazil."

They left the restaurant and headed toward their gate. Once they had boarded the plane, Jacqueline laid her head back on the plane seat. It was the first time she could even think about what had happened to Mark. She wondered if her heel had not slipped on the balcony, would she would be dead and Mark still be alive? Jacqueline had been the target and she knew it. After all, who would want to kill Mark? Just as she began believing that she could be happy and let the government find these rogue agents on their own, someone from that world took Mark away.

What Jacqueline could not figure out was how Maxwell had been there to help her escape. Since Max was seated elsewhere on the plane, she would have to wait to find out. She ran his words over and over in her head. "Jacqueline, are you all right? I heard the shot! I couldn't get here any faster!" Well, she knew that Max was not the shooter, but that did not mean that he did not know who fired the shot. Jacqueline did not believe in coincidences. The bullet must have come from the rooftop of a tall building across the street. Her training in Israel had taught her to instantly identify the location from where a shot originated.

Then, even in the devastation of losing Mark, she realized the truth. Max was Charles Dahl! She needed to stay calm and play this out in Brazil!

She had not seen Max for many years, not since she left him naked in bed, never to return. What in the hell was he, of all people, doing there at that moment? It was clear – he was looking for the money. It was obvious to her that he knew a great deal about her life with Rose and afterwards. She knew how deeply Max was involved in this mess. What did he mean that he made a "gentlemen's agreement" with Rose? Did they flip a damn coin? She could not imagine Rose agreeing to such a thing, but what did it matter now? Rose was dead, Mark was dead, and she was on a plane with the one person who was looking to harm her. Of that she was sure! Well, at least Marie had tossed the cell phone he had pinged at LAX.

The plane landed at Rio de Janeiro-Galeão International Airport. Together, they passed through customs in only a short time. Max and Jacqueline took a taxi to a small house, just a few blocks from a town square. All Jacqueline knew for certain was that one of the B6 assassins had taken the life of Mark, an innocent man. His death was collateral damage, and Max was Charles Dahl.

She was determined to get as much information as possible from Max and then get out of Brazil alive. That meant she would have to play along. She knew that she could no longer flee from the remaining members of B6. She turned to Max. "Do you know who all the members of B6 were?" He responded, "Yes, of course I do."

"Max, I think one of them killed Mark." He told her, "Jacqueline, I agree. I believe one of the remaining members of B6 killed Mark. However, I also believe that the shot was meant for you – and they know about Rose's tapes." Jacqueline did not respond.

She really was exhausted, and so she pretended to fall fast asleep on the sofa immediately. Within minutes, Max was on the balcony, using the telephone. All she could make out of the telephone conversation was, "Give me a few days with her. One way or the other, I will get it.... No, remember that trigger will release. Just give me a few days."

Jacqueline immediately knew all she needed to know. She had a few days to get away; he was interested in getting the recordings and the money from her, by her cooperation if possible. So, she would live to fight another day. She fell asleep immediately, knowing that Max planned to manipulate her to get the money and the location of the tapes in next few days. She would need her strength.

It was late the next morning when she awoke. Standing over her with a cup of coffee was Max. Appearing startled, she jumped to her feet, knocking the coffee all over him. "Jacqueline, it is me – you are safe." Jacqueline had knocked the coffee on him intentionally. She did not trust Max enough to believe that he would not try to drug her with the coffee. She remembered Sun Tzu's lesson – when strong appear weak, and when weak appear strong. Max was not fooling with the same woman he had met long ago.

At that moment, it hit home that Mark was dead and that everything was real. Max believed her act that she was in shock, and walked her to the balcony in a very attentive and concerned manner. Max was buying right into Jacqueline's frail woman routine. Appearing emotionally distraught was the perfect ruse to control Max. Yes, Jacqueline was devastated by Mark's death, but she knew she needed to get out of Brazil alive. This was not the right time to mourn the loss of Mark. "Jacqueline, are you all right?" Tearfully, she said, "No, Max, I'm not. Mark is dead. You know more about B6 than anyone should, and I'm in Rio, I think. Am I in Rio?"

Max sat down next to Jacqueline, slowly taking her hand as he said, "Yes Jacqueline, you are in Rio, and you are safe with me. Jacqueline, I know everything – the tapes and the money. Meier contacted me just before he died. I'm going after the rest of B6 – one of them is Mark's killer. That is the only way you will be safe." Jacqueline cringed at the thought that she had boarded the plane with Max. It was his face on the video – the one she could not make out! And it was clear he had no idea that Meier had recorded and e-mailed that video to her. There was no other explanation. It was all too clear now.

Just then, a small black bird perched itself on the rail of the balcony, and looked directly into Jacqueline's eyes. It was as though it had come to warn her, to confirm her belief about how much danger she was in with Maxwell. However, she knew that she must stay calm and pretend to trust him. "I'm going to help you Max – they killed

Mark." Max said, "Jacqueline, I know you have some training, and we will find them. However, I do need the tapes. By the way, how much of the B6 money did Meier pay you? We could never get him to part with any of that money for the remaining members of B6." She could not give in too easily, so she said, "We will talk about the money and tapes later, okay? Max, we are in this together." Max pressed her, "Don't you think it would be best if I knew now?" Jacqueline was evasive and answered, "It's in the States, but I want to recover for several days before we go get it." Max seemed pleased that she had agreed, saying, "Sure, Jacqueline; I know you are exhausted, so just relax, and we will go to the States the day after tomorrow. You just rest." Jacqueline was worried, but she knew that she did not let it show. "Yes, that sounds perfect."

Jacqueline knew that she needed to get out of Brazil. She had boarded that plane with Max while she was still in shock from Mark's death. That was a grave error. Now, she would have to act with extreme caution. Suddenly, she saw the Statue of Christ the Redeemer off high in the distance, just as the bird flew off the balcony. It was as though while the bird was there, Maxwell, who was standing less than two feet away from Jacqueline, disappeared. Suddenly, she remembered the words in Rose's letter, "statute," "Christ," "redeem," just as Max's voice intruded on her thoughts.

"Jacqueline, you are an amazing woman. I honored my gentleman's agreement with Rose, but I never stopped caring for you." His voice brought her out of her trance, and her training to survive kicked in with his words. Jacqueline knew that her survival rested exclusively on her ability to exterminate the entire B6 unit.

She asked Max for one of his T-shirts; Jacqueline told him that she wanted to feel more comfortable than she could in her new Chanel outfit. He got one for her, and then she went into the bedroom and changed. She then carefully laid out her outfit on the bed for later. Shoeless, she rejoined Max on the balcony.

"Max, I have been able to find information about all of the remaining members of B6 but one. It appears that Charles Dahl never even existed." Max told her, "Charles Dahl exists, and you are standing next to him." Jacqueline's blood ran cold, as Rose's words from the tape, "Trust no one," played in her mind. With Max confirming that he was the man on the video, she had no doubt what she needed to do. Jacqueline knew that she must keep her friends close and this enemy closer. She listened to the loud music from Carnival become even louder, as the dancing in the street intensified. "Let's go inside, Max. I can barely hear what you're saying over the music. It should be a little quieter inside." They walked back in from the balcony.

At that very moment, she realized Max had been able to locate Marie in order to follow her to LAX. Marie had spent her adult life under a different identity Rose had created. Max had already killed Mark. Now Marie was in jeopardy. Jacqueline picked up Max's Glock from the end table. Stunned, his eyes cold with fear, he asked with a cracking voice, "What are you doing?"

"You tracked my cub – now meet mama bear!" She fired the gun. Max fell to the floor, a bullet hole in the center of his forehead. Jacqueline walked over and felt for a pulse. She knew that there would not be one. However, her training was to verify a kill if possible.

No, there was no life. No, he was dead; the blood flowed from the back of his skull. It almost appeared stuck to the hard oak floor in the pooling red. His forehead was barely bleeding from the perfect round hole she had placed so carefully with a bullet from his own gun. No, the room's silence did not overcome her mind – she was quite peaceful. No, her hand was not shaking as she expected, like when she was training in Israel. No, she found she had no remorse as she laid the gun back on the table. Emotionless, she took a sip of wine.

Yet, still looking at the death before her eyes, she felt no need to further justify taking his life. She walked slowly back to the balcony where his fate had already been sealed minutes before she lifted the gun. No, she knew at some moment on that balcony, ten minutes earlier, that he was going to die. She had even changed out of her new clothes, to avoid getting gunshot residue on them. She saw no other choice; he knew one thing too much – how to find her daughter, who had been so carefully hidden from the men of C Street for so many years. Mentioning that had been a careless mistake for Maxwell. Really, he should never have told her that he tracked Marie. No, it was simply unacceptable.

It seemed that she went on automatic pilot after the shooting – her training kicking in. She analyzed the situation. She was alone in Brazil, but music from the street appeared to have drowned out the gunshot. For now, she felt safe. As her thoughts returned to the reality at hand, she walked back into the room of the dead from the balcony. Maxwell's briefcase was open on the chair. She would look inside it, but there were things to do first. Thinking quickly, she washed her hands several times and then used alcohol on them, to get rid of any gunshot residue. Then she grabbed plastic bags from the kitchen for her hands, careful to touch nothing else before she slipped the bags on her hands. There was no need to rifle though the briefcase; it only had one thing below the yellow legal pad – the file on Jacqueline from Meier's study in Washington.

She looked through his desk and his pockets; then she grabbed the memory card from his cell phone and the hard drive from his computer. However, the damn plastic bags kept falling off her hands! Jacqueline looked around and found one large envelope and then another, and placed everything she had taken from Max inside. She addressed and marked the package, "Do Not Open – Hold." She sealed one envelope inside the other. Jacqueline found stamps and put plenty of postage on the package. She was going to send it the solicitor in London, whose address she had stored in her head when she hired him to hold Rose's documents. She addressed the envelope to him, and put it beside her purse.

Nothing else in this house was hers but her purse and clothes. Thoroughly, she wiped her fingerprints from the gun. Unsure if she wiped every spot, she wiped it again.

With the meticulous nature carefully crafted at Mossad, she knew to wipe everything with a cotton cloth and alcohol, which she found in the bathroom. Jacqueline changed back into her clothes and put the T-shirt, the plastic bags, and the towel into another bag. She would dispose of all of them later.

Then she began to search for hairs – that damn long hair of hers – it was easy to find. On the pillow of the couch, sure enough, she found some hairs. Locating a roll of tape, she rolled every inch; she put the tape roll and the tape she had used into her purse, deciding to dispose of it later. The next order of business was to take care of fingerprints – she wiped the table, her wine glass, all of the chair arms, the sofa arms, the balcony, the bathroom, the door handles and the tape dispenser from the desk. She wiped them all again and for a third time, and finally she wiped the alcohol bottle and was done. Jacqueline knew that some of the members of B6 were still alive, at least for now. With Max's death, there was one less to kill.

Jacqueline knew that she had cleared every trace of her presence from the house. She took one last look around, and then she picked up her purse, the bag of items to throw away, and the envelope. Using the cotton towel, she first opened, and then closed and locked the door. As soon as she exited the door, she walked directly off the property. Not a person noticed her leave the house in all of the commotion of Carnival. Within a few minutes, and after just a few bumps and jostles from the crowd of people, she was well up the street and away from the house. In the huge crowd, she was invisible. Jacqueline entered Carnival. Loud music filled the air.

She tossed the cleaning towel a few blocks away, over a fence into a backyard that had laundry hanging on the clothesline. She saw a bonfire burning. It was surrounded by people celebrating and dancing. She worked her way through the throng of people, and threw the T-shirt and the tape onto the fire. She shoved the plastic bags down a storm drain another block away. That left only the envelope to mail. In another block or two, she found a mailbox on the sidewalk's edge, just two feet in front of her – she put the envelope inside it and she was done!

Appearing calm, fear buried deep, she quickly slipped into a seat at an empty table in the center of the crowded party of Carnival. It was people, music, dancing and drinking, all in a haze of lights. No one heard the shot over the music – of that she was sure, which meant she had time to think. She needed to get out of Brazil. If she made it alive, Sid would have to hear this story!

Thinking fast, she checked the false compartment of her purse – her passports and money were intact. Suddenly, her mind was blasted with thoughts. Rose referred to the statue in Brazil. She was getting distracted, but for the first time, the words in Rose's letter made some strange sort of sense. He wrote in the letter about a Jew looking for redemption from Christ. Something Rose said in an earlier conversation about the CIA bothered her. It happened when they were still at home together. After his cancer diagnosis, Rose said that to protect them from the CIA, he might have to leave them. The argument that ensued in the house that day was fierce.

Jacqueline became lost in old thoughts, trying to remember what had happened back then. Rose had changed Marie's identity when she left for school. They had agreed to fight it out with the CIA together, as long as Marie would be safe. Eventually, Rose promised not to do anything crazy, like run – even to protect her and Marie. That was weeks before he went psychotic and nearly killed her with the knife. She only saw him twice after that, and both times his eyes were still empty.

That was a year before he died. He had ordered direct cremation in 24 hours, as would any good Jew. Maybe if she had seen his body, this foolishness would not creep into her mind. She kept wondering if Rose was trying to tell her something in the letter he left with the tapes and in the hologram. After all, no Jew would be looking for redemption from Christ, especially Rose. However, Rose had clearly stated in the letter, "I will be waiting for our next dance under the statue in heaven, if Christ allows me to redeem myself."

Jacqueline knew Rose was dead, but an unsettled feeling, the feeling she was missing something in this entire CIA mess, was convincing her to confirm that he was not waiting at the statue of Christ the Redeemer before she left Brazil. Spending extra time chasing a ghost instead of fleeing for the airport while she had the chance could result in someone finding Maxwell's body. Being foolish was not part of her Mossad training. She had to stop letting her mind run wild! She thought, "He is dead!" Jacqueline was wasting time sitting at the table. There was no time for a trip to the statue on a futile quest. She needed to find a cab for the airport. She looked around for a taxi to get the hell out of there.

Jacqueline was trembling inside with fear. Somehow, she thought she still appeared calm to the outside world. Her imagination was running rampant, a dead man lay a few blocks away because of her, and she was on foreign soil! Her thoughts were in turmoil. The commotion in the street echoed the commotion filling her head. Dancers in costumes circled the tables, voices echoed, lights flashed, and music blared. There she sat, alone at a table in the midst of Rio's Carnival, attempting to gain her composure. She looked around at the characters of Carnival. There were Zulu Warriors dancing, clowns juggling, and hundreds of people samba dancing in the street. That was only the beginning of the party mood that filled the streets around the tables where she sat with her thoughts in disarray.

She noticed a tall, dark haired, good-looking doctor wearing wire rimmed glasses, his white coat and stethoscope worn proudly, walking toward her table. Strolling through Carnival, he was smiling a Cheshire cat grin. Jacqueline was positive that smile was because he was accompanied by gorgeous blonde twins who looked like they came straight out of a chewing gum commercial. They were so scantily clad that they were nearly naked, and each was all over him. The twins were obviously either his latest conquests, or more likely, they were about to be part of a wild romp with him. The sight of the three of them just added to the overall chaos, making it impossible for Jacqueline to concentrate on what to do next.

Amid the noise and confusion of the crowd, fireworks cracking, bright lights filling the sky, smoke filling the air, she was completely unaware of three large men dressed in bright colored shirts who were approaching her. Suddenly, they were there and abruptly sat down at her table without saying a word to her. She was startled but wanted to seem calm – after all, it was Carnival and everyone was friendly. She turned to the man at her left, expecting to engage him in casual conversation.

He spoke first, in a strong English accent, "Jacqueline Rosenberg, Inspector Letterbaugh, from Interpol. Please remain calm," as he discreetly flipped open a leather case to show her his Interpol Special Agent badge and photo identification. At the same time, he laid his hand across Jacqueline's purse. He asked, "Are you armed?" Her heart raced even faster than it had been before. "No, I have no weapons." She had seen Interpol badges before, so she knew the badge and his identification were real. Letterbaugh – that was the name of the man who argued with Günter! So, they had been after him, too! Jacqueline's mind came to a complete stop! They must have heard the shot! It was over! It only took a second to evaluate the situation. There was no way to take out all three of them and escape though the crowd of Carnival. She remembered what her Mossad training told her to do in a situation like this. Jacqueline would have to surrender for now, so she could live to fight another day.

Inspector Letterbaugh authoritatively told her, "We do not want any trouble here, so stay completely calm and this will go smoothly. In a moment, a man dressed in a costume will come to the table. Go with him. We want you to go with him without any reaction. If you cause a scene, the Brazilian Military Police will arrest you – or perhaps they will simply shoot you here. They are quite trigger-happy this time of year. Do you understand?"

Still in shock at the reality of being caught by Interpol, Jacqueline knew she had to cooperate for now. Her mind began to work again. Should she seek help from the American embassy? Probably not – maybe this was about C Street Underground, and if so, she might not survive the Americans. Jacqueline was sure that she was on several hit lists in America, and could no longer trust that the men whose plan she thwarted would not kill her on sight.

Jacqueline decided that she would need the help of Meier's survivors at Mossad. "Yes, but I want to speak to someone from the Embassy of Israel and a lawyer before any questioning." Inspector Letterbaugh acknowledged her request. "You will have that opportunity if you just go quietly, and do not create a disturbance. Do we have your cooperation?" He looked sincere, so perhaps there was a chance that she could use her Mossad rescue phrase with someone at the embassy. She told him, "I will not give you any trouble, Inspector." However, her mind did quickly assess that the Interpol officer had just said that "a man" would be coming to the table. That could make her odds of getting away much better; after all, the officer's English was quite precise. If she really was taken away by only one man, there was still hope. Perhaps Jacqueline could overpower him or, since she was wearing her venom bracelet, maybe she could quietly kill him and escape.

On the other hand, Jacqueline knew she had wiped that place clean – they had no evidence that she pulled the trigger. It was not as if there were many other options. Inspector Letterbaugh said, "You must remain calm, Jacqueline." She responded, "Let's just get this over with; I'm not going to run." With an edge to his voice that she had not heard before, he said, "Whatever you do, don't try to flee!" At the same time, the officer gave a sharp head nod to a group of men dancing near the table, as he removed his hand from Jacqueline's purse.

Suddenly, one of the dancers circling the table came to an abrupt stop and firmly stated, "Come with me." Jacqueline turned toward the voice, penetrating the blaring music that echoed through the smoke-filled air. A tall slender man costumed as a Zulu warrior, wearing so much face paint that he was unrecognizable, stood next to her at the table. Expressionless, she slowly picked up her handbag.

The painted-faced man grabbed her arm and pulled Jacqueline's body tightly to his side. She felt the hardness of a gun carefully concealed at the waist of his costume. A moment seemed like forever as Jacqueline scanned for an exit route. She could not figure out how to break his death grip, much less how to escape. Jacqueline could see no choice but to follow wherever he led. He moved her through the crowd, toward the center of the dancers in the street. Then everything seemed to stop – the music, the dancers, and Jacqueline's heart – when the warrior pulled her tighter. The band began to play *La Vie En Rose*. "I hope you don't mind – I asked them to play our song."

Jacqueline looked deeply into the eyes of her captor, as she spoke but a single word, "Rose."

Acknowledgments

To David E. Siar, Esquire, my husband, who always finds the time to read my contracts and provide his legal skills on a moment's notice, and who possesses the humor and stamina to edit my work throughout the creation process. Thank you for your unconditional support at every bend in the road.

To NeCole, my daughter, a woman who provides endless ideas for the characters in my books based on her remarkable wit. Thank you for your inspiration and the continuous joy you bring to life.

In loving memory of my mother and sister,

Lois Irene Walker
May 13, 1927 – August 23, 2005

Deborah Ilene Walker
December 18, 1954 – June 18, 2009

They were women liberated by hard work and perseverance before liberation was in vogue.

Editors: David E. Siar & Katrina Ruth, Ph.D.
Cover Design: Claudette Walker
Original Silhouette Photography: NeCole

Abacus Books, Inc.
Abacus Books, Inc., P.O. Box 55302
St. Petersburg, Florida 33732-5302, U.S.A.
www.abacusbooks.com

Claudette Walker is the world-renowned author of:

"To Love The Rose (Is Washington Stoned?)"

"C Street."

"The Casey Anthony Murder Trial"

"Decompression Map"

Claudette Walker's interest in literature began with the writings of James Joyce & Ian Fleming. She found herself inspired to write about the world of espionage. With her unforgettable interweaving of love, sex, drugs, and politics, Claudette's unique approach to her subject matter has entertained and inspired readers throughout the world. She writes and lives quietly on the west coast of Florida with her husband, an attorney, and her daughter.

For more information visit www.AbacusBooks.com

www.ingramcontent.com/pod-product-compliance
Lightning Source LLC
Chambersburg PA
CBHW071111290626
47170CB00018B/53